Advance Praise for Always Hope

"Deeply poignant and emotionally stirring, this fast-paced read—with plenty of surprising twists and turns—will resonate with readers."
—Emily Liebert, bestselling author of *Pretty Revenge*

"Jessica Schorr is a dedicated doctor who brings new babies into the world. When one delivery goes very wrong, several lives are forever changed. *Always Hope* is an important story about how lives can be altered in the space of a few moments and how trauma can reverberate throughout families. Tackling professional issues like medical malpractice and workplace stability, as well as marriage stressors like aging parents, caring for the differently abled, and teenage emotions, Frimmer's story moves forward with grace and heft. A serious and insightful examination of what happens when obligations become too big to handle on one's own, this expertly crafted tale will have readers thoroughly engaged throughout!"
—Jacqueline Friedland, *USA Today* bestselling author of *He Gets That From Me* and *Counting Backwards*

"Each of our lives is composed of intersecting storylines, as our choices and fates become inevitably intertwined with those of others. *Always Hope* portrays this so well—showing how humans hurt, love, and need each other. Poignant, moving, and heartfelt—get ready for all the feels."
—Kim Hooper, author of *Woman on the Verge*

"Heather Frimmer's third novel, *Always Hope*, is an absorbing, heart-wrenching story that asks the reader to embrace our humanness and need for connection, self-forgiveness, and empathy. Told from three intertwined characters, all caught in the wake of the aftermath of a traumatic birth from two years ago, Frimmer skillfully weaves an honest and thought-provoking exploration into how past trauma can point us toward a new path paved with its own beauty and grace. I adored this book."
—Sarahlyn Bruck, author of *Light of the Fire*

"*Always Hope* is a gripping, thought-provoking story about three families facing the fallout of a delivery room disaster. Told from the nuanced perspectives of the obstetrician now questioning her own skill, the mother of the harmed infant, and the malpractice lawyer who takes the case, this is not a book that takes sides, but rather dives deeply into the humanity of each character. It's a story that will resonate with anyone who's ever set foot in a hospital, asking the complicated question of who should be held responsible when good doctors make all-too human mistakes."

—Hadley Leggett, author of *All They Ask is Everything*

"A compelling story, *Always Hope* explores the complexities of trauma, forgiveness, and the resilience of the human spirit. Frimmer masterfully crafts richly developed, relatable characters who will imprint on your heart. This profound, transformative tale about finding hope amid despair is perfect for book clubs!"

—Dara Levan, author of *It Could Be Worse* and host of *Every Soul Has a Story*

"With a physician's eye and a mother's heart, Heather Frimmer has written a timely, topical novel in which no one is right and no one is wrong and nothing is easy. *Always Hope* is full of flawed characters fighting flawed systems in a flawed world who, in ways heartfelt and heartbreaking, maddening and inspiring, offer — always — hope."

—Laurie Frankel, author of *This Is How It Always Is*

"*Always Hope* is a heart-stopping family drama that explores guilt, secrets, and the dangerous edges of forgiveness—an unforgettable story of how far we'll go to find peace."

—Rea Frey, #1 bestselling author of *In Every Life*

ALWAYS HOPE

a Novel

HEATHER FRIMMER

Always Hope
Copyright © 2025 by Heather Frimmer
SC ISBN: 9781645385790
Always Hope
by Heather Frimmer

Cover design and interior art by Dana Breunig

Published by Ten16 Press, an imprint of Orange Hat Publishing

www.orangehatpublishing.com
Wauwatosa, WI

This book is a work of fiction. Names, characters, places and incidents are the product of the author's imagination or are used fictitiously.

To Alli, Marisa, and Michele,
two radiologists and a neurologist.
What we do is hard. Your support, love, and laughter keep
me going every single day.

Chapter One

JESS

Only one more to go. It seemed like a straightforward delivery. The labor was progressing normally, the tracings regular, and the baby in cephalic presentation. Jess removed the metal speculum and dropped it back on the tray. It had been a doozy of a shift, but her twenty years of experience had served her well.

"All looks good, Nicole," Jess said to the expectant mom. She adjusted the nose piece on her mask to keep her glasses from fogging up. Over two years since the start of the pandemic, Jess wished the hospital would eliminate the mask mandate already, so she could breathe easy. "This baby will be here before we know it."

"The tray's all prepped, Dr. Schorr," Eve said, her tone all business.

Jess's jaw clenched at the sound of Eve's voice. The delivery nurse used to be one of her best friends, the two of them working together smoothly in the delivery room and celebrating the new lives they had brought into the world over cocktails after work. Since the Carlson delivery two years ago, the friendship had cooled.

"I'll scrub up, and we'll get going." Jess matched her tone to Eve's, walked over to the sink, and stepped on the foot pedal. She waved a hand under the automatic dispenser and gathered the foamy soap in her palm, summoning her energy to make it through the last delivery of the shift. Overnight calls hadn't always been so exhausting. Then again, at forty-eight, Jess wasn't young anymore. It took her longer to bounce back. As Jess rinsed her hands, she caught her reflection in the mirror over the sink.

Her eyes were dark and puffy, and a deep groove traversed the bridge of her nose. She turned away, trying to focus on the task at hand. Get this baby out so she could go home. At some point this weekend, she needed to write her part of the article due to a medical journal in less than two weeks. With the reminder texts from her coauthor Ken Smart morphing from polite to direct to borderline rude, Jess had to get her act together before he went postal. A full professor in her department, he ranked above her; Jess had been stalled at assistant for more years than she cared to admit.

"Dr. Schorr, did you hear me?"

Jess snapped back to reality. "What?"

"Should I set up the stirrups now?" Eve said, tapping her foot.

"Yes, please."

"Eight centimeters dilated," Eve said. "You ready, Nicole?"

"Alone?" Nicole said, her eyes wide with fear. "Fucking business trip."

Eve took Nicole's hand. "You're not alone. Our team is right here with you."

Jess dried her hands with a paper towel and walked over to the window, training her gaze on the McDowell Mountains in the distance. A group of clouds hovered over the mountains, creating a pattern of dark shadows on the land below. Jess couldn't remember the last time she'd laced up her hiking boots and hit the trail. It was time to get back out there, but she would have to wait for the heat of the Arizona summer to dissipate. A clunking sound interrupted her thoughts. Eve fit the stirrups to the end of the bed, preparing for the baby's arrival.

Jess walked back over to the bedside and slipped her arms into the paper gown Eve held out for her.

"You remember how to do this?" Jess asked Nicole.

"I think so…" Nicole said.

"Don't worry. Eve and I will help you through it."

"I can't do this by myself," Nicole said. "I'm not strong enough."

"You're stronger than you think." Jess tried to take her own words to heart, push through her exhaustion for the sake of her patient. She had no choice.

Jess sat on the stool and rolled forward, positioning herself between Nicole's legs to do one last manual exam. The cervix had further softened and dilated, a sign of active labor. As Jess removed her fingers, she felt a bumpy ridge along the vaginal wall. Something about it felt familiar. Could it be the umbilical cord? This couldn't be happening again. Sweat dampened the edges of Jess's surgical cap as scenes from the Carlson delivery looped through her mind. Her heart hammered in her chest. *Just let me get through this delivery. Enough with the ridiculous cord obsession.* She squeezed her eyes shut, trying to erase the disturbing images.

Eve gave Jess a questioning look, her brow furrowed.

Jess responded with a quick nod, trying to convince Eve, and herself, that everything was in order. If she could stay focused for a few more minutes, everything would be fine. She had delivered thousands of babies. What was one more? Sweat dripped from her armpits down her sides. Why was this happening now? Even if this was a similar presentation to the Carlson delivery, that didn't mean this one had to end the same way. In the time since then, Jess had delivered hundreds of babies successfully. But she couldn't deny she was struggling more often in the delivery room lately. She thought back to the instructions from the meditation video she'd watched on YouTube a few nights ago. Breathe in for four seconds and out for six, or was it in for eight and out for ten? Thoughts raced around in her brain, colliding into each other like bumper cars.

"Dr. Schorr." Eve's voice sounded far away. "Nicole is ready. Can she push?"

"Um…" All of a sudden, the beeping of the fetal monitor slowed, and spots appeared in Jess's vision. No, not now, please. Jess's heart raced, her breathing ragged. She looked at the instruments on her tray, but she couldn't recognize anything. It was like peering through a film, everything reduced to vague shadows and rough silhouettes. All her training evaporated in an instant. She couldn't trust her senses to tell her the truth or her body to do things it usually did on autopilot. Her hands felt thick and clumsy.

"Uh…all set," she managed, her voice a hoarse whisper.

"Is everything okay, Dr. Schorr?" Nicole asked.

Jess wanted to reassure her patient, but she couldn't. Her throat tightened.

"Yes, fine." Eve eyed the tracing on the monitor. "You got this. Now bear down as hard as you can, and don't let the breath escape. All your energy should go to your pelvis."

Nicole tucked her chin to her chest and pushed, her cheeks flushing. After several seconds, she released her breath with an elongated grunt.

Jess exhaled along with her, trying to gather her wits. The baby's head appeared, the crown covered in whorls of dark hair, like one of those Rorschach inkblot tests. Was it a zebra or maybe a donkey? Everything was up for interpretation. Saliva pooled in Jess's mouth. She tried to swallow, but she couldn't remember how. Her muscles wouldn't cooperate.

"Good one," Eve said. "Keep going like that."

Jess tried to focus on the baby's head. She had the sense she was supposed to do something now, but she wasn't sure where to put her hands. The more she tried to calm herself, the faster her breaths came, one after another with no reprieve. Heat collected inside her mask, making her feel trapped. She ripped it off and wiped the sweat from her nose with a sterile towel. It didn't help. Jess still couldn't force air into her lungs.

When Nicole pushed again, Jess tried to make room around the baby's head, but her hands wouldn't cooperate, her fingers numb and tingly. She tried opening and closing her fists to make the feeling go away. No such luck. Newborns could be so slippery.

She couldn't trust her hands to hold firm, to grip the baby and not let go.

"Nicole is ready for one final push," Eve said.

"Not yet," Jess said, stalling.

Eve bent down next to Jess. "What's going on?" she whispered.

"It hurts!" Nicole screamed. "I need to push."

"One minute. Dr. Schorr is getting the clamp ready." Eve leaned back down. "Can you do this?"

"Yes, yes…" Jess tried to inhale, her heart galloping violently in her chest. The pins and needles in her hands intensified, and the room whirled around her. Jess wanted to pretend she was okay, but she wasn't. Far from it.

"Where is my fucking husband?" Nicole wailed.

Jess stood up from the stool, holding on to one of the stirrups to keep her balance. She had to get out of here. Now. Before she passed out on the linoleum. Staggering into the hallway, she slid down the wall and buried her face in her lap. Her heart pounded in her ears, drowning out everything except the faint sound of Eve's voice and the piercing cry of a newborn.

Chapter Two

KENDALL

"Have you been giving Hope her tummy time?" Dr. Hill asked, standing over Hope at the examining table. The developmental pediatrician bent and straightened each of Hope's legs.

"Every day." Kendall looked up at the painting on the wall, the cartoon llama giving her a disapproving look. The smell of rubbing alcohol burned her nose. With Hope turning two next month, Kendall had wanted to be done with these visits by now. She had never expected them to be an ongoing thing. "We do twenty minutes in the morning and again in the afternoon."

The doctor checked Hope's reflexes in her elbows and knees. "Good. Any signs of crawling or maybe scooting? Does she ever use her arms to try to move herself?"

"Not really. It takes all her energy to hold her head up, but maybe soon?"

"And how's it going on the food front?" Dr. Hill asked. "I'd like to see her graduate from pureed to soft foods like avocado and banana."

"I'm not sure she's ready. She still spits it out."

"Swallowing is a complex process. And her prominent lingual protrusion doesn't help."

Kendall hated the way the developmental pediatrician used complex medical terms instead of regular words, as if intentionally creating distance between them.

Dr. Hill sat Hope up, a hand on either side for when she toppled.

"Does it affect her speech as well?" Kendall asked.

"Absolutely. It's all interconnected. Speech is a dance between the tongue, the lips, and the throat. It takes many muscles to say a few simple syllables."

"I'm waiting," Kendall said. Every week at playgroup, the other children's vocabularies grew exponentially, simple sounds and short words turning to longer words and two-or three-word sentences. She pretended to be happy for the other moms, proud of their babies' development, but sometimes it was hard. Really hard. Dr. Hill had suggested a group for parents with disabled children, but Kendall refused to pigeonhole her daughter. Maybe being around able children would push Hope to reach farther and climb higher. "Being patient isn't always easy."

"I understand." Dr. Hill picked Hope up. "She's certainly gaining weight nicely."

"Yes," Kendall glanced at the plastic button protruding from Hope's belly. "The extra feedings are working."

Dr. Hill passed Hope over to Kendall. "I'd like to have a talk in my office once you get Hope dressed." He washed his hands at the sink before leaving the room. Goosebumps popped up on Kendall's arm. She'd been taking Hope here for nearly a year, and Dr. Hill hadn't invited them to his office since their first visit. What made today different? When Kendall had gotten pregnant at twenty-six, the double line on the pregnancy test had thrown her for a loop. Married for just a year and a half, she hadn't felt ready for parenting a baby of any sort, and definitely not one with cerebral palsy. KC Events, the party planning business she had started after college, had just begun picking up steam. She'd planned only a handful of successful parties before she had to slide it to the back burner. With all of Hope's appointments and therapy sessions, it had been nearly impossible to make time for her company. In her element as KC, the name she used for work, she felt smart and organized. Kendall was barely keeping her head above water.

Kendall shifted Hope's weight on her hip and then laid her back on the exam table to dress her. Running her hand over the rigid plastic button sticking out from Hope's stomach, Kendall felt her throat tighten with guilt. She hated administering the feedings, the thick liquid dripping into the tubing before disappearing through the button. Maybe if she'd chosen a different doctor, another hospital, things would have turned out differently.

She sighed and pulled Hope's onesie over her head. Hope threw an arm out and groaned. With the click of the snaps, Kendall wished for the umpteenth time Hope would say a word. Just one. She wasn't asking for *mama*—any word would do. Kendall finished dressing Hope, then lifted her from the table and cradled her in her arms. Swaying back and forth, she sang Hope's favorite song. *You are my sunshine, my only sunshine*—something about the melody calmed Hope right away, worked like a charm every time—*you make me happy when skies are gray.* Hope quieted and cooed along with the song. Placing a gentle kiss on Hope's forehead, Kendall settled her into the stroller, secured the straps, and tucked Posy, her favorite toy, in next to her. The plush butterfly had been one of those strange anonymous gifts on the doorstep, back when Kendall was still opening them. It went everywhere with Hope.

Pushing the stroller down the hall to Dr. Hill's office, Kendall heard laughter from the front desk, Nancy and Olive probably sharing funny stories about their grown children, perfectly healthy kids who'd grown into fully functional adults with jobs and homes and dogs in their fenced-in backyards. They both talked about their children incessantly, oblivious to the fact that many of the patients here might never be able to live on their own, go to college, or even hold a pencil. A few times, Kendall had nearly scolded them for their insensitivity, but she'd thought better of it. If she acted like a bitch, the staff would take it out on her daughter.

She knocked on the door to Dr. Hill's office, and he invited her in. The room was lined with dark bookshelves, and certificates covered the walls. A sense of claustrophobia enveloped

Kendall, her face flushed with heat. The only other time she'd been here was when Dr. Hill had confirmed Hope's diagnosis. Everything about that day was stamped on her memory forever. She pictured Dr. Hill's mouth moving in slow motion, his lips curling slowly around the words as he'd enunciated each syllable with unnecessary emphasis.

"Is it okay if I leave the door open?" Now, Kendall took a seat facing the desk and parked Hope's stroller next to her by the window. "I'm a little warm."

"No problem. My wife says I'm cold-blooded."

"You never ask me to come in here." Kendall grabbed a pamphlet from the window ledge and fanned her face. "It's making me a little nervous."

"I understand." He paused and took off his glasses. "I've been seeing Hope for almost a year, so I have a much better sense of what's going on with her. It takes a bit of time to get to know a child, to predict what the future will hold."

Kendall tugged at the Hermès drop earrings she'd secretly ordered last month. "The future? But she's not even two yet."

"I'm certainly no fortune teller, but I do have a lot of experience," he said.

"We've been doing everything you suggested," Kendall said. "Physical therapy, speech therapy, music therapy... am I forgetting anything? It's a full-time job."

"Caring for a child with special needs is a major undertaking," Dr. Hill said. "You have to make sure you're nurturing yourself too."

"I'm fine," she said.

"I like to have a meeting after seeing a child for one year, to be as honest as possible, so that families know what to expect for their child's development. A reality check of sorts."

Kendall's breath caught. This didn't sound good. She wished Troy were here to hold her hand, but he was at work. Always at work. How could selling solar panels be more important than his family?

9

"The honest truth is," Dr. Hill continued, "the more time I spend with Hope, the more concerned I am. Cerebral palsy is a broad diagnosis. When I first saw Hope, she was too young for us to know how she would fare, but now I have a better sense."

"You do?" Kendall's stomach churned, the banana she'd choked down in the car threatening to make a reappearance.

"Two things stand out for me. The first is her speech delay. At this point, she should have some sounds and maybe one or two words, but even with intensive speech therapy, she's shown little improvement."

"But there's still time, right? She could start any day." Kendall searched Dr. Hill's face for any sign of encouragement.

"Also, the muscle tone in her arms and legs is significantly increased," he continued without acknowledgment. "It's called spasticity. This can make it hard for the child to coordinate walking and other motor functions."

"Her muscles are so strong. Isn't that a good thing?" Kendall thought about how hard it was to get Hope dressed sometimes, how she had to fight just to get her arms into the sleeves.

"Not exactly. Her muscles have strength but no coordination. It's like a weightlifter who's not able to pick up the barbell. All the energy has nowhere to go." Dr. Hill paused, his expression serious. "Mrs. Carlson, what I want to say is this."

Kendall took a deep breath, trying to remain calm.

He glanced out the window before meeting her eyes. "There's a high likelihood Hope may never walk or talk."

Kendall tasted sour banana in the back of her throat. "No. That can't be true."

"I know it's not what you wanted to hear—"

"It can't be true." Kendall stood up and slung her cream Louis Vuitton bag over her shoulder. She needed a doctor who championed her daughter, not a naysayer.

"Mrs. Carlson, let's talk this through." Dr. Hill stood and beckoned with his arms for her to sit back down. "I want what's best for Hope. Same as you."

The doctor's soft voice made Kendall pause. Maybe she should listen to what he had to say. She sat back down, gripping the sides of the chair. Hope flailed her arm and dropped Posy onto the floor.

"Waaaaaaaaaa!" Hope yelled.

Kendall bent down and scooped up the toy, tucking it next to Hope, who quieted right away. "See? She has a favorite toy. She loves cookies and hates carrots. I can see her sparkle."

"It's not personal. My predictions are based on experience and data."

"I'm her mother." Kendall's voice sounded too loud for the small room, but she couldn't help herself. "Doesn't my opinion count for something? There must be something we can do. Some other treatments we can try?"

"We always wish for the best, but I believe in honesty, to prepare you for the difficulties your family may face in the coming years."

The doctor's constant talk about honesty grated at Kendall's nerves. She needed to hear the truth, but at the same time, she didn't feel ready to process the reality of what he was saying. Her eyes strayed to a silver frame turned sideways on the desk, the photo of a little girl smiling on a beach, a deep dimple in her left cheek and grains of sand in her wavy hair. Kendall knew Dr. Hill saw children like Hope every day, but he had no idea how it felt to parent one, no idea how demoralizing it was to give and give and give and get so little in return.

"Is this because of her delivery?" Kendall asked, her voice wavering.

"It's hard to determine," he said. "A lack of oxygen can damage the brain. It's hard to know the effects of hypoxia until the baby grows up a little, until the brain develops more."

His answer was frustratingly vague, but Kendall could read between the lines. She balled her hands into tight fists, digging her manicured nails into the soft flesh of her palm, the sharp pain strangely satisfying. Dr. Schorr's face appeared in Kendall's

11

mind—the dark mole over her left eye, the panicked look in her eyes in the delivery room. She was still practicing medicine as if nothing had happened. "So, Dr. Schorr—"

"—is an excellent doctor," Dr. Hill backtracked. "One of the best we have."

So much for his supposed honesty. Hope started crying and kicking her legs against the desk. Kendall offered a pacifier, but the baby knocked it to the floor. "Do you think Dr. Schorr is responsible?"

A piercing pain started in Kendall's forehead and spread to her temples. She massaged her forehead to try to relieve it. The day Hope was born was a blur, but she knew he wasn't being straight with her. Troy was convinced Dr. Schorr was at fault, bringing it up often, but Kendall wasn't sure. What about her birth plan? Maybe the choices she'd made there, the boxes she had and hadn't checked, had also played a part in how the delivery unfolded. She shook away those thoughts. Pinning blame wouldn't change anything now. It wouldn't make Hope's disability go away.

"I'm honestly not sure," he said quietly.

If the doctor used the word 'honest' one more time, Kendall might throw up.

"This must all come as a shock." Dr. Hill opened his desk and handed her a pamphlet. "We do have a clinical trial going on, looking at a new drug to treat spasticity. To relax the muscles without causing sedation."

"I need to know the truth."

"I know you want answers," Dr. Hill said, "but sometimes there are none to be had. What I can offer is excellent therapies and the best medicines available."

Kendall struggled to breathe, as if she were being held underwater.

Dr. Hill handed her the pamphlet. "Take a glance. It looks promising."

Kendall scanned the glossy photos of healthy kids in bright outfits and the marketing write-up on the inside: Better range of motion, less pain, improved ability to walk. The last part stood out from the rest.

"Do you think this one is worth it?" Almost from the day Hope came home from the hospital, the doctors have been suggesting various trials and experimental treatments. Desperate to do everything she could, Kendall had grasped at every straw. But now, sometimes she felt like she was playing a never-ending soccer game on a team of one, covering both defense and offense. How long could she keep running before she collapsed from utter exhaustion?

Hope began screaming again.

She couldn't imagine signing Hope up for another trial only to find out she'd been getting a phony placebo pill. The disappointment would be too much to bear. Kendall stood up and began moving the stroller back and forth to calm Hope down. The band of pain now wrapped all the way around to the back of her skull.

"The good news is," Dr. Hill continued, "if the medicine is shown to be effective, all participants will be offered the drug as soon as the trial ends, well before it goes on the market."

Kendall wasn't sure what he'd just said. She'd reached her limit. On one hand, the trial sounded encouraging, a glimmer of sunlight peeking through the storm clouds, but on the other, it could be a false promise, just like all the others.

Chapter Three

ABE

Abe took a notepad from his desk drawer, *Goldman and Silverberg, LLP* printed across the top in navy blue lettering. He leaned across his wooden desk and began the interview. "Before we get to talking about your potential case, I'd like to get to know you a bit."

Sean Barclay slouched in his chair, dressed in a flannel shirt, baggy jeans, and work boots, his face weathered from the sun. "Alright, shoot."

"Let's start with your home life. Are you married? Do you have any children?"

"Nah," Sean said. "My last girlfriend tried to rope me in, but I escaped."

Strike one. Single men were a bad bet. A wife and kids engendered empathy with a jury. "What type of work do you do?"

"I'm a roofer. In the business for twenty-five years." He held up a freckled arm as evidence of his sun exposure. "It's all I know."

Now this sounded a bit more promising. It was always good when the client worked in a specialized field and couldn't earn a paycheck any other way.

"My house needs a new one," Abe said, "but that's not in the cards for me anytime soon." He glanced at the filing drawer in the right side of the desk, wishing the pile of bills inside would magically disappear. "So, what brought you in today?"

"I want to sue my surgeon. He fucked up my back. I met your lady assistant at my neighbor's pool party, and she said you can help."

When Norah, Abe's paralegal and right-hand woman, had told Abe she'd booked a new client, he'd felt his face flush with shame. What kind of attorney couldn't recruit their own clients? But he was in no position to turn business away.

"What brought you to the surgeon?" Abe asked.

"Slipped disc. 'Easy fix,' he said. Made it seem like no big deal."

"Okay. Did he recommend surgery?"

"Yup. Claimed I'd be slinging shingles in no time. I haven't worked in a year."

"I'm sorry to hear that," Abe said. "How have you been making ends meet?"

"My sister's been helping me out. She lives up in DC Ranch, you know that rich people place up in North Scottsdale? I told her I'd pay her back, but she and I both know that's a crock."

"Did you bring in your medical records?"

Sean took a folder from his backpack and handed it over the desk. "It's all there. Just like Norah said. She's a fine piece of ass, by the way."

Strike two. Abe ignored the crude comment. He opened the folder and scanned the documents inside. As he turned the pages, his mind strayed. Focusing on work had been difficult in the past ten months since Risa's death. Who was he kidding? Since his wife's death, *everything* had been difficult. Abe tried to take in the details of the MRI report. Typical post-operative stuff. Scar tissue, a little bit of hemorrhage, and expected surgical defects in the bones. Nothing that clearly pointed a finger at the orthopedist. You needed patience to find the diamond in the mine, but with this case, Abe might dig to China and come up empty-handed.

"Tell me more about your recovery," Abe said.

"After the operation, the pain got worse. That butcher maimed me."

Abe wasn't buying it. This schmo had walked in the door on his own without assistance. A walker, a cane, or at the very least, a prominent limp lent credence to a case. Subjective pain was difficult to hang your hat on.

"Did the surgeon have any suggestions?" Abe asked.

"He said some shit about physical therapy. I've shelled out enough already."

If Abe didn't take on some jerks as clients, he'd never earn a living, but this guy was rubbing him the wrong way. Flipping over to the next page, Abe skimmed the surgeon's notes. He stroked his goatee, searching for helpful nuggets. The handwriting was neater than most, and the notes thorough. This wasn't going to be an easy nut to crack, but it was the only one he had. He couldn't make a habit of requesting extensions on the office rent.

"Mr. Barclay," Abe said. "What are you trying to achieve here?"

"I expect that sucker to pay." Sean raised his voice. "He owes me bank for what he did to me."

Strike three. This guy was full of malarkey, just out for an easy payday. From his brief review of the chart, Abe didn't see any evidence of neglect or abuse. Surgery may have failed to solve the problem, but that didn't constitute malpractice.

"I'd like to take some time to comb through the documents. I'll get back to you in a few days." He needed to get this clown out of his office. Maybe he'd have Norah make the call tomorrow, clean up the mess of her own making.

Once Sean left, Abe turned his chair to the window. Shoppers in sunglasses and baseball hats crossed North Scottsdale Road. Abe wished he could be so carefree, that he didn't have to worry about keeping the lights on. Somehow, he'd have to bring in cases with a semblance of merit. Turning back to his desk, he closed the Barclay file. His eyes burned, but he tried to hold back. Crying in the office wasn't going to help the situation. The merciless Arizona sun seared the back of his neck. At sixty-seven, Abe didn't tolerate the heat well anymore. He wiped the sweat from his neck with a tissue. A framed photo from Eliza's college graduation caught his eye. Abe's daughter was in the center wearing her red cap and gown, Risa and their son, Ross, on either side. Abe remembered focusing the camera and getting the light just right, blissfully unaware his wife would be gone too soon. He buried his face in his arms.

Norah knocked at the door. "I have some mail, Mr. Silverberg."

Abe sat up and gathered himself, thanking his lucky stars Norah had agreed to stay on after Marty announced his retirement six months ago. This was her first job after she graduated paralegal school more than twenty years ago, and she'd become a fixture, an essential ingredient in the recipe. Running the firm without his longtime partner made Abe feel unmoored, but Norah's continued presence offered some comfort. Nearly ten years younger than Marty, Abe had always followed his elder partner's orders. Marty had been the manager and Abe more of a worker bee, but now Abe had to steer the ship.

"Is everything okay?" she asked.

"Yes, fine," he said, trying not to raise concern.

She dropped a pile of envelopes on his desk. Abe needed to dam the raging flow of bills before he got carried away in the current. Norah used to manage the accounting, but when Marty left, Abe had taken over. If Norah had insight into the sorry state of the finances, she'd be on the hunt for a new job in no time. He couldn't bear to lose her too.

"I'll take care of them," he said. "Paying bills relaxes me."

"Are you serious?"

"I could have been an accountant in another life," Abe said. In truth, he was so bad with numbers he could barely balance his checkbook.

"Let me know if you need help. How's the Barclay case?"

"A dud."

"I'm sorry." Norah pulled her auburn hair into a ponytail and secured it with a tie. "I thought he might be the real deal."

"I appreciate your effort, but the guy's a con artist. I hate to say it, but it might be time to pound the pavement."

"Mr. Goldman excelled in that arena."

"Believe me, I know." Abe sighed. Marty had had no shame—handing out his card at cocktail parties, coaxing people to share sob stories about loved ones with mesothelioma or silicosis, even pulling over at car accidents on the highway. Schmoozing didn't come naturally to Abe. He had always been the one to put his head down and get the work done.

"Big shoes to fill."

"Enormous." Abe turned to the window so Norah wouldn't see his eyes filling with tears, again. Losing Risa and adjusting to work without Marty in the same year had been a horrible one-two punch. At some point soon, Abe would have to figure out how to dissolve the partnership. He couldn't allow Marty to continue collecting half the money for doing bupkis.

"I miss him too," she said. "Who's going to make the tasteless jokes around here?"

"I guess I'll have to spiff up my repertoire. But no promises," Abe said. It felt good to joke around.

"I'll keep my expectations low. No offense, but you're no Jimmy Fallon."

"No offense taken," Abe said.

They were both quiet for a minute.

Norah leaned her elbows on the desk and peered over the top of her geometric glasses. "I'm not trying to be pushy, but—"

"Listen, Norah." Abe needed to allay her fears before she put into words what they were both thinking. "There's been a lot of changes around here, but I don't want you to get the wrong idea. Goldman may be out perfecting his golf swing, but Goldman and Silverberg is here to stay. There's no need to worry. I have a plan."

Now Abe would have to figure out what this supposed plan entailed. Maybe he'd sneak out a bit early today. A change of scenery might help him come up with ideas.

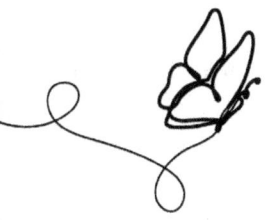

Chapter Four

JESS

Jess entered the kitchen, her mind reeling from the morning's delivery. The panic attacks had been happening for months, but she'd never had to abandon a delivery room before. Somehow, she'd always managed to muddle through. Thank goodness Nicole and the baby seemed okay when she'd snuck past the room on her way out. How could she continue working as an obstetrician if she lost her shit at the sight of an umbilical cord? It wasn't something she could avoid. She'd been hoping the attacks would go away as quickly as they'd begun, but no such luck. Jess needed to figure out how to make it through the next month and a half without going insane. Once the Carlson baby turned two, the statute of limitations would expire, and Jess would breathe easier.

She dropped her purse on the counter with a thud.

Drew looked up from a pile of coupon flyers. "That bad?"

No matter how horrible her day, Drew's hazel eyes and caring smile always lifted Jess's spirits. "Bad doesn't even begin to describe it." She gave him a kiss. If Jess told Drew about the episodes, he'd go into social worker mode, therapizing her up one side and down the other. With both a mother and sister in social work, he came by it naturally, but Jess was in no mood to talk about her feelings right now.

"What happened?"

"Oh, you know. It was busy."

Drew patted the chair next to his. "Tell me a story." This was the same line he used at the hospital, the one that had made her take notice when they met on the wards during her intern year. He had a talent for getting people to open up in a gentle and unassuming way, but Jess hated when he used his social work tricks on her.

"No stories today." Jess sat down.

"Tough shift, huh?"

"It wasn't the best." Jess took a sip from Drew's water glass. "I'm too tired to go into the details."

"Sounds like there was a lot going on at the hospital."

That was an understatement. Jess had to change the subject before he tried to probe deeper. Enough with Drew's empathy statements and annoying reflective listening. "Just deliveries left and right. How are the girls?" she asked.

"Maddie's on her phone. Vivian's still asleep."

Jess looked at her watch. It was almost noon. Her twelve-year-old used to be up with the sun, but lately she'd been sleeping in later and later.

"I didn't want to wake her," he said. "I think she was up last night watching videos."

"What kind of videos?"

"Something on YouTube, I think. I don't know."

"You didn't ask?"

"I'm trying to give her some privacy. She doesn't need us all up in her business."

"A few questions wouldn't hurt."

"She's fine," Drew said. "Don't worry."

As if on cue, Jess heard the toilet flush in the girls' bathroom, followed by the sound of Vivian's footsteps on the stairs. She wore fuzzy pajama pants decorated with movie reels and buckets of popcorn and a loose t-shirt, her short hair sticking out over her ears.

"Hi, sweetie." Jess yawned and stretched her arms over her head. "How was your night?"

Vivian shrugged and took a seat at the kitchen table next to Jess.

Opal, their orange tabby, brushed against Jess's legs. She scratched the base of her tail.

"What's on the agenda for today?" Drew asked. "Maybe the zoo?"

"Dad, please." Viv rolled her eyes. "I'm over it already."

"Okay, then maybe the Diamondbacks game? They're at home today."

Viv sighed. Opal jumped onto Viv's lap and curled up like a cocktail shrimp as Viv ran her hand over the cat's body.

"Jess, you want to step in?" Drew said. "I need a pinch hitter."

Jess looked up from her phone. "Oh, I don't know. I'm going to bed, but you guys could hike at Tom's Thumb?"

"Are you kidding?" Viv said. "It's hot as fuck out there."

"Vivian Stella Rubin," Drew said. "You know we don't talk that way in this house. I'm not sure what's gotten—"

"I have an idea that might cheer us both up," Jess said, trying to let Viv off the hook. She wasn't sure why her daughter was changing in so many ways, but getting on her case wasn't going to help. "How about we go out for sushi tonight after I wake up? I can make a reservation at SumoMaya."

"Yes." Vivian's eyes twinkled. "I'm going to get the sushi burrito and the rock shrimp tempura."

Bingo. Jess had known this would work. Like her namesake, Jess's Grandma Vivian, her daughter loved food. "I'm leaning toward the yellowtail crudo and the spicy tuna hand roll," Jess said.

"The two of you are ridiculous with the food talk," Drew said.

"Everyone has their passion." Jess tucked a piece of hair behind Viv's ear. What had inspired her to chop off her hair? "Right, sweetie?"

"Yeah, Mom."

Drew grabbed a spatula from the drawer under the range and held it in the air. "If food is the key to your heart, how about a plate of Chef Rubin's famous cheesy eggs?"

"Make some for me too," Jess said. A few hours ago, she couldn't have imagined putting anything in her stomach, but now she was actually hungry. Hours of anxiety had taken a lot out of her.

"Anything for my girls," he said.

A brief cloud passed over Vivian's face. Drew took the eggs from the fridge and cracked them into a bowl. Maddie galloped down the stairs, her tight tank top exposing too much breast. Her eyes were outlined in black, wings curling up at the outside edges, and her lips cherry red. Jess didn't love the cleavage or the make-up, but these days she picked her battles.

"Hi, Mom," she said. "When did you get home?" Because of Jess's long hours at work, her children were often surprised to see her here. Like a scorpion crossing your hiking trail, you knew they lived there, but you still didn't expect to encounter one.

"A few minutes ago," Jess said. "Where are you headed?"

"Talia's family is doing a staycation at The Fairmont. Ella and I are going to hang out at the pool."

"Will Mason be there?" These days, they were on a need-to-know basis. Maddie never told them the whole story, but Jess had a sneaking suspicion Maddie's boyfriend was part of the deal.

Maddie rolled her eyes. "Mom, not everything's about Mason."

Jess would beg to differ. When she checked the texts on Maddie's phone, everything was indeed about Mason. "It's a simple question, Madeline. No need to pull an attitude. Don't forget, you need to work on your college applications this weekend."

"I'll do it later, Mom."

Drew poured the eggs into the pan. "Maybe your sister would like to join you?"

"Dad, she's in seventh grade."

"That's irrelevant. She could use something to do," Drew said.

Jess's phone buzzed, Eve's name flashing on the screen. She quickly pressed ignore, too exhausted to deal with this now. Eve would have to wait. Jess needed some time to figure out what to say to her anyway.

"I don't need a pity party," Vivian said.

"I'm always doing things for her," Maddie said. "Helping her with her homework, driving her to cooking class and soccer practice. Who do you think helped her find a picture of her haircut *and* drove her to the mall to get it done?"

"You knew about that?" Jess asked.

Maddie glanced at her phone. "Ella's here. See you later." She swung her tote bag over her shoulder and flew out the door.

"*Her* friends are not my kind of people anyway," Vivian said.

Jess noticed a frosted cake under a glass dome on the counter, the perfect excuse to change the topic. "What's your latest creation?"

"Almond cake with honey lavender frosting. I was feeling inspired."

"Delicious," Jess lied. The combination sounded questionable, but she'd already done enough to piss off her girls for one morning.

Drew slid a plate in front of Vivian. "My lady, your breakfast is served."

Vivian looked down at the pile of eggs with a frown. "I'm not hungry anymore." She pushed her chair back and ran upstairs, Opal landing on the ground with a thump.

"What happened?" Drew asked. "Did I say something wrong?"

"I have no idea," Jess said, listening to Viv's heavy footsteps above her head. She wanted to chalk it all up to hormones, but she couldn't shake the sense something more was going on. A few weeks ago, after Viv refused to leave her room for an entire weekend, Drew set her up with a psychologist colleague. An impartial listening ear couldn't hurt, he'd told her. Viv hadn't said much after her first couple appointments, but she was still indulging her passion for baking, so things couldn't be too bad.

A chime rang out from her phone. Jess pressed play to listen to the voicemail.

23

"Jess," Eve said. "I've been trying to cover for you, but today was too much. Nicole is fine, and the baby is doing well in the nursery, but that wasn't okay. You put me in a terrible position. Enough is enough. You can't keep pretending—"

"Everything okay?" Drew asked.

"Yes, all good." Jess buried the phone in her pocket. "I'm going to go grab some rest."

Drew held up the frying pan. "What about your breakfast?"

"I guess I'm not hungry either," she said, climbing the stairs to her bedroom.

O   O   O

Upstairs in her walk-in closet, Jess took off her scrubs and pulled on her favorite sweatpants and an old t-shirt. Closing the closet door, she collapsed to the floor and curled into herself, her body instantly wracked with sobs. Today Jess had deserted her patient in her moment of greatest need. What if Eve hadn't been there to cover for her? Tears ran down her face onto the carpet.

Eve's voicemail played on repeat in Jess's head. *Today was too much. Terrible position. Enough is enough.* She couldn't call her back. Not now. Jess was in no shape to form a coherent sentence, much less apologize in any meaningful way. Two years ago, the Carlson delivery had put their friendship on life support, and with today's fiasco, Jess had single-handedly pulled the plug. Her thoughts turned back to the minutes immediately following the Carlson delivery.

Eve had ducked her head into the operating room. At Valley Health, the delivery nurses stayed on labor and delivery, leaving the duties in the OR to surgical nurses. Blood-soaked gauze pads, crumpled drapes, and used instruments had littered the floor. "Jess, is the baby okay?"

Jess had stood frozen along the side of the room, unable to process how everything had gone sideways so quickly. "I don't know."

"What do you mean? Where's the baby?"

"The NICU team shipped her out. Phoenix Children's."

"Why?" Eve asked. "For cooling?"

Jess leaned on the wall, the tragedy of the situation becoming clear. "I think so."

"Shit. I was praying she was getting enough oxygen."

Jess took off her cap and tucked in her scrub top. "You better keep praying. Because this mess is your fault."

"My fault? Wait a minute, Jess—"

"If you'd done your job, if you'd examined her properly, maybe this all would have turned out differently."

"Hold on," Eve said, her tone sharp. "You're the doctor and you were missing in action. And now you're blaming your nurse?"

Jess blinked away the bad memories. At the time, she had lashed out at Eve in a state of exhaustion and panic. She didn't know if she had believed what she was saying or if it was a knee-jerk reaction to the events of that day. Now, she cringed as she remembered accusing her friend so bluntly. Jess's belly ached from crying, and her eyes burned. She pushed herself up and used a nightgown from the drawer to wipe her face. How had she let things fall apart? She'd spent years building her career—medical school, residency, rising through the ranks at Valley Health—and now everything she'd worked so hard for hung in the balance. Jess had always wanted to be a doctor. Her parents had gotten her a doctor's kit for Hanukkah at age five, and she'd worn the plastic stethoscope everywhere. Once she got into medical school, obstetrics had been her hands down choice. Bringing babies into the world was a happy business, and Jess liked it that way. She had never expected the rare sad days to haunt her the way they did. Memories of the Carlson delivery had taken up residence in her soul.

Jess desperately needed some rest, but first she had to ratchet down her anxiety. Why were the panic attacks suddenly worse? Right after the Carlson delivery, she'd barely had time to think about what happened. The frenzy of the day had never faded though, and she found herself rehashing the details at odd moments. What if she'd done something differently? What if Eve had called her in earlier? Or maybe Eve had called, and Jess couldn't remember? The more she thought about it that day, the cloudier it got, her breath quickening as she struggled to pin down exactly what had happened. A few months after the Carlson delivery, the panic attacks had started, increasing steadily in frequency the closer she got to the two-year deadline. Now it was happening at least once or twice a week, if not more. Jess didn't know how much longer she could fly under the radar, especially with what had gone down this morning.

How could she explain her panic attacks to Eve now? Would Jess be able to do her job, never knowing when it would happen again? What if she couldn't work? Drew's meager social work salary wouldn't come close to covering their bills. Her stash called out to her from under her shoe rack. If she indulged, Jess knew it would help calm her nerves. Reaching under the bottom shelf, she pulled out a large Tupperware container and popped off the lid. Jess took a moment to admire her supplies, neatly lined up and organized. It was a spectacular collection.

Rolls of wrapping paper with brightly colored patterns were stacked in one section, and various ribbons, bows, scissors, and tape filled the other two. She took a wide satin ribbon from the box and ran it between her fingers, feeling her breathing calm as the fabric grazed her skin. She got onto her knees and lifted the lid off the extra laundry basket. There were a few gifts waiting to be wrapped—the adorable Noah's Ark shape sorter she'd found at the little toy store in downtown Scottsdale and the set of pretend food she'd ordered on Amazon a few weeks ago. At the beginning, Jess had picked out things for newborns. Rattles, teething toys, and board books. Splurging on an activity gym that played music and had eye-catching plastic charms hanging from the top may have been a bit much, but it was important for Hope to have lots of tummy time to strengthen her neck muscles. After she'd learned about Hope Carlson's diagnosis through the labor and delivery grapevine last year, she'd become more careful to choose developmental toys. Kids with cerebral palsy ran the gamut from mildly affected to severely impaired, and Jess had to make sure Hope was given every opportunity to thrive.

Glancing down at the rolls of paper, Jess chose a white one covered in lime green alligators and pink giraffes, a perfect pairing for the ark toy. She unrolled the right amount and cut a straight line with the scissors. The sound of the blade cleaving the crisp paper took Jess down another notch. She centered the box on the paper and carefully folded the sides over to line up in the back, securing it with double-sided tape. Then she moved on to the hard part, folding the ends into neat hospital corners. Before she started wrapping for Hope, she'd been abysmal at it, her seams crooked and corners bunchy and uneven, but now she'd become a pro. Once the paper was secure, Jess encircled the box in a green ribbon with white polka dots and tied it into a neat bow. As a finishing touch, she picked a small card and wrote a note with a pink marker.

Dear Hope,
I can't believe you're turning two. Time has flown. I'm sure you're skipping and jumping and doing all sorts of other tricks to make your parents smile. I think you'll enjoy Noah's Ark. It will help you learn about shapes and develop your fine motor skills. Have fun!

The notes were more for Kendall Carlson than for Hope, but Jess didn't want to come on too strong. If she spoke to Hope, the message came across better. She didn't want to seem creepy. Jess wanted Hope to grow into a healthy, happy child. If that meant leaving gifts without signing her name, so be it. Every time she dropped off a gift at the Carlsons', she noticed something else that needed upkeep. Hope deserved the best, and the family could use all the help they could get. She moved on to the box of play food. The picture on the outside showed various fruits and vegetables, condiments, and a pizza broken up into triangular slices. Hope may not be ready for pretend play, but she would be soon. Better to get ahead of her than to play catch-up. She picked out a turquoise paper covered with gem-tone balloons and finished it off with a large rosette bow.

Jess exhaled with a sigh. She felt much better. The voicemail from Eve briefly popped back into her mind, but she pushed it away. She'd still have to figure out how to respond, but for now, she needed to crash. Climbing into bed, she pulled the cool sheet up to her chin and let her eyes drift closed.

Chapter Five

KENDALL

After the meeting with Dr. Hill, Kendall couldn't make herself drive home. Not yet. With Troy still at work, Kendall couldn't be alone with Hope, her mind spinning on all the things her daughter couldn't do, all the milestones she hadn't reached. She picked up her cell phone and looked at Troy's name, the four letters blurring into a fuzzy black blob. Nope, she couldn't do it. He'd answer with his clipped work voice and try to rush her off the phone. Typical Troy. When he arrived home from work, she'd have to find the strength to tell him, to repeat Dr. Hill's horrific predictions out loud.

She pulled into a spot at Trader Joe's and flipped down the mirror on the visor. Even at the grocery store, Kendall liked to look her best. She ran a comb through her shiny blond hair and applied a coat of Dior coral lip gloss, the one she kept hidden in her purse. If Troy saw the designer label, he'd have a fit. With all the stress she was under, she deserved a few guilty pleasures. Kendall unbuckled Hope from her car seat and hoisted her onto her hip.

As she walked toward the entrance, she ticked through her shopping list in her head. She needed more of the honey-flavored yogurts Hope liked, the only kind she didn't spit out, and something easy to make for dinner. Troy expected food to be ready when he walked in the door, just like his mother had done for his father. The difference was his mother had been a stay-at-home mom and didn't have to care for a disabled child. Sometimes Kendall felt pinned under the weight of her husband's unrealistic expectations. He was a good husband in so many ways, loyal and steadfast, often bringing her a bouquet of spring tulips, or surprising her with a night out at her favorite farm-to-table restaurant, but he could also be so old-school. The only cooking he ever did was on the grill, and the Arizona heat made that unbearable for months on end.

Outside the entrance, Kendall spotted the last of the shopping carts with the booster seat built in and headed toward it, adjusting Hope's weight on her hip. A woman coming from the other direction clutched a wild-haired, screaming toddler to her chest, her sights set on the same cart. No way was Kendall letting her get there first. Not today. She picked up her pace to an awkward gallop, her purse sliding down her arm. As she reached the cart, she grabbed the handle, relishing the feel of the smooth plastic in her palm.

"Really? I was going to use that," the other woman said. Her baggy sweatpants and plaid shirt didn't do her any favors. She put down her child, who fell to the ground in a fit. The woman grabbed hold of the cart and gave a firm tug, but Kendall wrenched it out of her grasp. She wasn't about to let this stranger add fuel to her garbage fire of a day.

"Are you serious?" Kendall said. "It looks like you should pay attention to your kid instead of fighting over a stupid cart."

The child was now in full meltdown mode, wailing and pounding the pavement with his tiny fists. Kendall turned and rolled away, her head held high. It was a small win, but one she desperately needed.

"Who do you think you are?" the woman yelled after her.

Kendall ignored her and kept going, hoisting Hope back up onto her hip.

"Bitch," the woman said. She wrangled her squirming child into the front of a regular cart and wheeled around.

This wasn't the first time someone had slung that word at Kendall. Deep down, she knew she was a nice person, but sometimes she didn't come across that way. Even when she tried to be sweet, she often couldn't smooth out the hard edges. Once she'd gained some distance, Kendall centered Hope in the red plastic chair and fastened the straps around her, fishing a burp cloth from her purse to wipe the drool from Hope's chin. As the automatic doors whirred open, the chill of the air conditioning cooled her face. She shook off the woman's nasty comment and pushed the cart to the produce section.

Stopping next to a pile of avocados, Kendall reached out to squeeze them, finding each one firmer than the last. She moved on to the pineapples and brought one up to her nose, smelling nothing at all, not even a hint of sweetness. A few packages of the firm tofu she liked sat in the refrigerated case, but just before she got there, a young man wearing a Pride shirt swooped in and snatched them up. As she moved on, Kendall looked at Hope. She was fast asleep, her tongue protruding from her mouth, her neck shiny with drool. Kendall tried her best to straighten Hope's body and tighten the straps for safety. She tucked the burp cloth under her chin and parked the cart next to the dairy case.

The woman from the parking lot stood in her way, reading the labels on two different containers of almond milk. Her hellion of a toddler had quieted down with the help of an iPad. Maybe Kendall had been too quick to judge her. She was about to apologize when the woman looked up.

"You again?" she said. "What are you trying to do now, steal my almond milk? Here, take it." She shoved a container at Kendall, sarcasm dripping from her voice like the condensation on the side of the carton.

"I wasn't—"

"Oh, I know your type. Always out for yourself. Never thinking about anyone else."

"Hold on a minute." Kendall didn't know what had climbed up this woman's ass, and she didn't care to find out. It's not like she'd robbed a bank or killed her firstborn. They'd argued over a shopping cart for fuck's sake. "You don't know the first thing about me or my problems."

"It's not hard to see," the woman said.

31

"Oh, yeah?" Was she referring to the way Kendall dressed? Or maybe she was commenting on her hair or makeup. What this bitch didn't know—yes, the woman had just earned the same title she'd so easily slapped on Kendall in the parking lot—was that taking pride in her appearance was one of the only things keeping her sane, one of the few ways she had to cope with Hope's challenges and the stress accompanying them. Did having a French manicure make her a bad person?

"I wasn't clear enough for you?" The woman slammed both cartons back onto the shelf. Her eyes darted to Hope. "Maybe your kid's not the only retard."

The sound of the word made Kendall's heart slam against her ribcage. Say what you want about her, but no one insulted her baby. Kendall reached out and put her palms on the woman's chest. When she pushed, the woman staggered backwards a few steps and then regained her balance.

The woman's face scrunched into an angry grimace. "Who do you think you are?"

Kendall grabbed a fistful of hair and pulled. When a few strands came out in her hand, she stopped. Looking down at the dark hair, she was horrified at what she'd done. This wasn't like her.

"Augh!" the woman yelled, lunging to grab Kendall.

Kendall brought her arms over her face for protection. The woman scratched at Kendall's forearms and tried to pull her arms down while Kendall held strong. Out of nowhere, an older man with a goatee stepped away from his cart and put himself between them. "Ladies, there's more than enough milk to go around." He gently separated them, a friendly smile on his face.

"It's not…" Kendall didn't know how to explain. The room whirled around her. "It's not what you think."

"Whatever the problem is," he said, "I'm sure it's gotten out of hand."

"She started this whole thing," the woman said, as if they were having a grade school argument.

"There are always two sides to every story," the man said. "Believe me, I know."

"Whatever. I don't have time for this." The woman wheeled around and sped toward the register, her toddler wailing again as he dropped the iPad into the cart.

Kendall's face was on fire, her breath uneasy. She wasn't sure she could drive home.

"You don't look so good." The man guided her over to a bench in front of a door labelled *Employees Only.* "Let's take a seat for a minute." He motioned for Kendall to sit on the bench, then went back and retrieved the cart holding Hope.

"Things got out of control," she said.

He took a seat next to her. "That's why I stepped in. I'm no stranger to confrontation."

"What do you mean?" Kendall hoped he would keep talking. His soft voice was helping cool her temper. She took a few deep breaths, trying to calm her nerves.

"Not sure I want to share in mixed company," he said.

"I'm in no position to judge."

"Sometimes my job gets a bad rep. You won't hold it against me?"

"I don't think so," Kendall said.

"I'm an attorney, specializing in personal injury." He said the last part quietly, as if he didn't want anyone to hear.

"Personal injury?" It sounded like something she'd heard on a TV commercial, but Kendall wasn't sure exactly what it meant.

"I help people sue when they've been harmed in some way or another. Car accidents, falls, things of that nature."

While he continued to elaborate, Kendall looked back at the stacks of different colored yogurts. Hope's favorite, the honey-flavored one with the sunshine yellow label, stood out from the rest. With all the commotion, she'd forgotten to put them in her cart. In fact, her cart held only a single bunch of bananas and a ripped store newsletter. Kendall couldn't take her eyes from the yellow label. It made her think about Hope, about all the things she might never be able to do, about everything Dr. Schorr had stolen from her and her baby on the day of her birth.

"Including people who've been hurt by doctors?" she asked.

"Medical malpractice is one of my areas of expertise."

"You help people sue?" She sat up and stared into his eyes. Kendall wasn't sure why, but something about this man made her feel safe. The wrinkles at the corners of his eyes gave him a wise look, and a trim goatee softened his chin. Suddenly, Kendall broke down sobbing, all of the emotions she'd been holding in since her appointment with Dr. Hill flooding back in a rush. Tears blurred her vision.

"It's all right. We need to get you home."

"I'll… be… fine," Kendall managed between gasps. When she tried to take a deep breath, the air caught in her chest.

"I'm sure you will," he said. "You seem like a put-together young woman."

Kendall sat for a moment and tried to gather herself. She still had to finish the shopping before she could go home. "Thank you for helping me," she said once her breathing came back to normal.

He opened his wallet and pulled out a business card. "If you ever need anything."

Kendall took the card.

ABRAHAM SILVERBERG
Personal Injury Attorney
Goldman and Silverberg, LLP

She tucked it into her purse with a weak smile. In a twisted way, this chance meeting was the highlight of her day.

Chapter Six

ABE

Abe carried the groceries into the house and dropped his car keys on the dryer. In the kitchen, there was no free space, the counters covered with dirty dishes, newspapers, and stacks of junk mail. Abe put the bags on the floor, opened the dishwasher, and attempted to load the dishes, many of them stained with dried-on egg yolk and smears of peanut butter. He couldn't get the glasses to sit right on the top shelf, and the mixing bowl didn't seem to fit anywhere. When Abe tried to close the door, it kept popping back open. What the hell? He had a law degree, for Pete's sake. Giving up, he left the door open. He'd have to hand-wash the dishes later when he had more time. When Risa was alive, Abe hadn't given much thought to household tasks. There'd always been underwear folded in his drawer and clean glasses in the cabinet. Now, he was a one-man show.

While stacking groceries in the pantry, Abe noticed a bag of Risa's walnut granola on the shelf. Ten months after her death, it was surely stale by now, but Abe couldn't throw it away. Everything in this house reminded him of Risa—her face cream on the bathroom vanity, her *World's Best Teacher* mug on the floating shelf in the kitchen, old issues of *The New Yorker* filling the magazine rack by the couch. Ross and Eliza had been trying to get him to downsize to a condo, but Abe couldn't imagine leaving this house. Sure, it would help his bank account, but it would feel like a betrayal of Risa. He heard Bea rustling in her crate. The dog wouldn't want to move either. She loved running circles in the yard, paddling across the heated pool, and sunning herself on the stone patio.

35

Bea's tail thwacked against the side of her crate. Four years ago, right after Risa had been diagnosed with ALS, she'd become obsessed with browsing adopt-a-dog sites. When she came across a photo of the beagle mix, she'd fallen in love in an instant. Abe had reservations about taking in an animal, but he couldn't argue with a dying woman. Broadway, the dog's full name, had also been Risa's idea, a tribute to the city they'd left behind when they moved west all those years ago. It didn't exactly roll off the tongue, so they'd shortened it to Bea. The spunky nickname suited the dog perfectly.

Abe slid open the latch, and Bea made her grand entrance, whimpering with joy and wagging her tush along with her tail. Her earnest eyes, black nose, and spotted belly got him every time. The dog jumped on the couch and covered his face with slobber. He needed this today, a hefty dose of unconditional love.

His mind turned back to the woman he'd met at Trader Joe's, the way he'd so brazenly handed her his card. He must have been feeling the pressure of the overdue rent. Prostituting himself was not his style. Why was she contemplating a lawsuit? Did it have something to do with the baby in the cart?

He let Bea out for a quick pee and then scooped a cup of dog food into her bowl, mixing in a spoonful of canned salmon. He spoiled her rotten. Bea buried her snout in the bowl, making a chomping noise as she sucked down the kibble. While she ate, Abe glanced over at the wheelchair in the corner. He'd been putting off getting rid of it. In nicer weather, Abe used to push Risa past the clubhouse and around the pool, the desert air and small talk with neighbors providing a brief distraction from her awful disease. Everyone had heard of ALS, the ice bucket challenges filling everyone's Facebook feeds a few years back, but it was impossible to comprehend the reality of the disease until the unthinkable struck the love of your life.

Bea licked the sides of the bowl and jumped onto the couch, wiping her face against the cushions. Once the dog was satisfied all traces of her meal had been transferred to the fabric, she sat up and looked at Abe.

"Good news." Abe checked his watch. "We're going to meet Uncle Ross and Harley."

Abe met his son at the dog park at least once a week. Ross claimed it gave them a chance to catch up, but Abe knew his son wanted to lay eyes on him, make sure his widower father was taking care of himself. Clicking on Bea's harness and attaching the leash, Abe led her to the mudroom, the dog's nails clicking on the tile floor. Before he closed the door behind him, Bea let out a desperate yelp. Her mouth was empty. Bea never took a car trip without Mr. Squirrel, her favorite toy. He opened the car door and secured the dog inside, then rushed back into the house. He thought he'd seen the purple toy on the kitchen floor, but it wasn't there, nor was it in the crate or out on the patio. Where was the darn thing? If he didn't find Mr. Squirrel soon, he'd be late to meet Ross.

Maybe Bea had left him in bed. He pulled the covers off and let them fall to a heap on the floor. No dice. He jogged to the bathroom. Mr. Squirrel had to be somewhere. There was one last place Abe hadn't checked. Risa's closet.

In the months since her death, Abe had tried to pretend the closet didn't exist. Looking at Risa's brightly colored blouses hanging on the rack and her collection of sneakers on the floor made him lightheaded. Abe used the doorknob to steady himself. Focus, he told himself. Find Mr. Squirrel and get the hell out. He couldn't think about cleaning out the closet now, not with Ross waiting for him. Besides, going through Risa's jewelry or taking her clothes to Goodwill wasn't in the cards anytime soon. Abe wasn't ready yet.

Abe looked under a bunch of sweaters, behind two piles of t-shirts, and on the floor behind a tower of shoeboxes. No Mr. Squirrel. Bea was surely getting antsy out in the car. Abe knelt on the floor and reached his arm into the plastic laundry basket in the corner. Pulling out Risa's favorite gray sweatshirt, he brought the worn fabric to his face and breathed in the familiar smell, a mixture of Dove soap and vanilla. To the very end, Abe had asked the aides to use Risa's favorite body wash and perfume, so she'd still smell the same even as she was disappearing a little more every day. He couldn't bring himself to put these clothes in the laundry, to wash her familiar scent down the drain. When Abe put the sweatshirt back, he saw purple fuzz and a glassy eyeball peeking out from underneath a bunched-up pair of leggings.

"You little rascal." Abe should have known. Not only had Bea hidden the toy here before, but Abe had even found the dog curled up in the basket, her nose buried in Risa's clothes. Motivated by Risa's smell, she'd learned how to push the door open with her snout. Abe wasn't the only one grieving. He rushed back out to the car and offered Mr. Squirrel to Bea, who grabbed the toy quickly, bouncing in her seat with excitement.

At the park, the sun was low in the sky, the heat of the day dissipating. When they reached the dog park, Abe saw Ross sitting on a bench outside the fenced area, his back curved and head down. At the sight of his father, he sat up straighter and cleared his throat. Abe let Bea in through the gate and took a seat next to his son.

As Abe curled the leash on his lap, Bea scampered over to Harley, Ross's Bernedoodle. The fancy-schmancy breed was yet another opportunity for Ross to judge his father. He'd warned Abe against adopting a shelter dog, expounding on the possible behavioral and health problems. Abe could have turned around and berated Ross for paying over three grand for a designer mutt, but it wasn't his style. Ross was wired one way and Abe another.

"Bea's looking a little rough around the edges," Ross said. "When's the last time you gave her a bath?"

"I'm not sure." Risa used to bathe Bea in the tub, testing the temperature of the water on her wrist and lathering her up with expensive doggy shampoo. Now, Abe let her take an occasional dip in the pool and called it a day. "Did you work today?"

"I'm on at eight. Overnights this week."

When Ross had headed east for medical school, Abe had thought he would never look back, but after finishing his emergency medicine residency in Philly, he'd accepted a job at The Mayo Clinic here in Scottsdale. In theory, it was nice to have Ross so close, but sometimes Abe wished he were farther away. Connecting with his son didn't come easy. They talked often, but rarely communicated.

"That's rough," Abe said. "I don't know how you do it. My head hits the pillow at nine every night."

"Emergencies don't respect the clock, Dad." Ross pointed at Abe's belly. "You have a stain."

Harley jumped on the fence and barked, revealing two rows of pointy teeth. Ross's dog was unpredictable, while Bea was all belly rubs and wet kisses. Unfortunately, Harley was the closest thing to a grandchild Abe would ever have. Ross and Gavin didn't seem interested in going the surrogacy or adoption route, and Eliza was collecting master's degrees in lieu of children. Abe regretted Risa never held a grandchild in her arms, and he sometimes felt sorry for himself too. He would have been a marvelous grandfather. The loss hit him hardest at night in bed, his mind spinning with loneliness.

"Go play, Harley," Ross said. The dog sprinted over to pounce on Bea.

"How'd you do that?" Abe asked.

"I don't know. When I talk, people listen. Animals too."

"You've always been that way."

"I guess. So, how are you doing, Dad? How's work?"

"All good." Abe wasn't sure what else to say. He didn't want to bore Ross with the mundane details of his office.

"You've had a solid run. Maybe it's time to relax a little."

Watching the dogs, Abe tried not to take offense at Ross's suggestion. He was too young to be put out to pasture. "Believe it or not, I still enjoy working. The challenge and mental stimulation are good for me."

"You busy since Marty left?"

"Never better." Abe wished he could confide in Ross, but they'd never had that kind of relationship. They skimmed the surface. Diving deep was too scary.

"That guy could run down an ambulance." Ross forced a chuckle.

"Go easy on him. His heart's in the right place." Abe wasn't about to admit Ross's assessment was fair. "How's Gavin?" Abe hadn't been thrilled when Ross came out back in college, mostly because he knew it would make Ross's life harder, but Abe had come to care for his son-in-law. He was a kind man, a successful radiologist, and he clearly loved Ross.

A commotion erupted from the dog park. Harley had pinned Bea, her neck in his mouth, while all the other dogs gathered around barking. Abe and Ross stood up. Abe yelled and waved his arms until Harley released his prisoner. Bea ran away, unscathed.

"You need to get your dog trained," Abe said.

"Seriously, Dad? I've got a lot going on right now."

Abe sat back down and patted the seat beside him.

Ross collapsed onto the bench with a sigh. "Gavin's being sued."

"Oh… I see." Abe tried to squeeze Ross's shoulder, but his son pulled away.

"He didn't do anything wrong, but it doesn't matter," Ross said. "His whole life has become about defending himself. He's afraid to go to work."

"I'm sorry to hear that. What's the case about?"

"A missed lung cancer. The thing was barely a speck on the old scan. I don't understand how this can be valid."

"Sounds like a tough one. Did the patient follow up?"

"I'm not sure. Gavin is a good radiologist, Dad. He reads the journals, goes to conferences, and is always a team player. It's not fair."

"The insurance company will provide an excellent attorney. They always do." Abe had been up against enough of them over the years to know. Those defense attorneys made Harley seem docile in comparison.

"It's hard to know," Ross said. "Do you think you could take a look? Give an opinion from your side of the fence?"

Abe couldn't read a file for someone who wasn't his client, even if that someone was his son-in-law. "I'm not sure that's a good idea."

"I can get copies of the files. No one would ever know."

That wasn't the point. It wasn't the right thing to do. "I can't, Ross. It's not allowed. Gavin is family, and I'm not the attorney on the case. I'm sorry you're both going through this, I really am. And I'll be supportive in any way I can, as a father. But I can't look at the case."

Bea came over and put her paws up on the fence, her tongue hanging from the side of her mouth. Abe released the dogs and poured water into Bea's portable dish, the dog lapping it up until her chin was dripping.

"I think Bea's tired," Abe said. "Thanks for meeting me today. I'll see you soon. Give my best to Gavin."

Ross's shoulders slumped before he straightened and stretched to grab Harley's collar. Nodding once, Ross clipped on the leash and started walking to the car without looking back at Abe. If Risa were here, she would have known just what to say, the right words to soothe their son without forcing Abe to violate his ethics, and the meet-up would have ended with hugs all around.

Chapter Seven
KENDALL

Kendall unloaded the shopping bags from the trunk, her hands trembling with nerves. Dr. Hill's words echoed in her ears, the scene she'd made in Trader Joe's playing on repeat across her mind.

"What's going on?" Troy stood by the door, a serious look on his face. She'd called him from the car and asked him to leave the office early, something she'd never done before.

"We'll talk in the house. Why don't you grab Hope?"

Troy lifted Hope out of her car seat and brought her gently to his chest. Her face lit up in a lopsided smile, and Kendall's stomach fell. Her daughter rarely responded to her that way. It wasn't fair.

"Is everything okay?" he asked as they walked to the door.

"Give me a minute." Kendall adjusted the heavy groceries on her arm. A large, wrapped package sat outside the garage. Her heart sank.

"Another random package," Troy said.

"I saw it," Kendall said.

"This is getting ridiculous. What kind of whack job does this? And with weird, anonymous cards to boot. It might be time to call the police."

Kendall put the bags on the garage floor. "I'm sure they have bigger things to deal with."

"I've been researching security cameras. The one with the best reviews is on back order."

Once Troy disappeared through the door, Kendall picked up the box. She was sort of curious but unwrapping it would be a bad idea. The toys always made her feel sad about all the things Hope couldn't do, all the milestones she might never reach. Opening the storage closet in the garage, she added the present to the growing pile.

In the kitchen, Troy strapped Hope into her adaptive highchair and gave her a teething biscuit. He unpacked the bags, stacked milk and yogurts in the fridge, and filled the crisper drawer with vegetables.

Kendall motioned for him to have a seat at the island. "We need to talk."

Troy put away a carton of eggs. "I'm almost done."

Kendall shot him a look. He pulled out a barstool, the chair legs making a scraping noise on the floor, rehashing the grooves in the tiles. She wished he would pick up the chair, but she was too tired to remind him again. The kitchen badly needed to be redone, but there was no way they could swing that now.

"Kendall, what's going on?"

"It's about the appointment. You know the one you couldn't go to because you had a meeting?" Kendall still couldn't understand how a meeting about solar panels took precedence over their daughter.

"I had to be there. This new client could keep us in the black for the year. Did Dr. Hill suggest another type of therapy? What's the hourly rate for this one?"

"That's not fair." Kendall hated when Troy said things like that in front of Hope. Yes, the bills added up, but if these things could help Hope, how could they deprive her? "You know she needs it."

"I know," Troy said, his brow furrowed. "But sometimes I'm not sure it's doing any good."

"Dr. Hill shared some news today." Kendall paused, summoning the courage to repeat the doctor's predictions. "He wanted to discuss the future."

Troy took his phone from his pocket and started scrolling.

"Put your phone away," Kendall said.

"Christ, Kendall. Enough with the beating around the bush."

"Dr. Hill is not sure Hope will ever walk or talk."

His eyes widened. "Are you serious?"

"I couldn't believe it either."

"He can't be right. She's eating some foods, and she'd holding her head up so much better." Troy walked over to Hope's chair and planted a kiss on her cheek. "Our little pancake." Troy had started using the nickname a few months ago when he'd made pancakes on a Sunday morning. If they dipped tiny, little pieces in water and maple syrup, Hope was able to swallow them. Now just the sight of the griddle made her squeal with excitement.

Hope gave him another smile. It was so easy for him. Kendall took care of Hope every weekday—setting up her tube feeds and bathing her and exercising her tight muscles—and when Troy arrived home after work, Hope would light up. Troy got all the glory with none of the guts. Was that true? Kendall told herself it wasn't as skewed as it seemed. Hope loved her just as much, and there were plenty of smiles during the week. They just got lost in the grind of daily care, buried under Kendall's suffocating isolation and exhaustion. Sometimes it was hard for her to remember the good moments.

She watched her husband's hands as he played peek-a-boo with Hope. She'd always loved his hands, the way his fingers felt when he touched her. She couldn't remember the last time they'd had sex. Since Hope's arrival, they'd only done it a handful of times, more out of obligation than genuine interest. She was just so tired. What would happen if she took his hand now, touched the top of her tongue to his finger? Would he respond? Sweep her upstairs? No, they couldn't. Not with Hope right there. And honestly, if Troy took her to bed right now, she'd probably just fall asleep.

Troy shook his head. "I don't believe it. She's only a baby."

"We treat her like one, but she's not. Besides, he sees kids like her, day in and day out."

"You're acting like this guy walks on water. Do you have a crush on him or something?"

"Not funny, Troy. He's an expert in his field."

"That doesn't mean he's right. We should get a second opinion."

"Getting defensive won't do any good." Kendall softened her voice. "If you want to take her somewhere else, that's fine, but I don't think it will change anything."

Troy paced in front of the refrigerator. "Maybe he's wrong. There must be something he isn't seeing."

"Troy, you're making me nervous," she said.

He ran his hand through his hair and sat back down. "What else did he say?"

"He's been tracking her progress for a while. He said he doesn't make predictions until he's sure."

"And now he is?"

"Unfortunately, yes." She reached to touch his hand, but he pulled back to take his phone from his pocket. He typed something in and then scrolled.

"What are you looking for?"

"That damned Dr. Schorr," he said. "Looking for new reviews on RateMD."

"Obsessing about her isn't going to help." Kendall blew air out through her lips. "What's done is done."

"That doesn't mean she shouldn't pay. If she'd been more on her game, we might not be having this conversation."

"You don't know that." Kendall thought back to the day Hope was born, the pandemonium of beeping monitors, the staff yelling under face masks, the cacophony of medical jargon. Memories of her birth plan lurked in the back of her mind. Choosing not to have cervical checks had seemed like the right decision at the time—a way to reclaim a bit of control of her body in the face of her unplanned pregnancy—but maybe it had been a terrible choice, even a tragic one. "There was so much going on."

"Maybe this is just the thing we needed to kick us in gear. No more pretending." Troy had been pushing to sue since Hope was born, but Kendall couldn't deal with that complication. Figuring out how to care for Hope was more than she could handle. When Troy had brought it up again a few times, while paying bills or after another failed experimental trial, Kendall had found ways to deflect, to turn the focus from negative to positive. She wanted Hope to get better, but a lawsuit seemed so scary and nebulous. What if the defense attorney questioned her about the birth plan? Kendall didn't know if she could handle any more guilt on top of what she was already carrying.

"Dr. Hill also mentioned a new trial," Kendall said.

"Another bullshit trial?"

"He said it could help relax her muscles," Kendall filled Troy in on what Dr. Hill had said about the experimental medicine.

"I don't know. We've been in this merry-go-round too many times." He sighed and ran his hand over the cracks in the countertop. Pulling her in for a hug, he caressed the back of her head. "We need the money, Kendall. It's that simple. It's scary to think about, but I think it's time to get a lawyer. We've been going it alone for too long."

"I know it's all so expensive, but we're doing okay, right?"

"Not so much. Solar Strides hasn't seen the growth we'd expected, and from what you've said, KC Events isn't exactly flush with cash either."

Kendall's face burned at the mention of her company account. "That's not fair. You know it's been hard for me."

"It's time." Troy pursed his lips, a sign of determination. He was a loving father, and he wanted to do what was best for their child. There was nothing malicious about it. She felt a surge of love, for him and for Hope, but she still wasn't sure the lawsuit was the right way to go. She was a nice person, not a money grabber who used her child for financial gain.

Kendall thought again about the man from Trader Joe's, the one with the goatee and the kind eyes. Reaching into her back pocket, she pulled out the business card. Before she had a chance to show it to Troy, a harsh gasp came from the highchair. When Kendall looked over, Hope's face was swollen, and her eyes wide with panic, half of the biscuit on the tray in front of her. Kendall released the straps and grabbed Hope under the arms, adrenaline pulsing through her veins.

"She's choking!" Kendall screamed. Hope had to be watched carefully, especially when she had things in her mouth.

Troy laid Hope face down on his forearm and pounded her back, his large hand making a slapping sound. Kendall reached under and swept her finger in Hope's mouth, trying to remember what she'd learned in the baby CPR class.

"Keep going," she yelled.

Kendall watched, paralyzed with fear. Hope's skin had turned pale, her usual pink color faded to white. After all they'd been through, she couldn't lose Hope. She'd never be able to recover from that.

"Don't stop," she said. "You have to keep going."

Troy's breath was ragged, fear in his eyes. After several more desperate slaps, a piece of biscuit shot out of Hope's mouth and across the kitchen, landing in front of the refrigerator.

Hope gasped and started wailing. "It's okay, Pancake." Troy cradled her to his chest, covering her with kisses. "You're better now. You're going to be all right."

"I thought we could lose her," Kendall said, her voice shaky.

Troy rubbed circles on Hope's back. "This girl is stronger than you or I know. Stronger than anyone knows." He paused and looked directly at Kendall. Still holding Hope securely, he reached out with one arm and touched Kendall's shoulder. "It's time, Kendall. Hope's birthday is next month."

"I know." Only a few months after Hope came home from the hospital, Troy's boss had mentioned he had a cousin who'd brought a birth injury lawsuit, throwing in that Arizona law said they had to make the decision by age two. Would choosing to sue be an admission of defeat, an acknowledgment of Dr. Hill's predictions? But what if the lawsuit gave them the cushion they needed to give Hope every possible treatment? If Kendall deprived her child, she'd never be able to forgive herself. Maybe it was time to listen to Troy, before they lost the chance forever.

"We need to find an attorney," he said.

"I'll do some digging." Putting her hand in her back pocket, Kendall fingered the sharp corner of the business card. She still wasn't totally on board, but when she was ready, she knew exactly who to call.

Chapter Eight

JESS

On her way to work, Jess headed to the Carlsons' house to deliver the latest gift. She usually made the drops under cover of darkness, but today she was running late. Her hairdryer had decided to call it quits, and she'd had to sort through the mess under the sink in the girls' bathroom to find another one. Still, the sun was just peeking above the horizon, the desert air pleasantly cool. Though she'd given Hope a big box of wooden puzzles a couple days ago, the shape sorter was wrapped and ready to go. Better Hope have the toy than let it collect dust in Jess's closet. Besides, Hope was probably recognizing colors and shapes by now, and Jess didn't want to miss her window.

She turned left off Scottsdale Road and passed through the entrance to the Carlsons' neighborhood. Slowing down as she pulled onto Solano Lane, Jess took care to make sure no one was outside. The optics wouldn't be good if she got caught, but she felt compelled to make sure the gifts arrived safely. Jess's hands were clammy on the steering wheel as she coasted to the curb. She took a deep breath and held it for a moment, scanning the house for lights. Nothing. Her heart pounding, she slipped out of the car and removed the gift from the passenger seat, trying to close the car door without making any noise. Jess tensed up every time she came here, but the visits were the one thing that kept the guilt from pooling in her stomach. She tried to push the thoughts away. She'd done the best she could in an impossible situation. She was a good doctor, but she wasn't superhuman. Dwelling on what-ifs wasn't going to change anything now.

Walking up the driveway, Jess took in the state of the house. It looked even worse than it had last time. Chips of tan paint had peeled off the stucco walls, several shingles were missing from the roof, and the windows needed a good scrubbing. The landscaping wasn't much better, the coverage in the rock gardens thin and the cactuses shriveled. Jess didn't know what Kendall or her husband did for a living, but based on the state of the property, they struggled to make ends meet.

Jess placed the wrapped package outside the garage. As she walked back to her car, her muscles unclenched. Giving Hope gifts was the highlight of her day. Though she would never be able to see Hope play with the toys, imagining was the next best thing. When Kendall unwrapped the ark toy, Hope's face would light up. Kendall would open the box, take out the ark, and empty out the colored animals, the plastic clicking on the wood floor. Hope would clap her hands together and giggle, the sound of her laughter filling the room. At first, Kendall might need to help Hope learn which shape fit in which hole, but with practice, Hope would surely get the hang of it.

She took a deep breath, relishing the fresh air in her lungs. Early morning in the desert was her favorite time, before the sun began its torturous ascent. As she reached her car, she noticed motion next door. A middle-aged woman was doing lunges in the neighboring driveway, her hair held back with a thick headband. She gave Jess a questioning smile. This woman had never been here before. Jess cursed her hair dryer for fritzing out today, when she had places to be. Fixing her eyes on the pavement, Jess moved toward the driver's door with purpose, trying to avoid an interaction.

"Everything okay over there?" the woman asked.

Jess tried to open the door, but found it locked. Where had she put her keys? "Yes, fine."

"I read an article that early morning exercise is better for your body." The woman walked down the driveway toward her. "Gets your day started right."

Jess plunged her hand into her purse, rooting around for her keys. "Sounds very ambitious."

"Do you live in the neighborhood?" The woman stopped next to the car. "I haven't seen you at the pool."

"Um, no. I was just—" Jess couldn't come up with a quick excuse for why she was here so early. Nothing made any sense.

"Just delivering a present for little Hope?" The woman motioned to the box outside the garage. "Kendall's been wondering about you."

Oh, shit. This woman was quite a busybody. Jess prayed she wouldn't tell Kendall she'd seen her delivering the gift.

Jess retrieved her keyring from the depths of her bag and pressed the unlock button, the beep piercing the morning stillness. "No, I… I have to go."

"What's your name?"

Jess jumped into the car and threw it into drive. She had to make herself scarce before this woman asked any more questions.

O   O   O

"Today's lecture is about the umbilical cord, the normal anatomy, and what can go wrong." Jess aimed the laser pointer at the slide. This was the last thing Jess wanted to discuss, but the residency director had assigned her the topic, so she had to run with it.

The residents sat in a few rows of chairs, some of them attentive and others more focused on their free lunch than on the screen.

"The normal cord has three vessels, one vein and two arteries. It's coated in Wharton's jelly, which protects the vessels from compression. But there are a lot of ways things can go wrong."

Anita, the chief resident, took a bite of pizza, a string of cheese hanging from her chin. Looking at the cord of cheese, Jess forgot her line of thinking for a moment. What had she been talking about?

"Oh… where was I?" Jess asked.

Anita wiped her mouth with a napkin. "Things going wrong."

"Yes, right. Cord abnormalities fall into two broad categories. Anatomical and external. Problems from the inside and problems from the outside." Jess tried her best to make her voice animated, keep the residents on board.

Hudson, one of the first years, raised his hand. "By inside, you mean malformations of the cord?"

"Exactly. The cord can be too short or too long, too coiled or not coiled enough, and then there are problems with abnormal insertion. There's a complete list in your handout."

Hudson lowered his hand and shoved a bite of salad into his mouth.

"When we talk about external problems, the one you've all heard of is the nuchal cord. It shows up in movies all the time. Someone gets to be the hero, freeing the cord from around the baby's neck. You can only pray it's a sliding loop instead of a locked cord."

"What's a locked cord?" Hudson asked.

"When the cord is wrapped so tightly it can't be slid off. Pray that never happens. And if it does, fire up the operating room ASAP."

A few of the residents' mouths dropped open.

"Don't worry." The phrase was easy for Jess to say, but much harder to follow. "If you do your homework and log enough deliveries, you'll know how to handle the situation."

Anita raised her hand. "I'm graduating in less than a year. There are never enough deliveries."

"You'll continue on the job, for sure. Medicine is about life-long learning." Wasn't that the truth? Jess had learned things she'd never wanted to learn, seen things she could never unsee, no matter how hard she tried.

"The cord can also be completely normal, but in the wrong place. The main one in this category is prolapsed cord. If the cord extends into the birth canal, it can be compressed by the baby's head, cutting off blood supply." The laser pointer dot quivered on the screen. Jess's mind drifted back to the Carlson delivery, her heartbeat hammering in her ears. Kendall Carlson had had a prolapsed cord. If Jess allowed herself to relive that day right now, she'd never finish this lecture. No. Not here. She took a breath and tried to calm her trembling hand.

"The most important thing to do is stay calm. If you panic, mom will too." The Carlson delivery had been the opposite of calm, the delivery room a frenzied chaos. "And, uh… I'm not sure…" The red dot on the screen blurred into a fuzzy red orb. "I don't…"

Anita stood up from the front row and took hold of Jess's elbow. "Dr. Schorr, are you okay?" She guided Jess to a chair in the front row. Jess tried to calm her breathing and quiet her hands. Hudson handed her a plastic cup of water, which Jess sipped slowly. After a few minutes, the shaky feeling passed.

"My blood sugar must be low." Jess stood and slipped her computer into her work bag. She had to get out of here before the residents started asking questions she didn't care to answer. "I'll email out my slides so everyone can review."

Retreating to her office, Jess slumped into her desk chair and rested her head down on her arms. She tried the meditation breathing again. In for four, out for three. Was that right? Damn it. How could she have blown it again? To be well-trained, the residents needed to learn about the umbilical cord, and Jess had failed them. She was letting people down everywhere she turned. At work, for sure, and her home life wasn't smooth sailing either. She couldn't remember the last time she and Drew had gone out for dinner, she'd been avoiding visiting her father in the nursing home, and something was going on with Vivian. Looking up at the time on the computer, Jess realized she was late to meet Mai for lunch in the cafeteria.

Downstairs, Jess spotted her best friend near the back of the seating area. Giving her a *wait one minute* finger, Jess ordered her usual salad at the counter.

"Took you long enough," Mai said, once Jess sat down. "I was about to eat my own arm." Ninety pounds at most, Mai could really put it away. Hours spent in spin class allowed her to eat her weight in food.

Jess opened the plastic container and poked the salad with her fork. "I'm not having the best day."

Mai took a bite of her sandwich. "What's going on?"

"Feeling off my game. I'm not sure what it is." Jess hadn't told Mai about the Carlson delivery or the panic attacks, but maybe the time had come. Eve might have already told Mai anyway, and it would be good to have someone to lean on, especially now that the panic attacks were becoming more frequent.

"Something with work?"

"That's part of it, but I just feel off. In the OR, in clinic, even at resident lecture. Something's not right."

"Sounds stressful."

Jess wasn't ready to talk about the panic attacks, but she could at least share what was happening with Viv. "It really is. Vivian just started seeing a psychologist. Drew insisted. At first, I thought it was overkill, but I think it was the right choice after all."

"What's going on?"

"She's always in her room behind closed doors. Doesn't go out with friends or do anything fun. Baking is the only thing that makes her smile."

"Better to get help early. You never know what's going on in her head."

"I know. I just want to get both my kids through their teenage years alive and intact."

"Agreed. And what about work?"

"I don't know," Jess said. "My enthusiasm isn't what it used to be. I certainly don't look forward to coming here."

"Maybe it will pass. I go through phases too," Mai said. "Medicine isn't all it's cracked up to be. If another patient complains of thumb pain, I swear. It's from scrolling on your stupid phone, dumbass. Rheumatology doesn't offer much drama."

Jess took a bite of salad. "If I'd known you in med school, I could have steered you to a more exciting field." The two women had become instant friends during an orientation session at the hospital for new residency staff. Instead of watching insulting videos about patient confidentiality, they'd spent the afternoon passing notes back and forth.

"Can't complain. My schedule is good, and the journals keep accepting my papers."

"You're killing it," Jess said. Mai had risen through the academic ranks at remarkable speed. She'd likely be awarded full professor before fifty, while Jess would still be rewriting the same mind-numbing article. Preeclampsia in teenagers had seemed like an interesting topic at first, but now Jess had trouble feeling inspired. Every time she sat down to write, her mind wandered to other things—Maddie's college essays, the magic cookie bar recipe Vivian had come up with, the inane reality dating show she'd been binging on Netflix—anything besides formatting statistical charts and discussing results she cared nothing about. "I can't meet a deadline to save my life. Ken Smart is probably hiring a hit man as we speak."

"How do you get in the zone? Classical music works for me. Maybe herbal tea or meditation?"

"I find every excuse not to write. I'd even rather take the cat to the vet."

"Don't get down on yourself. Everyone has low points."

"This could be more than that. Maybe publish or perish isn't for me." Jess should never have taken an academic job. Her father's voice had been echoing in her head, telling her it was the only choice. Not only had he insisted she become either a doctor or a lawyer, he'd also constantly touted the prestige of academia. A math professor, he'd expected his daughter to follow in his footsteps, but seeing her name at the top of a journal article left Jess cold. She preferred face-to-face clinical interactions over research. If she'd gone into private practice, she wouldn't have had to worry about churning out the journal articles to claw her way up the academic ladder. The job would be focused on caring for people, the reason why she'd chosen medicine to begin with.

"What else would you do?"

"Take care of people. Without having to churn out papers."

"Keep your eye on the prize. If it takes you longer to get there, so be it."

Jess cringed at this suggestion. Sometimes Mai sounded like Jess's father, or like her father used to sound, his single-minded focus on grades and status above all else. For him, talking about emotions was a frivolous waste of time. As long as Jess made honor roll, aced her exams, and got into the best college and medical school, nothing else mattered. He was all business all the time. Come to think of it, Jess hadn't visited her dad in several weeks. Had she been subconsciously avoiding it? Finding things to talk about with him was never easy.

"I'm not sure I'm even headed in the right direction," Jess said.

"What do you mean?"

"Remember rotating through the public hospital during residency? I really liked it over there."

"That dump? I couldn't get out of there fast enough."

"It doesn't have the same resources," Jess said, "but seeing pregnant teens made me feel useful, like I'd done something worthwhile."

"No teens in your practice now?"

"Few and far between. I can't remember the last one I saw."

Mai's phone pinged, and she picked it up. "Have you seen this?" She showed Jess the screen. A fat-bottomed bear waded into a backyard swimming pool. The camera shook. There were whispers in the background while the bear paddled across and back, before climbing out and shaking off. Red tags stamped with the numbers 311 protruded from both ears.

"Wow," Jess said. "Is that in Scottsdale?"

"Yeah, up north. Weird, isn't it? He has his own Facebook page."

"Why is he tagged?"

"To keep track of him. They look like little earrings."

Jess felt a flutter in her chest. "This isn't cute."

"Don't overreact, Jess. It's just a harmless black bear. Probably only weighs a couple hundred pounds."

"Of wild animal."

Mai slipped her phone back into her purse. "Is something else bothering you? You seem on edge."

"No, all good."

"Come on, Jess. You think I don't see through that?"

Jess glanced around to make sure no one was in earshot. Maybe she would feel better if she told Mai about the panic attacks. "Don't tell anyone, okay?"

"My lips are sealed."

"I keep having these episodes."

"Episodes?"

"I can't catch my breath, and things get all blurry. When it comes on, even simple things are hard. It's so scary."

"How long has this been happening?" Mai's expression radiated concern.

"For about two years, but only once in a while. Lately it's been more often."

"And you didn't tell me until now?"

"I haven't told anyone," Jess said quietly.

"Not even Drew? I know you're strong-willed, but it's okay to ask for help. You are married to a social worker after all."

"I don't want to make a big deal."

Mai finished her sandwich and closed the container. "What do you think started it?"

"There's this one patient I can't get out of my mind. Nothing's been the same since that day."

"What happened?"

Jess slumped in her chair, exhausted by the conversation. This was more than enough for one day. "It's too much. I can't get into it now."

"Maybe you should see someone," Mai said.

Jess took a sip of iced tea. "What do you mean? A therapist?"

"Therapist, psychiatrist, social worker. Spin the wheel and take your pick."

"I've never needed that—"

"Asking for help doesn't make you weak. You know that."

"I never expected to be the one in the chair."

"And I never thought I'd spend my life treating arthritis. Sometimes, you have to go with the flow."

Going with the flow had never come easy to Jess. She always liked to know which end was up, but lately everything seemed upside down. Jess thought of Claire, the psychologist Vivian had started seeing recently.

"I'm sure I can dig up some names, if you want." Mai said.

"No need," Jess said. "I think I've got it covered."

○ ○ ○

Jess muddled her way through the rest of her workday, trying her best to get the journal article in order. The results section was in mediocre shape—many of the tables were disorganized and the statistical analyses less than clear—but she'd take what she could get. She cursed Ken Smart for roping her in as a co-author. Though she'd had to say yes, Jess had really wanted to take a pass. She squeezed her eyes shut and back open, trying to make sense of the numbers swimming on the screen. No dice. Tackling the discussion section would require too much processing for her late-afternoon brain. She decided to go home and start fresh tomorrow. On her way out, she pushed the button to open the hospital automatic doors and was slammed with a wall of heat. Today was a real scorcher. Jess put on her sunglasses and tried to remember where she'd parked. When she pressed the unlock button on her key fob, a honk sounded from three rows away.

When she'd nearly reached her car, Eve pulled into the next spot. Jess ducked down behind a pickup truck, hoping the nurse would rush past her. Jess had been avoiding Eve since that horrific delivery last Saturday morning. She knew she'd fucked up, but the last thing she needed was more guilt. She heard the car door close and the confirming staccato beep of the locks. Jess turned her head away from the sound of the approaching footsteps, as if to make herself invisible.

"Jess?" Eve said. "What are you doing?"

"Oh… I dropped my keys. But I found them now." Jess stood up, jingling her keys in the air.

"Were you in clinic today?"

"Academic day. I have a paper due soon."

"Part of the deal, I guess," Eve said.

"Yup." An awkward silence followed. Jess wished Eve would go away. She didn't have the mental strength to deal with her, on top of everything else.

"I left you a message," Eve said.

"My phone's been acting up." Jess was digging a hole for herself. Why couldn't she just tell Eve the truth? She'd listened to the message, but she had no idea how to respond, what to say to make things right between them.

"Did you get an email from risk management?" Eve asked.

"Not yet." Jess hadn't checked her work account for a few days, but the email was surely lurking in her inbox. With two accounts for the hospital—one for patient correspondence and one administrative—plus her personal account and the old med school account, it was hard to stay current. Maybe she'd been subconsciously avoiding that one.

"They're going to close the file soon. If the Carlsons don't bring a suit by next month, they've lost their chance."

Jess looked around to make sure the coast was clear. This wasn't a good place to talk about this. A bead of sweat rolled down her neck. Jess looked longingly at her SUV, wishing she could get in and turn the AC on full blast.

"I also wanted to check in with you," Eve said. "See how you're doing."

"I'm fine, honestly." Jess wasn't about to tell Eve she'd nearly passed out while lecturing about umbilical cord prolapse. It was a miracle Eve hadn't reported her already, so she didn't want to give her more ammunition. "You don't have to worry about me."

"You need to take care of yourself."

"Believe me, I am. I'm still hiking every weekend," Jess lied, trying to reassure Eve she was practicing self-care.

"That often?"

"A bunch, yeah."

"Remember the time we summited the pyramid trail together?" Eve said with a smile.

Jess couldn't remember the last time she'd seen Eve's face light up. "We told each other jokes to get to the top."

"Bad jokes and so many energy gels," Eve said. "Gross."

"Not so appetizing."

"Brunch afterwards was always much better."

"The hash browns and waffles with mounds of fruit on top —"

"And don't forget the Bloody Marys with olives and pickles—"

"And extra horseradish!" they said together.

"I could use one of those right about now. Maybe next weekend?" Jess asked. Suggesting this made Jess feel vulnerable, but the easy banter between them encouraged her to take the leap. She wanted to patch things up between them, not only because she missed their friendship, but also because keeping her emotions bottled up had taken a toll.

"Oh…" Eve cast her eyes downward. "I'm not sure that's a good idea."

"It would be fun. Give us a chance to catch up." Jess knew she sounded desperate, but she couldn't help pushing.

"I don't know," Eve said. "That episode last week scared me. You put me in a terrible position. A nurse shouldn't be delivering babies on her own."

"I'm not sure what happened, but it won't happen again." Jess feigned confidence.

"We're both lucky it turned out okay."

"You don't need to panic. Everything's fine." Jess's stomach flipped over. She had to figure out a way to get out of here before she lost all composure. "I promise."

"Jess, I can tell something's not right. I was hoping you'd get better, but you need to get help." Eve's eyes shone with determination.

"Don't worry about me. I have everything under control."

Chapter Nine

KENDALL

The women sat in a circle under the shade of the playground canopy. The other babies crawled or toddled while Hope sat propped on Kendall's lap, her head resting on her chest. Kendall was glad Jeanine Koch had suggested they meet at the railroad park today rather than at her perfect house. The pristine flowered wallpaper and monogrammed hand towels in the bathroom gave Kendall an inferiority complex.

"Bir-die," Tyler said, pointing to a brown bird perched on the edge of the slide. "Birdie, Mama."

"Yes, sweetie, bird. Good job." Jeanine smoothed Tyler's hair off his forehead. "He's learning so quickly now. The words are coming fast and furious."

Why did Kendall keep coming to this group? After every session, she told herself this would be the last. The monthly reminders of the milestones Hope might never reach did no favors for Kendall's mental health, but she always found a reason to return.

"It's incredible," Liv Marshall said. "They're these amazing flowers. They start from tiny seeds, and with a little water and a lot of love, they blossom. A true wonder." Liv's daughter grabbed a handful of rocks and stuffed them into her mouth.

"No." Liv pried open the baby's mouth and brushed the rocks from her tongue. "Dirty. That's dirty."

Kendall thought back to Hope's choking episode a few days ago. What if she hadn't glanced over when she had?

"How's Hope doing?" Jeanine asked.

Kendall shook away the awful memory. She didn't want to think about what could have happened.

62

Aubrey Lawlor handed her son an applesauce packet. "Yes, we want to hear the news."

"Thank you for asking," Kendall said. As painful as these meetups were, these women were Kendall's only friends. She didn't count her neighbor, Marisol, who was twenty years older, more mother figure than friend. Though Kendall had grown up and gone to college in Arizona, many of her friends had dropped away. They'd shown up to the baby shower with burp cloth cakes and bottle warmers and board books, offering phony smiles and words of congratulations, but soon afterwards, her phone went silent. Her parents' response hadn't been much better. With no idea how to deal with a disabled grandchild, they visited Kendall's brother in Minneapolis more often than they drove less than an hour to see her.

"The news was not good."

"Whatever it is, we're here to support you," Aubrey said.

"That's what this group is for," Jeanine said. "To celebrate the good times and prop each other up in bad ones. This parenting thing is no joke."

"Airplane." Tyler pointed at the sky. The plane etched two parallel white lines against the vivid blue sky.

"You're right," Kendall said. Jeanine's heart was in the right place, but sometimes she could be tone-deaf. Her son was practically speaking in full sentences, so it didn't sit right when she went on about how difficult parenting was for her.

"Amen to that." Liv opened her daughter's fist and brushed more rocks to the ground. "Can't take your eyes off them for a second."

Hope listed to the left. Kendall shifted her position to give her more support. When she was alone, she would have used the nursing pillow, but she didn't want to invite extra attention. Stares of pity only made her feel worse.

"So, what did the doctor say?" Aubrey asked. Her son squeezed applesauce onto his neck and down the front of his shirt.

"He wasn't optimistic." Kendall's chest tightened. "About Hope's future, I mean."

"What do you mean?" Jeanine asked.

Kendall's eyes filled with tears. "He said she may never walk or talk."

The group fell silent.

"That's a shock," Jeanine said.

"You don't have to accept that," Liv said. "Be your child's best advocate. Don't take no for an answer."

"But isn't he a specialist?" Aubrey wiped her son's shirt with a burp cloth. "Maybe Kendall should listen to what he has to say."

"I'm not suggesting she ignore it," Liv said. "I just mean Kendall shouldn't let it get her down. There could be other ideas—like homeopathic medicine or acupuncture. There's a whole world of alternative treatments out there."

Kendall had had more than enough of Liv's off-the-wall suggestions. Reiki and essential oils weren't going to cure cerebral palsy.

"What about a second opinion?" Jeanine asked. "See if another doctor says something different."

"That's what Troy suggested. When I told him about the appointment, he went into fight mode. Started talking about other stuff too."

"What other stuff?" Aubrey said.

"He got really angry." Kendall wasn't sure she wanted to mention the possible lawsuit here. On one hand, it seemed so personal, something that should be whispered about, but on the other, she needed input. She and Troy had been going around in circles for too long. Maybe other opinions would help her come to a decision. "I think he wants to sue. We've talked about it in passing before, but it never seemed right to me. It might make things worse rather than better."

"Think about the costs of what Hope might need," Liv said. "It would be nice to have some extra money."

"If the doctor made a mistake, she should pay," Jeanine said.

"I'm not sure," Kendall said. "Maybe the early labor was my fault. Pilates class or the sushi the night before. I'm not sure it should all fall on her." She hadn't told the other moms she'd declined cervical checks, so mentioning it now would only make the conversation more confusing.

"That's crazy talk. You can't blame yourself," Jeanine said.

"I don't know," Aubrey said. "She's a good doctor. Maybe she doesn't deserve it." Dr. Schorr had delivered Aubrey's baby too, and everything had gone as planned. Aubrey often described the delivery as if it were a stroll in the park on a sunny day.

"It's your decision," Liv said. "But don't write it off too quickly. If not for you, then for Hope."

Kendall tried to take a breath, but she couldn't, the drowning feeling washing over her again. She needed to change the topic. She stood up and centered Hope's weight on her hip.

"How about a ride?" Jeanine suggested. "We can't come to the railroad park without getting on the train."

Leave it to Jeanine to redirect. She often had a sixth sense about what Kendall needed. The ladies had given her a lot to think about, but she needed a break to digest their advice. Once they'd gotten their tickets and claimed seats in the open-air train, Kendall breathed easier. The conductor stood up and gave a speech about the park. Though she'd heard it countless times, she still loved everything about it—his ironed uniform with the buttoned vest and pocket watch, the resonance of his voice, the animated way he told the story.

The train started up with a loud horn and screeching of wheels on the track. As it picked up speed, Kendall welcomed the fresh air on her skin, the wind whipping her hair around her face. She loved the rhythmic click-clack of the wheels, the vibrant, primary-colored train cars, and the hum of the engine noise, but what she loved most of all was the look on Hope's face. Her eyes closed and her mouth open to catch the wind, she seemed perfectly at peace. Anyone looking at her wouldn't know she'd yet to take her first steps or say her first word, that her parents paid hundreds of dollars a month for therapies that might never make a difference, that she'd been sentenced to a life with disability before she'd taken her first breath. Was Dr. Schorr at fault? Kendall wasn't sure. Maybe if Dr. Schorr had paid more attention, reacted faster, Hope would be toddling across the circle, eating rocks, or squeezing applesauce onto her clothing.

A tap on her shoulder snapped Kendall back to the moment. Jeanine sat behind her, Tyler on her lap.

"How are you holding up? You're dealing with a lot."

"I'm fine."

"Kendall, you don't have to pretend. You've got a tough decision to make."

Kendall buried her nose in Hope's curls and took a deep breath. The smell of baby shampoo grounded her.

"It's okay to be unsure. To live with uncertainty for a little while."

"That's not easy for me," Kendall said.

"No kidding," Jeanine said. "You don't have to be perfect all the time. Sometimes it's okay to just be you."

"I do so much for Hope, but none of it seems to make any difference. Maybe I've found something that might."

"Maybe," Jeanine said. "But don't make any rash decisions. Let the idea percolate for a bit."

Kendall wiped Hope's face with a cloth.

"Listen, we're all going for frozen yogurt. Why don't you join us? Take your mind off things."

"I have to get Hope home for her nap,"

"If she sleeps later, is that the end of the world?"

"No…" Kendall pictured the scene. All of the other kids eating ice cream with a spoon, while Hope would thrust the treat from her mouth and be wearing the entire cup within five minutes. No, she couldn't bear it. Not after everything else she'd been through in the past few days. "Troy invited some colleagues over for dinner. I have to get home to start cooking."

○　　○　　○

With Hope finally napping, Kendall's shoulders crept down from around her ears. She walked from room to room, assessing where to tidy up first. The mudroom was a disaster zone—Hope's shoes and toys strewn all over the floor, Troy's dirty softball uniform on the dryer, and desert mud ground into the tiles. Kendall didn't have the energy to take this on yet. She'd start with a smaller task, score an easy win. Kendall headed to her walk-in closet and breathed in the woodsy scent. When they'd toured the house, Kendall had ignored the cracked floor tiles, dated kitchen cabinets, and broken sliding glass doors. The closets had sealed the deal—his and hers with cedar walls and top of the line organizing systems.

Picking up random shoes from the floor, Kendall lined them up on the rack, organizing the pairs together. Then she turned to her sweaters, refolding each one and stacking them in the pull-out drawers. Just as she was moving on to her pants, one of the dust bags on the top shelf caught her eye. She grabbed a stepstool and took a few down. Now was the perfect time to take stock of her collection, give the girls some air.

Kendall sat down on the stool and removed her first darling from its silk bag. Her eyes welled up, as often happened when she held the classic Chanel flap bag. Running her hand over the black, quilted leather and heavy gold chain, she twisted the iconic clasp and opened the flap to make sure the authenticity card was still inside. It was there, safe and sound. She patted the pocket and zipped the bag back into the protective case. Next, Kendall moved on to a Louis Vuitton. The designer's utilitarian totes and monogram patterns had never been her favorite, but this one was a true beauty. The rectangular shape, cream-colored leather, and curved caramel handle epitomized timeless elegance. Plus, this one had a microchip sewn into the lining, so she'd never go astray. Kendall took a deep whiff of the leather, then tucked her away.

Just one more and she'd get back on task. She couldn't be caught on the floor surrounded by designer handbags. When Kendall wore them in public, she assured Troy they were quality fakes, deals she'd found on a special website. A little white lie never hurt anyone, right? She tried not to dwell on how she'd paid for them, to pretend KC Events wasn't in the red. Unzipping another dust cover, she pulled out a flirty lady. The Bottega Veneta bag was a playful yellow color with padded fabric in a woven checkerboard pattern. If the others were fine French pastries—chocolate croissants or delicate éclairs—this one was a marshmallow Peep. An impulse purchase at Fashion Square last year, this bag always put a smile on Kendall's face.

An important piece was missing from Kendall's collection. She didn't yet have an Hermès, the holy grail of handbags. With no store in Arizona, this one posed a bigger challenge. After some online research, Kendall had scored the phone number for Jeffrey, a sales associate at the Beverly Hills store. She'd also bought earrings, a pair of sandals, and a Twilly scarf—you needed to establish a purchasing history to be considered for a bag—but no offer yet. Maybe if she told Jeffrey the story about Hope's delivery, he might acquiesce. Why hadn't she thought of that sooner? She'd leave a heart-wrenching voicemail for him later this week. Kendall stepped back onto the stool and slid each girl back into place. It had been a lovely visit, but it was time to get back to reality.

Chapter Ten
ABE

It was Saturday, but Abe couldn't steer his mind away from work. No matter how hard he tried to read the newspaper, his thoughts kept drifting back to the firm's pile of outstanding bills and the limited income to cover them. There would still be some collections from prior cases, but not enough to move the needle in any meaningful way. Retrieving his weathered briefcase from the mudroom, Abe removed his laptop and a file folder full of mail. If he was going to perseverate about work, he might as well make himself useful. Bea plunked herself down at his feet.

Abe took the envelopes from the folder and flipped through them. Most of it was chazerei, trash destined for the junk bin: various sales mailers from legal billing companies, banks, and retirement planners. The last one was official correspondence from the office condo board. Abe ripped open the envelope and scanned down the letter to the bottom line. Because the carpets throughout the building were in dire need of replacement, there would be an unexpected special assessment. Goldman and Silverberg owed ten thousand smackers, due by the end of next month. For Pete's sake. This was the last thing he needed right now.

Pressing the power button on the computer, Abe whispered a silent prayer for it to boot up. It was long overdue to be replaced, but he'd have to limp along with it for a while longer. On the home screen, he clicked on his firm management software and opened the accounting tab, the screen populating with a rainbow of graphs and numbers. Despite the colorful display, this was far from a pretty picture. The balance in the account was the lowest in Abe's memory, and he hadn't yet added the assessment expense.

69

His morning coffee churned in his stomach. He couldn't bring himself to type in the number and watch the balance dwindle before his eyes. If he didn't land a good client and fast, rent would only be covered for a few months. He briefly thought of Marty, how easily he used to whip up business out of nowhere, but that wasn't going to help now. Abe had to tackle this problem on his own. It was time to start knocking down doors and handing out his card to anyone who would take it. Maybe the Sean Barclay case was a stinker, but that didn't mean Abe was down for the count. He still had some fight left in him.

Abe closed the laptop and got up to refill his coffee. Enough wallowing for one day. He needed to find something to occupy himself, anything to get his mind off the dismal state of affairs at the firm. His work shirts had been lingering in the dryer since Wednesday, so it was high time he fired up the iron to press them. Abe set up the board in the living room and laid the first shirt down, smoothing out the fabric. He slid the hot metal over the shirt, then sprayed some water from the squirter. The more he ran the iron over the fabric, the more the wrinkles multiplied. When he smelled a burning odor, he lifted the iron to see a singed, brown hole in his favorite shirt. Darn it all. Buying new shirts wasn't in the cards right now. Somehow, Risa always had his shirts pressed to perfection while Abe couldn't do it to save his life. Enough already. He unplugged the iron with a harrumph. Norah didn't care what he wore to work anyway.

Bea gave a sharp bark for attention.

"What is it? You want to play?"

The dog's eyes sparked with life, her time-to-play-fetch face. He grabbed her favorite orange ball, the one that fit perfectly in her mouth, and lobbed it over the couch. Bea scampered around and retrieved her prize, dropping it proudly at her master's feet.

"Good girl. Again?"

Taking a seat on the couch, Abe prepared for a long game of fetch. After several repeat performances, Bea tired herself out and flopped into his open arms, her tongue lolling out the side of her mouth. When he buried his face in the scruff of her neck to give her a kiss, he smelled a foul odor. Clearly, her quick rinse-offs in the pool weren't doing the job. She was long overdue for a proper bath.

Abe headed to his bathroom and stopped in his closet to grab a few towels. Glancing at the hanging bar, he noticed a suit covered in a clear plastic wrapping with blue writing on the outside. A bell clanged in his head. It was the same covering that used to be over his work shirts back when Risa was alive. Her ironing prowess had been a figment of his imagination. Abe had spent months trying to figure out how to use the darn iron when he could merely have dropped his shirts off at the dry cleaners. He'd have to bring in a big bagful this week to make up for lost time. The expense would be less than having to replace the shirts he burned holes through.

When he reached the bathroom, Bea was ready, her tail thwapping a rhythm against the porcelain tub. Abe turned on the water and adjusted it to the perfect temperature, testing it on his wrist the way Risa had. As the tub filled, he rifled through the closet to find the doggie shampoo and rinsing cup. Lifting the dog into the tub, he settled her in the center and lathered up her fur, making sure to pay special attention to her tuchas and undercarriage.

"Yes, you're such a good girl," Abe talked her through the unpleasant experience. "You know that, right? The best girl ever."

Bea looked up at him, her eyes even more prominent in her wet, scrawny face. When Risa had first seen Bea at the shelter, she'd gazed into those soulful eyes and beamed with joy. A woman who used to have a smile for everyone—the clerk at the post office, the seamstress who altered her slacks, and of course, always for her family—she'd had a hard time finding it since her diagnosis. As she lost the ability to do so many things she'd taken for granted, joy had become much more elusive. If adopting this creature would make Risa smile, then Abe accepted it was meant to be.

Pouring cupfuls of water over Bea's fur, Abe sniffled at the memory. He missed Risa's smile and friendly demeanor, the way she could chat it up with anyone and everyone. She used to gently coax him into the world, out to dinner with other couples, to museum exhibits and neighborhood block parties, holding his hand firmly in hers. Everything had been easier and more fun when Risa was around. Abe wiped his nose with his hand. Enough wallowing. Risa was gone, so he'd have to learn to do things on his own. He drained the bathtub and lifted Bea onto the mat. Well, that hadn't been so bad. Sometimes he underestimated himself. Just as he reached for the towel, Bea decided to shake off. Fat droplets of water flew in all directions, soaking the floor, walls, and Abe's whole body. He used the towel to wipe his face and dry off his glasses. The next thing he knew, the dog had made herself scarce.

"Wait, Bea!" Abe chased after her, the towel slung around his neck. As she rounded a corner, she careened right into a large ceramic planter, which toppled into the window, sending a jagged crack up the glass. Oy vey. He couldn't catch a break today. Fixing this would cost a pretty penny. Abe caught up to Bea and scooped her up into a towel.

"You little rascal. Enough with the shenanigans." Abe rubbed behind her ears and looked into her sweet eyes. It was hard to stay mad at her. When he placed his nose to her head, he took a whiff of oatmeal and honey, the dog funk successfully eradicated. Abe opened the patio door and watched Bea scamper after a bushy-tailed squirrel.

Abe grabbed the yellow pages from its perch on top of the fridge. Admittedly old-fashioned, it was the most efficient way to find what he was looking for. Flipping to the W section, he perused the options and chose Superior Window Repair, the one with the most professional looking ad. After he called and left a message, Abe's stomach sank. He wasn't looking forward to seeing this quote. As he turned back to the sink, a pile of dishes gave him the stink eye. He looked away, but the tower of pans and dishes kept drawing his focus. Handwashing the darn things with a sponge was getting old. It was high time he learned to run the dishwasher. This old dog could learn new tricks.

Stacking the plates and cups and lining up the silverware was no easy feat, but eventually Abe finagled all the dishes inside. He took the Dawn liquid from the counter, filled the chamber, and clicked the cover. After he closed the door, he pressed start, and a whirring noise began, assuring Abe he'd done everything right. He gave himself a mental pat on the back for a job well done, collapsed onto the couch, and turned on CNN. A few minutes later, the dishwasher made an unfamiliar sputtering sound. When Abe got up to investigate, he saw clouds of soap pouring from the bottom and sides of the machine.

"Holy mackerel." Abe's first instinct was to cover the crevices, to try to push the suds back inside, but that was no use. The harder Abe pushed, the more the bubbles billowed from all sides, creeping across the kitchen floor like a soapy monster possessed. He should have quit while he was ahead. In theory, Abe wanted to handle this crisis by himself, solve the problem of his own making, but he'd had more than enough housework for one day. He was running on empty. Wiping an errant tear from his cheek, he took his phone from his pocket and dialed Norah. She'd know how to clean up the mess he'd created. If this fiasco didn't bankrupt him, he'd consider himself lucky.

Chapter Eleven

JESS

Passing through the entrance gates to the botanical garden, the muscles in Jess's shoulders tensed up. Usually her favorite place, today she wasn't feeling it, maybe because she'd used up all her energy convincing Vivian to come. The air was thick with dust and the sweet smell of agave. Jess had suggested this outing to get Viv alone, to try and suss out why she'd been so moody lately, but maybe that had been a mistake. Shaking off her doubts, Jess tried to stay optimistic.

"These are so cool," Viv pointed to sculptures installed between the plantings. Leave it to her daughter to fixate on brightly colored plastic in a botanical garden.

"Yes, and look at this crazy cactus." Jess reached out to touch one of the spines, allowing it to indent the flesh of her finger.

Viv clicked her nails on a yellow sculpture, then snapped several photos with her phone. "They look like balloon animals."

They wandered out of the cactus garden onto the Sonoran loop trail. Jess stopped at a plaque about desert wildflowers, hoping the brightly colored pictures would pique Viv's interest.

"This purple one is nice," Jess said. She often wondered how anything grew in the desert, yet these hearty plants flourished despite significant challenges.

"Yeah," Vivian said, her eyes still on her phone.

"And this long one looks like a brain."

"Uh-huh."

This wasn't going well. Jess had never felt more distance between her and her younger daughter.

When Vivian took off her sweatshirt and tied it around her waist, something caught Jess's eye. Peeking out from the edge of her short sleeve, there was a stepladder of red lines on her arm, the skin surface crusted with bumpy scabs.

"What the hell—" Jess stopped herself. She'd have to gather her wits so she didn't alienate her daughter even more.

"What?"

"I thought I'd lost my phone, but it's here." Jess patted her purse.

They stopped along the trail at another flowerbed. Jess pretended to read the plaque, her mind swirling. Was Viv cutting herself? Why would she do that? A turquoise hummingbird hovered in midair, burying its beak in a honeysuckle blossom.

"Amazing," Viv said. "I don't know how they do it."

The bird's wings were moving so fast Jess's eyes couldn't detect motion. The bird made it look easy. Jess ran from one task to another, putting out one fire and moving onto the next, dealing with her kids and her father and work, and then waking up and starting it all again. Like she was chained to a constantly spinning treadmill, Jess had no choice but to keep on running. She certainly didn't do it with such grace.

"A feat of nature," Jess said.

They stood together, watching the bird feed. Jess tried to peek at Viv's arm, but the area was now under her sleeve. After a few minutes, they continued on the path. Jess couldn't stop thinking about the marks and what could have driven Viv to cut herself. She'd read this phenomenon was becoming more common with teens, but she'd never thought her girls would fall prey to it. When they came upon Gertrude's, the garden café Jess stopped in front of the hostess stand.

"How about we stop for brunch?" Jess said. Maybe if they sat down and looked at each other, they could have a real conversation.

"Okay," Viv said. Since she was little, Viv had loved Gertrude's French toast with prickly pear jam.

The hostess showed them to a table on the patio. After they ordered, Jess began digging.

"I'm glad we made the time for this today," Jess said. "I know you've always loved this place."

"Yeah, I have."

"You seem a bit down. Is it about the bat mitzvah? I know you're under a lot of pressure."

"I don't know."

"Maybe if we get some things crossed off the list, you'll feel better."

"Like what? I'm doing the Torah tutoring, and I know all my prayers."

Jess took her phone from her purse and pulled up the website she'd found last week. "You'll need a dress. I want to put in the order, in case it needs tailoring." Jess showed Viv the one she'd saved in her cart, a pale pink one with a tweed top, a satin band at the waist, and a flared skirt. Modest, yet pretty.

"This would work for both the service and the party, with a wrap to cover your shoulders on the bimah." Jess couldn't believe Viv would be on stage at synagogue reading from the Torah in only a few short months. Having both of her girls' bat mitzvahs behind her would be bittersweet, a relief for sure, but also tinged with sadness. They were growing up so quickly.

"I don't like it," Viv said.

"What do you mean?" Jess took another look. "It's classy."

"It's not my style, not who I am."

Jess didn't know how to talk to Vivian anymore. Something that used to be so easy was now a major challenge. She sensed the disapproval of the dress was about something more, maybe the reason she was cutting herself, but she wasn't sure what. "What's going on with you?"

"What do you mean?"

"Vivian, I saw your arm," Jess said. "I need you to be honest with me."

Viv tugged her sleeve down over the scars. "It's nothing."

"Oh no, you don't, young lady." The second the words were out of her mouth, she wanted to take them back. She needed to change her tack. If Viv was harming herself, Jess needed to radiate concern, not judgement.

The waitress appeared. "I have huevos rancheros and a prickly pear French toast."

"The huevos are for me," Jess said.

The waitress placed the plates down in front of them. "Anything else I can get for you?"

"How about some sanity?" Jess said.

"If I was selling that, I'd be a millionaire." The waitress laughed and moved on to the next table.

Jess sighed. "How long has this been going on?"

Viv refused to make eye contact.

Jess pointed to Viv's arm. "This is not something we can brush under the rug."

"I don't know," Viv mumbled. "A while."

"Did you tell Claire about this?"

"Yeah. She's been helping me. Giving me other ways to deal with stuff."

"I'm glad she's been there for you." Jess meant it, but she couldn't help feeling like a failure. Why couldn't Vivian lean on her? Maybe it was her fault Viv was struggling. Had she passed on her anxiety to her daughter? Or maybe she'd been so distracted by work that she'd failed to see the warning signs. "Have you told her what's going on?"

"A little... I don't know."

Jess tried to soften her voice. "What is it?"

"It's hard to talk about. I don't know what to say."

"Whatever it is," Jess said, "it can't be that bad. You don't need to hurt yourself. That's so extreme." Jess was trying to be supportive, but she knew her words sounded judgmental. She didn't mean it that way, but she was genuinely worried. She'd learned during her psychiatry rotation in medical school that cutting provided an emotional release, but she didn't really understand it. How could making yourself bleed solve anything?

"Seriously, Mom? It's not like I want to do it. I don't have a choice."

"Don't have a choice?" Jess pressed her fingers to her temples. She didn't understand. How could you have no choice but to take a knife to your own skin?

"It's the only thing that takes away the pain, makes me feel better. That's what Claire said."

"Pain from what?" Jess said. "What's bothering you?"

Viv picked up her knife and sawed off a piece of French toast. "Mom, can we not do this now?"

"Listen, honey," Jess said, steeling herself. "I want you to know Dad and I love and support you, no matter what. I don't know what's bothering you, but I'm here whenever you're ready to share." Holding her breath, Jess waited to see how her words would land. She didn't want to table this conversation, but if she kept prodding, it would only push Viv farther away.

"I know," Viv said.

Jess exhaled. The smell of poached egg and black beans turned her stomach. It had sounded good earlier, but now she couldn't think of eating. All she wanted to do was hold her daughter tight and make everything all better.

Viv popped a strawberry into her mouth and cut off another bite of French toast. Jess pushed her food around her plate and waited for Viv to finish.

After lunch, Vivian suggested they go to the butterfly pavilion. Exhausted from their conversation, Jess would have preferred to call it a day, but she agreed. Anything for Vivian. They reached the exhibit and entered through the double set of screened doors.

Vivian tilted her head up, taking in the spectacle. Hundreds of butterflies fluttered over her head, her eyes wide. "I love this place," she said.

"Yes, I know." Jess didn't feel the same. The way they started out as a simple caterpillar, and then transformed from chrysalis to butterfly in a matter of weeks seemed deceitful, nature's bait and switch. You thought you were getting one thing, but you got something else entirely.

Viv pointed to one perched on a branch. "That one is so pretty."

It reminded Jess of the toy she'd given to Hope soon after she was born. Despite Jess's feelings about butterflies, the fun pink of the plush toy had caught her eye, and the crinkly noise had sealed the deal.

Jess followed Viv through the pavilion, Viv's face full of joy as she watched the monarchs and swallowtails and painted ladies. If her daughter could find joy so easily here, then surely she would be all right. As soon as she got home, Jess would call Claire. Maybe the therapist would shed some light on the situation.

O   O   O

Jess sat on hold with Claire's office, the annoying Muzak worsening her pounding headache. Her muscles ached from the stress of the day. The receptionist had said the doctor would pick up in a minute, but it had been much longer. Until the last year, Vivian had been her easy child, the one who went with the flow, bounced back quickly, and had a smile for everyone. What kind of mother was she to miss something so serious?

"Hello, Mrs. Rubin?"

"Yes, I'm here." Jess answered to anything these days. Keeping her maiden name for professional purposes had been the path of least resistance, but after the kids were born, the two last names created confusion.

"I'm connecting you with Claire now. Hold on."

After a few seconds, a confident voice came on. "Hello, this is Claire."

"Thank you so much for taking my call," Jess said, comforted by the psychologist's casual approach. "I'd like to talk about my daughter, Vivian Rubin."

"Yes, I'm glad you called."

"I'm checking in on how therapy is coming along." Jess knew this sounded vague, but she didn't know how to ask the question.

"I've enjoyed getting to know her. Is there something specific you'd like to address?"

"Something happened today... I'm hoping you can help me sort it out."

Jess heard paper rustling in the background. "What has you worried today?"

Jess told Claire about seeing the scars on Viv's arm and their subsequent conversation at Gertrude's. "Did you know about this?" Jess asked.

"We've been exploring this issue together," Claire said. "If I thought there was any danger, I would have contacted you immediately."

Jess rested her forehead on her hand. "I can't believe I didn't know, that I had to find this out by chance. The old Viv would have told me."

"Teenagers change in so many ways. It's their job."

"Well, these changes feel scary."

"That's a common feeling. When they're little, parenting is overwhelming but manageable. As your children grow up, their world becomes bigger and more frightening. I hear the same thing from parents all the time."

"Do you have any idea why she's hurting herself?"

"Many things have come to light through our discussion. I think it would be better if we talk in person."

"What do you mean?"

"I suggest all of us sit down, Mr. Rubin included. I'm hoping with my encouragement, Viv will be able to share what's bothering her. I'd like you to hear it directly from her."

"All right. Can't you tell me anything more? I'm really concerned."

"This needs to come from your child, not from me."

"Can you fit us in tomorrow?" Jess asked. "I don't want to wait."

"I'll slot you into my first opening." The conversation had run its course. Jess booked an appointment for Thursday, ended the call, and exhaled with a sigh. Something told her she'd have to brace herself for whatever Vivian had to share.

Chapter Twelve

KENDALL

"You really have a way with her." Kendall took two cans of Diet Coke from the fridge.

"She's doing so well," Julieta called back from the living room floor.

Marisol's seventeen-year-old daughter had been a godsend. She'd often come over at a moment's notice, helping Kendall prepare Hope's tube feeds, playing with Hope, and organizing the living room.

Marisol sat at the kitchen island. "Julieta loves helping with her. She's definitely meant to work with children."

Julieta turned Hope's neck gently from side to side, then moved on to leg raises to strengthen her hip muscles. When she squeezed Hope's thighs, the baby giggled with glee.

How would Kendall have managed if she didn't have such great neighbors? The Herreras were the only people Kendall invited into her home, the only ones she allowed to see her dated kitchen cabinets, scratched floor tiles, and chipping countertops. Before she'd gotten pregnant, she'd heard people talking about needing a village to raise a child, but now she actually understood the saying. Since Marisol didn't work, she was usually available to answer questions or lend a helping hand.

"I have no doubt she's found her calling." Kendall handed a soda to Marisol and opened the other. "How's the college application process going?"

"It's a lot. I'm not sure how she's going to put it all together in time."

Kendall nodded, but she had no frame of reference. Growing up in Casa Grande, halfway between here and Tucson, attending the University of Arizona had been a given. Her father ran a fairly successful plumbing business, but her parents couldn't afford to send her out of state. "One step at a time, I guess?"

"I keep telling myself that, and in a few months, it will be in God's hands."

"Julieta's a wonderful girl." Kendall took a sip of soda. "I'm sure she'll get in where she wants to go. And what's been going on with you lately?"

"Oh, not much. Aldo and I just got back from a couple days in Sedona. Retreat for his investment firm."

"Sounds painful."

"It wasn't so bad," Marisol said. "One of the ladies brought some gummies, so that didn't hurt. Helped us tolerate all the talk about mutual funds and asset allocation. And it made the spa day much more enjoyable."

Kendall laughed. With marijuana legalized here, she'd have to think about getting in on the action. A gummy now and then might help her get through the worst days.

"Not saying I want to go every year. It might be a one-and-done situation. And oh—I forgot to tell you something. Between packing for the trip and traveling, it almost slipped my mind. A couple days ago, I was outside before dawn doing my morning routine, and I saw someone."

"Who was it?"

"She parked in front of your house and put a present by your garage. I guess she's the secret admirer. I left you a voicemail right away."

Kendall was so bad with checking her voicemail. She couldn't believe Marisol hadn't tried her again. She'd been trying and failing to catch the secret Santa in the act for two years. "You actually saw her? What did she look like?"

"I don't know. Brown hair, not too tall."

Kendall waited, but Marisol didn't say more. That sounded like the majority of women. "That's it?"

"She was kind of regular, wearing some sort of hospital outfit."

"What do you mean?"

"You know, the ones that match?"

Was Marisol saying she was wearing scrubs? Kendall wasn't sure what to make of that. "What kind of car did she drive?"

"An SUV of some sort," Marisol said. "A Trailblazer or maybe a Pilot?"

Kendall sighed. Nearly half the cars on the road fit this description. "What else? Did she say anything to you?"

"She was in such a rush. I asked her name, but she didn't answer. Couldn't get away fast enough."

"That's bullshit." Kendall's face flushed with heat. "She's been delivering gifts for two years, and she can't even own up to it? What the hell?"

"Language," Julieta said from the living room. "Innocent ears. We wouldn't want someone to pick up bad habits." She tickled Hope's belly.

"I really need to know who she is," Kendall said.

"Well, I'll do my part, keep my eyes peeled. If she comes back, I won't let her off so easy."

This whole situation made Kendall feel vulnerable, as if she'd left the house without her make-up on. Some random woman was sneaking around outside her house before dawn, leaving gifts with weird notes. She was tired of being a victim. For a moment, she thought about asking Marisol her opinion on the lawsuit but then decided against it. She'd heard more than enough opinions already. Troy was right. It was time to call an attorney.

Chapter Thirteen
JESS

The blinking cursor on the screen taunted Jess. Goose bumps covered her skin, the air conditioning in her office turned up full blast as usual. Academic days were the bane of her existence. So many hours to fill with research, drafting, and proofreading articles, the seconds ticking by in slow motion. The dread took hold days in advance, the thought of sitting alone in her office making her jittery. It was nearly noon, and she'd managed to edit one chart and come up with the first two sentences of the discussion section. There was a good reason she was on Ken Smart's shit list. At this point, he was probably whispering in the department chair's ear, telling her to stall on putting Jess through for promotion, again. In Ken's last email, he'd offered to bring on another co-author to finish the work, but Jess refused. She'd written plenty of boring papers in the past. What was one more? Jess scanned the words on the screen—preeclampsia, cardiovascular, meta-analyses— until one of them stood out from the rest.

PRESSURE.

Her thoughts turned to Vivian and their trip to the botanical garden on Sunday. What was going on with her? Maybe she was under too much pressure at school. Pushing her to take honors algebra might have been a mistake. Her girls had a nice life—a beautiful house abutting the preserve, good friends, and more love than any child could ask for—but lately, conversations with Viv ended with her either storming off or clamming up completely. Jess had assumed it was normal teenage girl behavior. Other girl moms had reported their daughters had morphed into drama queens as well. But if Viv was cutting herself, it must be more. The appointment with Claire couldn't come soon enough, yet Jess also wished it would never arrive. When Jess had been pregnant with Maddie, people kept telling her to sleep now because she'd never get the chance again. She'd pictured a colicky newborn, but the warning applied more to parenting teenagers. If one of the girls was out, Jess lay awake with worry until everyone was home safe and sound.

Jess took a gulp of water. Damn this article. It wasn't going to happen today. Jess squeezed her eyes shut, trying not to imagine the next scathing email from Ken Smart. Opening the Notes app on her phone, Jess reviewed the items on her to-do list. She might as well be productive in some way. The first item on the list was to donate to the Cerebral Palsy Foundation. Jess gave a couple of times a year, and for her last birthday, she'd even asked her friends and family to donate in lieu of gifts. It was a drop in the bucket, but maybe all these small donations would help make some progress. It certainly wouldn't hurt. Plus, it gave Jess some measure of peace to know she was doing something to help Hope and other children like her. Opening the website, she clicked on the pink *Contribute* button and made her donation. When she looked back at her list, another item glared at Jess, one that had been languishing there for weeks.

→ BOOK PARTY PLANNER

Jess had been stalling on planning Viv's bat mitzvah. Three years ago, Maddie's celebration had been a breeze. Her older daughter had learned her Torah portion without complaining, written a thoughtful speech interpreting the meaning of the passage, and even helped choose the theme. For the party, she'd looked adorable in a strapless white dress with a flouncy, tulle skirt, the tight bodice embedded with Swarovski crystals. Everything with Vivian had been needlessly difficult. Insisting she didn't want a big party or a fancy dress, Vivian had even threatened to forgo the whole thing. Jess made it clear that wasn't an option. If Maddie had had the big soirée, so would Vivian. Drew's parents had already booked their flights from DC. Saul and Myra Rubin would never live it down with the Bethesda set if their daughter-in-law put the kibosh on their granddaughter's big day. With less than six months to go, it was time to get down to business.

Jess opened the web browser on her computer and googled KC events. Rachel Schneider, a member of the synagogue, couldn't stop raving about this company. Every time they ran into each other, Rachel figured out ways to throw in more details from her daughter's party—the etched plexiglass invitations, the candy bar spanning an entire wall, and the Beats headphones and wireless speakers as prizes to keep the kids dancing. It sounded over the top, but Jess did need a new party planner. The one she'd used last time, Toni of Toni Affairs, was a busybody, constantly gossiping about her clients. Jess didn't care that Saylor Weinstein's dress had cost eight thousand dollars, that Gary Reiter had shtupped Aline Simon in the bathroom during his son's candle lighting, or that Nancy Finkel had imported South American parrots for her son's zoo-themed shindig. Plus, Toni overcharged for everything. With Maddie going to college next year, Jess needed to keep the budget in line.

The KC Events webpage had a photo gallery of various parties, broken up into sections for anniversary parties, weddings, and b'nai mitzvahs. She clicked on the last one and perused the photos of extravagant affairs—women with caked-on makeup and shiny blowouts, massive clusters of colorful balloons, and elaborate centerpieces featuring everything from sports to movies to video game characters. One of the photos featured some familiar faces—Maddie had gone to preschool with Ethan, the bar mitzvah boy—and the event looked tasteful and low-key.

She dialed and waited for an answer.

"Hello?" a woman answered.

"Hi," Jess said, gathering her wits. "Is this KC Events?"

"Yes, it is. I'm sorry," the woman said. "Sometimes I forget which number is ringing. KC speaking."

"My name is Jessica Rubin. I got your name from Rachel Schneider. You planned her daughter's bat mitzvah? She and I go to the same synagogue."

"Oh, yes, of course. That was sweet of her to refer you."

"From the way she talks, it seems like a party no one could forget."

"It was a big one," KC said.

"I'm not looking for anything like that," Jess said.

"That was all guided by her. I meet my clients where they are."

"Sounds wonderful." Jess had always had to talk over Toni to get a few words in. "Last time, things got a bit out of hand. The final bills came as quite a shock."

"That's not the way I work," KC said. "I provide you with a spreadsheet of all the proposed components and the costs, and you can approve or not, as you wish. Totally transparent. No surprises at all. I assume we're talking about a bar or bat mitzvah?"

"Yes." Jess could tell by the way the woman pronounced the Hebrew words she wasn't Jewish, and maybe it was better that way. As a member of the synagogue, Toni had been privy to everyone's business. "My daughter Vivian will turn thirteen in December. Her bat mitzvah date is January 22nd."

"Five months. That's a bit of a crunch."

"I know. I'm not sure why I waited so long to call," Jess said. So many other things had taken priority, but Jess wasn't about to admit that to KC. Who wanted a client who was a hot mess?

"Do you have a venue?" KC asked.

"Yes, I reserved Hangar One Scottsdale."

"Oh, that place takes a lot of extra legwork," KC said. "Everything has to be brought in. I'm not sure I can fit you into my schedule."

"You've come so highly recommended. I know you would make the party a great success." Jess laid it on thick, hoping to check off this task so she could move on to other things. KC had to say yes. A baby cried in the background. "I don't have time to plan it myself. Between parenting two teenagers and working full time at the hospital, my plate is pretty full."

"Which hospital?"

"Valley Health." Jess kept her answer brief. She'd learned long ago not to share the details of her work in casual conversation. Either people asked how she looked at vaginas all day or they waxed poetic about their harrowing birth experiences.

"I'm very familiar with it," the woman said. "My daughter sees several doctors there. Feels like a second home."

"Really? I hope she's okay." Jess was sorry to hear this woman was dealing with a sick child, but she didn't have time for a sob story. The discussion section wouldn't write itself.

"She's getting there, little by little," she said.

"Never a dull moment in parenting." Jess's thoughts turned to the scars on Vivian's arm, the angry red slashes marring her pale skin.

"You're so right."

The baby's cries intensified. Jess needed to seal the deal before the woman excused herself. She had an idea. "From one mother to another. Please, I know you'll make this celebration a success."

There was silence for a moment followed by a long sigh. "It sounds like you need my help."

"Yes, to focus on the details. Big picture I can do, but I'm not the kind of mom who puts the favors together in her dining room. I've learned to delegate, in order to survive."

"There's only so much you can take on, right?"

Jess thought she heard a wobble in KC's voice, but maybe it was just a bad connection. The baby had quieted down.

"One last thing," KC said. "Do you have an idea about the theme? Or any other details you had in mind?"

"I'm not sure," Jess said.

"We'll come up with something," KC said. "Why don't you send me some photos? Pictures of your daughter, of her room, of any things special to her. The photos could spark some ideas."

"Sure, but I'll have to fly under the radar. Anything could set Vivian off these days."

"She's becoming a teenager. It all sounds normal." Her voice wavered on the last word. Jess was sure she wasn't imagining it this time.

"I guess." Jess clicked on the *Contact* section of the website to make sure she had KC's email address. "So, I'll send the photos, and we'll touch base in a few days?"

"Sounds great."

Jess hung up the phone, feeling confident she'd made the right choice. KC seemed warm, competent, and most importantly, reasonable. It felt good to place Vivian's bat mitzvah party in such capable hands. Energized from the small win, Jess decided to pay her father a visit after work. It had been too long since she'd checked in on him.

O   O   O

Walking to the front entrance of Sun Terrace Memory Care, Jess admired the well-tended gardens and manicured shrubbery. It didn't erase the guilt she carried for not being able to care for her father herself, but at least it was a high-quality place. After her mother died unexpectedly, Jess had known there was no way he could live alone. Between the funeral, packing up and selling their Scarsdale home of fifty years, and moving her father across the country, she'd had to take over a month off from work. Drew had flown back with the kids right after the funeral and taken on the task of finding a memory care facility with an opening. He'd done a commendable job. Contrary to the news reports, this home had somehow managed to avoid a major outbreak during the pandemic. She was grateful, even though it meant she hadn't seen her father face to face for months on end. The parking lot visit had been a complete failure, her father staring at her through the window in total confusion. She reached the door and pushed the button on the intercom.

"How can I help you?" a woman said.

"Hi, I'm Jessica Schorr. Alvin's daughter."

The long beep from the speaker made Jess's pulse gallop. She hated coming here, but it was a necessary evil. As she opened the door, the familiar odor hit her immediately, a mix of strong disinfectant and overcooked meat with an undercurrent of urine. Her father had been living here for nearly two years, but Jess would never get used to that smell.

The woman at the front desk handed Jess an electronic fob to get her into the locked ward. Jess made her way to her father's area, scanning the common space and then his room. It was August, but *It's a Wonderful Life* played in the living room area, and a woman with a bird's nest of white hair sat immobile, her mouth agape. Where was her dad? He wasn't watching TV, sitting at a table, or in his room. He must be wandering again.

She approached the desk. "Hi, any idea where Alvin might be today?"

"He's a tricky one. Always on the move. Check Shirley's room."

"Again?" Jess wasn't sure why her father found Shirley's bed more appealing than his own, but he definitely did.

"If you find him, coax him out here for dinner."

As she walked down the hall, Jess took note of the names on the doors. Elsa, Harvey, Ruth. Toward the end, she reached Shirley's room, a photo on the door of a middle-aged woman on the tennis court in a snappy outfit. Jess pushed the door open, not sure what she would find.

Someone was in the bed, the covers pulled up over their head. Was this Shirley? Jess stood for a moment, listening to the familiar breathing pattern, two short snores followed by one long. No, this was her father. Alvin Schorr had a perfectly nice room of his own, but he preferred to bed hop.

She pulled down the covers and placed her hand on his warm body. "Dad, it's me, Jess."

He opened his eyes and smiled. "Oh, it's my girl."

Jess's heart lifted. She knew her father would never say her name again, but on the good days, there was a glimmer of recognition. "It's time to eat. Let's go sit down."

She guided him by the elbow to the seating area. He looked thinner and more stooped than the last time she'd visited. The smell of beef stew permeated the air.

Jess got her father situated at a table next to Shirley.

"So, let me see," Jess said, trying to fill the silence. "Work is busy, but good. Drew and Maddie are chugging along. Vivian's going through some teen drama, but it's all settling down." This update was a sugar-coated version of the truth, but he couldn't handle anything more.

"What's that? Oh, look." Her father pointed out the window. "A flying contraption. A whosa-ma-jig."

A bluebird hovered outside the window, then landed. "It's a bird. Remember?"

No, he didn't remember. Who was she kidding? He didn't remember his home in Scarsdale, his decades-long career as a college math professor, or his only daughter. The one name still imprinted on his brain was Rhonda. He didn't recall his wife per se, but her name still lived within him.

He scrunched his eyebrows together. "A bird?"

Shirley wore her perpetual smile. "Yes, yes."

An aide placed two plates in front of her father and Shirley. "Would you like a plate?" she asked Jess.

"No, thank you." Jess tried to visit during mealtimes, so she and her father would have something to talk about, but she never ate here. It was too depressing.

He picked up a cantaloupe ball and squeezed it between his fingers.

"How about some stew?" Jess asked.

The meat looked less than appetizing, but she needed to encourage him to eat. He couldn't afford to lose any more weight. She offered him a spoonful. "Take a bite, Dad."

"I don't want it."

"You used to like this. Just try a little."

He accepted the offering, then immediately spit it into the fruit cup.

"I can bring you food, Dad," she said. "Just tell me what you'd like."

He watched the bluebird take flight.

"Let's see." Jess thought back to the foods he used to enjoy. "Cinnamon oatmeal, noodle kugel, cheesecake with cherry topping?"

At the last suggestion, his eyes lit up. "Yes!"

Bingo. From now on, Jess would make a habit of stopping off for cheesecake before she came to visit.

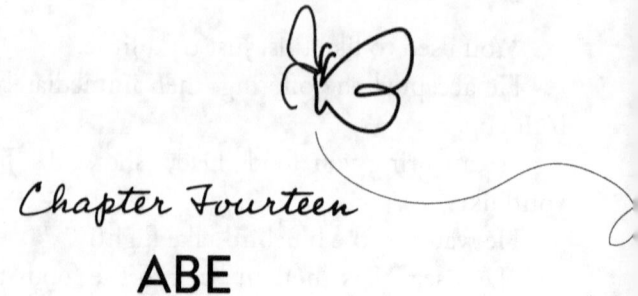

Chapter Fourteen

ABE

"So, what do you think?" Norah asked, looking at him over her glasses.

She wanted a pat on the back, but Abe couldn't do that in good conscience. He looked back down at the poster. The background was black, white capital letters filling the center of the page.

WE HOLD DOCTORS AND HOSPITALS ACCOUNTABLE

The bold font made the phrase sound angry. On the right side, Abe stood in a gray pinstripe suit, his arms crossed and a broad smile on his face. He didn't remember having this photo taken, and when he looked more closely, his ensemble didn't look familiar. He hadn't owned a double-breasted suit since the eighties, and he'd never sported a pocket square.

"This is something," Abe said.

"I know, right?"

"That isn't even me."

"A little photoshopping goes a long way. I found a photo of a guy in a suit and popped one of your head right on top."

Abe was appalled. Marty had never even stooped this low. With this travesty plastered on a billboard on the side of the 101, motorists would take one look and assume the worst of him. Ross would disown him in a hot minute.

Norah read the words from the bottom out loud. "You pay nothing unless we win. Over 100 million collected. This will definitely bring in more traffic."

"Or cause traffic accidents." Abe blew air out through his lips. "This doesn't feel right." The words were accurate, but the presentation was all wrong. Abe wanted his clients to hire him because he was a skilled attorney who got them what they deserved, not because he wore a cheesy suit and paid a mint for advertising.

"You don't like it?"

"I can't do it this way. I know we're a bit lean, but it's going to turn around. I'm willing to hustle, but not like this."

Norah's lip trembled. "I was trying to help."

"I know. I truly appreciate your effort." The last thing Abe wanted to do was offend Norah. He was truly thankful for everything she did, both for the firm and for him personally. After all, she'd found him a reasonable deal for window repair, and his dishwasher would never have recovered without her vinegar and vegetable oil trick.

"I did receive one call," she said.

"Oh yeah?"

"They're coming at eleven."

Abe didn't need to check his calendar. He knew it was wide open.

"It's a young couple with a child. They said something about suing a doctor."

Had this client found the firm through a Google search? Or maybe Marty was busy chatting people up at the golf club? The woman from Trader Joe's appeared in Abe's mind, the despondent look on her face as she asked him whether he took on malpractice cases, tears running down her cheeks. The way her baby slouched over the side of the cart. Perhaps she had called to make an appointment?

Once Norah went back to her desk, Abe organized the pens in his drawer by color, straightened up the pile of file folders on his desk, and surfed around the internet for some clothes. Marty had booked a tee time for next Saturday morning, and Abe's golf shorts had seen better days. If he was going to stand up to Marty, insist they negotiate an end to their partnership, he had to look the part. This website was a no-go, each pair more hideous than the last.

Norah came back into the office. "They're here. The mother is Kendall, and the father's name is Troy."

"And the child?"

"Hope. She seems delayed. More like a baby than a two-year-old."

Yes, it must be the one from Trader Joe's. "I gave the mom my card."

"Excuse me?" Norah raised her eyebrows. "*You* handed out your card?"

"Yes." Abe puffed up his chest. The feeling of shame from the store was still there, but it was mixed with a sense of pride. No matter how difficult, he'd done his duty to keep the firm afloat. "Ms. Wilkes, please send in my clients."

"I'm proud of you. Don't let this one off the hook." Norah closed the door behind her. Abe straightened his tie and sat up straighter in his chair.

Norah led the attractive, young couple into the room. Mrs. Carlson was more dressed up than she'd been at the store, wearing heels and a slim pantsuit, her face fully made-up. Her husband, tall with a square jaw and a cleft chin, looked ready to talk business.

Abe stood and came from behind his desk to greet them. "Abe Silverberg. Nice to meet you."

"Troy Carlson," the man said, reaching his hand out. His handshake was unnecessarily firm, like he had something to prove.

Abe rescued his hand and shook it out behind his back. The woman parked the stroller between the two chairs facing the desk while Mr. Carlson tucked a blanket around the child's legs.

"I'm Kendall. Thank you for fitting us in." When she returned his handshake, her grip was much gentler.

"All righty then, why don't you make yourselves comfortable," Abe said, trying to sound friendly.

"Would anyone like a drink?" Norah asked. "Coffee, tea, water?"

"Thank you. We're fine." Kendall took a seat, motioning her husband to do the same.

Norah left the room, leaving Abe to conduct the interview.

"It's nice to see you again." Abe took a seat at his desk. "You seem to be doing better than the last time we met."

Kendall's cheeks flushed. "That was so unlike me. It was a particularly stressful day."

"We all have our moments. Believe me." Abe understood feeling overwhelmed. During Risa's long illness, there had been plenty of days when he'd barely been able to drag himself out of bed.

"I have my doubts about hiring an attorney my wife met in the grocery store," Troy said. "But your reviews are excellent."

"I'll try to live up to my reputation. Shall we get down to business?" Marty had done most of the client-facing meetings, so Abe had expected to be out of his element, but he felt surprisingly comfortable.

"Yes," Troy took out his phone. "I have a list of questions."

"Go easy on the third degree, Troy."

"He's our potential attorney. We need to make sure he's up to par." The golf term made Abe think about his upcoming date with Marty. If he could tell Marty about his new case, it would make the outing much more palatable. Otherwise, he'd spend the whole nine holes listening to Marty condescend about how to get potential clients to sign on the dotted line.

"Tell us about your experience," Troy said. "What percentage of your work entails malpractice work? What is your win/ loss ratio? Do you typically settle, or do your cases go to trial?" He scrolled farther down his phone, looking for more probing questions.

Abe loosened his tie. "You've done your homework, but I think we're putting the cart before the horse. Before we discuss my qualifications, I need to weigh your case, see if it has merit."

Troy placed his phone on the desk, unbuckled Hope, and lifted her onto his lap. The child didn't have the strength to sit up without support, and her arms seemed fixed in a bent position. If this case had any merit, Abe would take it on.

"I understand Hope has a disability," Abe said. "Has she been given a diagnosis?"

"Cerebral palsy," Kendall said.

Abe opened his notebook and started jotting things down. "And when did you learn of that?"

"Early on," she said, "but we recently received some disturbing information. Her prognosis doesn't seem good."

"That's putting it mildly," Troy said. "Our child may never walk or talk. We've been going through a lot."

"I'm sorry to hear that," Abe said. "Why don't we start from the beginning? What happened to Hope, and why do you think a doctor is to blame?"

"It's a clear-cut case of negligence at Kendall's delivery," Troy said. "Open and shut."

"It sounds like you're feeling angry," he said, dusting off the listening skills he'd learned in a continuing education course a few years back. "That's a natural response, but if I'm going to take this on, I need to learn what happened. I'd like to hear about your pregnancy first, before we talk about the delivery."

"I guess I had the typical complaints. Heartburn and swollen legs, nothing out of the ordinary. In the last few weeks, my blood pressure went up, but my doctor said it was nothing to worry about."

"Alright," he said. "And what was the name of your doctor, the obstetrician who oversaw your care?"

"Dr. Meghan Felix."

"But she's not the one who caused this mess," Troy said.

"My water broke at thirty-two weeks," Kendall said. "We called Dr. Felix's office, and her nurse sent us to the hospital. The baby needed to be delivered within a day. To prevent infection."

Abe scribbled the details and circled the word infection. Could this be the crux of the case?

"At the hospital, it was all orderly. They had me change into a hospital gown and started monitoring the baby—"

"Then they started giving her some medicine in the IV, to start the contractions and some other things too. If everything had been handled correctly, Hope's life would have been so much easier." Troy ran his hand over Hope's curls, his eyes shiny.

Kendall met Troy's eyes, then reached out and squeezed his hand.

"You can't pin everything on one person," Abe said. "These cases can be so complex, more than one provider involved. Also, don't forget about the hospital. They have deep pockets. The more defendants, the better chance of winning. So, what happened next, Mrs. Carlson?"

"Before we continue, there's something I should mention." Kendall twisted her hands in her lap. "At one of my prenatal appointments, Dr. Felix had me fill out a birth plan with my preferences for the delivery. I chose to opt out of cervical checks."

"Is that relevant here?" Troy said.

"Actually, if I'm going to take on your case, I would encourage you to be as honest as possible. Any and all information may be important."

"Do you think this is important?" Kendall asked softly.

"It may well be, but I don't know where it fits into the puzzle quite yet." Abe certainly wasn't thrilled with this little detail, but better to be aware of it than be ambushed in court. From previous cases, Abe knew cervical exams helped assess the progress of labor and the baby's position and could help diagnose unusual complications like hemorrhage and umbilical cord malposition. Foregoing this part of the physical exam could cause a delay in diagnosis. At least he had time to plan the best way to spin it. "Why don't you tell me what happened next?"

"The contractions started, each one more painful than the last. It felt like my insides were ripping open. The staff kept saying everything was fine, but one nurse kept talking about the monitor. She saw something."

"What was it?"

"She kept saying the same word," Kendall said. "It sounded like celery, but that can't be right."

Abe searched his mental database for the right word, something that would come up in the delivery suite. "Decelerations?" Abe wrote the word and circled it several times. If the baby had a dangerously low heart rate, this nurse could be at fault as well.

"Maybe," Kendall said.

"Did she tell the doctor?" Abe asked.

"If she had, we wouldn't be where we are today," Troy said. "Can nurses get sued too?"

"It's unusual," Abe said, "but not out of the question. I'll look at all possible angles."

"The doctor on call was assigned to deliver me," Kendall said. "I wanted my own doctor, but it wasn't her day to cover."

"Who performed your delivery?"

"Dr. Schorr. Dr. Jessica Schorr." Troy enunciated each syllable, then spelled the last name.

Abe wrote the doctor's name in capital letters and underlined it. He'd have to do some digging on her, see if she had previous settlements or judgments, surf the internet for negative ratings or illuminating comments.

Kendall continued telling her story. From what he'd heard so far, Abe wasn't sure how strong the case was, but it certainly held more promise than Sean Barclay's. He'd need to do the proper research, but the more he heard, the more optimistic he became.

It reminded him of a case from a while back, the baby with brain damage from a placental infarction. That payout had kept the lights on for years.

As Kendall was describing the trip from the delivery suite to the operating room, something made Abe's ears prick up. "Did you say the doctor was riding on the stretcher?" This detail seemed out of the ordinary.

"Yes," Kendall said. "Dr. Schorr instructed the resident to ride between my legs and keep her fingers inside me. Something about keeping the baby's head away from the umbilical cord."

"Are you positive? Troy asked.

"You don't recall that part?" Abe asked. "I thought you were there."

"I wasn't feeling—"

"Troy passed out," Kendall said. "He hit the floor before I had the C-section."

"Literally?" Abe asked. This little detail wasn't going to help the case. It was never good to lose a key witness at a crucial moment.

"No joke," Kendall said. "He missed the whole operation."

"So, tell me more about the delivery," Abe said.

"You want the gory details?" Kendall asked.

"Details are my job," Abe said.

"Well," Kendall continued, "as I said before, she had the resident put her fingers inside me, to keep the blood flowing, I guess."

Hearing this description again rang a bell for Abe. It sounded like a case Marty had won back in the nineties. "I'm going to throw out a term here. Umbilical cord prolapse. Does that sound at all familiar?"

"Yes," Kendall said. "That's it. That's what Dr. Schorr said."

"I'm starting to get the picture. It was a bit fuzzy, but it's becoming clearer."

"What do you think?" Kendall asked quietly.

"Do we have a good case?" Troy said.

"Preliminarily, yes. I'll need some time to go over the details and review the supporting documents, of course."

"The sooner the better," Troy said. "Hope's second birthday is next month. I understand we need to file suit before then?"

"That's correct, but it shouldn't be a problem. I'm glad you came in when you did."

"And what is your typical payment arrangement?" Troy asked.

"I work on contingency. That means I don't get paid unless I win your case."

"And if you do?"

"Then, my fee is forty percent of the settlement or judgment."

"That's a lot," Kendall said.

"That's why we only take on the ones we think we can win. What do you hope to get from the suit?"

"We need to recuperate our costs," Troy said. "It's taken a lot out of us."

"Understood. I'll be back in touch as soon as possible."

Once the Carlsons left, Abe looked out the window, collecting his thoughts. A massive cloud covered most of the sun, but a few rays peeked out from the edge. Turning back to his computer, he resumed searching for golf shorts, more than ready to take a swing with Marty now.

Chapter Fifteen

JESS

Thursday afternoon, Jess, Drew, and Vivian sat in the waiting room of Claire's office. Jess stared at the black and white photograph on the wall of two little girls playing on a swing set. The photo brought her mind back to the simpler times, when her girls used to play together, when their fights were about who got the bigger scoop of ice cream or who was on whose side of the car. Fearing she'd reached the *big kids, big problems* phase of parenting, Jess's stomach churned with anxiety. The two antacid tablets she'd taken weren't helping, and she couldn't quiet the hurricane of thoughts ravaging her mind.

"It's going to be okay," Drew said. He rested his hand on her thigh, but she brushed it away. How could he be so sure? Usually, Jess would be comforted to have him by her side, but today she couldn't calm her nerves. Viv sat on the other side of Drew, chewing the corner of her lip while she scrolled on her phone. Maybe the damn phone was the problem. Jess had read an article in *The New York Times* about the unrealistic expectations social media placed on girls. No one could ever be as perfect as the digitally enhanced images they were bombarded with every day.

"Hello, Rubin family." Claire stood in the doorway to her office, her petite body dwarfed by the large potted plant by the door. Jess had forgotten how young the therapist was, just out of graduate school. "I'm so glad you could all make it today."

The three of them stood and followed Claire into her office. A charcoal loveseat and matching armchair sat at right angles to each other with a desk chair turned to complete the seating circle. Lavender throw pillows, table lamps, and a soft grey wall color created an inviting space. Jess and Viv took a seat on the couch.

"I'd prefer you sit in the chair," Claire said to Viv. "To make eye contact with your parents."

Once they'd all rearranged themselves, Claire turned over a new page on a yellow notepad and gave them a warm smile. "I want you to know a meeting like this is quite common. When working with teens, it's often useful to include family members. A holistic approach allows my clients to get more meaningful results."

Vivian looked at the floor, chewing her lip.

"I can't promise any of this will be easy," Claire continued, "but you've taken an important step by coming in today."

"I don't think we're your typical clients," Drew said. "A physician and a social worker."

"It does help that you know the lingo and have an understanding of what we're trying to do here. But if I'm being honest, sometimes professionals like yourselves come with more baggage. It can require some serious unpacking."

"That won't be the case with us." Jess noticed Vivian picking at her cuticles. "So, why did you call us in? Is it about the cutting? We need to know what's going on."

"I think it will all be clear in a few," Claire said. "The cutting is a symptom, not the root problem."

Jess grabbed one of the throw pillows and hugged it to her chest.

"Remember how we rehearsed?" Claire said to Viv.

"I think so."

"Go ahead," Claire said softly.

Viv angled her body to face Jess and Drew. "I guess it's now or never. So, Mom, you know how I didn't like the bat mitzvah dress you picked out?"

"That's not a problem," Jess said. "There are so many dresses out there, plenty of other places we can shop—"

"Hold on a moment," Claire said. She gave Viv a nod.

"What I'm trying to say is I don't want to wear a dress at all."

"You're the bat mitzvah girl," Jess said. "You need to wear a dress."

"No, I don't want to wear a dress, like ever. That's the reason I've been so upset."

"What's the issue?" Jess asked. "That you don't like tulle and lace?"

"No, that's not it," Viv said.

"Then what is it?" Jess said.

"That I don't feel like a girl," Viv mumbled. "Usually, I don't feel like a girl or a boy. Most of the time, I'm floating somewhere in between."

"We call that nonbinary," Claire said with exaggerated enunciation. "A sense that neither of the defined gender roles feels like a fit."

Suddenly, the room felt much too warm. Jess wanted to ask Claire to open a window, but she couldn't interrupt the conversation. Of all the things she'd worried Vivian might be going through—anxiety about grades, bullying at school, and God forbid, thoughts of suicide— this was never on her radar. Drew took her hand. This time, Jess allowed it, relieved to feel his skin against hers.

"I want to wear a suit when I read the Torah," Viv said. "A navy suit with brown oxfords." A slide show of family photos flashed across Jess's mind. Vivian in the newborn nursery with a pink knit hat on her tiny head, on her first day of kindergarten in her favorite twirly dress and sparkly ballet flats, and at the fifth grade moving up ceremony, her long hair in a French braid tied off with a ribbon. That last one was only two years ago. How could things have changed so fast?

"Nonbinary children often have a feeling of gender dysphoria, the sense that their assigned gender role is uncomfortable, even painful." Claire handed Jess a pamphlet. A glossary of terms filled several pages. "The cutting gives a sense of relief, a way to dull the pain."

"This is coming out of nowhere," Jess said. In an instant, the child she'd known so well was someone else entirely.

Drew rubbed her back. He didn't seem nearly as shocked as she felt.

"I've known something wasn't right for a while," Viv said. "Then last year I read a book with a nonbinary character, and it all became clear. It put a label on how I'd been feeling."

"Sweetie," Drew said, "you're brave for telling us this news. Mom and I want you to know we love you and are so proud of you."

"Thanks, Dad."

"Can we get a hug?" Drew pulled Jess to stand, and Viv joined them. Everything was moving too fast. Jess wasn't ready for a group hug. She barely understood what was going on, but Drew seemed to have digested this information without a moment of questioning or confusion. He'd been awfully quiet this whole time. Was it possible he'd already known this news, that Viv had shared with him and not with her?

"Have you told any of your friends?" Drew asked once they'd all sat back down.

"I've been helping negotiate the coming-out process, deciding who to tell and when," Claire said. "This whole thing can be scary and intimidating, especially for someone so young."

"I told Xander last week. He was okay with it," Viv said. Jess wasn't surprised. The two kids had been inseparable since second grade, but how much support could a twelve-year-old boy possibly give?

"What about Maddie?" Jess said. "How are we going to tell her?"

"She already knows. Kids in my generation just get it."

Jess didn't know what to say to that. On one hand, she was happy her kids were leaning on each other, but she also wanted Viv to come to her in times of crisis. Was she failing as a mother?

"Now," Claire said, "before we ask your child to step out so we can chat a bit more, there's one more thing to share."

"Yeah," Viv said. "This part is hard."

"Do it just like we practiced," Claire said.

"Okay, I'm just going to say it. I want to change my name."

"What do you mean?"

"My new name is Vox."

"That's a name?" Jess couldn't help herself. Drew squeezed her hand. They had spent months poring over baby name books, trying out and rejecting hundreds of names, before settling on the perfect one. Five-year-old Maddie had even given her stamp of approval, and now it was all for nothing.

"I wanted to keep the V, to honor Grandma Vivian."

Drew seemed unperturbed by this bombshell, as if their daughter had told them she got a C on a math test, not that she wanted to change who she was entirely. "What do you think about this?" Jess asked him.

Drew raised his palms in the air. "I think we need to let our child speak the truth."

"Choosing a name can be an important step in the coming-out process. Vox did a lot of thinking about their new name," Claire said.

"Their?" Jess said.

"Vox has chosen different pronouns," Claire said. "They and them instead of she and her."

Vox shifted in the chair.

"I can see you're tapped," Claire said to Vox. "Why don't you sit outside in the waiting room? I'd like a few minutes with your parents."

Vox rushed out of the office. Once the door clicked shut, Claire launched back in. "So, I know this can be overwhelming. It may take some time for the dust to settle."

"I don't love the pronoun part." Jess had read articles online and heard stories on NPR, but she had never met someone in person who used they and them.

"It's a thing now," Drew said.

"They and them seem clunky. They is plural. It's not grammatically correct."

"It may sound odd at first, but you'll get used to it," Claire said.

"I'm not so sure." She turned to Drew. "How did you manage to climb on board so fast?"

"I don't know. Years of training?" The corner of Drew's mouth twitched a little, a sign he was hiding something. When they got home, she'd have to dig a little, figure out the real story.

"Vox is counting on you both to support them through this transition. I have no doubt you're up for the challenge."

"Of course we are," Drew said.

"Maybe if you focus first on using their new name, the pronouns will fall into place." Claire ended the session with pleasantries, encouraging them to book another family session, as needed.

Fastening her seatbelt in the car, Jess realized she'd forgotten to ask Claire for a referral to a therapist for herself. In the jumble of gender labels and names and pronouns, it had slipped her mind. She could only handle so much. Her child's mental health had to come before her own.

Vox. Of all the names in the world, why did she, or *they*, pick one that sounded more like an appliance brand than a name? Their easy child, the one who had always been quiet and obedient, had found their voice, and Jess had no choice but to listen.

○   ○   ○

As soon as they arrived home, Viv—*Vox*, Jess mentally corrected herself—disappeared upstairs. Her daughter confounded Jess on a daily basis. Wait, could she still say daughter or was it child instead? Within minutes, she escaped to the mall with Xander. She must have been planning their escape on the way home from Claire's office. Who could blame her? She'd done a hard thing. They, not she, Jess reminded herself again. *They* needed to blow off some steam, hang out with their best friend, eating greasy

French fries and buying unnecessary crap. Jess was glad to be left alone with Drew. He opened the fridge and started rearranging containers, trying to hide behind the open door. She closed it and pointed to a kitchen chair.

"Park it. Now."

"I'm just as upset as you are," he said, obeying her order. "Why are you taking it out on me?"

"There's something you're not saying. Did you know about this already?"

Drew scratched at a streak of dried-on food on the countertop.

Jess stared at her husband. "Come on, Drew. After over twenty years together, I know when you're hiding something. Your responses were too polished, as if you already knew what was going on. You came off smelling like a rose."

"I wanted to show Vox we're always on their side."

"See, you're used to the new name and pronouns already. You didn't even skip a beat. How long have you known?"

Drew sighed, abandoning the countertop stain. "A few days."

"Are you serious?"

"They swore me to secrecy."

"When you say they, do you mean just Vox?"

"Both of the kids. Vox told Maddie first, and then they came to me together."

"That production number in Claire's office was for my benefit?"

"Vox was scared to tell you," Drew said. "I let them go at their own pace. It's been torture keeping it from you, but I had to honor their wishes."

Now that she knew, Jess flashed back to dinner with Drew a few days ago. He'd said *they*, but he hadn't been talking about both girls. At the time, Jess had blown it off, but now it made sense. "Did you know about the name change too?"

"Yes."

"What the hell kind of name is Vox? I've never heard of it."

"I'm not sure," he said. "But it's their choice, not ours."

"Aren't we allowed to name our own child?"

"Listen, I understand you're upset. There's a lot to take in here."

"You've had time to come to terms with it. I had it thrown in my face without warning."

"I thought about telling you so many times, but I didn't want to betray Vox's trust. They never would have forgiven me."

"And what about the bat mitzvah? They're going to wear a suit and a yarmulke? What will the rabbi think of that?"

Drew pulled out the chair next to his. "Jess, sit and breathe for a minute. You're spinning in circles. We need to come to terms with these changes for ourselves before we worry about the rabbi or anyone else."

Jess collapsed into the chair with an exhale. "I don't know how to do this, Drew. We've always had two daughters. Now everything I thought was a given has been thrown into question. Where do we go from here?"

"We don't have to solve it all tonight."

Her chest ached for coming up short. She wished Vox had confided in her, trusted her to guard the secret and guide them along the way, but she'd gone to Drew instead. If Jess had been home more, been more focused on what was going on with her family rather than distracted by work, maybe Vox would have come to her.

Jess looked at Drew, the man who'd had her back for so long. He'd been by her side through the grueling years of residency and beyond. Together, they'd figured out breastfeeding, diaper changing, and how to install car seats. Now, faced with the daunting task of parenting teenagers, he was still her sounding board and rock. Though Jess felt slighted, Drew had kept the secret to protect their child. His heart was in the right place. She wanted to go to him, to rest her head on his chest and melt into his embrace, but her body wouldn't move. The betrayal was too raw.

"I know what might help," Drew said.

"What?"

"Takeout from The Sicilian Butcher. Drown our sorrows in tagliatelle and Tomaso's meatballs." Drew opened the Uber Eats app on his phone, squinting while he placed the order.

Jess sighed, willing her guilt to float away with her breath. They'd talked enough about this tonight, and she hadn't eaten since breakfast. "Did you add a piece of chocolate Nutella cake to split?" she asked.

Drew smiled. "Do bears poop in the woods?"

Chapter Sixteen

KENDALL

With Hope down for her morning nap, Kendall tried to get some work done for the Rubin affair. Taking on a new client had seemed like a good idea at the time, but now she wasn't so sure. Since Hope's birth, Kendall had only planned two simple events, a small retirement party and a tasteful sweet sixteen. No mitzvahs yet. She hadn't felt ready for the high expectations and demanding parents, but Jessica Rubin seemed pretty chill. With any luck, Vivian's bat mitzvah would be the perfect way to dip her toes back into the water. She stared at her computer screen, the numbers on the spreadsheet blurring into a swirling mass of black. Kendall couldn't stop thinking about the lawsuit. Attorney Silverberg had said it would take a few days to file with the court and serve the defendants. Kendall pictured a waiter in a tailcoat and tie presenting Dr. Schorr with a pile of papers on a silver platter.

Shaking away the ridiculous image, Kendall opened up Facebook to gather information about the bat mitzvah girl. Jessica had only sent a few generic photos, so Kendall didn't have much to go on. Maybe if she found some pictures of the family, she'd be struck with inspiration. She typed Jessica Rubin into the search bar and scrolled through the results. The first one lived in Houston and wore a tacky purple dress showing a generous amount of side boob. Another was a zookeeper from Anchorage with oversized black glasses and a pointy nose. A third in Orlando sported a Disney t-shirt and Minnie Mouse ears. None of them lived anywhere near Scottsdale. No luck. Maybe Jessica Rubin was one of the *holier than thou* types who'd opted out of social media.

A murmur came through the baby monitor. When Kendall reached the nursery to check, Hope was fast asleep in her crib, her hand curled around Posy. Soft light filtered through the gauzy curtains, giving the room a soft glow. She remembered decorating this room the month before her due date, she and Troy filled with optimism for the future. Dipping their rollers into the pale pink paint, they had coated the walls together, chatting about the day they would meet their baby. Kendall longed to turn back time, to recapture the innocence she'd had before everything changed. They'd never envisioned incubators and ventilators and arterial lines, the first several weeks of their baby's life spent in the sterility of the neonatal ICU, and then everything that followed.

Blinking away the bad memories, Kendall returned to her desk, clicked the last email from Jessica Rubin, and opened the attachment, a folder which contained a few photos of Vivian. In the first one, the girl wore a magenta party dress, long hair framing her face. Her smile was uncomfortable, as if all she wanted to do was rip off the dress and put on comfy pajamas. The next one was of Vivian on a beach with her dad, both in white shirts and jeans. Staged family photo shoots were a bit cliché, but Kendall was a sucker for them. The crinkles at the corners of the man's eyes made him seem kind, a good dad. There was something awkward about Vivian in this one too, like she wasn't sure where to put her hands. The last photo in the folder was different. Vivian's hair had been cut short, but her face was different too, her smile broader and more confident. She seemed more at peace with herself, at home in her body.

Hope cried out. Nap time was sadly over. Kendall lifted Hope from her crib and tried her best to soothe her. After taking many laps around the house, turning on the music on the play mat, and offering various snacks, Hope's screams only intensified. Sometimes sleep set Hope's nervous system on high alert.

Kendall was sinking further underwater. When the light from the surface was barely visible, an idea struck her. Tennis. Something about watching people play calmed Hope down. Grabbing the diaper bag, she secured Hope into her stroller and pushed her down the street to the community courts.

It was a hot one, the midday sun directly overhead. Kendall pulled the shade over the stroller, walking briskly to get out of the sun. As Hope continued to wail, Kendall ignored the questioning look of a man jogging by, then turned down the path to the clubhouse and parked Hope in the shade. Two women were in the midst of a game, the ball volleying over the net at rapid speed. Hope fixated on the ball and immediately stopped crying. Worked every time. After the next point, the player closer to Kendall gave a friendly wave. It was Aubrey Lawlor, from playgroup. Kendall hadn't seen her since the last meeting at the train park, when Aubrey had been so adamantly against the lawsuit.

"Let's take five," Aubrey said, coming over to greet Kendall at the fence. "I've been meaning to call you."

Kendall wasn't sure why. They'd never spoken outside of group.

"With Jacob into everything, I barely have a moment, but that's no excuse."

"So crazy." Kendall's throat burned with jealousy. She could put Hope down on a blanket on the floor, go make a cup of coffee, and the baby would be in the same place when she returned. Listening to this in play group was torture enough. She wasn't sure why Aubrey had to rub it in.

"I wanted to apologize for what I said at group," Aubrey said. "My behavior was out of line. My first instinct was to stand up for Dr. Schorr. I've been happy with her, but that's irrelevant—"

"No, I understand—"

"Let me finish. Just because I had a good experience doesn't mean you weren't wronged. I was biased, and I'm truly sorry."

"Thank you. That means a lot," Kendall said. It wasn't often that someone spoke so honestly with her. The incessant platitudes— it's all up from here, what doesn't kill you makes you stronger, it's all part of his plan—made her want to punch someone. There was no sunshine after the storm.

"What did you decide? About the lawsuit, I mean."

"We're going ahead with it," Kendall said. "I wasn't sure, and I'm still not, but it's important to Troy. I think it's helping him process, in his own way."

"I can't even imagine how I'd feel. I have a hard enough time taking care of Jacob. The hours stretch in front of me, and it feels like Marcus will never be home, and then when he arrives, he claims exhaustion. As if I haven't had a long day too."

"I know. It's overwhelming," Kendall said.

"Did you find an attorney?"

"He comes highly recommended." Kendall would never admit to Aubrey or anyone else that they'd crossed paths in the dairy section of Trader Joe's. "He has an excellent record."

"Does he think you have a good chance?"

"He seems quite positive. Wants to loop in the hospital and maybe a delivery nurse too."

"Interesting. I never knew you could do that."

"Me neither," Kendall said. "It's a steep learning curve."

"Not a course you signed up for, I'm sure."

"You ready, Aubrey?" her tennis partner asked.

"One more minute," she called over her shoulder. "Listen, this whole thing sounds super stressful. I'm here if you need anything at all." Aubrey took her place on the court and returned the first serve, her stroke confident. The ball launched over the net and whizzed past her opponent.

Later that evening, Kendall perused Instagram while sitting on the couch next to Troy. On the Hermès page, there was a video of a woman with severe bangs, her face hidden by a green Birkin. Kendall had left a message on Jeffrey's voicemail nearly two weeks ago, her eyes welling up by the end of her monologue. Oh well.

It had been worth a try. Opening the search bar, she typed #partythemes, the screen filling with photos of frosted cookies, charcuterie boards, and giant lawn lettering. Sometimes this trick gave her inspiration, but today it all seemed overdone and trite. Coming up with a theme for the Rubin affair was no easy task. There was so little to go on. The sound of gunshots and wailing sirens from the TV made Kendall jump. This show was about firefighters in Chicago, or was it Boston? All of Troy's shoot-em-up shows were basically the same.

Her phone rang. As if she somehow sensed Kendall was grasping for a theme, Jessica Rubin was on the line.

She stepped into the kitchen. "Hello?"

"Hi KC, It's Jessica Rubin. I hope it's not too late."

"Perfect timing, actually. My husband has claimed the remote."

"I have some news to share with you, about the event. Our child has some major changes going on. Apparently, she's been struggling with her gender, not feeling comfortable in her skin."

"What do you mean?"

"Last week, she told us she's nonbinary, kind of in between male and female. She wants to use they and them pronouns. Clearly, I'm having trouble getting used to the change."

"Okay…" Kendall wasn't sure what Jessica Rubin expected her to say. In college, she'd known people on all ends of the gender spectrum. It wasn't a big deal.

"And here's the kicker. Their name is no longer Vivian. Now it's Vox." Jess's voice caught.

"Unusual. I haven't heard that one before."

"I don't want to burden you, but my laundry list of stressors could fill a phone book."

Maybe this was Kendall's opportunity to bow out of this commitment. Simplify her life. "You sure a party still makes sense?"

"It's important to me. It may sound silly, but it is."

"Sometimes we can't do it all." If Kendall followed her own advice, she'd be honest with Jessica Rubin, tell her she'd taken on more than she could handle, but something wouldn't let her quit. The woman sounded needy, almost desperate. Kendall didn't want to let her down. Plus, an affair with two hundred guests would bring in good money. She couldn't turn that down.

"In theory, I know you're right, but I still want to do it."

"I get it." As women, they'd been programmed to think they could do it all, but in reality, that was a farce. "I can't remember the last time I made dinner outside the microwave. There's not enough time in the day."

"How many kids do you have?"

"Just one, but she takes a lot of energy. I give her everything I've got."

"It's exhausting. And a long haul to boot."

"Definitely. My daughter is still young, but when I look out at the horizon, it stretches on forever." There was a lump in Kendall's throat. She had to change the topic before she broke down in hysterics. "So, what does this mean for the party?"

"I'm not sure. We need to tone down the girl stuff for sure. No pinks or purples or glitter. And Vox wants to wear a suit."

"I haven't come up with a theme idea yet, so it's all good. I can definitely choose more neutral colors." This could be a good opportunity for KC Events. Maybe grow a new market, show prospective clients her inclusive and open-minded attitude.

"There's something else I forgot to mention. Vox is obsessed with baking. They even have an Instagram account with photos of their creations and recipes."

"That's a great idea. What's the handle?"

"Cake It 'Til You Make It."

"That's adorable." Kendall jotted the name down on the whiteboard by the fridge, to remind herself to look it up later. "Don't worry, the event will be fabulous. I've got you covered."

After the call, Kendall gave herself a mental pat on the back. Walking away from this client wouldn't be right. Now that she had an idea for a theme, the rest of the planning would fall into place.

Chapter Seventeen

ABE

Abe pulled his Toyota Camry into the Desert Mountain Club and parked next to Marty's convertible. The tasteless vanity plate, RUHURT, made Abe's blood boil every time. Tone-deaf choices like this gave plaintiff attorneys a bad name, another reason Abe needed to separate himself from Marty as soon as possible. He grabbed his clubs from the trunk and threw the bag over his shoulder, making sure the coffee stain on the side faced in. If he was going to stand up to his partner today, he had to put his best foot forward.

Marty stood at the first hole in pressed khakis, a pristine white polo, and a braided leather belt. He tapped on his watch, the cart already loaded with his clubs and a cooler full of cold drinks.

"Sorry I'm late," Abe said. It was only a few minutes past nine, but he felt the need to apologize anyway.

Marty shaded his eyes with his forearm. "Those shorts are blinding."

"What, these? Had them hanging around." Abe had spent too much on these darn plaid shorts and light blue polo, hoping to look like a boss. Now, he felt silly. No item of clothing would help him get a leg up with Marty. After all these years, the unwritten hierarchy between them was too firmly established.

"You ready to roll? Let's get ahead of this group." He motioned to two couples walking towards them from the clubhouse. "Don't want to get stuck behind them."

"What's the rush?" Abe hated when Marty pressured him.

Marty checked his watch again. "I made a reservation at the Outlaw clubhouse for 11:30. To beat the lunch crowd. We need to play with purpose."

Abe wasn't sure why Marty insisted they eat there. The dark wood and Western-themed decorations made Abe feel like he was at a Wild West theme park. Marty hopped into the driver's seat, and Abe slid in beside him. As they sped to the first hole, Abe felt every bump, his breakfast doing flips in his stomach. When they'd opened the firm together over thirty years ago in a whirlwind of ambition and excitement, exit strategy hadn't been a priority. Abe had been thankful for the law school alumni network connection, and Risa thrilled to say goodbye to the snowy winters and ridiculous cost of living in the New York area. But how could the contract be silent on dissolving the partnership? They were attorneys for Pete's sake. Marty stopped the cart at the first hole.

"So, how's business?" Marty asked. "Anything new and exciting?"

"If I say yes, will you come back? It's too soon for you to be put out to pasture." Abe cursed himself silently. What the hell was he saying? Abe was supposed to be convincing Marty to dissolve the partnership, not tempting him to come back.

"I have to say the grass tastes pretty good."

"Oh yeah?"

"But you know, I'm always here for advice if you need help."

"I'm doing all right on my own," Abe said.

"When you're ready to close up shop, I can help you with your portfolio." Marty launched into a monologue about his investments, droning on about index funds and earnings reports. Abe's mind wandered. Financial terms had never made any sense to him.

"Norah would never let me retire." Abe couldn't tell Marty the truth. He could barely afford his monthly bills, so retirement was not on the table.

"How is Norah? I miss kidding around with her."

"She and I are working on bringing in more clients. She's got some good ideas." Abe needed Marty to know the firm would live on, that Silverberg would thrive while Goldman was perfecting his short game or sitting by the pool with a martini.

"Oh yeah?" He raised his eyebrows. "Like what?"

The way Marty asked the question sounded dismissive. Being a salesman didn't come naturally to Abe, but he was making it work, doing things his way. "I just signed a new case last week. I think it's a strong one."

Marty's eyes widened. "Really?"

"What? You thought I couldn't do it?"

Marty placed his ball on the tee and pulled out his three-iron, taking a moment to line up his swing. "Not at all. I'm proud of you. Now you're the BSD at the firm."

Abe had seen Marty naked in the locker room any number of times, and his dick was neither big nor swinging. It was no coincidence Marty insisted on driving a banana yellow Maserati convertible. "Not sure that term fits either one of us."

"It's all about attitude." Marty took a swing, sending the ball into a sweeping arc onto the fairway. "If you act like you're in control, then you will be. If you start feeling defeated, it's a self-fulfilling prophecy."

"I guess so," Abe said, placing his ball on the tee.

"Where'd you find the case?"

"Pressing business cards. Trader Joe's, of all places."

Abe gave it his best shot, the ball falling far short of Marty's, as usual.

"Business is everywhere," Marty said. They hopped in the cart and drove to the fairway. "What is it? A missed cancer? A surgical error? Nasty hospital infection?"

"No, childbirth case. It seems to have merit."

"Ooh. A bad baby case," Marty said. "Is the baby alive?"

"Yes, she's almost two. Serious disabilities."

"Even better," Marty said. "It'll be easy to get the jury on your side. Park her right in front of the jury box and watch them weep. Pass out tissues before your direct. It's a nice touch."

As callous as it sounded, there was a kernel of truth there. This type of case could be a goldmine, but Abe didn't like to see it through that lens. Reducing these poor people to dollar signs seemed callous and greedy. Yes, he had to make a living, but that didn't mean he should forget there were real people involved.

"I'm not sure exactly what went wrong," Abe said. "The parents are hard to pin down. The mom doesn't seem fully committed, and the father is quite direct."

"Hunt down everything you can. Notes from everyone. OB doc, nurses, neonatologist, anesthesiologist, respiratory therapist. Leave no stone unturned. You never know what you could find. Are you bringing in any codefendants? That's always a good strategy."

"I don't know yet," Abe said. "I'm still looking everything over."

"And don't go soft on me," Marty said. "These cases have large awards for a reason. Tally up all the damages. Therapies and care for a lifetime, lost wages. And don't shortchange the pain and suffering."

Sweat collected under Abe's cap as he climbed out of the cart. He'd mentioned the case to prove himself, but Marty had turned it around, making it all about him, his own expertise. No, Abe couldn't let him get the upper hand. He'd come here with a goal in mind, to rewrite the well-worn script. It was now or never.

"I've been thinking—"

"Always a dangerous thing," Marty said with a guffaw.

"Seriously, I think it's time to take a look at our partnership. Figure out a way to move forward from here." Abe underpowered his approach shot, falling short of the green.

"It's only been a few months." Marty made his chip look like a cakewalk, the ball landing within a foot of the hole. "Let's let the dust settle first. Plus, I'm still here for advice, when you need to bounce things off someone."

Abe's face flushed. "It's been longer than that and—"

Marty gave Abe a slap on the back. "I'm sure we can hammer something out in due time. The buyout will cover—oh, Cy Berkowitz is on the next hole. We'll have to grab a bourbon with him at the clubhouse later."

Abe didn't want to table the discussion. He needed independence to run the firm on his own once and for all. "I'm not sure—"

"That group is creeping up on us." Marty indicated the foursome waiting for them to clear the course.

Feeling like he had something to prove, Abe managed to send his ball just barely onto the green. Marty then putted his ball in for par, while Abe needed four putts to coax his ball to the hole. As he bent to retrieve it, Abe was overcome with a wave of dizziness, the tall cactuses on the course swaying in his vision. He placed his hand on the ground to steady himself.

"You okay?" Marty asked.

Pushing himself up, Abe walked slowly to the cart. He wasn't sure if it was the heat or Marty's blasé attitude getting to him. Marty took a soda from the cooler and held it to the back of Abe's neck. "How's that? Nothing like a cold can of Coke to make everything better." He opened the can and handed it to Abe.

Abe took a sip and collapsed into the seat, the shade of the canopy allowing him a moment of reprieve. His whole body was coated in sweat, his golf shirt soaked through.

"I have to say, you're looking a bit worse for wear," Marty said. "Your stamina's in the shitter these days."

Abe held the cold can against his cheek. "I don't think I can push through today." He felt embarrassed cutting the game short, but he didn't have much choice. Pushing through the round was out of the question.

"Why don't we go to the clubhouse to cool down? I have an extra shirt in the car. You can change and clean up."

At the clubhouse, Abe used hand towels in the bathroom to dry his chest and underarms and pulled Marty's golf shirt over his head. It was a bit tight over his paunch, but it would have to do.

When Abe reached the booth, two iced teas and a breakfast quesadilla sat on the table. A portrait of a settler aiming a rifle hung over a large stone mantle. The man stared Abe down, daring him to make eye contact. A wooden wagon wheel turned chandelier loomed over their heads.

"You look much better," Marty said. "It was a bit dicey back there."

Abe took a gulp of iced tea. "I don't know what happened."

"One minute we're having a nice conversation, and the next, you need to be airlifted off the green."

"Let's not exaggerate." Okay, Abe hadn't been at his best, but it hadn't been a life-or-death situation. He didn't want to be immortalized in a story Marty told at parties. "I'm not ready to throw in the towel quite yet."

Marty laughed. "Good, I need to keep you around. To have someone to beat on the course."

Chapter Eighteen
JESS

Jess should have been thrilled to have a Sunday morning free. Now that she'd proofread the article, gotten Ken Smart's seal of approval, and sent it off to the Green Journal for review, Jess had more wiggle room with her free time. She tried to read the cover article in *The New York Times Magazine*, a dismal feature about elephants in captivity, but she kept reading the same sentence over and over. She'd already gotten up to refill her coffee twice, loaded the dishwasher, and thrown in another load of laundry. When Drew and Maddie first planned to hike Camelback with a few of Maddie's friends and their dads, Jess had been looking forward to some alone time with Vivian. Since the session with Claire, Jess had been doing her best to say Vox, but in her head, her daughter was Vivian. That's the way Jess thought of her. *Them*. Damn it. It was going to take some time to get used to the new name, and the pronouns were even more difficult. Every time Jess said they or them, it sounded wrong, but she had to keep at it. For the sake of her child.

Now, with Vox holed up in their room, Jess wished she'd made plans to go out. She had no idea how to connect with the child she used to know so well. The chime of the doorbell pulled Jess out of her head. Maybe it was Laura Cartwell, the neighbor across the street who liked to pop in unannounced. Jess usually found her annoying, but today she would be grateful for any distraction. Before she stood up, Jess heard the door opening. A man's voice filled the entryway. Who was here? She wasn't expecting any deliveries.

Vox came into the kitchen. "Mom? There's a policeman at the door."

"What? Why?" Jess thought of Drew and Maddie. No, that couldn't be it. One of them would have called from their cell if something was wrong.

"He didn't say. He just said he needed to speak with Dr. Jessica Schorr."

Jess only used her maiden name at work. Why would a police officer be using her professional name here? Of course, she knew why, but she didn't want to admit it to herself.

The man's large frame filled the doorway, his head nearly touching the top. He wore a tan uniform and a black tie, the morning sunlight glinting off a gold badge pinned to his left breast pocket.

"Good morning," Jess said. "Is everything okay, officer?"

"Morning, ma'am. I'm Officer Zavala from the Maricopa County Sheriff's office. How are you today?" His tone was even. No emergency here.

"I'm fine," Jess said. "What can I do for you?"

The officer bent to pull a green envelope from a black bag at his feet. "I'm sorry to be the one to do this, but you've been served."

"Served?" Jess's pulse pounded in her neck. She'd been dreading this moment for two years. Now that it was here, it didn't seem real.

"A complaint has been lodged against you in Arizona State Court. The details and a summons are included in the envelope."

"I don't understand." This wasn't right. Lawsuits happened to other people, the unfortunate doctors who sweated it out on the witness stand while opposing counsel attacked their training, expertise, and clinical choices. What if she refused to accept the envelope? She could just close the door and go back to reading about depressed elephants, pretend no one had ever come to the door. Her heart pounded against her ribcage and sweat collected along her hairline.

"I'm required to deliver this in person," he said, extending the envelope toward her.

Jess didn't want to take it, but she had no choice. As she grasped the envelope, it shook in her hand. A bead of sweat slid down the side of her face.

"And I'll need you to sign this log." He pulled a clipboard from his bag. "To prove I did my job."

Jess's hand trembled as she scrawled her signature, even more illegible than usual. Patient encounters flashed through her mind—deliveries that hadn't gone as expected, clinic patients whose babies had congenital heart defects, women with preeclampsia or placenta previa who hadn't followed her prescriptions for strict diets or bed rest. Which one of them had done this? As the images played back, Jess knew she was kidding herself, hiding in a den of denial. There was no question who'd brought the suit. Jess froze on an image of Kendall, her smooth blond hair and perfect manicure, the look of fear on her face as she was rolled to the operating suite. Squeezing her eyes shut, Jess tried to calm her racing heart and clear away the bad memories.

"What do I do now?" she asked, her voice shaky. "I don't know what to do."

"Call your lawyer, I'd think," the officer said, "but I'm no expert."

"It's okay, Mom," Vox placed a hand on Jess's shoulder. Jess had forgotten they were standing behind her. Their touch grounded her, reminding her to keep on breathing.

The officer tucked the clipboard away. "Good luck, ma'am. I'm sure it'll turn out okay."

He walked down the path to his cruiser. As he backed out of the driveway, Jess felt numb, as if she were watching a scene in a TV movie. How could this be happening to her? She was a good doctor who'd gone to a competitive college, a top-tier medical school, a highly ranked residency. She'd studied for long hours into the night, took copious notes, and made countless flashcards, scoring over the ninetieth percentile on all her board exams.

Jess closed the door, leaned her forehead against the panels, and tried to take a deep breath. Every time she tried to inhale, the air caught in her throat, and she ended up taking quick, raspy breaths, one after another. After a few seconds, the familiar tingling in her fingers and toes returned. She needed to sit down before she passed out.

"Mom, are you all right?"

"I'm sure this is all a big mistake," Jess said, the sharp corner of the envelope digging into her skin. She wanted to hide it away, stash it under her mattress, and reclaim her peaceful Sunday morning. "I'll be right back."

Jess sat down on the closed toilet lid and closed her eyes. Hanging her head over her knees, she tried to make the dizziness go away. When she opened her eyes, black spots swirled in her vision. Shaking her fingers, she tried to make the tingling sensation dissipate. The gasping sounds of her choppy breaths echoed in her ears. Willing herself to slow her breathing, Jess concentrated on deliberate inhales and exhales, trying to allow a few seconds for each. Once she'd calmed down a bit, the spots faded from her eyes and the tingling in her hands went away.

"You okay, Mom?" Vox said.

"Yes, almost done." Jess sat up and gathered her damp hair, thankful she'd made it to the bathroom before Vox had to witness her panicking. It would have been scary for Vox to watch their mom fall apart. Opening the envelope, Jess removed the crisp and formidable stack of papers inside. The one on top had an official seal in the left corner, the word SUMMONS in capital letters at the top. As Jess scanned down the page, one section jumped out.

To Jessica Schorr, MD,

A complaint has been filed against you in civil court by PLAINTIFFS Troy and Kendall Carlson. The details of the complaint are outlined in the following documents. If you were served this summons in the state of Arizona, you are required by Arizona state law to respond to this complaint within 20 calendar days.

Jess's breath caught. This was the name she was praying not to see. Had she been deluding herself? Babies with Hope's dismal Apgar scores usually had an uphill battle, but Jess had tried to remain optimistic. Without admitting it to herself, Jess had prayed the gifts would grant her freedom, let her off the hook. Jess shoved the papers back into the envelope, sour liquid filling her mouth. Standing up, she opened the toilet lid. She retched, a violent noise erupting from her as the vomit hit the water with a loud splash.

Vivian knocked on the bathroom door. "Mom? I'm worried. Should I call Dad?"

"No, honey. I'll be right out." Waiting for the nausea to pass, Jess pictured Drew and Maddie at the summit of Camelback, the panoramic views of the mountains in the distance and the valley laid out below. How would she share this awful news? She'd have to figure that out by the time they got home.

Chapter Nineteen

KENDALL

"It's going to be a great event. I look forward to working with you." Kendall hung up the phone with a smile. With her second new client this month, things were looking up. After a rough couple of years, Kendall could now see a ray of light. Maybe KC Events would stay afloat after all.

She opened a new spreadsheet and typed the name *MILLER* at the top, excitement fluttering in her chest. Weddings often made Kendall feel like a pinball, pinging between bride, groom, and their respective parents, but she loved the process anyway. All about joy, celebration, and hope for a lifetime of happiness, Kendall bought into the fantasy wholeheartedly. She knew from experience that marriage wasn't always easy, but she could still give her clients the picture-perfect day they'd always imagined.

Just as she started filling the spreadsheet with information, a loud cry from the monitor pierced the stillness. Shit. Short nap days were the worst. She turned the volume down on the monitor so she could hear herself think. Kendall had thought she'd hit the ground running for the Miller wedding and make some progress on the Rubin affair, maybe source components for the baking-themed centerpieces and compare prices. Plus, she needed to order the tablecloths and speak with the florist about the most affordable florals for a January event. So much to do, and never enough time.

Hope's urgent cries now travelled down the hall to Kendall's office without the aid of the monitor. Work would have to be put on hold, once again. Pulling open the curtains in the nursery, Kendall smiled at Hope and lifted her onto her shoulder. After a few minutes bouncing her up and down and rubbing her back, Kendall realized Hope was overdue for a feeding. That's why she was so hysterical.

After she secured Hope into her highchair, Kendall began preparing the set up. She chose a blended meal from the fridge, the fruit one featuring a boisterous cartoon mango and an indifferent strawberry on the packaging. She poured the thick liquid into the kangaroo bag, attached the plastic tubing, and hung the bag from the top of the metal IV pole. Once everything was ready, she lifted Hope from her chair and laid her down on the couch. After cleaning the button on her stomach with a moistened cotton swab, Kendall clicked in the fastener and opened the roller clamp, allowing the pinkish-brown liquid to creep down the tubing.

Kendall settled Hope onto her lap and launched into her favorite Laurie Berkner song, the one about seeing a butterfly. Keeping Hope calm and distracted was important so she wouldn't squirm and yank out the tubing. While she sang, Kendall kissed her smushy cheek and stroked her soft curls, relishing the smell of baby shampoo. Once the feeding finished, Kendall dragged the highchair into her office, fastened Hope inside, then turned on a Peppa Pig video on the iPad. Something about the cutesy animal characters with posh British accents made Kendall feel okay about letting Hope zone out for a bit. Maybe it would allow her a few minutes to get some work done.

Clicking back open the Miller spreadsheet, she tabbed down to venue and typed in *Silverleaf Country Club*. Kendall closed her eyes and pictured the stone patio festooned with lights, the warm spring breeze fluttering through the bride's veil as everyone raised their glasses in a toast to the happy couple. The hightop tables would be decorated with simple vintage bud vases and there would be a signature cocktail on offer at the bar, something to honor the unique personalities of the bride and groom. Kendall would come up with something once she got to know them better. The sound of something crashing to the floor and a cry from Hope brought Kendall back to reality. When Kendall retrieved the iPad, there was a diagonal crack across the black screen. She jammed the button several times, but the damn thing wouldn't turn back on. She called Troy, trying to ignore the sound of Hope's desperate screams. Malfunctioning electronics sat squarely in his domain.

Troy answered. "Is everything okay?"

"Yes, I mean no. Not really. I was trying to work, but the iPad fell and now Hope's upset."

"What?"

"She knocked it over, and it cracked. It won't turn on, and I just need to get some work done."

"Did you try pressing both buttons at once?"

"I think so. She's screaming and—"

"Kendall, I have a meeting in three minutes. I can't deal with this right now. See you when I get home."

He ended the call without saying goodbye. Because she worked from home, Troy expected her to run her business and take care of Hope simultaneously, while he had the privilege of a quiet, distraction-free office. Getting anything more done today seemed unlikely. Maybe she should go out for some fresh air. She called Marisol and asked her to watch Hope while she ran downtown to order a birthday cake for next week's party, neglecting to mention she also planned to stop by Fashion Square. The bakery was so close to her favorite mall, it would be a crime to pass up the opportunity. Once Marisol arrived, Kendall ran out the door with a wave.

Kendall put on her Cartier sunglasses and climbed behind the wheel. It felt good to be free for once. Sometimes it felt like she went back and forth from home to work, all within a few feet of each other, and failed miserably in both roles. Luckily, the bakery errand proved to be a breeze. The second Kendall saw the photo of the cake, she knew it was perfect for Hope's second birthday. That left more than enough time to peruse the new fall items on display at the mall.

The parking lot was blissfully empty, so Kendall snagged a spot right by the entrance. She did a lap around the upper level, relishing the bland, instrumental music and the aroma of freshly baked cinnamon rolls. This was her happy place. No client emails to check, no fussing toddler, and no husband demanding a hot meal. Here she could just be Kendall Carlson, the woman who loved pretty things. On the lower level, Kendall stopped at the Gucci store and gazed through the window. A display on the front held several of the mini bags with the signature print, gold accents, and double G hardware. Entering the store, she approached the rack, took a beige one into her arms, and cradled it to her chest. She stroked the textured leather and fingered the linked gold chain strap. The bag was flawless. What were the chances Kendall would fall in love at first sight on the exact day she landed a new client? It was meant to be. Ferrying the baby safely to the cash register, she handed over her business credit card and watched the cashier swaddle the bag in tissue paper and ensconce her in a pale green box with the classic diamond crisscross pattern. Kendall's heart was full. It had turned out to be a good day after all.

Chapter Twenty

JESS

Jess picked up Drew's hiking clothes from the floor and tossed them in the hamper. He and Maddie had arrived home a half hour ago, exhausted but proud of reaching the summit for the first time. Maddie chattered on about how they'd boosted each other up, raving about the views from the top. When Jess had heard enough, she suggested the kids watch a movie together, and to her amazement, they listened. Ever since Vox came out, they'd been getting along better.

Opening the bathroom door, Jess admired Drew through the shower glass. Even after so many years of marriage, he still looked good. More importantly, he cared more about people than things, prioritizing relationships over investments. Jess didn't mind working to pay the mortgage if it meant having someone like Drew by her side. Her stomach dropped. Could this lawsuit jeopardize their marriage? Their bond was so solid, but no relationship was unbreakable. Jess had heard stories of doctors who'd lost everything from a malpractice case, the lawyers coming after their cars, their property, even their homes. Nothing was sacred.

Jess knocked on the shower door.

Drew wiped the condensation from the glass with his fist. "You have to pay for a peep."

"When you're done, we need to talk."

"Sounds serious. More bat mitzvah decisions? Wait, do we still call it that?" He squirted shampoo into his hand and lathered his hair.

"I'm not sure." If there was another term, Jess didn't know what it was, and she couldn't focus on it now anyway.

Drew tipped his head back to rinse. "That spreadsheet from the planner was a bit much. You said this one was more laid back."

"I thought she was," Jess said. KC's spreadsheet had seemed a bit over the top, but Jess didn't have the bandwidth for the mitzvah right now. She had to tell Drew about the sheriff and the summons. After reading the first two pages, she'd stashed it in her nightstand, but that wouldn't make the problem go away. "Finish up so we can talk."

Opening the drawer, Jess took out the thick envelope. It was probably just lots of legalese, but the weight of the envelope scared her. Had she spent years in school and training, all for nothing? She put her hand to her chest to calm her racing heart. What had happened to Hope? In her mind, she pictured a spunky little thing who loved burying herself in the sandbox and playing with shape sorters. Was this not Hope's life?

The details of that day were a blur, so many questions careening through Jess's head. If she'd made different choices, taken time to discuss the case with Eve, insisted on a cervical exam, maybe she could have prevented disaster. Jess wasn't sure if she was at fault, but she couldn't shake the guilt. Would the lawsuit force her to examine that day, putting every one of her choices under a microscope? If the news got out at the hospital, everyone would talk, second-guessing what she did and didn't do that day. Jess feared it would change the way Drew looked at her, the way he thought about her. He'd always placed her on a pedestal, but maybe those days were over.

Drew emerged from the bathroom in a cloud of steam, a blue towel wrapped around his waist. When he saw her, his smile fell. "Is everything okay?"

"Far from it." Jess paced in front of the bed. "I've been working my ass off for over twenty fucking years. I've been eating crap from the vending machine, missing chorus concerts and soccer games, and reading all the stupid journals. I've done what I'm supposed to do and then some. I don't have anything more to give."

"Jess, why don't you sit down?" He guided her to the bed.

She handed the envelope to Drew. As his eyes trained across the first page, his brow furrowed.

"When did this happen?" he asked.

"Today, while you were out. A sheriff in a uniform came to the door. Vivian answered it. I mean, Vox. Fuck. If I'd known who was at the door, I never would have let them open it."

"Okay, let's start from the beginning. Do you remember this patient?"

Jess didn't know what to say. She'd never told Drew what had happened at the hospital that day. With the chaos that followed, Jess had barely had time to breathe. The more time passed, the more tightly she held the secret. How could she tell Drew after two weeks, two months, and now, two years? It was too late, and now Jess was dealing with the aftermath.

He waved the papers in the air. "Do they have a case?"

"I'm sure it's nothing," Jess said, trying to keep her voice even.

Drew flipped through the pages. "Does it say what the damages are? What's the reason for the suit?" He stopped on a page, his eyes widening. The look on his face made Jess's heart flutter.

"What is it?" she asked.

He pointed to a spot in the middle of the page. Jess grabbed the papers from him. In a box labelled co-defendant, a name was typed in all capital letters, a name she knew all too well. EVE MARCUS. Her colleague, trusted nurse, and friend was also being roped into the suit.

"Nurses get sued?" Drew said. "What the hell happened?"

"I'm not sure…" It was bad enough Jess was dealing with this nightmare. Now Eve too? When she tried to take a deep breath, the air caught in her throat. With Eve also being charged, they might be pitted against each other.

"We'll figure this out together." He wrapped his arms around Jess. "You're not the first doctor to go through this, and you won't be the last. We'll take it one step at a time."

The warmth of his skin, the tickle of his chest hair on her cheek, and the smell of soap calmed Jess, her heart slowing and her stomach settling down. She wanted to be even closer to him. The sound of the doorbell, the image of the sheriff's body filling her doorframe, and the feel of the heavy envelope in her hand all fell away. It was just Jess and Drew, alone in their bedroom. She hooked her fingers under his towel and let it drop to the floor.

"What are you doing?" Drew asked.

Jess locked the door, took Drew by the shoulders, and pushed him down onto the bed. She climbed on top of him, bringing her lips to his. Her world may be spinning off its axis, but sex with Drew was one thing she could control. In all their years together, he had never refused her advances. She needed to feel his skin against hers, his breath hot in her ear, and most of all, in this moment, she needed to feel him inside her. Everything else could wait until later.

O   O   O

Afterwards, Drew went to the kitchen to prepare dinner. Lying in bed, Jess took a few extra minutes to plan what to say to the kids. Freaking them out unnecessarily wouldn't help anything. Jess let her eyes drift closed.

In her dream, she lounged on a chaise in her backyard in an oversized hat and sunglasses. She gazed at the mirrored surface of the pool, the midday sun reflecting dots of light onto the tiles. Opal leapt onto Jess's chair, her tail forming an S shape in the air. Turning in circles a few times, the cat finally curled up in a ball and relaxed.

The dream shifted focus, and Jess now had an overhead view of Jasmine Drive. A bear lumbered down the street, big green tags protruding from his ears, the color the same as the sheriff's envelope. Stopping to sniff the rock daisies at the edge of the road, the bear then found his way between their house and the Paciello's. He paused to commune with some bumblebees and chew a few mouthfuls of grass. Why had Jess been so concerned when Mai first told her about the bear? This creature seemed perfectly docile, not threatening at all.

Opal appeared in the backyard on the other side of the fence. She arched her back and hissed, her long tail swishing back and forth, daring the bear to take a swat. In an instant, the bear transformed. He growled and took off at full speed, scaling up and over the fence in a split second. Opal sprinted away, and the bear chased her, ripping holes in the grass with his thick claws. Foam dripped from his flapping jowls. Opal emitted pained screeches as she ran for her life, desperate to escape the bear's wrath.

Jess watched from above, powerless to help. Before long, the cat began to tire. Her pace slowed and the volume of her yowls decreased. With each passing second, the bear got closer and closer to Opal until only a short gap remained.

"Noooooooo!" Jess screamed. She was back on the ground now, outside the fence. Jess rattled the gate, but it wouldn't budge. When Opal's tail was only a few inches from the bear's face, the beast opened his mouth wide, ready to chomp down.

Jess felt a tickle under her nose. She tried to scratch it away, but the sensation continued, something furry brushing over her face. Opening her eyes, she saw Opal sitting on her chest, her hazel eyes staring her down. Jess caressed the cat's back, relieved to feel the soft fur between her fingers.

"Mom?" Vox stood next to the bed.

"Hmmmmm," Jess mumbled, a sour taste in her mouth. Sweat pooling under her breasts, she covered herself with the sheet. Opal jumped off the bed, hitting the floor with a thump.

"Are you awake?"

"Just had a bad dream."

"Was it about me?"

Teenagers thought everything was about them. "No, actually. It was about Opal."

Vox bent down and picked up the cat, snuggling her to their chest. "Was she cute as ever?"

"Adorable," Jess said.

"Dad's grilling dinner. He said ten more minutes."

"I'll be down soon."

Vox left, clicking the door closed. Jess stretched her arms over her head and groaned. She had to face reality. Today, her real life had become a nightmare in its own right.

Chapter Twenty-One
ABE

Abe sat back in his chair and took a sip of his drink, enjoying the bustling energy of the crowded brunch restaurant. Servers balanced trays of golden pancakes, eggs Benedict, and crisped hash browns, and there were children everywhere, screaming and generally running amok. Still, Abe adored a good brunch. It gave him a break from his daily bagel with cream cheese routine and made for good people-watching, not to mention the crowning glory: the Bloody Mary bar. Something about the dizzying array of pickled vegetables, cured meats, and citrus wedges kept him coming back for more.

Ross and Gavin were running late, as per usual. Abe felt a twinge of nerves in his gut. Since their meeting in the dog park over a month ago, he and Ross had been at a stalemate. The few half-hearted voicemails Ross had left sounded more obligatory than genuine. He spotted the two of them coming through the door, Gavin holding the door open for Ross. Abe stood and waved his arms up and down, as if directing a plane to land. Leading with humor certainly couldn't hurt. They approached his table, and Gavin leaned to give Abe a warm hug, while Ross offered a stiffer one.

They all took their seats and arranged their paper napkins on their laps. Abe looked over at the kitchen, waiting for one of them to start the conversation.

"So, how are you, Abe?" Gavin broke the awkward silence. "It's been a minute."

"Sure has. You two are hard to pin down."

"With our schedules, working nights and weekends," Ross said, "Gavin and I barely even share a meal as it is. It's a small miracle we made this work."

Abe picked up the laminated menu. "Then let's make this one count."

"It's all delish. You really can't go wrong," Gavin said.

Abe took a bite of the celery stalk from his drink. "Forgive me for noshing. The Bloody Mary bar was calling my name."

"Very tempting. I think I'm going to help myself to one of those." Gavin headed over to check out the offerings.

"So, how have things been going?" Abe kept the question vague, hoping Ross would take the ball and run with it. Maybe this would give them a chance to clear the air.

"It's been a struggle. I'm not going to lie. Gavin and I are both fighting to keep our heads above water."

"What do you mean?" Abe didn't want to assume Ross was referring to Gavin's lawsuit. A small part of him held out hope it was something else stressing them out. He wanted to enjoy a nice meal with his son and son-in-law without having to defend his line of work.

"This suit has really thrown a wrench in the works," Ross said. "Gavin has lost all confidence in his skills, second-guessing every call he makes. He's at work hours longer than he used to be, which leaves me to deal with meals and the dog and pretty much everything else."

"I'm sorry for your troubles." Though they were adults now, Abe hated to see his kids in distress. Still grieving the loss of his mother, Ross didn't need any more tsuris right now.

"He's never been an anxious person before," Ross said. "And now everything puts him on edge. Every conversation revolves around affidavits, witnesses, and depositions. I'm trying to be supportive, but it's hard. Working in the ER, then coming home to legal conversations takes a lot out of me."

"I can imagine." Abe's thoughts drifted to the Carlson case. The sheriff's department had just served the papers to Dr. Schorr.

Had the surprise attack launched the doctor into a tailspin? He'd been so focused on getting the paperwork in under the two-year deadline, he hadn't stopped to think about the downstream effects.

"It's just brutal, Dad. Gavin's started seeing a therapist last week. To help him process everything."

"That sounds like a wise choice. Prioritizing mental health is important. Maybe you should do the same?"

"I honestly don't know how I would fit it in. My plate is full."

Gavin returned and set down his creation, a drink with a skewer of bacon and several spears of asparagus poking from the top, and a large shrimp clinging to the rim. "How could your plate be full? We haven't even ordered yet."

Ross shot Abe a look. If Ross wanted to change the subject, that was his prerogative.

"Yes, let's order," Abe said. "I'm thinking about the grand slam. Go big or go home, right?"

Gavin waved down one of the servers. As they'd ordered, acid churned in Abe's belly. Maybe vodka and tomato juice on an empty stomach hadn't been the best idea. He felt badly, guilty almost, that Ross and Gavin were going through such a tough time. It made him think about his life's work. Did his actions condemn the defendants he came up against to the same emotional turmoil as Gavin and Ross? Was Jessica Schorr crying in a corner right now because of his actions? Maybe he'd been turning a blind eye to the suffering he caused for the sake of self-preservation. As Abe shook away these thoughts, his phone dinged with a new email from Kendall Carlson.

Dear Attorney Silverberg,

I wanted to check in to see if the suit has officially been filed. Is there anything we should be doing at this point? This whole thing is a bit overwhelming, so we might need some guidance along the way.

Also, I want to thank you for taking our case seriously and agreeing to represent us. The past two years have been a whirlwind of highs and lows, but the fact that you believe in us makes me feel so much better. Truly, thank you for that. It's done a lot to start the healing process for me, and for Troy as well. I know he comes across as a bit rough, but that's because he loves Hope so much and would do anything for her. I appreciate your patience and understanding as we navigate the next few months together.

Let me know the next steps when you get a chance.

Best,
Kendall Carlson

As Abe put his phone back in his pocket, his stomach quieted. Though he might cause anxiety for those on the other end of the lawsuits, he'd devoted his life to personal injury work for a reason. Good people like Kendall and Troy Carlson deserved fair representation, and he was uniquely skilled to help them. He made a mental note to respond to her email when he got home.

"Everything okay, Dad?" Ross asked.

"All good." Abe rubbed his hands together. "Now how long until we get our grub? I'm famished."

Chapter Twenty-Two
JESS

Jess opened the door to her office and crossed the waiting area. One receptionist gave her the side eye as she scanned in a patient's insurance card, while another started whispering. Was Jess imagining it or had her staff gotten wind of the lawsuit? If so, the reputation she'd so carefully built could be destroyed in the blink of an eye. Saying a quick good morning, Jess sped down the hall, hoping to avoid other doctors or coworkers. If they asked about the suit, she would have no idea how to respond, and if they didn't, she was in no mood for small talk.

She took cover in her office, closing the door behind her. Pulling out her desk chair, she sat straight-backed and squeezed her thigh with her hand to try to calm her trembling muscles. How was she going to make it through the day, the weeks, the months ahead? The ringing of her phone brought Jess back to the moment. She took a breath and answered.

"Dr. Schorr? Mira Taback from risk management."

Mira had been the one to answer Jess's call on the night of the Carlson delivery. After Hope was transferred to Phoenix Children's, she'd checked on Kendall in the recovery room, then made a call to risk management, as per hospital protocol. Whenever a baby was transferred for a higher level of care, risk management opened a file.

"We just received notification of a malpractice claim," Mira said, "and a subpoena for medical records. I wanted to touch base with you immediately. I'm sure your mind is reeling with all sorts of thoughts."

"It's a bit overwhelming, yes."

"When this happens, many doctors don't know which way to turn. That's only natural."

Jess tried again to still her quivering leg. "Yes, I've never been through this before."

"You've had a good run. I've informed your malpractice carrier, and they have already assigned you representation, Attorney Angela Caputo. She's quite experienced in the field. You'll be in good hands. I've also sent you an email. Nothing specific to your case. Just some helpful guidelines for how to conduct yourself. To paint yourself in the best possible light. Please peruse it at your earliest convenience."

"I understand," Jess said. "Does anyone else know this is happening?"

"It's certainly not public knowledge. Unfortunately, sometimes people get loose-lipped. Whether it comes from the plaintiffs or other defendants, one can never be sure."

Jess's morning coffee swam in her stomach. She didn't want to think about who was saying what to whom. Had Eve already been served her papers? After decades of friendship, Jess didn't think her friend would badmouth her around the hospital, but she wasn't sure. Gossip spread through the hospital like a grass fire over parched earth. Once it started, it was nearly impossible to quench.

"Try not to obsess," Mira said. "I've taken the liberty of setting up an initial appointment for you with Attorney Caputo. I think sitting down with her will calm your nerves." Mira filled Jess in on next Monday's appointment time and ended the call.

Turning on her computer, Jess clicked open her hospital account and typed in the password. Her inbox was filled with unread emails—reminders for weekly tumor board meetings, invitations to networking events, and sales pitches from various medical device companies. She opened the one from Mira. It was a generic list separated into two sections: Dos and Don'ts. Jess scanned the list of dos. It said things like contact your malpractice carrier, choose your attorney and meet personally with them, and continue practicing medicine as usual. Jess exhaled. She'd done or at least scheduled those things, so she wasn't failing as miserably as she'd thought. In the don'ts column, she noticed don't contact the plaintiff, don't speak to anyone about your case, and don't alter the medical chart. Jess scanned her eyes over the remaining bullet points but couldn't digest any more information. She'd have to circle back to it later.

It was almost nine a.m. and both of Jess's first patients had failed to show. Two in a row was a rarity. Was it possible they'd heard about the lawsuit somehow? Jess shook away the doubts. Paranoia wouldn't help anything. Maybe she'd use the time to do some research on umbilical cord prolapse, make sure she was up to date and could speak eloquently on the topic. Printing out three articles, she read every word, her yellow highlighter squeaking over the page. Her stomach flipped over again. All this reading about umbilical cords was making Jess queasy. She finished putting stars next to the relevant references and looked back at her computer screen. The icon for the hospital electronic medical record, a white hexagon with red letters in the center, glowed as bright as the North Star. She clicked on the program, typed in Kendall's name, and waited. If she did the proper research, she'd make a better first impression with her attorney. When the chart popped up, Jess scanned down the page of visits. Kendall had only been in the hospital twice, for the delivery and for an allergic reaction to a bee sting several years earlier. Clicking on the delivery encounter, Jess took stock of the notes going down the page, three from her, including the operative report from the Caesarean section. The rest of the notes were from Eve.

Jess clicked on her initial note.

9/24/2020 1:22 p.m.
G1P1, 32 weeks gestation presenting with premature preterm rupture of membranes. Vital signs within normal limits, as are the fetal heart tracings. Patient declined cervical checks per documented birth plan. Nothing of concern on exam.

Review of systems was unremarkable, and nothing in her prenatal history to cause alarm.

Jess scanned down to the management section and noted she'd prescribed Pitocin to induce labor, corticosteroids to promote fetal lung development, and magnesium to decrease the chance of fetal brain injury. Everything seemed to be in line. Maybe she had been blowing this whole thing out of proportion. Could the case be defensible after all? She clicked on the next note.

9/24/2020 10:04 p.m.
G1P1, 32 weeks gestation who presents with premature preterm rupture of membranes. Vaginal exam demonstrates umbilical cord prolapse. Stat C-section is indicated.

The documentation was appropriate, but the delay wasn't a good look. Nothing about that day had gone as planned. Her mother's panicked voice rang in Jess's ears, as clear as if it were yesterday. The even keel of the dispatcher's voice, the wail of the sirens, and then the accident, all while Kendall was in the hospital. So much had been out of Jess's control.

Jess moved on to Eve's notes. The first one seemed routine, as did the next several. She skimmed down the page to a later one.

9/24/2020 7:54 p.m.
The fetus had several runs of prolonged heart rate deceleration. Oxygen administered by face mask and fetal scalp stimulation performed. Dr. Schorr informed.

Jess didn't remember anything about scalp stimulation to get the baby's heart rate back up. A shiver coursed down her spine.

9/24/2020 8:48 p.m.
The fetal heart tracings continue to be erratic, despite previous

interventions, concerning for fetal hypoxia. Lactated Ringer's solution hung for patient support. Dr. Schorr again notified.

Jess tilted back in her chair. Eve had mentioned the tracings on the phone, but she'd never said anything about hypoxia. Or had she? Jess had been pulled in so many directions. Maybe she'd missed something? She remembered reassuring Eve the irregular tracings were related to the magnesium. Tacking on a short addendum to one of Eve's notes would clear that up. She knew she wasn't supposed to do this, but she needed to clarify her thinking. It wasn't altering the medical record exactly, just setting it straight, making her intentions clearer. As her fingers flew over the keys, her heart lifted. She was being proactive, doing something to dig herself out of this hole.

Addendum 9/19/2022 9:32 a.m.

In reviewing the chart, I would like to clarify the communication between Nurse Marcus and myself on the day of delivery. Nurse Marcus informed me of several runs of deceleration. I felt this finding was likely an effect of the magnesium sulfate administration, rather than a sign of fetal distress. Once I detected the umbilical cord prolapse on physical exam, the patient was immediately transported to the OR for stat C-section.

As she hit save, Jess's jaw clenched with tension. No amount of explaining would change the fact that Jess had failed. Sure, Eve had played a part too, but as the obstetrician on record, Jess was ultimately responsible for overseeing the case. If she'd monitored Kendall more closely instead of relying on Eve, would Hope have been born healthy? Maybe, but not necessarily. And what about Kendall Carlson's birth plan? Deciding to forgo cervical checks had been her choice. She must have known declining an important part of the physical exam wasn't without risk. Didn't that mean she owned some of the responsibility too? If Jess admitted to any blame, she'd risk her career, but if she tried to cover up, she would buck up against what was right. Jess shook her head, trying to clear the warring thoughts. Second-guessing wouldn't change anything. Her career and family had to take precedence over Hope, as callous as that may sound. As much as Jess wanted Hope to grow up strong and healthy, she had to put her own family first.

Jess turned her attention back to Kendall's chart. The operative note was succinct and unremarkable. Once Jess had made the call, the C-section had been quick and relatively easy. No blood transfusions or pressors were required. The baby, on the other hand, was a different story. As soon as Jess freed the infant from the uterine incision, she'd had a sickening sense of dread. The baby was pale and limp, her cry barely audible. Before Jess knew what was happening, the pediatric team had whisked her away, transferring her to Phoenix Children's for a higher level of care. Jess would never forget Kendall's screams, the way she kept saying, "Where's my baby? What's wrong with my baby?" over and over. Was that the first moment, Jess wondered now, when the stone had started to form in her stomach? A burden she'd been carrying around with her for nearly two years. Jess wiped a tear from her cheek.

"Dr. Schorr?" Jess's medical assistant stood in the doorway.

Jess clicked to minimize the EMR. "Yes, what's up?"

"We have two patients checked in. Mrs. Todd is here for an abnormal glucose challenge test result and then a preeclampsia follow-up after that."

"Okay, I need to take care of one more thing."

"Mrs. Todd is all set in room three."

As soon as the door was closed, Jess opened EMR again. There was one more thing she needed to check. Her pulse quickened. Videos from HIPAA trainings played in her head, warning against accessing a patient's chart out of curiosity, but she ignored the internal alarm bells. If she were going to defend herself, she had to know more about Hope's condition. Jess took a deep breath, trying to clear her head and slow her racing heart. With trembling hands, she typed the name into the search bar.

CARLSON, HOPE

As soon as Jess hit return, the whole screen filled with words and documents. In her two short years, Hope had racked up countless visits with doctors and nurses and therapists. The most recent visit was with Dr. Hill, a developmental pediatrician. Jess clicked and read down the page. By the time she reached the middle, her mouth dropped open. Ever since learning of Hope's cerebral palsy, Jess had been telling herself it must be a milder case, that maybe Hope would need speech therapy to encourage her to pronounce her R's properly or physical therapy to improve her muscle coordination. Nothing to stop Hope from living a full life. The child Dr. Hill described in his note was far from the one Jess had pictured. This Hope needed help sitting up, had a feeding tube in her stomach, and hadn't ever spoken a word.

More tears stung Jess's eyes. When she'd recited the Hippocratic oath at her medical school graduation, she'd focused on the good she would bring to the world. But now, she couldn't stop thinking of all the ways things could go horribly wrong, the problems she could cause rather than solve. Enough of this. She blinked away her tears, closed the chart, and put on her white coat. There was a patient waiting for her in room three.

O O O

While Jess reassured Kalyn Todd her abnormal glucose result was likely a false positive, she longed to be somewhere else. For her next patient, Jess sent labs and increased the dose of her blood pressure medication. After answering her questions with as few words as possible, Jess successfully extricated herself and returned to her office, exhausted. Her clinic days used to feel like a welcome break from the mayhem of labor and delivery, but since the sheriff had darkened her doorstep two days ago, the simplest things had become a slog, familiar ground now shaky and unstable. Jess felt like a fraud. If her patients heard about the lawsuit, would they look for another doctor? Her muscles ached. She shook out her arms and then clasped her hands behind her back to stretch out her chest.

Her assistant came in carrying a tablet. "Checking in, Dr. Schorr."

"Break it to me gently," Jess said.

"Your last morning patient rescheduled, so you have a break until one."

"Excellent." The lunch break would give her a few minutes to get her bearings.

"Brenda and I are going for a power walk. Care to join us?"

"I'm going to lay low. Eat my lunch and catch up on charting." Jess was in no mood. Her medical assistant and office nurse would have a more pleasant walk without her.

Jess opened up the calendar on her phone to get a sense of what the week had in store. Drew had a staff meeting after work tomorrow, so Jess would have to cook dinner and make sure the kids did their homework. Maddie had a piano lesson after dance on Wednesday evening, and Vox had their session with Claire after school on Thursday, but other than that, it was pretty quiet. As she was about to close the calendar, Jess noticed an event next Monday.

HOPE'S BIRTHDAY

Jess had entered it in capital letters so she wouldn't miss the date. Last year, she'd given Hope a baby walker personalized with her name. She couldn't imagine letting the day pass without acknowledgment, but she couldn't give a gift now. Could she? The email was clear on that point. Any contact with the plaintiff is forbidden. No phone calls, emails, or texts. An anonymous birthday gift would definitely be considered contact. Something tugged at Jess. She'd been giving the gifts to placate her guilt, to frame herself as a generous benefactor rather than the doctor, at least partially responsible for Hope's disabilities. If she stopped, Jess would be forced to face her guilt head-on. She wasn't ready to do that.

Thinking back to the note in Hope's chart, Jess was overcome with a wave of nausea. She grabbed the garbage bin and held it on her lap, waiting for the feeling to pass. She thought back to all the gifts she'd delivered over two years—wooden building blocks, puzzles, and board books. The child from Dr. Hill's notes wouldn't be able to use any of those. Maybe deluding herself had been Jess's coping mechanism. Living in a fantasy world where Hope could sort shapes, jump rope, and learn Spanish words was better than facing reality.

Her cell phone chimed. A group text from Mai.

"Girls' night out tonight?"

The group included Mai, one of the nurses from her clinic, a physician's assistant from the OR, one of the pulmonologists, and Eve. It had started a few years back when they'd all ended up in the same bar near the hospital one evening after work, and then Mai had carried on the tradition, sending a text a few times a year. Since the Carlson delivery, Eve had avoided Jess at those get-togethers, pretending to be engrossed in other conversations. The timing on this one wasn't great. At work, Eve had been keeping things professional, but a social setting was a different story. Mai didn't know about the Carlson delivery or the lawsuit, so the three of them at a bar would prove awkward.

A few of the ladies responded with excuses. A kid with a fever, too many charts to catch up on, an anniversary dinner. Jess waited a few minutes for Eve's response. Eve texted that she had a haircut scheduled after work. Looked like she was out.

"Jess?" Mai typed.

"I'm in," Jess texted to Mai only. She wasn't sure if she should text with Eve and she'd broken enough rules already today. "Agave?"

"Wanted to try this axe throwing place downtown. You game?"

"Sounds good."

"Random Axe of Kindness. After work at 6?" Mai typed back.

When Jess responded with a thumbs up, she felt lighter somehow. Maybe getting out her aggression was just what Jess needed. It wasn't all her fault. So many forces had converged that day, so many distractions pulling her focus from patient care, but that didn't mean she deserved to take the fall. Eve had been involved too, and now she was avoiding Jess at all costs. She turned back to her computer and opened Google. Surfing around a little wouldn't hurt, right? A tricycle was the gift she'd had in mind. Maddie and Vox had each gotten one around the same age, but for Hope, instead of choosing a red Radio Flyer with the silver bell and ribbons on the handlebars, Jess would look for a more appropriate one. She'd meet Hope where she was, rather than dwelling in denial. In the search bar, Jess typed, "Tricycle for Kids with Cerebral Palsy." The first article looked promising.

"The five best tricycles for children with special needs."

Jess scrolled down the page. One of the trikes caught her eye. Bright pink with a tall back support and lots of straps to keep Hope safe and secure, it was too perfect to pass up. If she kept her wits about her, risk management would never know. Hope needed this gift. Adding it to her cart, Jess filled in her information and checked out with her credit card. Once she received the email confirmation, she breathed easier. The gift should arrive by this weekend, just in time for Hope's birthday. Far from a cure, maybe it would spark joy in Hope's difficult life. Only someone who genuinely cared would pick out such a thoughtful gift.

Chapter Twenty-Three

JESS

As soon as Jess arrived, she was glad she'd decided to come out tonight. The place had a fun vibe, packed with people chatting, laughing, and throwing axes at the targets. Though it was only she and Mai tonight, it felt good to be out in the world.

Scanning the room, Jess spotted Mai in one of the cubicles, chatting with a guy with a shaved head and a tattoo of barbed wire encircling his neck. Jess had always gone for the nerdy guys, as evidenced by Drew's obsession with sorting the ValuePak coupons from the mail. This dude was no coupon clipper. As Jess got closer, Mai threw her head back and laughed.

Jess joined them and stashed her work bag in the corner. "Sorry I'm late. My last patient took forever."

"No worries," Mai said. "Just getting a safety briefing."

"You'll have to fill in your friend," tattoo guy said, "and don't skip any details."

Mai flashed a flirty smile. "I'm a quick study. Had lots of practice over the years."

He eyed the white coat peeking out from Jess's tote bag. "You ladies nurses?"

"Doctors, actually," Mai said.

"Impressive," he said. "What can I get for you today? For safety, there's a two-drink max."

"I'll have a Blue Moon," Jess said.

Mai ordered a gin and tonic, her old standby.

"That was some award-winning flirting," Jess said once he headed back to the bar.

"You know I don't get out much. What Tom doesn't know won't hurt him."

"I guess. That tattoo is hard to resist."

Mai laughed. "So, what's been going on with you? I feel so out of the loop."

"Life just gets busy sometimes," Jess said. "We've had some interesting developments in the Rubin household."

"Oh yeah?" Mai said. "Do tell. Helping Tanner do fifth-grade math is less than scintillating, so I'll take whatever you're dishing out."

Tattoo guy returned, placing their drinks and a bowl of tortilla chips on the table. "You ladies ready? I want to see some axes flying," he said before moving on to the next group.

"Yes, sir." Mai picked up an axe from the stump, lined up the target, and heaved. It bounced off the wooden board and clattered to the floor.

Jess tried next. The axe missed the board by a foot, clanging off the metal cage.

"Good try," Mai said. "So, what's happening with you? You left me hanging."

Jess wasn't sure how to phrase it. "Um, I guess I no longer have two daughters."

"What do you mean?"

"A few weeks ago, Vivian came out as nonbinary." Jess went on to explain Vox's name change and new pronouns. "It's been a major adjustment, to say the least."

"Wow." Mai took a sip of her drink. "How's Drew taking it?"

"On the surface, he's in social worker mode, spouting things like 'that must be hard' and 'sounds like you're dealing with a lot,' but I know it's not easy for him either. We're mourning the child we knew, the one we thought we had. Like her childhood, I mean *their* childhood has been erased. It's bizarre."

"So Drew's putting on a tough exterior?"

"He's also had longer to digest the information. Vox came out to him first." Jess felt a pang in her chest as she admitted this out loud.

"You pushed that baby out of your vagina, and that's the thanks you get?" Grabbing another axe, Mai used two hands to give her throw more power. The handle side struck the board and fell with a clunk.

Jess took a long sip of her beer. "We're all coming to terms with the new normal."

"What does that look like?"

"Today? Short haircut, formless t-shirts, and baggy jeans. Tomorrow, who knows? We're taking it day by day. For the bat mitzvah, they don't want to wear a dress. The party planner wasn't thrilled." In reality, KC had pivoted more smoothly than Jess had expected. In her head, Jess wanted to be accepting, but her heart wasn't quite there yet.

"She'll get over it. It's not about her."

"I guess," Jess said. "There's something else I need to tell you. It's about work."

"Oh no. That doesn't sound good," Mai said.

"Remember when I told you about the panic attacks, the patient I couldn't get out of my mind? Well, it happened."

Mai's eyes widened. "*What* happened? Now you're really scaring me."

The email from risk management flashed through Jess's mind. The instruction to avoid talking about the case didn't include her best friend, right? Jess looked around to make sure no one was within earshot. "She's suing me."

"Oh, Jess, I'm so sorry. That really sucks." Mai pulled Jess in for a hug. In the warmth of her embrace, Jess realized how much she needed it today.

"It's a nightmare," Jess said. "Honestly, I don't know which end is up these days. It's too much."

"I'm sure it's stressful, but you can't let it derail you. You're an excellent doctor who's delivered hundreds of healthy babies. Your patients adore you. Think of all the holiday cards tacked to your bulletin board."

"I know, but sometimes it's hard to keep my chin up."

"Are you still having the episodes?"

"Once in a while, but since I got served two days ago, I've mostly been in my head. Wondering how things would have turned out if I'd made different choices. What would have happened."

"Maybe you need a breather," Mai said. "Take some time off work to regroup. For you and for your patients."

"I can't," Jess said. "I'm booked six months out. Plus, we'd never be able to pay the bills without my salary."

"Did you ever find a psychologist?"

"Sort of. I've been seeing someone." Jess left her answer deliberately vague. The only psychologist she was seeing was her child's, but it was the best she could do right now.

Mai looked past Jess to someone behind her. "We didn't expect you tonight."

Jess turned to see Eve standing there, her hair shorter and blown straight, her mouth open in surprise.

"I didn't know…," Eve stammered, checking her watch. "But I just realized I have to pick up Isla from her track meet."

"You just got here," Mai said.

"I know. We'll have to catch up later." Eve turned on her heel and walked back to the front.

Jess felt her pulse quicken. Eve was literally running away from her. Before the lawsuit, she'd had trouble mending their friendship, and the situation was even worse now. She had no clue how to untangle the complicated knot she'd tied, but she knew she couldn't let Eve disappear so fast.

"Give me a minute," Jess said to Mai.

Pushing the door open, Jess saw Eve on the sidewalk. "Eve, wait."

Eve turned around. "I can't do this now. Anyway, we're not supposed to talk to each other."

"I know, but we have to," Jess said. "You can't just run away. This whole thing has gotten out of hand."

"That's the understatement of the year. A sheriff showed up at my house, Jess. Nurses never have to deal with this shit."

"It was awful, right?"

"Beyond horrible. I cried for a good twenty minutes."

"I couldn't stop vomiting," Jess said, "but we need to figure out a plan."

"What do you mean?"

"If we're on the same page, everything will fall into line."

"Same page?"

"Instead of pulling each other down. If we launch a lifeboat together, we can both be saved, but if we're only in it for ourselves, one of us will go down with the ship."

"This isn't the fucking Titanic, Jess."

"I think about Hope every single day." A lump formed in Jess's throat. "About what-ifs and maybes. You're making it seem like I don't care, but that couldn't be farther from the truth."

"Me too," Eve said, "but I'm not sure what the truth is anymore. I was so sure it was your fault, that the delay in getting to the OR was the reason for Hope's cerebral palsy, but now I'm not sure. What you said right after Hope's delivery keeps coming back to me."

"What did I say?"

"You said it was my fault—"

"I didn't mean that. The baby had just been shipped out, and I didn't know which way was up. Pointing fingers was easier than facing the truth."

"This could get ugly. You know that, right?"

"What do you mean?"

"I mean we're not in this together."

"Aren't we? We both work hard and try to do what's best for our patients."

"That has nothing to do with it. This is all about how the lawyers can spin the story to their best advantage. My lawyer wants to throw you under the bus."

"What are you talking about?"

"That's the way these things play out. Pit the defendants against each other and let them duke it out to figure out where the money lies."

Jess's heart rate picked up. "You wouldn't do that, right? We've been through so much together."

"I don't want to, but I may have no choice."

Mai came outside to check on them. "Is everything okay?"

Jess wiped her eyes with a tissue from her purse.

"I have to go." Eve gave a quick wave and walked to her car without a backward glance.

"That was odd," Mai said. "I wonder what's up her butt."

"I'm not sure."

"How about a few more throws? We still have twenty minutes on the clock."

Back inside, Jess chose an axe and took a moment to line it up just right. Bending her right arm, she flung the axe into the air. The head rotated over the handle, revolving in the air several times until it struck the target with a thwack. The next few months were going to be difficult, but she had to do her best to keep her chin up and stay strong.

Chapter Twenty-Four

KENDALL

With a stack of paper plates in one hand and a large bowl of fruit salad in the other, Kendall opened the sliding door to the patio. She took a moment to survey the scene. Several of the kids from the playgroup sat on the patch of fresh sod she'd convinced Troy to have installed. It hadn't been an easy argument to win, but Kendall had ultimately prevailed. Everything should be lovely for Hope's second birthday party. Jeanine Koch tossed a beach ball in the air while her son Tyler pointed and yelled "Ball!" over and over.

Marisol slid the door closed behind Kendall and took the tray of fruit. "You're doing too much. Let me pitch in."

"Thank you. I want everything to be just right." Kendall couldn't get over how pretty the yard looked. Fuchsia streamers draped along the wrought-iron fence and white balloons floating over the patio table made everything festive, a fitting celebration for their little girl. "Julieta was such a help this morning."

Marisol placed the fruit on the table. "She's always happy to lend a hand. You know she adores your little *mariposa*."

Hope sat in her highchair at the patio table, wearing a pink and white striped dress with two watermelon slices appliquéd on the front pockets. She looked adorable. When Kendall had come across the dress last month in the Mini Boden catalogue, she'd known it was the one, immediately placing the order with her debit card so Troy wouldn't discover how much she'd spent. Leaning over at Hope's side, Julieta turned the pages of a board book. Hope pointed to each page and garbled with glee.

"Your sweet girl is loving this," Marisol said.

"She sure is, and so are our husbands," Kendall said. Troy stood next to Hope, running his hand back and forth over her blond curls while talking with Marisol's husband, Aldo. Taking a long pull of beer, he laughed loudly at one of Aldo's jokes. It was nice to see Troy letting loose a little. With the stress they'd been under lately, the Carlson family deserved a celebration.

Aubrey Lawlor turned from her conversation with the president of the neighborhood association, a look of exasperation on her face.

"You've had enough?" Kendall whispered. The president set her eyes on her next victim, making a beeline for Jeanine. "A minute-by-minute playback of the last meeting isn't your idea of a fun time?"

"I need a supersized piece of cake. When are you bringing that bad boy out here?"

"Do you think it's time yet?"

Hope banged her hands on the table, smiling at the noise she made on the solid wood.

"Hope's demanding it," Aubrey said.

"Everything's better with sweets," Marisol said.

Catching Troy's eye, Kendall mouthed, "Go get the cake."

He nodded and headed inside. Kendall checked the table, making sure she had brought out all the paper goods and utensils.

"Do you need anything else?" Marisol asked.

"I think we're all set." She'd spent the last few weeks obsessing over the yard, the invitations, the refreshments, losing count of the number of trips to Party City and Costco. Kendall was surprised at how well the afternoon had gone, but she couldn't shake a nagging sense of unease. Something could go wrong at any minute.

"Do you have a minute to catch up?" Aubrey asked. "What's happening with the lawsuit?"

"Oh, that. I'm not sure…" Kendall brushed Aubrey off. This topic wasn't appropriate for a birthday party.

"I've been thinking about you. Wondering if there's anything I can do to make things easier."

"Isn't the cake gorgeous?" Marisol said.

Troy held the enormous custom cake Kendall had ordered from the overpriced bakery downtown. On one hand, Kendall felt guilty about spending so much money on flour and sugar, but on the other, she was glad she'd splurged. It had two large tiers, covered in smooth yellow buttercream frosting with white piping along the edges and pink and blue fondant butterflies flitting over the surface. Two rainbow candles sat in the center, the flames wavering as Troy passed under the outdoor misters.

"Everyone," Marisol announced, "please gather on the patio to sing to little Hope."

Kendall's skin bristled. She didn't allow anyone to condescend to Hope, but she knew Marisol meant it as a term of endearment, so she let it go. The guests gathered around the patio table. As Troy presented the cake to Hope, she lunged for it with both hands.

"Troy!" Kendall cried out, but it was no use. He was too busy straightening the candles. Hope grabbed a fistful of cake and smeared the frosting and chocolate crumbs across the front of her dress. Jeanine Koch started snapping photos, cooing over how adorable she was.

"No, it's ruined." Tears pricked Kendall's eyes. She'd spent hours planning and preparing for this moment, imagining a posed shot of the three of them, the light from the candles illuminating their faces, but now Hope's dress was a mess, and the cake was a disaster. So much for the photo op.

While the guests sang an off-key rendition of *Happy Birthday*, a slideshow flashed through Kendall's mind. Tiny Hope in the incubator, her arms and legs spindly as sticks. The day they'd brought her home from the hospital, Kendall frozen with fear at the thought of caring for her child. Hope's first birthday, when she'd started wailing mere minutes after the guests arrived.

"We need one with the parents. Put your arms around your girl." Jeanine held the phone up, waiting for Kendall to find her brave smile. Frosting coated Hope's cheeks and streaked her hair. Kendall did her best to strike a pose, planting a kiss on Hope's cheek while Troy did the same on the other side. After Jeanine got several shots, Kendall licked her lips. The buttercream tasted just sweet enough.

Troy cut the cake onto paper plates. Guests mingled and chatted as they enjoyed the dessert and helped themselves to fruit salad. Kendall accepted a slice of cake from Marisol and looked around. There were large divots in the brand-new sod, a few rocks at the bottom of the pool, and popped balloons drooping along the railing, but Kendall tried to ignore the imperfections. Everyone was having a good time, especially Hope, and that's what was important.

A loud splashing sound broke through the chatter. What was that? Had one of the kids fallen into the pool? No, the surface was unbroken.

"Did you hear that?" Marisol asked.

Kendall made eye contact with Troy. She didn't know what had made the splash, but it was her husband's job to figure it out. With their unspoken division of labor, unexplained noises fell squarely in his territory. He started across the patio. Just as Troy stepped onto the grass, a large black animal climbed out of the Herrera's pool, his enormous paws leaving prints on the stones. The bear stopped next to the grill and shook himself off, droplets of water flying in all directions.

Marisol turned to her husband. "It's a bear in our pool!"

Her husband stood frozen.

"It's bear 311," Jeanine yelled, hoisting Tyler onto her hip and dashing for the house.

Other guests screamed and scooped up their children. Within seconds, the party cleared out, the Herreras the only remaining guests. The bear lumbered across the yard and flopped down on the Herrera's patio, finding cool shade under the overhang. He rolled around and then licked the water from his fur. The beast wasn't going anywhere fast.

"Looks like we're staying for dinner," Aldo said.

"Maybe we should call the game warden," Kendall said, thankful for the tall iron fence between the two properties. There was no way he could scale that thing.

Troy and Aldo disappeared inside to find the phone number, and Julieta took Hope to the living room. Sitting down at the patio table with Marisol, Kendall kept her eyes on the bear. He lay on his side, his massive belly rising and falling with each breath. Right now, nothing about the creature seemed dangerous, but that could change in an instant. Kendall needed to remain vigilant.

"So, Aubrey was up in your business about the lawsuit?" Marisol asked. "What's her deal?"

"I'm not sure," Kendall said, watching the bear out of the corner of her eye. She didn't understand how Marisol could be so chill about it.

Marisol scooped some icing from the side of the cake with her finger. "Seems a bit much if you ask me. It's none of her business."

"She goes to the same doctor. When I first brought up the lawsuit, she got on her high horse, crying about what a good doctor she is and how this could ruin her career."

"What does that have to do with it? You're doing what's best for your child."

"I guess." The more Kendall thought about it, the more comfortable she'd become with the decision. If it meant improving Hope's future, Kendall would face her fears about the legal suit. Taking things one step at a time made the complication much more manageable. Plus, Attorney Silverberg seemed to know his stuff, and they sure could use the money. "I keep telling myself we're doing this for Hope. Everything's for Hope, always Hope."

With a shuffling noise, the bear arose, took a few slurps of water from the pool, then climbed up and over the short chain-link fence at the back of the property and into the preserve.

Chapter Twenty-Five

ABE

"Let me talk this through," Abe said. Norah sat on the other side of the conference room table, papers covering the surface. "Everything needs to be in order before the deposition."

"Whatever works for you, Mr. Silverberg."

"Enough with the formalities," Abe said. Over the years, Marty had insisted any staff refer to them as Mr. Goldman and Mr. Silverberg. Abe found the custom odd. "It's driving me crazy."

"I can't call you Abe. It sounds weird."

"Then call me Abraham," he said. "Call me *hey, you*. Just don't call me late for dinner."

"Your routine needs some work."

"Risa laughed at all my jokes. Even the worst ones."

Norah lifted several file folders from a box onto the table. "You two were so well matched. Such a great couple."

Abe opened one of the folders. "Every pot has its lid, as my grandmother used to say. Corny, but it makes sense."

"I'm not sure what I think about that," Norah said. "I get the idea, but I don't believe in one soulmate. It's too limiting."

"Risa and I had something pretty special."

"You adored each other." Norah put the empty box on the floor. "But that doesn't mean you won't find love again. There could be someone else out there for you."

Norah had the best intentions, but Abe wasn't ready yet. Not even close. With Risa's wheelchair still living rent-free in his house, he needed more time. This was his new reality. He was a widower now.

Abe opened a folder containing copies of Kendall Carlson's medical records. "Enough kibitzing. We've got a lot of ground to cover."

Norah performed an exaggerated military salute. "Yes, sir."

Abe split the pile in half and handed a stack to Norah. "We need to go through these with a fine-toothed comb. Scrutinize every sentence."

"Should we put on some music to make this more tolerable?"

"As long as it's Broadway."

Norah clicked around on the computer and started the music. A trombone riff from *Chicago*, the musical, filled the air, one note sliding into the next.

"Good choice," Abe said. "Perfect for the task at hand."

They put their heads down. Abe's pile consisted mostly of the nursing notes, page upon page of vital signs, fetal heart tracings, and consent forms. Norah moved her lips while she read to herself.

"Anything good?" Norah asked after a few minutes.

"Not so far. You?"

"The notes and treatment seem appropriate. I think this case is going to hinge on one major point."

Abe waited. "Are you keeping me in suspense?"

"The timing. The diagnosis was made, but it seemed to take longer than it should have."

"Agreed, and we need to figure out why. Was that the fault of Nurse Marcus, Dr. Schorr, or a combination of the two?"

Mary Sunshine's song came on. The soprano sendup renewed Abe's energy. He took a moment to listen to the lyrics, going over the details he'd read about the Carlson delivery in his head. It was much better for the case if everyone carried some blame. Keeping the hospital, the nurse, and the obstetrician on the hook upped the chance for a big win. As Mary Sunshine said, no one was ever all bad or all good. Everyone falls somewhere in between black and white, made up of sundry shades of gray.

Abe flipped through the nursing documents. "The birth plan is not great for us."

"I saw that. We'll have to find a way to minimize that detail."

"Agreed," Abe said. "Maybe change the topic at just the right moment. And when was the prolapse documented? I don't see it here."

"It's here in Dr. Schorr's note. Kendall was admitted just after noon, and the diagnosis was made at ten p.m. What took the doctor so long?"

"Seems like the crux of the case," Abe said. "The late diagnosis led to a delay in moving to a C-section." Abe was missing something. A patient in preterm labor with worrisome fetal tracings. Why wouldn't the obstetrician be onsite hours earlier? He flipped through several more nursing notes, including summaries of a few phone calls to Dr. Schorr. Nothing too incriminating here.

The talky beginning of *Mr. Cellophane* came through the computer speakers. Abe had never liked this song. What kind of sad sack claims to feel invisible? Today, however, he felt a connection to the lyrics like never before. A dedicated husband for so long, he didn't know who he was supposed to be without his wife.

Abe turned to the last page of notes. Seven days ago, Dr. Schorr had written an addendum. Abe clapped his hands together. Jackpot. Nearly without fail, addendums were a gimme for the plaintiff, proof that someone was trying to cover up an error or oversight.

Norah looked up. "What did you find?"

"Dr. Schorr stepped in it." Abe had had a hunch this case was a goldmine, but the good doctor was making it even easier than he'd expected.

Chapter Twenty-Six
JESS

The conference room was much too warm. Jess wiped her palms on her scrub pants. Where the hell was her attorney? The meeting was set for noon, and it was already quarter past. Jess should have changed out of her scrubs after her last surgery, but she worried she'd be late. Yes, this lawyer was paid to represent her, but she wanted to make a good first impression. She grabbed a pen and clicked it open and closed. With Jess's next surgery in less than an hour, this was cutting things close. Finally, a tall woman in a tailored pantsuit breezed in, closing the door behind her.

"Good afternoon," she said, extending a long-fingered hand. "I'm Angela Caputo." As Jess stood, she was dwarfed by the attorney's height.

"Jessica Schorr. Thanks so much for coming." Why was she thanking her for showing up fifteen minutes late? Something about this woman made Jess fall in line.

While Angela took a seat at the opposite side of the conference table, Mira from risk management came in and pulled out her laptop. "Sorry I'm late. Busy day." She placed a box of tissues in front of Jess. That was odd. Was this meeting going to make Jess cry?

"'Before we dive into details, I'd like to provide some reassurance," Angela said. "The fact a suit has been brought doesn't say anything about you. It's often more about a bad outcome than the quality of the medical care."

"I've seen so many cases," Mira said, "and the doctors often second-guess their choices, even when everything was appropriate. Try not to go down that path."

Hot tears collected in Jess's eyes. Barely a minute in, and she already needed the damn tissues. She grabbed a few and wiped her eyes, leaving semicircles of black mascara on the paper. Jess appreciated what they were saying, but their canned speech didn't apply to her. She wasn't crying because she'd done everything right, but because she may have done something wrong. If she'd delivered the baby sooner, maybe Hope would be learning to jump and sort shapes and sing her ABCs.

"It's normal to be upset," Mira said.

"I'd be worried if you weren't," Angela said. "You spend years learning to be a good doctor, and then someone calls your skills into question. It can shake you to the core."

Enough with the emotional mumbo jumbo. Jess got enough of that from Drew at home. She wanted to focus on next steps, strategies, and tangible answers to her questions.

"We'll leave the details for a later meeting." Angela opened her laptop and started clicking. "Today's more about guidelines for the situation. I trust you received our initial informational email?"

Jess nodded. After her first skim through, she'd forgotten to circle back, but Angela didn't need to know that.

"I'll send it again, just in case." Mira clicked around for a few seconds. "Done."

"I expect you to follow our guidelines," Angela said. "I'll review the highlights. Everything you do from this point forward could be scrutinized by the plaintiff attorney, the judge, and the jury. And I mean *everything*."

Sweat dampened Jess's palms. She wiped them on her pants again. Before her next operation, she'd have to change into a new pair.

"Don't go crazy online," Angela said. "In fact, avoid reading altogether. Nothing good will come of it."

"Oh, I didn't know." Jess hadn't seen that bullet point. The stack of journal articles about umbilical cord prolapse was still in her work bag, one she'd read at least five times, highlighting in multiple colors.

"What have you done?"

"I may have done a bit of Googling, to be helpful."

"Well, that ends now. Shred anything you printed out and pretend it never happened."

Jess nodded.

"Second, the only people you speak with are me and my staff. No exceptions. Even your husband is on a need-to-know basis. Any and all conversations can be used against you."

"And because the hospital is also named in the suit," Mira said, "speaking with anyone could make the process unnecessarily complicated."

Jess had told Drew and the kids, of course, but no one else. Mai didn't count, right? Talking to your best friend was like talking to yourself. And Eve was named in the suit herself, so she already knew about it, of course.

"The more named defendants, the higher chance of a big payday," Angela said. "Plus, hospitals have bigger bank accounts, so they're always included, if possible. And I believe there's another defendant." She looked down at her computer. "Yes, here it is. Eve Marcus, delivery nurse."

"I know."

"I understand you two are friends?"

"How did you know?"

"Social media tells all. She was at your older daughter's bat mitzvah? Girls' night out? I saw photos."

"We used to be closer." Jess thought back to Maddie's party, the room decked out in dance décor, a ballet slipper on pointe in the center of each table, she and Eve clinking their champagne glasses together in celebration.

"Let me be crystal clear. You are not to have contact with her. No phone calls, no emails, not even a wave across the cafeteria."

"Understood," Jess said, thinking back to the girls' night last week. After that fiasco, Eve had no interest in speaking with her anyway. "But we do work together."

"I've spoken with your chairman," Mira said. "Every effort will be made to avoid scheduling you two together, whenever possible."

"Also, each defendant has been assigned different representation," Angela said, "to make sure everyone has the best possible defense."

"That's hospital policy," Mira said. "Otherwise, the hospital's defense would be prioritized over the named individuals."

"The last rule is this," Angela said. "Do not, under any circumstances, change anything in the medical record. Merely opening the chart makes you suspect."

"Um, I..." Jess wasn't about to share that she'd read both Kendall's and Hope's charts in their entirety and, to make matters worse, addended one of her notes. Of course, she knew the attorney would figure it out at some point, but she couldn't bring herself to deal with it now. Only ten minutes into the meeting, Jess was already depleted.

"Trust me, it will do more harm than good."

"How will I refresh my memory?" In truth, memories from that awful day were permanently tattooed on her brain. No reminders necessary.

Angela handed Jess a folder. "These are the records for you to review. All you need to prepare for the deposition is in this packet."

"The deposition?"

"Opposing counsel will question you. Your performance will be crucial, every word scrutinized to the nth degree."

"How will I know what to say?"

"We'll set up a separate meeting to discuss the details of the case. Go over how the deposition works."

"A coaching session?"

"Exactly. We can even practice out loud to help you get the wording right."

As the meeting wrapped up, Jess's stomach groaned with hunger. She thanked them both and headed to the gift shop for a candy bar. Standing in front of the display, Jess weighed the pros and cons of the various choices, finally landing on a Snickers. It would give her the boost she needed to finish out the day. At the check-out, she got in line behind Divya Pandey, another doctor in the OB/GYN department. Jess tapped her foot, hoping her colleague would walk out without noticing her.

Divya zipped her wallet, then saw Jess. "Oh my gosh, I haven't seen you in a while. How *are* you?" she said, emphasizing the second word in the question.

Her inflection made Jess wonder if Divya had heard gossip about the lawsuit. Or maybe she was imagining things. A wave of nausea overcame her, a mix of hunger and shame. If she was being honest, she wasn't great, but she couldn't admit that. All she could do was smile and nod.

"I'm fine, thanks." Jess swallowed hard. "How are you?"

"Crazy, as always. Shivani is applying early decision to an Ivy, so we're getting all her ducks in a row."

"Wow, which one?" Jess didn't really care, but she needed to pretend it was business as usual.

"I'm not allowed to say. Just in case." Divya shook her crossed fingers in the air. "Oh, did you hear about the overnight staff cuts?"

"No, what now?" Jess must have missed that email.

"They're eliminating in-house scrub nurses after midnight. So, we have to call them in from home if there's a case."

"You're kidding," Jess said. "That could mean major delays."

"All in the name of the bottom line."

"It's getting so predictable."

"Totally. Listen, I have patients waiting. Great to see you." Divya walked out with a wave.

O O O

Leaving the locker room, Jess pulled her phone out of her pocket. She'd finished an ovarian dermoid resection and a hysterectomy in record time. She briefly considered stopping to see her dad but decided against it. Instead, she'd swing by and drop off Hope's birthday gift. It wasn't like her to chance a drop-off in broad daylight, but today was Hope's birthday. If she waited until tomorrow, the present would be late. Deep down, Jess knew it was a terrible idea for so many reasons, but she decided to go for it anyway. She'd make it lightning quick. Get in and get out.

The tricycle had arrived over the weekend. She'd considered assembling it so Hope could ride it right away, but she couldn't do it on her own. Following assembly instructions wasn't up Jess's alley, the words barely in English and the diagrams even more baffling, so she'd wrapped it instead. It had taken forever to finagle paper around the enormous box, topping it off with a large rainbow rosette and sparkly streamers hanging down the sides.

In the car, Jess dialed KC, figuring she could multitask on her way. She had questions about some recent additions to the spreadsheet. The baking-themed centerpieces KC had designed were adorable, but the price was a bit steep. How could a few flowers, spoons, and spatulas add up to four hundred dollars each?

"Hello?"

"Hi KC, it's Jessica Rubin. Do you have a minute?"

"Sure, what's up?"

"I wanted to go over some of the numbers you sent. I hate to be a pain, but Drew thinks the centerpieces are too pricey." It was easier to blame her husband.

"I was worried about that," KC said. "I might have some more affordable options. Let me check what I have in storage."

Jess heard a door squeaking open and the sound of boxes sliding across the floor. "Whatever you can do to keep the cost down. I want it to look nice, but I need to save some money for

Vox to go to college." The new name had come out without conscious thought. She was starting to get used to the change.

A driver turned left, cutting Jess off. She laid on the horn.

"Everything okay?" KC asked.

Jess turned right onto Solano Lane. "Yes, sorry. I'm on my way home."

"I've found some things that may work. Let me price out different ideas."

Jess parked in front of the house and hopped out. A mylar balloon hung down from the mailbox. Opening the back hatch of her SUV, she tried to maneuver the box out with one hand. No dice. She put the phone on speaker, setting it down in the trunk. Even with two hands, this was no easy task. She grunted with the effort.

"What are you doing?" KC asked.

"Delivering…." She heaved the box to the edge of the trunk.

The busybody neighbor appeared next to the car. "You're back. Do you need some help?"

Jess startled. She tugged her baseball cap over her eyes and adjusted her sunglasses.

"For her birthday? That's so sweet. Are you friends with Kendall? I didn't get your name last time."

"Yes, um… Kendall and I go back a few years."

"Really? She said you don't sign the cards."

Coming here during the day had been a terrible idea. Jess would keep her answers vague and hope the nosy neighbor would go away. "I must have forgotten."

The woman gave Jess a questioning look but then moved on. "I'm Marisol Herrera. Ever since the Carlsons moved in, we've been tight. My daughter babysits for Hope. Let me help you carry that. It looks heavy."

"I'm fine, thanks," Jess said.

"You missed a crazy party."

Jess looked at her blankly. A deep dimple in Marisol's left cheek drew Jess's focus.

"Kendall didn't fill you in?"

Jess assumed she was talking about Hope's birthday party, but she had no idea what had made it crazy. She needed to find a way to get out of here. "We've been... missing each other."

"You didn't hear about the surprise appearance of Bear 311? A day to remember for sure."

All of a sudden, scenes from Jess's nightmare careened through her mind, Opal screeching as the bear gave chase, his massive jaw and gnashing teeth ready to tear the cat apart. Jess pushed the memory away. "Sounds like quite a day."

"It sure was."

Jess took a few deep breaths. The bear was long gone, so there was no reason to be afraid. She needed to deliver this gift and finish her conversation with KC. Wait a minute. Was the party planner still on speaker? "Hello, you still there?" No response. The call must have dropped. She'd try her back later.

Jess lifted one side of the box, and Marisol grabbed the other.

"Thanks so much. Let's leave it by the mailbox," Jess said. She put down her side, and Marisol followed her lead.

Jess's phone rang. The nursing home was calling. Her heart leapt into her throat. Even if they were only calling to say her father was running low on adult diapers or shampoo, Jess had a mini heart attack every time.

"Hello?"

"Dr. Schorr, it's Fiona, one of the nurses at Sun Terrace. No emergency, but your dad is more confused today than usual."

"Okay, what's going on?"

"He's been wandering around looking for Rhonda. I think a visit from you would help center him."

"Okay, I'll do my best to get there." With everything else going on, Jess wasn't sure how she would fit that in, but she'd have to make it work. Ending the call, she closed the trunk and walked over to the driver's side.

"Kendall's here," Marisol said, pointing to the car in the driveway. "You should go say hello."

"Sorry, I need to go see my dad." What she needed to do was get the hell out of here.

"Okay, then," Marisol said. "I'll tell Kendall you stopped by. What's your name again?"

This woman needed to mind her own business. "All good. Everything's in the card."

Chapter Twenty-Seven

KENDALL

"What the hell?" Kendall stared down at her phone, her hands trembling. She wasn't sure what had just happened, but something felt wrong. She looked out the garage window at the woman getting into her car. Large sunglasses hid her face, and a cap covered her hair. Why had Marisol's voice come through the phone? Jessica Rubin had been talking with Marisol about the bear at Hope's birthday party, and then the call dropped. The whole thing made no sense. She stepped out of the garage and took several gulps of fresh air. Marisol dragged a large box up the driveway.

"Special delivery," Marisol said.

Kendall grabbed hold of the other side and helped move it into the garage. "Who was that?"

"She wouldn't say her name. It's the same one who was here before. Always wearing a hospital outfit. Is she a nurse or something?"

Her mind spinning, Kendall couldn't deal with Marisol's questions right now. She needed to be alone so she could make sense of things.

"I feel a migraine coming on." Kendall draped her hand over her forehead for dramatic effect.

"Have you tried Botox? It works miracles for my mother."

Kendall endured more talk of acupressure, biofeedback, and warm compresses before she successfully evicted Marisol. Closing the garage door, she opened the card taped to the box, a big pink number two above a three-dimensional butterfly on the front.

Dear Hope,

Happy second birthday! What a perfect card for you. With lots of hard work, you will transform from a caterpillar into the gorgeous butterfly you're meant to be. You are strong, and you have an amazing mommy who helps you every single day.

I owe you an apology. My gifts have not always been right for you. Hopefully, this one will make you happy. You're going to love riding it around the neighborhood. This will be my last gift to you. I wish I could give more, but the universe has other plans. Please know I will never stop thinking about you and wishing you well.

Love always...

Kendall's mind spun. What the hell was going on? Why would Jessica Rubin be giving Hope gifts? And this note was different from all the rest. Why would this be the last gift? None of it made any sense. Kendall opened Instagram. Vox Rubin's baking account had a punny name. What was it again? She searched for *Batter Late than Never*, but that was a chubby guy jousting with a spatula. When she typed Vox Rubin into the search bar, *Cake It 'Til You Make It* came up. Yes, that was it. In the profile pic, Vox stood next to an intricately decorated cake centered on a china stand. If Kendall found a photo of Jessica Rubin, maybe this would all make sense. Scrolling down through photos of cakes, cookies, and breads with witty comments, Kendall found a family photo of Vox in front of a table full of pies, her parents on either side. Kendall enlarged the photo, Jessica Rubin's face filling the screen. They'd never met in person, but something about her face looked familiar. It was her eyes, the dark mole above her left eyebrow. Kendall recognized her. She racked her brain to figure it out. Did she live in the neighborhood? Or maybe she worked at Trader Joe's? No, she'd said she worked at a hospital.

A scene came back to her, one she would never forget. A doctor in a blue gown, a mask covering the lower half of her face, and those same eyes, the same dark mole above the left one. In Kendall's memory, those eyes had filled with fear as she told Kendall her baby had been sent to Phoenix Children's. Kendall's heart hammered in her chest. She quickly googled *Valley Health* and clicked on the Find a Doctor tab and OB/GYN. Scrolling through the list of doctors, she found Jessica Schorr. In the photo, Dr. Schorr wore a burgundy blouse. Though her eyes were rimmed with eyeliner in this staged photo, Kendall knew them immediately. They were the same eyes. Jessica Rubin was Jessica Schorr, one and the same.

Kendall yelled and ripped the birthday card into hundreds of tiny pieces, the bits raining to the floor. She tore the paper off the box in ragged sections, screaming with rage.

"Who the hell does she think she is?" she yelled. Was Dr. Schorr trying to gain the upper hand in the lawsuit? What was her end goal? Kendall tried to remember the details of the conversations they'd had in the last month, mostly centered on party details, but some had gotten more personal. Had she said anything to hurt their case? She'd been so stupid to fall into this trap.

Kendall looked at the box. On the outside, there was a photo of a bright pink adaptive tricycle, the exact same one Kendall had been eyeing online. She'd longed to buy it for Hope, but the price tag was way too steep.

Troy opened the mudroom door, Hope on his hip. "Kendall, what's going on?"

"Just organizing."

"I heard you yelling." He looked at the box. "What is *that*?"

"It's from the secret admirer." Kendall said, not sure she was ready to share the identity of the anonymous gift-giver. Knowing Troy's hot temper, he'd lose his cool and make things even worse.

"Come on. You've got to be kidding. Who would do that?"

Hope gurgled. Kendall sat down on the ground and opened her arms. After Troy settled Hope in her lap, Kendall pointed to the picture of the tricycle. "Look what someone got you for your birthday."

Hope reached out to touch the box.

"She likes it, Troy."

"Well, I don't," he said. "It's time to call this in."

"If we do that, they'll take it away. For evidence or something. That wouldn't be fair to Hope."

"It's weird, Kendall. Something feels off."

She took a deep breath and hugged Hope closer, trying to calm her frazzled nerves. Was Troy right about this? Maybe she shouldn't let this slide, but the boy in the picture on the box looked so happy, the wind ruffling his hair, his face filled with joy. They had to keep this gift. Hope deserved that happiness too.

"I know who gave this to us," Kendall whispered.

"What do you mean?"

"I just figured it out today. The pieces finally came together."

"Is it your parents? Your brother? The Herreras? They're great neighbors, but that seems a bit much—"

"No, Troy. It's Dr. Schorr." Her breath caught in her throat. It sounded too crazy to be true, but saying her name out loud made Kendall even more sure.

"What the fuck? Why would she do something so stupid?"

"I don't know. I'm so ashamed for not putting it together sooner. She took advantage of us."

"We can't let that happen. Now we really need to win this damn lawsuit. If you don't want to call the police, we have to tell our attorney, at a bare minimum."

"I guess so."

"Let's call him first thing tomorrow. Fill him in on this little development."

From the determination in Troy's eyes, Kendall could tell there was no arguing with him. At least Hope would get to keep the tricycle. Despite the ups and downs of this discovery, this gift had made one thing crystal clear. Any lingering doubts about suing Dr. Schorr had flown right out the window.

Chapter Twenty-Eight
JESS

"Is everyone ready?" Jess threw her keys on the table in the entryway, waiting for a response. Shabbat services started in less than an hour. The b'nai mitzvah families were required to usher three times, and today was one of their assigned days. The aroma of vanilla and cinnamon wafting from the kitchen made Jess nervous. What was Vox baking now? Had her family forgotten all about the commitment? In the kitchen, Vox brushed egg wash onto two loaves of braided challah.

"Hi, Mom," Vox said. "My fans are going to love this one."

Jess hadn't been thrilled when Vox asked to create an Instagram account to flaunt her baking successes to the world. After all, Maddie hadn't been allowed on social media until fourteen, but after lots of pleading and begging, Jess had surrendered. In just a few short months, Vox's photos and cute captions had garnered over three thousand followers.

"There's cinnamon and sugar worked into the dough. I can't wait to try it."

Jess checked her phone. "You don't have time to bake it. We need to be at services soon."

"All right." Vox opened the fridge and moved things around to make room for the tray. "The magic will have to wait."

Since they'd come out, Vox seemed so much happier. The way they flitted around the kitchen reminded Jess of the butterfly garden, the mesmerizing insects fluttering from flower to flower, defying gravity with their paper-thin wings.

Maddie flew down the stairs and grabbed her purse from the hook on the wall. Her ruffled floral skirt barely covered her tush, and her top clung to every curve. "Madeline Rubin, we're going to synagogue. Go back upstairs and change."

"But I'm going out with Mason afterwards. I have to look cute."

"You'll look cute in a longer skirt."

"Come on, Mom. Who's going to care?"

Jess pointed upstairs. "I care, that's who."

Jess followed her, trying to ignore Maddie's mumblings about how women were held to double standards, body positivity, and the unfairness of it all. In her bedroom, Drew was getting dressed in the walk-in closet, threading a leather belt through the loops of his pants.

She kissed him hello. "You almost ready?"

He flashed a cheesy smile. "Born ready."

"The kids don't seem to be in any hurry."

Drew placed his hands on Jess's shoulders. "It's all under control, Jess."

"There's so much to think about."

"You're making yourself crazy. Maybe you can relax for one night?"

"Can't make any promises, but I'll try."

○ ○ ○

Jess handed a prayer book to Rachel Schneider and leaned in for an air kiss. "Shabbat Shalom."

The rest of her family stood on the other side of the sanctuary doors next to a second rolling shelf of prayer books. Vox, dressed in a pair of khaki pants and a white polo, chatted with the youth director. An older man with a goatee accepted a prayer book from Maddie.

"How long until the big day?" Rachel asked.

"Less than four months," Jess said. "That's why we're here tonight. Required ushering."

"I remember it like yesterday. Now Avery's a senior. Can you believe it?"

Avery teetered up the center aisle in four-inch wedges and a short jumpsuit. Arm in arm with another similarly clad girl, they claimed seats and promptly turned their attention to their phones.

"That's wild."

"Did you hire KC Events? She was absolutely fabulous for our affair." Rachel used the word *our* as if she were the one who'd chanted Torah, when all she had done was shell out the bucks for an overly extravagant party.

"I did. Thanks for the recommendation."

"Isn't she terrific?"

"She seems nice. The spreadsheets are a bit much, but I'm leaning into it." Actually, KC owed her a call. She'd said she'd be back in touch with more reasonable centerpiece options, but Jess hadn't heard from her in a few days. She made a mental note to check her voicemail later.

Rachel glanced at Vox. "So... Vivian looks different these days."

"We've had some recent changes." Jess willed Rachel to move it along. She was getting better with Vox's name and pronouns, and slowly accepting the deeper changes they symbolized, but sharing it with a passing acquaintance didn't come easily.

"Her fashion sense is definitely *different*."

Jess stiffened. "They recently came out as nonbinary, so they're choosing to dress more masculine. Changed their name to Vox." That would shut her up, Jess thought, pasting a smile on her face.

Rachel raised her eyebrows. "They?"

"Vox is using they/them pronouns."

"That's something," Rachel said. "It's going to make your mitzvah challenging, to say the least."

"We've got it all figured out, thanks," Jess said, stretching the truth a bit. She had met with the rabbi to discuss Vox's new identity and how it would affect the ceremony, his openness and acceptance a welcome relief. But with the lawsuit, planning the party had moved to the back burner. Jess would circle back with KC later in the weekend to make sure things were still on track.

Cantor Hirsch stood on stage, strumming her guitar. The familiar melody of "We Return" filled the room. Hearing the song filled Jess with a sense of belonging. Though she'd felt completely out of sorts the past few weeks, she felt at home here in the sanctuary. In the months after her mother's death, she'd attended Shabbat services here once a month, the familiar place and people providing her comfort and a sense of peace.

"Shabbat Shalom all." Rabbi Glasser stood at the podium. He welcomed the crowd to Congregation Shalom and asked everyone to find a seat.

"We'll talk more later," Rachel whispered.

Jess scooted past a gentleman with a goatee to join her family in the second row.

The space wasn't fancy, but it emanated warmth. A large Jewish star made of slats of pale wood decorated the wall, and two rust-colored pendant lights beside the ark created a soft glow. Tonight, there was an elaborate flower arrangement in front of the podium, the lilies perfuming the air with a citrus aroma. Jess inhaled the sweet scent. With everything going on the past two weeks, she'd barely had a moment to herself. It felt good to sit down and just breathe.

"I would like to thank you all for coming," the rabbi said, "for taking time out of your busy lives to reconnect, both with yourself and with each other."

Vox stared at their lap, while Maddie scrolled on her phone. Jess elbowed Drew. "Tell her to put it away."

"It's important to step away from the chaos," the rabbi said, continuing as if speaking directly to Jess. "Take a break from the phones and the emails and the to-do lists. That's what Shabbat is all about. Focusing on what's truly important."

Jess took Drew's hand. He stroked her palm with his thumb.

"Here at Congregation Shalom, we believe in radical welcome. Everyone has a place here, no matter their color, gender, or

183

sexual orientation." The rabbi made eye contact with Vox. "Let's take a moment to connect. Please, turn to someone you don't know and introduce yourselves."

Making small talk had never been Jess's strong suit.

Turning to her left, she held out her hand. "I'm Jessica Rubin. I don't think we've met."

"I don't come often," he said, returning the handshake. His suit was a bit outdated, but his goatee was neatly trimmed.

"Me neither," she said. "My family's ushering today. A requirement for the big day."

"Big day?"

"My daughter's bat mitzvah." Jess ran her fingers through her hair. "I mean my child's."

"Putting in your time. Mazel Tov."

"Thank you. What brings you here today?"

"My wife's Yahrzeit, unfortunately. I can't believe it's been a year."

"I'm sorry for your loss." Jess's heart went out to him. His situation put her troubles into perspective. Sure, she had several stressful things coinciding in her life, but in the grand scheme of things, it wasn't anything she couldn't handle.

The service continued with Hebrew prayers. Though Jess didn't understand the meaning of the words, she had them all memorized.

"Now, we move into silent prayer," the rabbi said. "Please remain standing. You may use the words in your book or put the book aside and attend to whatever rises to the surface for you tonight."

The phrase made it seem like her thoughts were a bubbling stew, threatening to boil over onto the stovetop. Jess closed her eyes. Never one to talk to God, probably because she wasn't sure he, she, or they, for that matter, even existed, her current situation called for an exception. If she'd ever needed prayers, now was the time. *Please watch over me during this time of great stress.* That sounded so vague. She needed to be more specific. How could she ask for divine help if she wasn't clear on what she needed?

I'm in trouble, she tried again. *This lawsuit threatens my career and my family. Please help me weather the storm and stay strong. I promise, if you shepherd me through this crisis, I'll be the best person I can possibly be. I'll volunteer every giving day and make donations to the annual fund without fail.*

Jess opened her eyes. Some people had taken their seats, a few were whispering, while others were deep in thought. Jess remembered one more thing she wanted to say, one more prayer that needed answering. Closing her eyes again, Jess took a deep breath. *Please watch over sweet Hope. Help her grow and learn and develop into the child she's meant to be.* Jess sat down and folded her hands in her lap.

"You okay?" Drew whispered in her ear.

"Yes, fine." Jess didn't want Drew to worry.

When they reached the healing prayer, Jess breathed easier. Her immediate family was alive and well, thank God. Jess's thoughts then turned to her father. Because Alzheimer's only went in one direction, praying for healing seemed silly. After his diagnosis, Jess had asked Rabbi Glasser to read his name, but when they reached a year, she'd let him fall off the list. Praying for a miraculous recovery wouldn't do any good, and if she were being honest, she wasn't sure she wanted it. Most of the time, her father couldn't remember his own name, but he was sweeter and gentler than he'd ever been. She'd never admit it out loud, but she far preferred this version of him to the old one.

"And now we'll move to the conclusion of our service," Rabbi Glasser said. "The Mourner's Kaddish."

The man to her left wiped his eyes with a handkerchief. She recited the prayer with extra emphasis, in honor of her mother, of course, and of this man's beloved wife.

"V'al kol-yisrael, v'imru amen," the congregation finished in unison.

Jess turned to her neighbor. "May your wife's memory be a blessing."

Chapter Twenty-Nine

ABE

In the restroom, Abe splashed water on his face, dreading the gathering after services. He'd much prefer to cuddle with Bea in front of the TV, but he'd sponsored the Oneg in Risa's honor, so he couldn't skip out. In the social hall, there were two large tables, one with cold drinks and coffee, and the other offering platters of assorted cookies and bowls of fruit salad. Abe had selected teal tablecloths, Risa's favorite color. He spotted Marty and Gladys on the other side of the room, talking to the rabbi and his wife. They must have snuck in late. Knowing Marty, he was probably schmoozing the rabbi up one side and down the other.

Several congregants gave Abe their regards—teachers from the Hebrew school, people he'd met serving on various committees, and parents of Ross and Eliza's peers. Abe thanked them politely. He wished Ross and Gavin could be here, but they'd booked a non-refundable trip to Hawaii before they'd realized the conflict. And Abe would never expect Eliza to fly home from Boston for an hour-long service. She probably had a research paper due anyway.

Abe stepped up to the table and filled a bowl with fruit, perching a chocolate rugelach on top.

"A man after my own heart." A woman stood behind him in line. She had full cheeks and a broad smile, beaded earrings dangling from her ears. She didn't look familiar.

"You don't say," Abe said. "What part of my selection are you referring to?"

She helped herself to a few cookies. "The rugelach, of course. A more perfect cookie has never been created. Would you care to sit?" she motioned to a table by the window.

"Sure, why not?" Abe sat and took a bite of his rugelach, pastry crumbs falling onto his sweater. He brushed them off.

"I'm Francine Gans by the way. People call me Fran or Frannie."

"Fran Gans? That rhymes."

"I couldn't keep my maiden name. It wasn't a thing back then."

"Very true. It was a different time." Next to the coffee urn, Marty chatted it up with the woman who'd been sitting next to Abe during the service.

"And you are?" Fran asked.

"Abe Silverberg."

"Have you been coming here a long time?"

"It seems like forever. My children grew up here, went to the school from kindergarten all the way through confirmation."

"How nice. I just joined recently."

"You and your husband?"

"I lost Sheldon nearly four years ago," Fran said. "Tried staying in Illinois, but I was rattling around in that old house all alone. Six months ago, I made the move, to be closer to my daughter and her boys. Best decision I ever made."

A Midwesterner. No wonder she was so friendly. "Risa died a year ago. Today is her Yahrzeit actually."

"Oh dear, I heard her name read aloud. I'm sorry for your loss."

They ate in silence, joined by their common bond. Abe took a bite of cut-up pineapple, the taste sweet and sour at the same time.

"What's keeping you busy in the Valley of the Sun?" he asked.

Fran chuckled, her earrings swaying with her laughter. "Well, the synagogue has certainly been a boon. I play mahjong on Tuesdays, canasta on Thursdays, and once a month, there's a book club on Sunday afternoon. Novels with Jewish themes."

"You really dove in headfirst."

"I can't sit around my house staring at the walls. And my daughter and her family have their own lives. They don't need me showing up for dinner every night."

"I hear you. My son usually meets me at the dog park."

Marty and Gladys crossed the room towards him. Abe hoped his partner wouldn't lay it on too thick with Fran. Marty gave Abe a clap on the back. Abe's shoulder blade smarted from the blow, but he tried his best to keep a smile on his face.

Marty pulled up a chair. "How you doing, partner?"

"Yes, long time no see," Gladys said, claiming the seat next to her husband. "We should have you over for dinner soon. I've been meaning to invite you."

"Not a problem," Abe said. "I've been busy at work."

"You must be missing Risa's home cooking," Gladys said. "I can't even count the number of delicious meals she made for us over the years."

"True enough." Marty looked at Fran. "Marty Goldman. I don't think we've met."

"Fran Gans. I'm new in town. Abe and I were just getting to know one another."

Gladys moved over to sit next to Fran. "In that case, you'll have to join the sisterhood. We always welcome new members."

While the women chatted, Marty launched his interrogation. "So, how's business? Any new leads?"

Abe looked over at Fran, but she seemed engrossed. He hadn't told her what he did for a living, and he wanted to keep it that way, at least for now. Often when people found out, they gave him a wide berth. He'd only spoken to Fran for a few minutes, but her friendly demeanor put him at ease.

"Still working on the same one. There's a lot to unpack."

"The bad baby case?"

Abe bristled at the phrase. Hope was a human being struggling with disabilities, not a bad baby. It was more complex and nuanced than that. "It was a traumatic birth, yes." He itched to continue the conversation about breaking up the partnership, but this wasn't the time or place.

"So, did you crack it wide open?"

The women were still kibitzing. Gladys bragged about her coffee cake, challenging Fran to guess the secret ingredient. Abe knew the answer was mayonnaise, but he kept his mouth zipped. Better the women stay engaged and distracted.

"I've got some good intel," Abe said, keeping his answer intentionally vague, "but the proof is in the pudding. The deposition is set for early November."

"Excellent job." Marty gave Abe another resounding back slap. "You've always had a nose for blood in the water. I'm sure this case is no exception."

Abe grimaced but decided to keep his mouth shut.

Chapter Thirty
KENDALL

Zipping her suitcase closed, Kendall strapped her Chanel bag across her chest, slipped on her white Oran sandals, and tied a flower print Twilly scarf around her neck for good measure. She had to play the part. When she reached the kitchen, Troy seemed less than pleased.

"You all set?" Kendall said.

"Kendall, this isn't my first rodeo."

Hope moaned, as if siding with her father.

Kendall leaned down and kissed Hope's cheek. "Have a great time with Daddy. I'll be home tomorrow."

Troy lifted Hope from the highchair. "This bridal shower came out of nowhere."

"I know. Mara should have given me more notice." When Jeffrey from Hermès had called yesterday out of the blue, Kendall had immediately jumped at the chance. No one says no to Hermès. She'd told Troy her college friend was having a last-minute bridal shower and packed up in less than half an hour.

"You take on so much," Troy said, his tone softening. "You deserve a break. Maybe you'll get a chance to go to the spa and relax?"

"Maybe." Kendall felt a pang of guilt for lying to Troy, but she couldn't turn back now.

"We'll go to the park and then do lots of tummy time. Right, my little pancake?" He zerberted Hope's cheek. She emitted a tumbling laugh, the one only Troy could elicit. Kendall tamped down her jealousy. After all, she had more than enough one-on-one time with her daughter. Endless, creeping hours. So much time she often wore her pajamas until mid-afternoon and her business was circling the drain.

"You'll have fun together, I'm sure," she said.

"We always do."

Kendall's phone dinged. "Driver's here. I'll be back before you know it." She kissed them both and flew out the door. Usually, she'd feel a tug of guilt leaving Hope for more than a few hours, but today she had a one-track mind. Hermès or bust.

○ ○ ○

Kendall landed at LAX and went straight to the motel she'd booked, a ten-minute ride from chic Beverly Hills, but a world away. The online photos hadn't told the real story. Drab paint on the outside and faded brown carpeting in the lobby, this place needed more than a facelift, but the money Kendall saved would go toward her dream bag. If it meant snagging a Kelly, she'd ignore the frayed comforter, moldy shower curtain, and dusty baseboards.

Wetting a tissue in the sink, Kendall wiped spots from the mirror so she could apply her make-up. With two hours until her appointment, she'd use the time to make herself look fabulous, convince Jeffrey she was deserving. Kendall had packed all her high-end stuff. No drugstore cosmetics today. Once she'd covered her blemishes with foundation, contoured her cheekbones, and perfected her eyeliner, Kendall assessed her reflection. Not half bad. She'd go to Beverly Hills a little early and window shop, be there with plenty of time to spare.

In the backseat of the Uber, Kendall pulled out her compact. Her stomach doing cartwheels, she checked her eyeshadow to make sure it hadn't smudged.

"Rodeo Drive?" The driver wore a tie-dye hoodie, her hair pulled back in a messy bun.

"Please."

"You on your own?" she said.

"Yes, a solo trip. I live in Arizona." The view out the window was like Scottsdale with the color turned up, the palm trees more dramatic, the lawns greener, and the front gardens bursting with hydrangeas and rainbow snapdragons.

"Oh, yeah?"

"Shopping."

"Something here you can't find back home?"

"I like to get away. Take a breather for a day or two." Kendall wasn't about to tell the Uber driver she planned to max out her company credit card to buy a handbag that cost nearly as much as her car.

"A change of scenery can work wonders."

"Sure can." With so much going on in the past few days, it did feel good to get some distance. Jessica Schorr's face flashed through Kendall's mind. The nerve of that woman, trying to take advantage of her, and of Hope, with her convoluted scheme. Kendall still wasn't sure what the doctor's goal was, but the whole thing made her feel vulnerable. She'd been letting her calls go to voicemail for the past few days, but when she got home, Kendall would send an email, make up some excuse for why she couldn't plan the Rubin affair.

Kendall looked at the map on the driver's phone. They were close. After dreaming of this day for so long, she couldn't believe it was here.

The driver pulled up to the curb. "I hope this trip fills your cup."

Kendall thanked her and climbed out. The store was two blocks away, so she started walking in the other direction to kill time. Showing up early to an appointment at Hermès wasn't a thing.

The first store Kendall passed was Louis Vuitton, the window display wallpapered with the classic checkerboard pattern in shades of purple, sleek bags posed on lucite tables. She stopped a moment to admire, then moved along. Two of those already lived in her closet. Next was Goyard, one of Kendall's least favorite labels. The water-resistant fabric reminded her of the oilcloth lining her grandmother's kitchen drawers. No, thank you. Reaching the end of the block, Kendall checked her watch. Time to head over.

The Hermès store was a gleaming, ivory fortress with floor-to-ceiling windows and two palm trees standing guard at the entrance. Kendall pulled open the door and felt a rush of cool air.

A thin woman in a black pantsuit gave her a once-over. "May I help you?" she said, her tone dismissive.

"Yes, I have a three o'clock appointment with Jeffrey."

She slid her finger down a tablet. "Kendall Carlson?"

"That's me."

The woman pointed to an armchair and instructed Kendall to have a seat. "I'll tell Jeffrey you've arrived."

When the woman disappeared, a shiver crept up Kendall's spine. She felt exposed. Maybe she should have chosen a wrap dress instead of her dark jeans and bouclé blazer.

A young man rode down the escalator, adjusting the large bow on his fitted lavender shirt. He approached Kendall and extended his hand. "Kendall? Don't you look darling."

"Thank you. It's so nice to meet you in person." She grasped his hand, hoping he wouldn't be skeeved out by her damp palm. Up close, she could see his black eyeliner and shimmery purple eye shadow.

"Shall we?" He led the way to a hidden elevator at the back of the store.

In the quiet of the elevator, Kendall's heart pounded against her ribcage. The doors parted to a long hallway, sconces with small lamp shades hanging between doors on either side. Jeffrey led the way to a private room.

"Make yourself comfortable. May I offer you a glass of champagne?"

"No, thank you." Alcohol would not sit well in Kendall's stomach right now.

"Help yourself to treats. I'll be back in a minute."

Kendall sat in a tufted chair next to a Giltwood table with a marble top, crowned with a plate of delicate, swirled butter cookies. Her stomach did another somersault. Who could think about food at a time like this? The walls were covered in dark green wallpaper decorated with golden leaves, and a rich ivory carpet cushioned the floor. She'd never been in such an opulent place. What was she doing here? Kendall tried not to think about how long it would take to pay off her business credit card after today.

Jeffrey returned carrying a large orange box and placed it on the table. "Are you ready? I think you're going to be pleased."

Kendall oscillated in her seat. She couldn't wait to see what was inside.

He opened a drawer in the table, took out a pair of silken gloves, and slipped them on. Removing the lid and folding back the tissue paper, he reached inside and carefully shimmied a bag out of the dust cover, placing it on the marble surface for admiration.

Kendall's mouth fell open, and her heart dropped. It was a Birkin. Not the style she wanted, but that wasn't the problem. The issue was the color. Instead of a lovely neutral, Jeffrey was offering her a bubblegum pink purse. It was the most hideous thing she'd ever seen.

Jeffrey caressed the leather. "Gorgeous, right?"

Kendall couldn't make any words come out.

"A true beauty. I know she'll find a good home with you."

Then Jeffrey told her the price. When Kendall heard the number, she tasted acid in the back of her throat. This was even higher than she'd expected. She'd have to plan more than a handful of parties to pay off this debt.

"This wasn't exactly what I had in mind," she said.

"I'm sorry to hear that. What were you hoping for?"

"I've had my heart set on a Kelly bag. Maybe in black or tan?"

"Those are in high demand, reserved for our dedicated customers only. We don't offer those to just anyone." Jeffrey's voice sounded robotic, as if he said this phrase multiple times a day.

"I have a purchase history." She tugged on her scarf to make the point. "Check my account."

"It would be highly unusual, but give me a moment." He gestured to the Birkin. "I'll leave this one here so you can think it over."

Jeffrey closed the door with a click. The hideous Birkin challenged Kendall to a staring contest. The pink color reminded her of Posy, Hope's beloved stuffed butterfly. Her throat tightened, and a swell of shame flooded her body. What kind of mother was she? Purchasing a bag wouldn't be fair to Hope. How could she spend money she didn't have, depriving Hope of the therapies she so desperately needed? She'd let her priorities get all out of whack. For what? For a ridiculously overpriced handbag? No. This wasn't who Kendall was. This wasn't what she stood for. The madness had to end. Kendall didn't need the Kelly bag or Jeffrey or Beverly Hills. She had to get out of here. Finding the stairs, she made her way downstairs and to the front of the store.

"Leaving empty-handed?" The woman in the pantsuit asked. "Everything all right?"

Kendall rushed by her without a word. She had to get to the airport and fly back home to her family as soon as possible.

O O O

The next afternoon, Kendall opened the bedroom window to let in some fresh air. She hadn't been gone long, but it was good to be home. Outside in the pool, Hope bobbed in her square green float while Lucas, her occupational therapist, squirted her arm with a turkey baster. Hope gurgled with glee and squirted him back. Just a few months back, Hope wouldn't have had the coordination to do this, but now it was no big deal. A silly game. The next time Kendall felt down, she'd have to remember this moment.

With fifty more minutes in the session, Kendall could check off some household chores. The garbage needed emptying, and the shower was desperate for a good scrubbing. She lifted the plastic bag from her bathroom garbage can and tied the sides into a knot. Troy's heavy footsteps echoed on the tile floor in the hall. He opened the bedroom door, a scowl on his face.

"Weren't you going for a run?" Kendall asked.

"I was, but then I saw the light flashing on the answering machine. It was a guy." Troy said, his voice much too loud. "Jeffrey something. He seems to think you can work things out, that it's meant to be. Is that why you went out to LA? To go fuck Jeffrey?"

"No, it's not what you think—" Kendall felt a burning in the center of her chest. She thought she'd left this fiasco behind in LA, but now it was coming back to haunt her.

"Well, my mind is reeling, Kendall, so you better start talking."

Kendall released a ragged breath and patted the bed for Troy to sit next to her. He refused.

"I wasn't honest with you," she said.

Troy's face twisted with anger. Kendall didn't want to say more, but she had no choice.

"There was no bridal shower. It was an excuse."

"What the hell, Kendall?"

"I got a call from Hermès. It's a big deal. I thought an expensive purse would make me happy. But when I got there, it felt wrong. All I wanted to do was come back home to you."

"I don't understand. Then who the hell is Jeffrey?"

"A sales associate at the Beverly Hills store."

"Did something happen with him?"

"What? No, not even close. He's totally gay."

Troy sat down with a sigh. "So, you're not cheating on me?" he asked softly.

"I was having an emotional affair with a stunning handbag, but it's over. I called it off."

"Now I'm really confused." He squinted his eyes, his forehead traversed with deep lines. "You lied to me about going to LA to buy a pocketbook? That doesn't make any sense."

"You're right. It doesn't." Kendall glanced over at her closet, keenly aware of her precious collection on the top shelf just behind the door.

"So, you didn't buy anything?"

"Not this time."

"What does that mean? Have there been other times?"

"Maybe a few. I let it get a bit out of control."

"Where did the money come from? I haven't seen any charges."

Kendall's cheeks flushed, but for the sake of her marriage, she had to be honest. "I used my business account."

"You sabotaged your own company for the sake of some silly purses? That doesn't seem like you. At least not the Kendall I know."

"I got lost in a fantasy world, but I'm finding my way out. Enough with the frivolous distractions."

Troy collapsed back onto the bed with an exhale.

"I mean, can you blame me, Kendall? We barely spend any time together anymore. As soon as Hope goes to bed, we pass out. Every conversation revolves around her. I don't remember the last time we talked about anything else."

Kendall laid down next to him and reached for his hand, intertwining her fingers with his. "With everything going on with Hope, we've faded into the background."

"I wouldn't be surprised if you were cheating. Things haven't been good for a while."

"I know. How do we fix that?"

"I'm not sure, but at least we're taking the first step."

"What's that?"

"Talking about it. Acknowledging the problem."

"I can't take on any more problems. Our finances were already shaky. I'm not sure how we get through this."

"I'm not either." Kendall rolled over and tucked her head under Troy's chin, her cheek on his broad chest. "But we've come this far. We'll figure it out together."

Chapter Thirty-One
JESS

"I need you to check the patient in room five," Eve wheeled her medication cart up to the nurses' station. "Thirty-five weeks with abdominal pain. She's bought herself at least an ultrasound."

"All right. I'll go take a look." Jess avoided eye contact. The last few times Jess had been on labor and delivery, she'd been scheduled with other nurses, but today she'd drawn the short straw. The department administration had ignored their lawyers' instructions to avoid contact. Working so closely with Eve was no easy feat. Halfway through the twelve-hour shift, the two women hadn't devolved into arguments or finger-pointing, so Jess counted that as a win.

Jess reviewed the chart, then headed to room five. The woman in the bed looked quite comfortable, deep in a game of Candy Crush on her phone. A man with a lumberjack beard sat by her side, his lips pursed with concern. He stood up as Jess entered.

Jess shook hands with both the patient and her husband. "Hello, I'm Dr. Schorr."

"What's going on?" the husband said. "Her due date is five weeks away. Is she in labor already? When will she get an epidural?"

"Let's not get ahead of ourselves." Jess motioned for him to have a seat. "My nurse did the preliminary exam, and everything looks good so far. So, tell me what's been bothering you."

"I've been having pain for several hours," she said. "I wasn't sure if it was contractions or not."

"I made her come in," the husband said, "to make sure everything's okay."

"Any fever? Nausea, vomiting, or diarrhea?"

"No, none of that. Just these bands of tightness for a few seconds, and then it goes away."

"It sounds like Braxton-Hicks to me, but I'll do an ultrasound, to be extra cautious."

"Braxton Hicks?" the woman said.

"Normal uterine contractions to get ready for labor. Like biceps curls for the uterus."

Jess stepped up to the ultrasound machine and selected the patient's name. Lifting up the gown, she squirted a liberal amount of blue gel onto her rounded belly and began scanning. Performing ultrasounds used to be one of the best parts of her job. In the before times, Jess had loved seeing the baby on the screen, the little white fetal parts swimming in pockets of black amniotic fluid. She loved measuring the head and abdominal circumference and most of all, she loved showing expectant parents the healthy, pulsing hearts and adorable facial profiles. Today, her usual joy was tinged with a sense of unease, the thought of seeing the umbilical cord looming in the back of her mind.

Using the ultrasound probe to push on mom's belly, Jess created a window to view the baby's heart. It was beating at a healthy rate. Jess saved several shots and took a cine video loop.

"Now that's a good-looking heart," Jess said. "You can both breathe easy. This baby isn't going anywhere soon." She finished the required measurements, then documented the position of the placenta. "Would you like a picture of her face?"

"That would be amazing. We don't have one yet," the woman said.

Jess continued scanning until she found the face, then angled the probe to get the best view. As she saved an image, Jess caught sight of the umbilical cord next to the baby's head. No matter how hard she tried to ignore it, Jess felt her eyes drawn back to the cord undulating in the fluid, coiled like a rattlesnake ready to strike. In a flash, she was back at the Carlson delivery—the prolapsed cord, the utter chaos, and the suffocating heat behind her tight face mask. She tried to take a deep breath, but the air got caught in her throat. After a few shallow inhales, her fingers became clammy and prickled with pain, her heart hammering in her chest.

"Can you see it?" the husband asked. "We need a portrait for the fridge."

Jess dropped the probe to the floor and placed her fingers on her neck. Her pulse pounded against her fingertips.

"Are you okay, Dr. Schorr?" the patient asked.

Eve swept into the room. "I'm happy to report your labs are all normal. Are we ready for discharge?"

The second Eve saw Jess, she guided her out of the room and down the hall. Jess leaned her weight on Eve, her vision blurring more with each step. Before she knew it, she was on the couch in the staff lounge with a pillow under her legs. Jess heard the water running and then felt a cool washcloth on her forehead. The cold sensation grounded her, and the panicked feeling slowly dissipated. Her fingers stopped tingling, and her heart rate crept back down. When she opened her eyes, Eve stood over her.

"You feeling better?" Eve asked.

Jess squeezed her eyes closed and then opened them again, half hoping this was all a bad dream. "I think so, yes."

"What happened?"

"Everything's fine." Jess hoped Eve wouldn't notice the quiver in her voice. She didn't want to give her more ammunition to use against her. "I'm okay, really."

"Enough with the façade, Jess. You almost hit the floor in the middle of a patient's room. What's going on?"

Jess should have known she couldn't pull one over on Eve. The woman could smell bullshit from a mile away. "Everything was fine until I saw the cord. Then I couldn't focus on anything else." Jess sat up and looked around. Across the room, the cabinets and microwave looked normal again, the edges straight and details sharp.

"You're under a lot of stress." Eve sat down next to Jess. "We both are. It's only natural to feel overwhelmed."

"Sometimes it's too much. I can't stop thinking about Hope, and then my mind goes into overdrive. I know I can't change what happened, but that doesn't stop my thoughts from spinning."

Eve guided Jess's head onto her shoulder and gently stroked her hair. "This whole thing is so sad. We're never going to be perfect. Humans make mistakes."

Jess allowed the weight of her head to rest on Eve. It felt good to be supported for once. It had been so long since she and her old friend had hugged or even touched. "I wish things had turned out differently. For Hope, and for us as well."

"I know," Eve said. "Maybe once everything is behind us...I'm not sure. We probably should get back to work."

"Because we're not supposed to be talking?"

"We'll pretend this never happened." Eve stood and tucked her scrub top into her pants. "Now let's discharge that patient. Got to keep on moving."

O O O

After her shift, Jess stopped by her office to grab her sweater and backpack. The light on her work phone blinked with a message. All she wanted to do was go home, order take-out Chinese, and stuff her face with egg rolls, but she couldn't ignore the voicemail. What if it was something important? She collapsed into her desk chair and pressed play.

"This is Angela Caputo. I've been doing a deep dive into the documents and have come across an alarming piece of information. Please call me as soon as possible."

Angela sounded pissed off. Jess didn't know if she could take any more today, but at the same time, she couldn't leave this hanging. What could be so alarming? Had Angela gone through her computer search history? Discovered that Jess had googled umbilical cord prolapse, neonatal hypoxia, cerebral palsy, and countless other topics she wasn't supposed to be researching? Or maybe she'd figured out Jess had perused Hope's chart? Whatever it was, she had to return the call. She dialed the law firm and waited for Angela to pick up.

"I've been combing through Kendall Carlson's medical record, and I came across a disturbing detail."

Angela's mention of the medical record made Jess's jaw tighten. She waited for the lawyer to continue.

"On September 19th of this year, the day after you were served papers for this case, you added a note to Kendall Carlson's chart. Is that correct?"

Jess felt cornered, as if she were under attack by her own attorney. She wasn't sure what to say. "Um, I guess."

"What in the world were you thinking? Mira sent you explicit guidelines for a reason. Going rogue is only going to damage your case."

"I thought it would make things clearer. Explain my thinking at the time."

"Not at all," Angela said. "It makes it look like you have something to hide. If you'd elaborated at the time, that would be a different story. An addendum is never a good idea. It's self-sabotage."

"I wasn't trying to sabotage anything." Jess sighed. She really had done it with the best intentions. Could this one misstep really doom her case to failure? "Where do we go from here?"

"I'll try to come up with some way to deal with this. In the meantime, if I'm going to continue to represent you, we need to have a come-to-Jesus conversation, an intervention of sorts."

"An intervention?" Jess didn't like the sound of that. Angela was always serious, but now she sounded almost threatening.

"I don't tolerate funny business," Angela said. "From now on, I need you to follow the guidelines to the letter. If I hear of any other transgressions, I'll be forced to sever our working relationship."

Jess couldn't imagine having to hire a new attorney, and she wasn't even sure how that would work. Would she have to go through her insurance company? She didn't care to find out. Angela was good at her job, and it would behoove Jess to follow her lead. "I understand. From now on, I promise to fall in line."

"I'm glad we're on the same page. With the deposition set for a month from now, we'll set up some coaching sessions, so you're prepared for all possible lines of questioning. The more you practice, the better you'll come across."

"All right." With everything else she was dealing with, practicing would prove a challenge, but Jess would have to make time. Her reputation and future career depended on it.

"Hold on for my assistant. She'll get some dates on the calendar."

Chapter Thirty-Two
ABE

Abe took the bagel from the toaster and topped it with a thick layer of cream cheese, the aroma of fresh coffee filling the kitchen. He poured himself a large cup, stirred in two sugars and a splash of cream, and sat down at the table. Bea parked next to his chair, banking on a handout.

For once, it felt nice to be alone in his quiet house. Ross had texted earlier with an invitation to the dog park, but Abe had begged off. It was so much easier to do by text, one of the pros of the new-fangled technology. Plus, he had work to do. Opening his laptop, he reviewed the questions he'd drafted for the upcoming deposition. It was a good start, but far too civil, much too polite. He'd have to add in a few zingers. When the doorbell rang, Bea sprang up barking.

"It's okay, girl. You're fine." It was most likely an overeager political candidate canvassing the neighborhood. If Abe waited a few minutes, maybe they'd move on to their next victim.

Abe took a big sip of coffee and a bite of bagel. When the bell rang again, he stood up and walked to the entryway, Bea skittering around his feet. As he opened the door, Abe held her collar to stop her from baring her teeth, as she'd done with the UPS guy last week. Usually so sweet, she got anxious around people she didn't recognize.

Fran Gans stood on his doorstep in a flowered sundress and cardigan. Under his ratty bathrobe, Abe wore only his tightly-whities.

"Good morning, Abe." Fran held a cellophane-covered basket tied with a blue ribbon. Her yellow tassel earrings matched her dress.

Abe tightened the robe around his belly. "I'm not dressed for visitors."

"Sorry to stop in unannounced. I'm here on official business. From the caring committee."

"Oh, I didn't know. What's the occasion?"

"Your wife's Yahrzeit. The synagogue aims to provide comfort during this trying time. The one-year anniversary can bring up a lot of feelings."

"That's very thoughtful." Abe tried to peek inside. "What form does this comfort take? Please say it involves chocolate."

"You're free to open it and explore the contents."

"Of course," Abe opened the door wider. "Come in, but please excuse the state of the house."

Fran carried the basket inside and handed it to Abe. "No worries at all. I like a lazy Sunday, too."

As Abe took the basket, he released Bea's collar. He tried to call her back, but she ignored him, heading straight for Fran's leg.

"Nooooo, Bea."

Fran bent down to Bea's level. "And who's this beauty?"

Bea flopped down at Fran's feet and rolled over to expose her spotted belly.

Abe's mouth dropped open. He'd never seen the dog warm to someone so easily. "Oh, this is Bea, short for Broadway."

"She's quite a lover." Fran rubbed her belly and scratched underneath her chin. "You're a little mush, aren't you? A real sweetheart."

"She never takes to strangers this way."

"Well, I have a way with animals. Back home, we always had a menagerie. A rotating cast of characters. When Sheldon got sick, we stopped taking in new ones."

"You adopt them?"

"Always," she said. "I'm a firm believer in providing care for animals in need."

The more time Abe spent with Fran, the more he liked her. She was kind, easy to talk with, and down-to-earth. "Would you like a cup of coffee? I just made a fresh pot." He really needed to change out of this robe, but it wouldn't be polite to leave her standing in the foyer.

"That depends. Is it that fancy Starbucks or a regular cup of joe?"

"I'm a regular joe kind of guy." Abe led Fran to the kitchen. Passing the laundry room, he closed the door before she could see the piles of dirty clothes on the floor.

Bea stuck by Fran's side, whimpering with excitement. When Fran took a seat at the table, Bea jumped up, her front paws on Fran's thighs.

"She really likes you." Abe shooed the dog off. "Usually, she's more skittish. Do you mind if I go change into something more presentable?"

"Take your time."

When Abe went to his bedroom, Bea stayed by Fran's side rather than following behind him. She'd never done that before. He threw on a shirt and a pair of jeans, ran a comb through his remaining hairs, and did a quick swish with Listerine. Back in the kitchen, he cleared off the countertop as best he could, adding to the tower of dishes in the sink. He poured fresh coffee into two mugs. "How do you take it?"

"Light and sweet."

Abe brought the mugs to the table. "I don't trust anyone who drinks their coffee black."

"Never. There's something wrong with those people. How about we tear into this basket?"

Abe nodded for Fran to do the honors. "Be my guest."

"I believe there's chocolate-covered shortbread. I made the arrangement myself." Fran ripped open the cellophane wrapping, freed the package of cookies, and held it up in the air. "Sweet success."

Abe shook his head as she offered him one. "Ladies first."

Fran opened the package, dipped one in her coffee, and took a bite.

Abe helped himself too, biting off half. He couldn't remember the last time chocolate had tasted so sweet. Then, his gaze wandered over to the wheelchair, and he put down the other half. What would Risa think about this? She'd told him to find someone new, but had she really meant it? Guilt burned in his stomach.

"Did you see the adult education listings for the winter session?" Fran asked.

"Adult education?"

"At the synagogue. There are some interesting ones. I'm signing up for the Taste of Torah class."

"When does it meet?"

She wiped her mouth with a napkin. "Sunday mornings."

"Have you studied Torah before?"

"No, but Sheldon couldn't wait for his weekly class to come around. He always came home full of excitement."

"I always thought it sounded dull, but in fairness, I've never given it a chance."

"Rabbi Glasser is teaching it. He promises to make it interesting and relevant. Would you care to join me?"

Abe wasn't sure how to answer. The idea of going to synagogue on a Sunday morning didn't sound appealing, but maybe it would be good to get out of the house, meet new people, and break out of his comfort zone.

"Why not? Count me in." He didn't let himself look back at the wheelchair in the corner.

Chapter Thirty-Three
JESS

"You ready for this?" Angela swept into the waiting area, looking polished in a navy dress and sensible heels, a light blue leather tote over her shoulder.

Jess stood up and buttoned her tailored jacket. Used to wearing scrubs nearly twenty-four seven, her pant suit felt tight, but she needed to present herself as a professional.

"As ready as I'll ever be," Jess said. No matter how many times she read over her notes and practiced her answers out loud, she still felt shaky. She tried not to think back to the first practice session with Angela when she'd broken down sobbing after the first question, blowing her nose and wiping her eyes between unintelligible answers. Much improved since then, Jess didn't think she'd ever feel truly ready.

Angela sat down and patted the seat next to her. Jess sank back into the chair. "Listen, it's completely normal to feel anxious. Today, your job is to tell the truth as succinctly as possible. Answer the questions, but don't expand. If you don't know something, just say so. Speculation is never good."

"That's a lot to remember."

"You've got this."

An older man came in, followed by a woman wearing glasses and another woman in black pants and a button-down white shirt. Something about this guy seemed familiar, as if they'd met before. Jess racked her brain, trying to come up with where she might have seen him. Did he live in her neighborhood? Maybe they'd crossed paths at the clubhouse or the community pool?

Or maybe he had grandchildren at the same private school as her kids?

"Good morning, everyone," the man said, smoothing his goatee. "Give us a few minutes to set up, and we'll call everyone in." The three of them disappeared into the conference room.

"Is that the Carlsons' attorney?" Jess asked. In her imaginings, the plaintiff attorney had been a merciless shark, not a friendly older man with a warm smile.

"Yes, Abe Silverberg. With his paralegal and the court reporter."

"Is anyone else coming?"

"No, that's it. And remember, I'll be there the whole time. I won't let him pull any shenanigans."

The woman with the glasses opened the door. "Come on in."

Jess followed Angela into the room, her right eyelid twitching with nerves. She'd have to keep it together for the next few hours, if not for herself, then for her family.

"Ready to go?" Attorney Silverberg asked the court reporter who sat in front of a strange typewriter-like machine with about twenty unlabeled keys.

The reporter's hands hovered over the keys. "All set."

"Allow me to introduce myself," Abe said. "I'm Abraham Silverberg, and this is my paralegal Norah Wilkes. I will try to be as clear and fair as I possibly can. The first topic pertains to details about you, Dr. Schorr. Your education, licensing, and training. Please tell us your full name, your address, and where you practice medicine."

As Jess answered, she continued going through possibilities in her mind. When her thoughts turned to Congregation Shalom, she knew she'd found the answer. He was the man who'd sat next to her at Shabbat services, the one who'd recently lost his wife. What a small world. He didn't seem to recognize her, but the random coincidence gave her a boost. He was a nice man and a fellow Jew. He couldn't be out to get her.

So far, the questions were perfectly straightforward. Where did Jess attend medical school, residency, and fellowship? Which state licenses did she possess? Where did she have hospital privileges? Jess's lingering doubts melted away. She was doing fine. Angela leaned back in her chair, nodding along with the clicking of the court reporter's machine.

"Changing gears now," Abe said. "Let's turn to your relationship to the plaintiff Kendall Carlson and the details of her treatment. When did you first meet Mrs. Carlson?"

"On the day of the delivery of her baby, September 26th, 2020."

"You didn't have a relationship with the plaintiff prior to that?"

"No, she was a patient of Meghan Felix. I was covering for her that week."

"Did you have a chance to peruse her chart before she went into labor?"

She wasn't sure how to respond. Reviewing another doctor's charts in advance wasn't really feasible. If a woman came to the hospital in labor, Jess quickly got herself up to speed.

Angela sat up. "Objection. Relevance."

"Fine, we'll continue with questions about the delivery. I'd like to dig into the details now."

Abe Silverberg no longer seemed friendly. Deep frown lines crossed his forehead, and all traces of his warm smile were gone.

"You were the obstetrician on call that day, is that correct?"

"Yes."

"When were you made aware Kendall Carlson had been admitted to the labor and delivery floor?"

"I'm not sure of the exact time. Sometime in the afternoon."

Norah shuffled through papers in a folder and handed one to the attorney. His eyes scanned down the page. "Allow me to jog your memory. According to your cell phone records, Nurse Marcus first called you around noon. 12:14 p.m. to be exact."

"Objection," Angela said. "Dr. Schorr is answering as honestly as possible. It's not your job to provide evidence."

"Understood, counselor. So, what happened next?"

"I examined her and wrote an admission note."

"The note from 1:22 p.m.?

"That's correct, yes."

The attorney looked down at his notes, his brow furrowed. "Is it true your next note was entered at 10:04 p.m.? Were you made aware of Mrs. Carlson's status during the intervening hours?"

Jess twisted her hands in her lap. Angela had coached her to avoid answering two questions at once. "Can you please rephrase?"

"Yes, let me make my question clearer. Who was caring for Kendall Carlson during the nine-hour span between 1:22 p.m. and 10:04 p.m."

"Nurse Marcus was watching her closely and keeping me apprised of clinical developments."

"What sort of clinical developments? Please be as specific as your memory allows."

"I'm not sure what the question is." Jess didn't want to say too much. Keep it short, Angela had said. The room was much too warm. She ran a finger under the neck of her blouse.

"According to the security records, you left the hospital at 5:43 p.m. and didn't swipe back in until 9:35 p.m. Isn't it true you thought it unnecessary to monitor Mrs. Carlson closely?"

Jess's head spun. Was this one of the double negatives Angela had warned her about?

"Objection. Counselor, be reasonable," Angela said. "The defense requests a five-minute break."

Jess released her breath, thankful for her attorney's intuition. She followed Angela to the bathroom, the muscles in her legs quivering with each step. In the bathroom stall, she unbuttoned her blazer and fanned her chest with her hands. She sat on the closed toilet, using the time to gather herself. This wasn't going well. When she'd practiced in front of the mirror, her answers had been far more eloquent.

Angela waited with a cup of ice water outside the stall. Parched, Jess downed the whole cup.

"You're doing fine." Angela tossed the cup in the bin. "His job is to make you nervous. Don't let him get to you."

"I don't know if I can do this."

"You can, and you will. Going forward, he's going to ask more about the medical details, about your choices minute by minute. Trying to incriminate you. Be as honest as you can, without saying too much. You're going to go back in there, hold your head high and finish what you started. Got it?"

Fueled by Angela's tough love, Jess buttoned her blazer and followed her attorney back to the conference room.

O   O   O

When Jess came back in, Attorney Silverberg looked more like the gentleman she'd met at Shabbat services.

"Dr. Schorr," he said. "We may have gotten off on the wrong foot. I suggest we start fresh."

Jess nodded and took her seat.

"Please tell us about your first interaction with Kendall Carlson."

Jess's mind drifted back to that day two years ago. After a full day of clinic appointments, she'd been scheduled to cover deliveries overnight. When Kendall had arrived at the labor and delivery floor around noon, Eve assessed and admitted her. In between clinic patients, Jess scooted over to L & D to write her admission note.

Kendall Carlson was sitting up in bed with a full face of make-up and a flawless manicure, her square-jawed husband next to her. Eve entered nursing notes at the rolling computer.

"I'm Dr. Schorr." Jess reached out her hand. "I'm covering for Dr. Felix tonight."

Kendall's handshake was limp. Jess's father would never have let such a noncommittal greeting slide. "A strong handshake creates a good first impression," he often said.

"Troy Carlson," the husband said, his voice too loud for the small room. "Where's Dr. Felix?"

"She's away this week."

"My due date is eight weeks away." Kendall covered her face with her hands. "It's too early."

"Once your water breaks, we don't have a choice. If you don't deliver within twenty-four hours, you risk serious infection. I'd like to do an exam to assess how far along you are."

"Have you seen my birth plan? It's filed in my chart."

"I have. I understand you'd prefer not to have cervical exams?"

"That's right," Kendall said. "Is that a problem?"

Troy stood up. "It's our choice, Kendall. Dr. Felix assured us it was well within our rights to refuse."

"It certainly is, but with your water breaking early, it would be helpful to have that extra piece of information. Another data point to help us make the best decisions."

"I really don't want it," Kendall said, her voice raspy.

"Understood. I will honor your wishes. The good news is thirty-two weeks is manageable these days. We'll give you medication to promote your baby's lung development and another medicine to induce labor. There's also another treatment called magnesium to prevent cerebral palsy. You're right on the borderline, but I'd be in favor of it. There's emerging data showing it may be helpful."

"Will my baby be okay?"

"She might need a few days in our neonatal ICU, but I have confidence you'll be able to bring her home soon."

Troy paced next to the bed. "ICU? That doesn't sound reassuring. Dr. Felix never mentioned anything like this."

"Mr. Carlson, your wife is getting excellent care." Jess turned her attention back to Kendall. "I know this is scary, but I promise to take good care of you." Jess had had every intention of delivering on her promise.

Attorney Silverberg coughed, bringing Jess back to the stark conference room. "When you initially saw Mrs. Carlson, you wrote an admission note. Did anything concern you at that time?"

"It wasn't a straightforward case. She had premature preterm rupture of membranes at thirty-two weeks gestation."

"What made the case difficult?"

"I didn't say difficult."

"Fair enough, I'll rephrase. What made it not so straightforward?"

"Because of the ruptured membranes, she needed to deliver within twenty-four hours to prevent infection. I prescribed steroids for fetal lung development and magnesium to reduce the chance of brain injury. Plus, she declined cervical checks, which further complicated the case."

The attorney ignored the last comment and handed a paper to the court reporter. "I'd like to enter this into evidence." After the reporter placed a yellow numbered sticker on it, he showed it to Jess. "This is your initial admission note. You outlined that all here, correct?"

Jess scanned down the page. "Yes."

"Anything missing from this note?"

"Not that I'm aware of."

"Thank you. When was the next time you saw my client?"

It had been a busy afternoon in clinic. When Jess wrapped up her last appointment, she had stopped to check on Kendall.

"How are you feeling?" Jess asked.

"I'm getting these weird hot flashes."

"That's expected." Jess eyed the bag of magnesium dripping through the IV line. "Magnesium can make you feel wacky. Flushed and dizzy. No need to worry."

Troy stood up from his chair. "Dr. Schorr, this is taking too long. Is everything on track?"

"Having a baby is all about patience, both before and after they're born." Jess stood at the computer and clicked through the vital signs and nursing notes. Kendall's blood pressure was stable, and her labs all looked fine. According to Eve's notes, the baby hadn't yet descended, so the delivery was still hours away. "A little extra time is a good thing for your baby. Give the steroids a chance to work, so she won't have trouble breathing when she's born."

Eve came into the room carrying two bags of fluid.

"Why would she have trouble breathing?" Kendall asked.

"Hopefully she won't. We're doing all we can to make sure she's as healthy as possible."

"Dr. Schorr," Eve said. "I'm glad you're here. After I hang another bag of fluid, I'll meet you in the hall."

While Jess waited at the nurses' station, her phone vibrated in her pocket.

"Hi, Maddie, I'm at work. Is everything okay?"

"Mom…" Maddie broke down crying. "Something's wrong with Opal. She's just lying here. She won't stand up."

"I'm sure she's fine, honey. Maybe give her some tuna in her kibble. That should perk her right up."

"No, she's not…" Maddie hiccupped. "I don't…"

"Calm down, sweetie." Jess could hear her younger child crying in the background. "Tell me exactly what's going on."

"She peed on the floor earlier, and she just threw up. I even tried the catnip. Something's really wrong with her."

"Okay, maybe she needs to be seen. I'm at the hospital. Can you call Dad and let him know?"

"He's at a conference, remember?"

Crap. Jess had forgotten Drew was at a continuing education conference up in Flagstaff and wouldn't be home until later tonight. Maddie wouldn't get her driver's permit until next month, and Mai was allergic to cats, so she couldn't pitch in either.

"I guess I'll call Laura Cartwell." Jess hated to ask a favor of her annoying neighbor, but she had no other choice. She reluctantly dialed her number. When Laura picked up, she said she was in Mesa getting her car fixed, but she agreed to meet Jess at the vet within the hour.

Jess had no choice but to go home. She called Maddie back. "I'll be home in a few. Can you wrangle her into the crate so we can take her to the emergency vet as soon as I get there? Laura will meet us over there." Jess ended the call and slipped her phone back in her pocket.

Eve came out of the room and placed a long strip of printed paper on the counter. "I want you to see the fetal tracings. Something doesn't seem right."

Jess followed the squiggly line with her eyes. The fetal heart rate was a bit lower than usual, and there were occasional decelerations, but both could be attributed to the magnesium treatment. Nothing about the tracing looked particularly concerning. "I think it's all from the mag. The baby's in good position on exam?"

"I think so, but—"

"Everything's under control." Jess had faith in Eve's skills. Plus, Anita, the chief resident, was on call and fully capable of fielding any questions that arose. "I have to run home for a few. Call me or Anita if anything changes."

"Are you sure that's a good idea?"

"The husband is getting to you? He's all bark, no bite. I'll be back before you know it." Jess left the unit and headed to the parking lot. If all went smoothly, she could be back in less than forty-five minutes. Nothing would happen before then. She was already on the highway when she realized she'd forgotten to write another progress note in the chart.

Now, the sunlight streamed through the conference room windows, shining straight into Jess's eyes. She raised her forearm to block the light. Angela stood up to lower the blinds.

"So, what you're telling us, Dr. Schorr," Abe said, "is that your nurse raised a red flag, and you ignored it."

"That's not what I said." Something caught in her throat.

216

"Objection," Angela said sharply. "Questions only, please."
Angela sounded more serious. Why had her tone changed?
Was it because Jess had left the hospital while on call? With labor
sometimes taking forever, especially with first-time mothers, it
happened all the time. Maybe a jury of random people wouldn't
understand. They would merely see a young woman in preterm
labor and the callous obstetrician who'd abandoned her. Had the
irregularities in the tracings been a sign of fetal distress rather
than a side effect of the magnesium? Maybe if she'd insisted on
a cervical exam at that time, she would have diagnosed the cord
prolapse. If Jess had not left the hospital, would Hope have been
born healthy?

"Fine," Abe said. "Let me restate the question. Dr. Schorr,
after Nurse Marcus expressed her concern about the fetal tracings, why did you choose to leave the hospital?"

Jess tried her best to stay cool. If she lost her composure,
she wouldn't stand a chance. "At that moment, it seemed safe. I
thought we had more time."

"Time is a good choice of words." Abe turned over a few
pages of notes. "After you left the hospital at 5:43 p.m, where did
you go?"

Jess had driven home, loaded up the kids and the cat, and
made it to the emergency vet in record time, but the waiting
room was full to bursting. A listless Doberman lolled in the
middle of the room, a Siamese mewled relentlessly from one of
the chairs, and a scruffy terrier squatted in the corner to do his
business. As Jess checked in with the clerk, she explained the situation and begged for Opal to be taken as soon as possible. Then
Laura texted to say they'd found a problem with her carburetor,
so she wouldn't be able to make it after all. Jess checked her watch
and tapped her foot for the entire hour it took to move through
the pipeline at the vet. Once Opal finally received a diagnosis of
urinary tract infection and the first dose of antibiotics, Jess sent
the kids and the cat home in an Uber. She didn't usually allow

that, but she needed to get back to the hospital as soon as possible.

The court reporter stopped typing and looked up. "Can you repeat the last question, counselor?" she said.

"No problem," Abe said. "Dr. Schorr, where did you go after you left the hospital?"

"I had to go home. My cat was sick."

"Interesting..."

"Attorney Silverberg, please." Angela gave him a stern look.

"Fair enough. Dr. Schorr, when did you next see my client, Kendall Carlson?"

"I started back to the hospital around 7:30 p.m."

He whispered something to his paralegal. When she handed him a document, he scrutinized it for a moment. "I find that fascinating, because you didn't enter the security doors at the hospital until 9:35 p.m. An awfully long time to travel a few short miles."

Angela stood up. "Objection."

"I'll try again." He made eye contact with Jess. "Dr. Schorr, on the evening of September 26th, why did it take you over two hours to drive the six miles from the veterinary office to Valley Health Medical Center?"

There was no good answer to this question. As Angela had instructed, Jess needed to tell the truth, no matter what. That evening, as Jess drove to the hospital on North Scottsdale Road, the sun sank behind Camelback Mountain, making the rocks glow red. As she tried to ride a wave of green lights, a phone call came through the car speaker. Lately, her mother's phone calls had become a drag, their conversations revolving around Jess's father's progressive dementia and how difficult it had become for her mother to care for him. When they'd put down a deposit at a memory facility the previous month, Jess thought her mom would be relieved, but the closer they got to his move-in day, the more her mom seemed bogged down with guilt.

"Jessica, is that you?" Her mother's panicked voice filled the car.

"Mom? What's going on?"

"Something's wrong. I was on the phone dealing with your father's doctor when I got a pain in my chest."

"Okay, Mom. Calm down."

"Oh, Jessica, I'm so dizzy."

"Mom, I need you to lie down on the floor. I don't want you to pass out.

Rustling came through the phone and then a sickening pause.

"Mom? Are you still there? Where's Dad?"

"He's… right here."

"Can you call 911?"

"I don't think…" Her mother's voice sounded faint.

"I'll call the ambulance. Don't move. They'll be there soon."

Jess stopped at a red light. She wished she could keep her mom on the line, but that wasn't possible. Right after she hung up, Eve's name flashed on the screen.

"Hello?"

"Hi Jess, are you here? I need you to see Mrs. Carlson. The baby's descended, and her tracings are worrisome."

"What? I can't—"

"She's had a few profound decelerations. Not clear why."

"I'm on my way." Jess hung up. With her left hand on the wheel, she used her right to dial 911 on her phone.

A man's voice came through the speakers. "What's your emergency?"

"Hi, yes, it's my mother. She needs an ambulance."

"What's the problem?"

"Chest pain and dizziness."

"We'll get an ambulance out to her right away. Address?"

"That's the tricky part. The address is in Scarsdale."

"Ma'am?"

"New York. She called me, but she's not able to call an ambulance herself."

"I'm going to get the New York Troopers on the line and see if they can connect me with the right department. Hang on."

Elevator music came through her speakers. Jess pictured her mother unconscious on the living room floor, her father disoriented and afraid. He often didn't recognize her mother on a good day, so he wouldn't understand a medical emergency. As she passed through the intersection at East McDonald Drive, there was a screeching of tires and the sound of crunching metal. The impact slammed Jess against the driver's side door. The airbag punched her in the face, snapping her sunglasses in half. Her car spun in a circle and came to a stop under the traffic light facing oncoming cars. Sharp pain shot through her left arm. She rubbed her throbbing cheek. White smoke wafted from the steering column. It smelled like gunpowder.

The hold music stopped. "Hello?" Jess said.

"Ma'am, are you still with me?"

"Yes." Jess used her right hand to palpate her left arm, making sure it wasn't broken.

"I have the Scarsdale dispatcher. I'll stay on the line."

"Hi, yes. My mother is having a heart attack. Chest pain and… I don't remember. She needs help."

"We'll get an ambulance out to her," the woman said. "What's her name and address?"

Jess managed to recite the information. "My father is with her. He'll be confused by all this. Alzheimer's."

"The ambulance is on the way. Maybe you could get a neighbor to stay with him?"

Jess wanted to curl up in a ball, pretend this wasn't happening. There was only so much one person could handle. "Before you go, is the first man on the phone? I have another emergency to report."

"I'm still here. Go ahead, ma'am."

"There's been a car accident. North Scottsdale Road and East McDonald." The driver of the other car got out of her vehicle, holding a bloody tissue to her nose. "We need police and an ambulance."

The dispatcher assured Jess help was on the way. She got out of the car and waited for a break in traffic. When a gap opened, she made her way across the two lanes and stopped under the shade of an awning.

"Are you okay?" Jess asked the other driver. "I'm so sorry." She wasn't sure how the accident happened. Usually, she was a careful driver.

The woman took the tissue away, blood still oozing from her nostrils.

Jess dug through her purse but found only a few napkins from the hospital cafeteria. She handed them to the woman.

"Are you out to lunch? You ran the light." With her nose pinched, the woman's voice sounded nasal. "This is a complete mess."

Had the light really been red? With so much happening at once, Jess couldn't recall seeing the stoplight at all. She looked back at the intersection. The whole passenger side of her SUV was caved in, and the front of the woman's sedan was crumpled like a used tissue, waves of steam rising from the hood.

"I didn't mean to run the light. I have a lot going on." Jess's breath caught in her throat. Don't cry, she told herself. She had to sort this out quickly and get to the hospital.

"Like you're the only one?" The woman examined the napkin. The bleeding seemed to be slowing.

"The police should be here any minute," Jess said.

Jess's phone rang.

"Hello?"

"Jess, what's taking so long?" Eve said. "The tracings are crapping out, big time. You need to get in here. I tried calling a few other doctors but couldn't get anyone."

"I just got in a car accident."

"Oh my god, are you okay?"

"I'm fine, I think." Jess rubbed her throbbing arm. "But we're still waiting for the police."

"What should I do? I need a doctor to assess this patient as soon as possible."

"Let me see if anyone is around. I'll get back to you in a few."

Jess sent a text to her department group chat. "Have a situation. On call but can't get in right away. Anyone free to check on 32 WK PPROM on L & D?" There used to be a doctor on backup call for emergencies like this, but that had been slashed in a round of hospital budget cuts. While she waited for a response, she called Anita, the senior resident on call.

"Hi, Dr. Schorr, what's up?"

"I need you to check on Kendall Carlson in L & D." Jess filled Anita in on all the details. "Do an exam and report back with your findings. I'll be in as soon as I can."

Another call came in and Jess picked up. "Hello?"

"Is this Jessica Schorr?"

"Yes, it is," Jess said.

A police car pulled up by the curb.

"I'm a paramedic with Scarsdale EMS. We have your mother en route to White Plains Hospital."

"Oh, thank god," Jess said. "What's going on?"

"With her symptoms and EKG, I'm worried it's a heart attack, likely a big one. ETA to the hospital is three minutes."

The police officer got out of the car and hoisted up his gun belt. "And my father?"

"Right next to me. Couldn't see leaving him alone. I'll put you on speaker."

"Dad, can you hear me?" Jess wasn't sure what to say. "It's going to be okay. Mom's not feeling well, so she's going to the hospital. Try not to worry."

Jess couldn't hear a response.

"The ER team will call you with an update," the man said.

Jess thanked him and put her phone back in her purse.

"Good evening, ladies," the police officer said. "Looks like you're not having a great day."

"It was all her fault." The other woman waved a bloody napkin in the air. "She ran the red light."

"What happened?" The officer asked Jess.

"The light was clearly green," Jess said, avoiding eye contact. She needed to get out of here as quickly as possible. She fished around in her purse for her hospital ID, holding it out to the officer. "I'm an obstetrician at Valley Health. I was on my way to the hospital."

"We still need to do the required paperwork. If I blow it off, the chief will have my ass."

The officer instructed them to get their registration and insurance cards from their cars. Jess scurried back across the road, opened the glovebox, and found her insurance card. The expiration date was May of last year. Crap. The new card must be sitting in a pile at home. Could this day get any worse? Maybe the officer would take pity on her. She checked her phone. Several of her colleagues had offered up excuses about vacations and family functions. No one was coming in.

Jess texted Anita. "Did you check on her?"

"Yes, she agreed to cervical exam. I feel cord. Need to do STAT section."

"Shit. I need a few."

"Should I start the case?"

Jess paused. Anita was a good resident, but saying yes didn't feel right. What if something horrible happened with a resident at the helm? Waiting was risky, but giving the go-ahead felt even more dangerous. "No, I'll be there soon."

She made her way back to the curb. The tow truck driver loaded her mangled SUV onto the truck bed. By the time the officer completed a multiple-page accident report, it was almost 9 p.m. And to make matters worse, Jess didn't have a ride to the hospital.

The officer handed each of them a copy of the report. "Let's hope your insurance is up to date, for your sake. If not, this is an expensive mistake."

"Officer?" Jess softened her voice.

"Yes, ma'am?"

"Any chance you can give me a lift to Valley Health? There's a pregnant mother who needs my help as soon as possible."

Attorney Silverberg tapped his pen on the table, bringing Jess back to the present. "That's quite a story, Dr. Schorr. Thank you for sharing."

Jess wasn't sure how much she'd said out loud. It was all a blur. "It was the worst day of my life. My mother died while Hope was being born. I did the best I could in an impossible situation."

"I feel for you," he said. "It really does seem overwhelming, but one question keeps coming to mind. With all the stress you were under, did you think of passing this case on to a colleague? Surely, Kendall Carlson would have been better served with a more clear-eyed physician."

"Counselor," Angela said. "No editorializing."

The attorney cleared his throat. "Dr. Schorr, in the midst of the chaos you described, did you ever consider phoning a friend? There must be a protocol for this kind of situation."

"Um… I tried." Should she have done more? Second-guessing was easy. Should she have let Anita start the C-section? Maybe if Jess had called her chair, she would have assigned another doctor? In medicine, asking for help was frowned upon, akin to admitting weakness. Though Jess had pulled herself up by her bootstraps and done the best she could, it hadn't been enough. Despite her best efforts, she'd failed in the worst possible way, and she'd have to live with that for the rest of her life.

Chapter Thirty-Four

KENDALL

Kendall pushed the button on the plastic piano in the playmat, Hope cooing at the sound of the tinny ABC song. In the past weeks, things had been looking up. Hope had finally learned to maneuver from her back to her side. Her muscles were getting stronger and more coordinated. Humming along with the tune, Kendall's thoughts drifted to the Dr. Schorr's deposition, happening right now. She couldn't stop thinking about it. How was it going? Was Attorney Silverberg getting the answers he needed to win the case?

Hope kicked one of the hanging shapes and made a long O-sounding cry. It wasn't a word, but it sounded vaguely like one. Kendall's spirits lifted. Despite the slow pace, Hope was making progress. If they won the suit, they'd have the money to continue her therapies. Attorney Silverberg better be digging deep enough to prove the doctor had messed up. But was Dr. Schorr really to blame? Kendall shook away her doubts. Like a train with faulty brakes, the lawsuit kept gaining speed. There was no turning back now.

When the music stopped, Kendall pressed the button again. The familiar notes of the Brahms' lullaby brought Kendall back to the day of Hope's birth.

"I'm concerned about the tracings," the delivery nurse had said, "but Dr. Schorr is on her way in."

"Is everything okay? I feel fine." With the epidural running, Kendall was numb from the waist down.

"Where is the doctor?" Troy asked.

"I've been filling her in on Kendall's status. She's well aware."

"Shouldn't she be here?"

A flash of uncertainty crossed the nurse's face before she turned away. She brought over a little radio with a purple music note on the front and tucked it next to Kendall's belly. A sweet lullaby filled the room. "This will help your baby stay calm."

Kendall wasn't sure why the nurse wanted to calm her baby down. And where was Dr. Schorr? Something didn't seem right.

Humming the *lullaby and goodnight* melody, the nurse changed the IV bag, then typed away at the computer.

A drumbeat of kicks against her ribs reassured Kendall. Her baby was strong and full of life.

"Knock, knock." A woman entered the room. She wore a short white coat and blue scrubs, her dark eyes rimmed with eyeliner. "I'm Dr. Reddy. Dr. Schorr asked me to check on you."

"Another doctor?" Troy said. "Dr. Felix is MIA, and now there's someone new? Valley Health is not scoring high marks from us."

"Mr. Carlson," Eve said, "Dr. Reddy works alongside Dr. Schorr, as a team."

Troy eyed the doctor's short coat. "You're a resident?"

"Yes, and I'm fully capable of assisting in your wife's care."

"Well, you can assist somewhere else. No one practices on my wife."

The nurse turned from the computer. "I understand your re-action, but this is a teaching hospital. Dr. Reddy is one of our best."

"You said Dr. Schorr was on her way in."

"She is," Dr. Reddy said, "but she's been held up. I'm step-ping in."

"And what if we say no?"

Kendall shot Troy a look. He could be so stubborn. With her legs completely numb, she couldn't walk out if she tried, so she was in no position to refuse help. She reached out and took his hand, hoping her touch would bring him down a notch. "Let's hear what Dr. Reddy has to say."

He opened his mouth to protest but then thought better of it.

"Thank you." Dr. Reddy put on a pair of gloves. "Dr. Schorr would like me to do an exam. To figure out why the baby's heart tracings have been so erratic."

"I don't want internal exams. It's in my birth plan."

"Your baby is in significant distress," Dr. Reddy said. "At this point, it's important I check your cervix to get a sense of what's going on."

Kendall sighed. "All right."

Dr. Reddy lifted Kendall's gown and inserted two fingers. As the doctor wiggled her fingers around, Kendall focused on her expertly-shaped eyebrows, a set of parallel frown lines emerging between them.

Kendall squeezed Troy's hand. "What is it?"

The doctor recovered quickly. "Nearly fully dilated. Moving along nicely. Be back in a few."

Why had she left in such a hurry? Something had her worried, but what? The beeping of the heart monitor accelerated.

"Where did she go?" Troy asked. "Fully dilated means it's time to push. Enough with all the delays."

Kendall took a breath, trying to slow her racing heart. Eve organized basins, clamps, and bulb syringes on a draped tray. She poured water from a plastic container into a blue basin and added a pair of scissors and a pile of gauze.

"Sounds like we're ready," Eve broke down the bottom of the bed and fit the stirrup attachments into the holders on each side, helping Kendall lift her useless legs into the stirrups.

The monitor alarm sounded, and Eve looked over at it. The line on the screen dipped way down and stayed there for a long time.

"What's that?" Troy asked.

"The baby's heart rate is down. The doctor will take a look. Make sure it's safe for you to start pushing."

Troy paced by the bed. "What's the alternative?"

"If it's necessary, we'll recommend a C-section. To get the baby out more quickly."

Troy's face paled. For all his bravado, a simple paper cut made him queasy.

"It's a routine procedure. We do it all the time. You can stand by her head and watch."

Troy sat down and hung his head between his knees.

Kendall looked to Eve for help. "He doesn't have to, right?"

"No, whatever works for you."

Dr. Reddy rushed back in, her previous confidence gone. Her smooth ponytail was now mussed, and the frown lines between her eyes had returned. Kendall felt a warm rush from her pelvis. Red blossomed between her legs, spreading quickly on the white sheets.

Troy stood up. He looked down at the stain and began to sway. "I'm not feeling so good."

"Why don't you have a seat?" Eve placed her hand firmly on Troy's shoulder and lowered him back down.

An alarm shrieked. "There's been a change of plans," Dr. Reddy said. "You have a prolapsed umbilical cord. Your baby's not getting enough oxygen. We have to do a C-section."

"I can't push?"

"Pushing will make things worse." The doctor removed the stirrups, climbed onto the bed, and positioned herself between Kendall's legs. "I'm going to do something a bit unusual."

The shriek of the alarm pierced Kendall's eardrums. "What's happening?"

"The baby's head is pressing on the cord. I need to relieve the compression." She slid her fingers back in and pushed hard, the pressure causing a deep ache in Kendall's pelvis. After a moment, the alarm quieted.

Troy stood up quickly. "This is insane. I've never heard..." His eyes rolled back in his head. Eve lunged to grab his arm, but she wasn't fast enough. He collapsed to the ground.

"Call a code," Dr. Reddy said.

"Is he okay?" Kendall sobbed.

"He'll be fine," Eve said. "We need to focus on you right now."

"I need to push."

Dr. Schorr rushed into the room. "I'm here now, and I'm going to take good care of you," she said, short of breath. Kendall had never been so relieved to see someone she barely knew.

Eve grabbed the phone on the wall and paged the code team overhead. She then knelt and placed two fingers on Troy's neck.

A voice came over the hospital intercom. "Code blue, Labor and Delivery, 6th floor. Code blue, Labor and Delivery, 6th floor."

Dr. Schorr unlocked the brakes and pushed the bed to the door. "Let's roll. There's no time to spare."

"What about Troy?" Kendall asked.

"Nurse Marcus will attend to him," Jess said. "We need to get you in for surgery. Dr. Reddy will ride with you. To make sure the baby gets blood flow."

In the hallway, the code team rushed past them. "Second room on the left," Dr. Reddy shouted from the stretcher.

The overhead lights in the operating room hurt Kendall's eyes. When the anesthesiologist helped her move from the bed to the table, Dr. Reddy moved with her, crawling on her knees. An oxygen mask came down over her face, and a blue curtain rose up from her neck. All Kendall could see was the anesthesia machine. Dread bubbled up in her throat.

"It won't be long now," the anesthesiologist said.

Dr. Reddy was still between Kendall's legs, her fingers pushing her insides against her pelvic bones. Kendall gasped as pain shot through her belly, followed by violent pulling and tugging.

"It hurts," she said.

"It'll be quick," the anesthesiologist said. "The epidural isn't as effective as a spinal."

Kendall didn't understand. She was scared and in pain, and her husband was out of commission, missing the birth of their child.

"Anita, are you okay under there?" Dr. Schorr said.

"I'm fine," Dr. Reddy said, her voice muffled by the drape.

"I need your help here. Push the baby's head back up. Don't be afraid to use force."

"I'll try," Dr. Reddy said.

Kendall felt like her guts were being ripped open. "Ayyyyyyy, I can't take anymore."

The anesthesiologist took her hand.

"I see the head," Dr. Schorr said. "Keep going, just like that."

Biting the inside of her lip, Kendall waited for the cry.

When Dr. Schorr finally freed the baby and delivered her, the room was eerily quiet.

The anesthesiologist peered over the drape. The look on his face made Kendall want to vomit.

"What happened?" Kendall sobbed. "I need to see my baby."

"The NICU team is here," Dr. Schorr said, her voice panicky. "They're going to take good care of her."

"Why isn't she crying?" A team of doctors surrounded her baby, sharp commands flying. This wasn't the way it was meant to happen. Her baby should be lying on her chest, skin to skin, not alone on a sterile table under harsh fluorescent lights.

"I need to hold her. I'm supposed to put her on my chest. Let me hold my baby."

"Not quite yet," Dr. Schorr said.

"What about breastfeeding? For her health."

"Your baby is getting excellent care. Try to relax while we finish the surgery."

"What do I tell my husband?"

"As soon as we know more, we'll loop you in."

A loud cry brought Kendall back to her living room. It took Kendall a moment to come back to herself. Something looked different. The play mat remained flat, the lullaby music played on, and the zoo animal mobile still hung from the top. It was Hope that had changed. While Kendall had been reliving the worst day of her life, Hope had maneuvered herself onto her side and almost to her belly. She was doing it all by herself. Kendall held her breath. Even with the hours of therapy, Kendall had never thought Hope would reach this milestone. With a final effort, Hope freed her trapped arm from underneath her chest and completed the roll onto her stomach.

"You did it!" Kendall screamed. "You did it, my girl. You're going to prove everyone wrong!"

Hope lifted her head, grinning with pride.

Kendall covered Hope's face with kisses. "You're a fighter, just like your mama. I'll never let you give up." Kendall scooped Hope up and twirled her around the room. Hope tilted her head up to the ceiling, giggled, and released more O-shaped noises. It was a small step, but exactly the win Kendall needed right now.

Chapter Thirty-Five

ABE

"Dr. Schorr, thank you for sharing the details of Hope's delivery. Very illuminating, indeed. Now I'd like to hone in on the medical record."

The doctor finger-combed her hair. Something about the motion gave Abe a sense of déjà vu. Yes, he'd seen her photo on the hospital website, but that wasn't it. He tried to shake the feeling away and focus. Two hours into the deposition, Abe was feeling pretty good. To his surprise, the doctor had been fairly forthcoming. Always a tough adversary, Angela Caputo instructed her clients to tell the truth. Abe appreciated that about her. The less bullshit, the better. Unfortunately, Dr. Schorr's sob story could be a stumbling block. If the case went to court, the jury might feel sorry for the well-meaning doctor who'd faced an impossible choice. The jury wanted to root for someone, to empathize with the human being on the stand. Kendall, holding Hope on her lap, had an automatic advantage from the get-go, but that didn't mean Dr. Schorr was down for the count. Abe needed to keep his guard up.

"In your answers, you explained why the delivery was delayed until 10:47 p.m. However, the chart seems to have some gaps."

Dr. Schorr's eyes widened. Abe had to tread lightly. If he came down too hard, he would come across as a jerk.

"What's the question, counselor?" Angela said.

"The question is, why didn't you document your interpretation of the tracings?"

"I'm not sure what you're asking," Dr. Schorr said.

The doctor was stalling, but Abe would give her a pass. Maybe if he gave her enough rope, she would hang herself.

"In your testimony, you attributed the concerning fetal tracings to the magnesium treatments. Is that correct?"

"Yes, that was my conclusion."

"But in Kendall Carlson's chart, I see no mention of this." Putting on his reading glasses, Abe pretended to peruse the notes. He knew full well where this information resided, but he wanted to give the doctor time to stew.

Dr. Schorr grabbed a tissue. "I'm sure it's in there somewhere."

Abe flipped over pages, ostensibly searching for said note. He wanted to draw out this key point. Juries didn't take well to liars. Licking his index finger for effect, Abe took his time paging through the pile of printouts, allowing the seconds to tick away. She should be the one to break the silence.

"I think it might be towards the end," she said.

"When did you document your thoughts on the erratic tracings? Before or after your little jaunt?"

"Objection," Angela said. "Your sarcastic musings are out of line."

"Fine, fine. I'm trying to jog your client's memory. Dr. Schorr, please tell us. This information needs to go on record."

Dr. Schorr used a tissue to blot her forehead, her eyes darting around the room. "I... I wrote a short note about it."

"You did?" He flipped over to the doctor's addendum. "Ahh, are you referring to the addendum you put in the chart?"

"Yes," Dr. Schorr whispered.

"I need you to speak up," the court reporter said.

"Yes, that one."

"This note is time-stamped September 19, 2022. Nearly a full two years after Hope Carlson's birth. Is that correct?"

"Yes."

"So, nearly two years after the event, you took it upon yourself to make an addendum?"

"Objection," Angela said. "Badgering the witness. My client has had enough with your antics."

"With all due respect, Dr. Schorr, why did you write an additional note in Kendall Carlson's chart so long after the event in question?"

"I know it's not typical, but I felt the need to explain my actions. When I checked on Kendall Carlson in the late afternoon, she was doing fine. Her vitals were stable, and she was comfortable. Nurse Marcus mentioned the fetal tracings in passing, and I attributed them to the magnesium therapy. I must have forgotten to document my assessment."

"You forgot?"

"It slipped my mind at the time."

"And just to be clear, Dr. Schorr, this note was added to the chart on September 19th, 2022." Abe turned to the court reporter. "Remind me, what day was Dr. Schorr served with the papers for this suit?"

The reporter scrolled back through her notes. "Counselor, the papers were served on September 18th."

"Thank you for that clarification." Abe had hit nearly every point on his list. With his ball squarely on the green, he needed just one more clean putt. "Now, I'd be remiss if I skipped over one last topic. My client has recently shared a crucial piece of information with me. It has come to my attention that Dr. Schorr has been sending anonymous presents to Hope Carlson. Is that true, Dr. Schorr?"

Dr. Schorr's face froze. She began coughing, and Angela handed her a bottle of water.

Abe waited, knowing he'd lined up his shot with perfection. "Whenever you're ready, Dr. Schorr."

"Um…" She coughed some more, clearly attempting to buy time.

"Have you been dropping off anonymous gifts at the Carlson home for the past two years?" When Kendall Carlson had shared that little tidbit with him last week, Abe had felt like he'd won the lottery. It was just the shocker he needed to fortify his case.

Dr. Schorr looked at Angela, perhaps hoping for another baloney objection. Angela narrowed her eyes.

"Dr. Schorr? We're waiting."

"Yes, it's true."

"What types of gifts did you bestow on Hope Carlson?"

Dr. Schorr listed a variety of items—mobiles, puzzles, and learning toys of all sorts—and Abe let her keep going.

"And what was your reasoning? It's a bit unorthodox, to say the least."

"I'm not sure I can put it into words. I needed to do something for Hope. Something to make her life better in some small way."

Angela cleared her throat, signaling her client to zip it.

Abe approached the doctor, leaning down to her level. "So, you're saying you felt the need to buy expensive things for a child you'd irreparably harmed? If that's not an admission of guilt, I'm not sure what is."

"Objection, harassment. Attorney Silverberg, give my client some space."

Abe raised both hands in the air, palms out. "Fair enough. Let's talk about your most recent gift." He checked his notes. "It arrived on September 26th, one week after you were served with this lawsuit. Is that correct?"

"Sounds right."

"Please share with the court what you chose to give Hope, on the occasion of her second birthday."

"An adaptive tricycle. I couldn't let her birthday pass by. I just couldn't."

"It's quite generous of you to spend your hard-earned money on gifts, Dr. Schorr. I'm sure the jury will be impressed. That will be all for today."

The court reporter lifted her hands from the keys, her mouth open in shock. No doubt about it, Abe had sunk his ball into the cup.

"Not so fast." Angela stood. "I have a few points to cover before we adjourn. Dr. Schorr, please explain why you felt it necessary to place an addendum in Kendall Carlson's chart."

"After I examined Mrs. Carlson for the second time around 5 p.m., I immediately received a call about my cat. Normally, I would have written a note to explain my thought process."

"But you didn't have time. Is that correct?"

"Yes, that's right."

"Thank you for the clarification," Angela said. "I have one more question about Kendall Carlson's birth plan. Please fill us in on what that entailed."

Abe's high from his last two lines of questioning dissipated in an instant. He'd tried to gloss over this detail earlier in the deposition, but Angela wasn't letting him get away with it.

"She opted to decline cervical checks."

"What did that mean for her delivery?"

"Checking cervical dilation is an important part of perinatal care. It helps us assess the stage of labor and decide how to care for mom and baby in the best possible way."

"So, by the patient's own choice, you were missing a vital piece of information. Is that a fair summary?"

"Objection, providing testimony," Abe said. He couldn't let this nonsense continue any longer.

"Fine," Angela said. "No further questions."

Chapter Thirty-Six

JESS

Jess stood up. The door was only a few feet away, but she wasn't sure how to make her body move. Angela was speaking with the court reporter, so she was no help. It was over? The nerve of this attorney to end the deposition with two bombshells, acting as if he was above it all. And Angela's attempt to repair the damage hadn't gone far enough. The addendum was no big deal, the goal to clarify her thoughts rather than cover anything up. And the gifts. How did Kendall Carlson even know she'd been the one delivering them? Jess had been so careful, except for that one last time. Maybe that nosy neighbor had said something to her, but that still didn't make sense. Jess had been wearing sunglasses and a hat, and the neighbor didn't know her name. Picking out the perfect presents, wrapping them, and delivering them to Solano Lane had become part of Jess's routine. She couldn't help herself. On the days Jess gave Hope a present, she felt lighter. The guilt was always there, but on those days, she breathed a little easier.

Walking to the door, Jess's feet throbbed with each step. In the waiting area, Eve sat in a chair, her head buried in a notebook. Jess had been barely keeping it together, but the sight of her old friend sent her into hysterics. She gasped loudly, and then broke down in sobs, all the emotion she'd kept bottled up during the deposition escaping with her cries.

"I didn't mean for any of this. I didn't…" Jess dropped to her knees at Eve's feet. "I'm a good doctor. You know that."

Eve met her eyes for a moment. Maybe this lawsuit didn't need to tear everything apart.

A man seated at Eve's side shook his head. "She's not at liberty—"

"I can't talk to you," Eve said.

"I know, but—"

"Our cases are separate. It could damage my case."

"That's quite enough," her attorney said. "My client needs to focus on her own deposition."

Jess struggled to get up, her mind reeling. Had her attorney convinced her the tragic delivery was all Jess's fault? Was there anything she could do to stop Eve from pointing the finger at her?

Angela exited the conference room, grabbed Jess by the arm, and led her into the hallway. "What do you think you're doing?"

"I'm just talking," Jess said. "We've been friends for over fifteen years."

"I don't care if you're twins separated at birth. As far as I'm concerned, she's dead to you. If I catch you speaking to her again, you'll have to find yourself a new lawyer. Those questions raised a lot of red flags. You haven't been honest with me, or with yourself. All this sneaking around doesn't paint you in a good light."

"I wasn't… I didn't. I can't process this right now. Drew is waiting for me outside." The hallway seemed narrow, the ceiling much too low. If she didn't get out of here soon, she'd be crushed between the walls.

"I'll call you first thing tomorrow," Angela said. "We need to come up with a plan B."

O   O   O

On the car ride home, Jess remained silent. Drew peppered her with questions, but she wasn't ready to share her experience. The claustrophobic feel of the room, the blinding sunlight in her eyes, how the Carlson's attorney had morphed from a man with kind eyes into a vicious pit bull in an instant. If she gave voice to any of these things, it would become too real.

At home, Drew helped Jess up to their bedroom so the kids wouldn't see her bloodshot eyes and tear-stained face. The kids knew the basics of the lawsuit, but it was nebulous to them. They had no idea what was at stake.

Drew locked the bedroom door with a click.

"Jessica, you need to talk to me. I know you think this is all about you, but it's not."

Jess crawled into bed, burying her face in the pillow. She couldn't meet his eyes.

"You can't hide from me. What happened in there?"

"It'll be fine."

"Fine? Come on. Tell it to me straight."

She turned over onto her side to look at him. "I mean, I guess it could have gone better."

He sat down and swept the hair off her face. "You don't need to pretend with me. You know that."

"It was awful, Drew. Worse than I could have ever imagined. The attorney was all nicey-nice with the small talk, and then he changed in an instant. Like Dr. Jekyll and Mr. Hyde. He went straight for the jugular."

"What did he say?"

"He'd done his research. He twisted the facts to make me look evil. And I didn't even see it coming. I answered his questions as best I could, but he backed me into a corner."

"What do you mean?"

Jess grabbed a tissue from the nightstand and blew her nose. "He kept highlighting ways I'd failed. Nitpicking the things I should have done, places I should have been, decisions I should have made. I'm a good doctor, even if I sometimes make mistakes. But that attorney made it seem the opposite, as if I'm selfish, focused more on myself than on my patients." Her mind flashed back to the way the attorney had made her gift-giving seem strange and pathologic. She wanted Hope to have toys that helped her grow up to reach her potential. Was that so wrong?

She briefly thought about telling Drew, but then thought better of it. After that grueling deposition, she didn't have the energy.

Drew laid down next to Jess and pulled her close. "It sounds super stressful. I'm sure you did your best. That's all you can ask for."

Jess pushed him away. She didn't deserve comfort right now. "I'm not sure my best is good enough. I'm scared, Drew."

He cleared his throat. "You have an excellent attorney. I'm sure she'll have a plan of attack from here on out. Don't lose confidence in her. This is what she does."

"I can't help thinking about what could happen. These cases can have huge payouts. What if I lose? What if the settlement is higher than my insurance limits? They could go after everything —our cars, our house, the college fund. All because of one bad day." Jess hiccupped, a new round of tears pricking the corners of her eyes.

"You're getting ahead of yourself. We need to hear what your attorney has to say. I'm sure there's a way to spin this."

Turning over onto her belly, Jess screamed into the pillow. "It isn't fair! It isn't fucking fair. I give everything to my job. One mistake and it can all be stolen away."

"You don't know that."

"I can't imagine the hospital will look favorably on a multi-million-dollar payout."

"Don't give up so easily. You're an amazing doctor and your patients love you. You think I would have fallen for a heartless wretch?" He tickled her ribs, trying to get her to snap out of her funk. "Can we agree to table the *oh, woe is me* act until we know more about the options?"

"My mind keeps going in circles. They're making it seem like I don't care, that I'm cold and unfeeling, but nothing could be further from the truth. I think about Hope Carlson every single day."

"You do?"

"When I'm in the shower, brushing my teeth, watching the news. In clinic, at the hospital, during surgery, even in my dreams. That delivery will haunt me for the rest of my life. No matter what happens with the trial, I will never be free."

"Fixating on the past isn't going to help now. You can only move forward."

There was a knock on the bedroom door. "Mom?" Vox said. "Dad? What's going on?"

"All good." Drew said. "We'll be down for dinner in a few. How about Simply Thai? Can you put in our usual order with Uber Eats?"

"Got it." Vox's steps faded away down the hallway.

Drew offered his hand to help Jess up. He took her chin in his hand. "I suggest you change your lens. Instead of perseverating on what went wrong, focus on what you've done right. For your sanity and mine, it's the only way to get through this." He wiped tears from her cheeks with his thumbs.

"This is terrible," Jess said. "I never thought I could feel so low. Like everything I've worked for my whole life could disappear in a flash. I feel like such a failure, letting people down at every turn. I'm so glad my mom isn't alive to see this, that my dad doesn't understand. It would be too much for them, and for me."

Drew placed a soft kiss on her forehead. "They would love you no matter what, you know that. And you're stuck with me. I'm not going anywhere."

Chapter Thirty-Seven

KENDALL

Kendall slipped Posy under Hope's arm and tucked the blanket around her feet. After turning over for the first time, Hope needed her afternoon nap even more than usual. Turning on the music on her mobile, Kendall leaned over the railing and placed a gentle kiss on Hope's cheek. Kendall needed to get some work done, but she couldn't stop thinking about how the deposition was going. Was Dr. Schorr owning up to how things had unfolded in labor and delivery? Had Abe confronted Dr. Schorr about the anonymous gifts? When would he call with an update? To distract herself, Kendall stood in front of the shelf of photo albums in the living room. Honoring her mother's tradition, Kendall had made an album for each year of Hope's life. It had seemed like a good idea, an excuse to relive happy memories and be proud of her child's accomplishments, but her lived experience had proven more bittersweet.

Choosing the purple album, Kendall opened to the pages filled with shots from Hope's first year. Taking a seat on the stiff-backed sofa, her heart sank. Instead of the typical first photo of Mom and Dad holding a newborn swaddled in a pink and blue blanket, Hope was in an incubator in the neonatal ICU. Plastic tubes adhered to her sunken cheek with shiny plastic tape, and her eyes were covered with white cardboard patches. Eerie, blue light made Hope look otherworldly, almost alien. Though she'd seen this picture hundreds of times, it never failed to make Kendall feel guilty. What kind of mother would allow her baby to lie alone in a hospital on the other side of town? Needing skin-to-skin contact with her mother, Hope had been offered only a cold, plastic incubator. Of course, Kendall had had no other choice. Recovering from a major operation, Kendall wouldn't have been allowed to leave the hospital, even if she'd tried. Those first few days, Troy went to Phoenix Children's every day and reported back on Hope's condition, but Kendall wasn't clear what he did during those visits. Did he question the medical team about Hope's care? Did he ask to cradle the baby, talk to her, telling her Mommy and Daddy loved her beyond measure? Kendall couldn't picture Troy doing any of these things.

When Kendall turned the page, a black and white ultrasound printout fell to the carpet. Picking up the paper, Kendall looked at the grainy image of her baby's face, her little nose and lips outlined by amniotic fluid, not a gray, shapeless blob, but a real baby with a face and arms and legs. Underneath the picture, Lucy was written in Sharpie marker. After they'd found out the sex of the baby at twenty weeks, they'd gone round in circles arguing about names, finally settling on Lucy. It was trendy, yet classic. Cute, but sophisticated. The perfect name for their perfect girl. Kendall's thoughts drifted back to the day she was discharged from the hospital.

Kendall's postpartum nurse knocked on the door. "You okay in there?"

"Yes, almost done." The nurse had been her savior in the four days after the C-section. She happened to have a five-year-old son with special needs. Her honest words and touching stories gave Kendall courage to face the road ahead.

Kendall used the bars on both sides of the toilets to help herself stand. Her belly sore and bruised, she flushed and watched a bowl full of blood clots disappear down the drain. No one had warned her how much she would bleed, or that her breasts would become as hard as baseballs, or that the pills they offered would barely touch the pain. There was so much she hadn't known.

"Looking so much better." The nurse guided her back into bed. "Being home will be good for you."

Troy sat in a chair by the window, his attention on his laptop.

The nurse pulled the blanket up over Kendall's legs and used the remote to turn off the TV. "When you have a minute, I have some parental business I need you to take care of."

"What's that?"

"We can't let you check out without completing the birth certificate." She grabbed a clipboard from the tray table and presented it to Kendall. "It's hospital policy. No more procrastinating."

"Troy?"

"Huh?" he said, his eyes still on the screen.

"Please help me with this. We need to pick a new name." With the baby fighting for her life in the NICU, their chosen name no longer seemed to fit.

He closed the computer and pulled his chair up to the bedside.

"I'll leave you two to hash it out." The nurse closed the door behind her.

Kendall propped the clipboard against her thighs. Their names, address, and phone number were simple, but her hand still trembled, her handwriting wobbly and uneven. The three blank spots at the top of the form stared back at her. Child's first name, middle name, and last name.

Troy pointed to the last one. "This one is easy."

Kendall wrote CARLSON in all capital letters. Maybe once she'd filled in that section, she'd be struck with inspiration. Lucy was a fine name, but her baby needed one that would give her courage and propel her to face the inevitable challenges coming her way. But what? Faith? Too religious. Patience? No good nicknames. Joy? Too happy.

"Maybe we should stick with Lucy," Troy said.

"There's got to be a better one."

"Nothing's coming to mind."

"I've got it." Kendall said. "I don't know why I didn't think of this one earlier."

Kendall moved the pen to the first blank space. She wrote the letter H and looked to Troy for approval. He nodded as she finished the four-letter name. Troy took the pen and wrote the middle name, a genuine smile spreading across his face for the first time since their baby was born.

"Hope Lucy Carlson," Kendall said.

"It's got a nice ring to it."

"It couldn't be more perfect."

Kendall's phone startled her from her thoughts. She looked at the screen. It was Attorney Silverberg. Was the deposition over already? She took a breath and steeled herself for his report.

"Hello?" Kendall's voice wavered.

"Good afternoon, Mrs. Carlson. Abe Silverberg here. Is now a good time to talk?"

His confident voice made Kendall breathe easier. He wouldn't sound so assured if the deposition had gone off course.

"I wanted to report back to you as soon as we finished."

"I appreciate that. I've been waiting on pins and needles."

"Completely understandable. So, which would you like first, the good news or the bad news?"

Kendall looked at her watch. If she had to hear bad news, she wanted Troy here with her, but he wouldn't be home for another three hours. She'd have to deal with it on her own, as usual. "The bad, I guess. Break it to me gently."

"Unfortunately, I don't think the nurse angle is going to pan out. She responds well to questions, and her answers made sense. And ultimately, the doctor was responsible for overseeing your care. Chasing after Eve Marcus is a dead end."

"Oh…" Kendall's mood careened back toward the ground. She had liked the idea of naming more than one defendant, upping the chance of success.

"Don't worry," Abe said. "Defendants are often dropped. It takes time to figure out where the crux of the case lies. You have to dig in a few places before you strike gold. The hospital is still on the hook, for sure."

"And what about Dr. Schorr?"

"Her deposition went well. I lined up the traps, and she kept falling into them, one after another."

"That's the good news?" Kendall knew she should be ecstatic, but she was tentative. She changed her position on the sofa to relieve a cramp in her hip.

"Sure is. The deposition is a major step. A bellwether of sorts, to give us a sense of where the case is going."

"And where is that?" Kendall thought back to the last time she'd seen Dr. Schorr, the day she'd delivered the tricycle. In the month and a half since that day, Kendall had gone from confusion to anger to something closer to empathy. On even the best of days, working motherhood could be a shit show, and Kendall almost felt sorry for her. Had Dr. Schorr made mistakes? Medicine was a black hole, but Kendall had to assume so. Should Dr. Schorr pay for them for the rest of her life? Troy thought so, but Kendall wasn't so sure. She clearly felt remorse for what had happened the day Hope was born. The gifts on their doorstep spoke louder than words. Kendall also couldn't stop thinking about her birth plan and how much that decision had changed the course of the delivery.

"I'd be shocked if Angela Caputo pushes this one forward. Taking it to court would be a suicide mission."

"That's good to hear, I guess."

"We should know more in the next few weeks."

Kendall couldn't believe she'd have to wait that long. The sooner this lawsuit was over, the better.

Chapter Thirty-Eight

ABE

Late for the first meeting of Torah class, Abe rushed through the synagogue doors. He'd planned to arrive earlier, but Bea had refused to do her business, turning in circles without doing the deed. He jogged down the hall, peeking in each classroom to find the right one. With his head turned, he collided with someone. The woman fell to the floor, the contents of her purse scattering over the linoleum.

"I am so sorry," he said. "Are you okay?"

The woman looked up, her expression of annoyance changing to one of recognition. "Attorney Silverberg?"

"Do we know each other?" Right away, Abe wanted to take the words back. For Pete's sake. It was Dr. Schorr, the woman he was trying to take for all she was worth. Talk about awkward. He reached down to give her a hand.

"Jessica Rubin." She accepted his hand, stood, and dusted off the back of her shorts. "I mean Schorr."

That's why she'd looked so familiar at the deposition. She'd sat next to him on the evening of Risa's Yahrzeit. "I didn't expect to run into you here. No pun intended."

Abe forced a laugh and bent down to collect her belongings. A tube of lip gloss, a small notepad, and a fidget toy shaped like a butterfly. Turning the toy over in his hand, he pushed a few of the squishy silicone buttons. Surprisingly satisfying. Was this another gift for Hope? This lady was making things too easy for him.

Dr. Schorr opened her bag for Abe to put her things back inside. "I'm picking up my child from bat mitzvah lessons. I'm not dressed to see opposing counsel." She motioned to her frayed shorts and flip-flops.

"Well, again, I truly apologize. I have to get to class now." Abe started down the hall, relieved to escape this awkward interaction.

"Attorney Silverberg?"

He turned back.

"Can I ask you something?"

Abe looked around, praying someone would rescue him. Where was Fran? He needed to find some way to extricate himself from this situation.

"Do I have a case?" Her voice was meek, nothing like the self-assured physician Abe had deposed two weeks ago.

"I can't speak about legal matters here."

"Please, I need to know. For the sake of my family."

"That's for your own counsel to answer. Attorney Caputo is quite experienced."

"For some reason, I trust you. Even though you were ruthless at the deposition. Scary even."

When people called Abe a bulldog, it usually made him proud, but Dr. Schorr's comment brought on a wave of guilt. Though he'd been doing his job, and doing it well, he'd made this woman feel small and incompetent. Abe had to say something. But what? A classroom door opened and a group of kids spilled out. One of them stopped next to Dr. Schorr.

"Only two more months of this trash," the child said. "They don't even let us use our phones in class."

"Vox, you know Dad and I want you to finish out the year."

"Whatever. Can we go now?"

"We're going to visit Grandpa at the nursing home. For his birthday." Dr. Schorr handed over her keys. "Go wait in the car. I'll be there in a minute."

Another wave of guilt crashed over Abe. Dr. Schorr was a human being with a husband, children, and an ailing parent, and the lawsuit was placing a rotten cherry on the top of her stress sundae. Even if Dr. Schorr had played a part in causing Hope's disability, she was still a human being. Usually, Abe didn't have trouble siding solely with his client, but he felt a kinship with Dr. Schorr. After all, he knew what it was like to juggle work and home life, feeling like you were never doing enough in either place. For the years when Risa was sick, he'd tried to keep up with his work, but his thoughts often strayed to the tragic unfairness of her diagnosis and challenges of caring for her day-to-day. It was hard to focus on the tragedy of others when there was one unfolding right in his own home. He swallowed a lump in his throat. Though his heart went out to Dr. Schorr, he still couldn't give her legal advice.

"I understand you're in a difficult position," he said, "and that's where your attorney comes in. I'm sure she'll—"

Dr. Schorr interrupted. "It's all so sad. I know I played a part, but I don't want to give up without a fight. It's not the way I'm programmed."

"Abe?" Fran waved at him from a classroom doorway. "We're meeting in here."

Abe nodded.

"Listen, I know this seems overwhelming," he said to Dr. Schorr, "but it will be over before you know it."

The doctor looked at him, her eyes glassy. With any common sense, she'd be able to read between the lines. There was no reason to drag this thing out any longer than necessary.

Chapter Thirty-Nine
JESS

In the car, Vox nodded their head to the beat of a monotonous song. Jess put her hands over her ears. "What the hell is this?"

She wasn't sure what to make of her conversation with Attorney Silverberg, and this noise wasn't helping her think. When he said *it'll be over before you know it*, was he implying she should settle? She'd always been a Type A personality, so admitting failure didn't come easily, not to mention the possible effect on her career. Who would choose a doctor who'd lost a lawsuit? Settling would erode the hard-earned trust her patients had placed in her.

"It's Kid Cudi, Mom. You like this one."

Jess switched off the radio and put the car in reverse. "Today, I most certainly do not."

"Did that man have something to do with the lawsuit?"

"How did you know?" Jess put the car back in park. So much for shielding the kids from the lawsuit.

"Your face turned red. I could tell something was up."

"Yes, just a little chat. It's all good." Jess hoped this vague explanation would fly, that Vox wouldn't ask more questions she wouldn't know how to answer.

"Are you sure? It didn't seem so good."

Jess put her hand over Vox's. "Don't worry. I'm trying to figure things out. Listen, before we stop to visit Grandpa, how about we take a short hike on the Javelina Trail? We both could use some fresh air."

"Okay, I guess."

Vox used to love hiking with Jess. They'd set out together for at least three or four miles, stopping to smell wildflowers along the side of the trail or analyze animal footprints in the dust. Lately, Vox had been full of excuses—a paper to write, cookie recipes to test, *Great British Baking Show* episodes to catch up on—so today, Jess would take the *I guess* and run with it. If she waited for enthusiasm, she'd never spend time with her children anymore.

At the trailhead, Jess snagged the last parking spot, a sign from the universe. This is where they were supposed to be right now. Jess hopped out of the car and sat on the open trunk to put on her hiking boots.

Once she was all set, she handed Vox a plastic water bottle from the back. "You don't have your CamelBak, so we won't go too far."

"Ugh, Mom. Single-use plastic is the worst."

"Can we skip the lecture about sustainable materials? Just this once?"

Vox slammed the car door for effect.

They set off on the trail, enjoying the first several minutes of flat terrain. Jess wanted to talk with Vox about the approaching mitzvah, all the things left to plan. After KC had sent her a cryptic email begging off the job, Jess had taken on the task. Working a full-time job, dealing with the lawsuit, and planning a big party had been no easy feat. But now with the deposition finally behind her, Jess should have more time to plan Vox's special day.

A cloud passed over the sun, giving them a brief respite. Jess pointed at the sky. "Look at that one. What do you see?" Jess hoped the familiar game would break the ice, get Vox to open up to her.

Vox took a sip of water. "I don't know."

"Okay, I'll start. I see Papa Smurf on a jet ski." Jess made up the most outlandish thing she could imagine, trying to coax a smile.

"Are you serious?"

Jess laughed. "No, I just wanted to see if you would go for it."

"It looks like a marshmallow man to me. All puffy and chubby."

"Sounds delicious. Add some graham crackers and chocolate, and we're all set. Maybe we could have s'mores at your affair. That would be fun, wouldn't it?"

Vox's expression soured. "I don't know, Mom. This big party isn't sounding so great anymore."

"What do you mean? We've been planning it forever."

"I know, but things are different now."

"Like what?" Jess ticked through the tasks she'd accomplished since KC had gone AWOL—selected the menu with the caterer, met with the florist to pick arrangements for the bimah, and chosen invitations that didn't read too girlie. "I'm sure we can make it work. We've come too far to turn back now. Do you know how much time I've put into this party? I mean, the planner quit for who knows what reason, and I was left to pick up the pieces, like I didn't already have enough on my plate between Maddie applying to college and you coming out and Grandpa in the nursing home. I mean—"

"Mom!" Vox placed a hand on Jess's shoulder. "Take a breath. You're not listening to me. I'm not sure I want to come out while reading Torah. It's too much all at once."

Jess pictured Vox at the synagogue podium in a suit, tie, and shiny oxfords, their short hair parted to one side and combed flat against their head, Great Aunt Esther saying, "Why isn't she wearing a dress?" in a stage whisper while Vox's classmates snickered in the back row.

"I want it to be special," Vox said. "I don't want my gender reveal to ruin it. Too confusing, you know?"

"But we've already booked the venue and the DJ and the caterer." If Jess canceled now, she wouldn't be able to get back her deposits. She was in no position to throw money down the drain, especially with the lawsuit looming over her.

A man jogged past them down the trail, his tank top drenched in sweat.

"I know, but it's not what I want. Not anymore. I want to read the Torah and give my speech as me, as my authentic self, without anyone questioning what I'm wearing or what pronouns I prefer."

Jess started up the first incline, taking a moment to collect her thoughts. Her first instinct was to tell Vox they were being selfish, that the milestone was about the whole family and not just them, but she held her tongue. It was much more complicated than that. Jess hadn't thought of it as a coming out before, but of course it would be. The day would have a double meaning for Vox—an important Jewish milestone and a day to be out in the open as who they wanted to be. She owed it to her child to hear them out.

They reached the first small summit and sat down on the large, flat rock where they liked to take a pit stop. When Vox was little, Jess would pull out a juice box and a granola bar from her backpack, and they would sit for a few minutes to recharge. She took a moment to appreciate the vista now, the houses in the subdivisions below tiny compared to the jagged mountains in the distance. No matter how many times she'd been here, Jess never tired of the view.

"So, what do you suggest we do?" Jess asked. "If you don't want a party, then what *do* you want?"

"I have another idea."

Jess uncapped her water bottle. "Lay it on me."

"Let's do it in the backyard."

The second Jess heard the idea, a feeling of calm overcame her. Because they'd done a big party for Maddie, she'd felt Vox needed the same thing. Big on equity, she and Drew wanted to treat both children the same, but their children were different in so many ways. One size didn't always fit all.

"Asa Kellerman did theirs like that," Vox said. "They said it was the best experience."

"Who's Asa Kellerman?"

"A friend from the teen support group Claire connected me with. They're nonbinary and pansexual."

Jess had no idea what pansexual meant, but asking questions now would derail the conversation. "What are you picturing?"

"Just close friends and family. People who know me well."

"So, service at the synagogue and party at the house?"

"No, the whole thing at home."

Jess wasn't sure what that would look like. "The rabbi and cantor too?" she asked. Maybe their idea wasn't so crazy. If Vox wanted to keep things simple, forgo the big party, who was Jess to stand in the way? It would make everything so much easier. Jess pictured deleting the to-do list, fantasized about pressing the little garbage can icon and watching the list of tasks disappear into the ether.

"Of course," Vox said. "And I want to call it a B-mitzvah. That's the non-gendered term."

"B-mitzvah?" After the name change and new pronouns, Jess could roll with this change, but she'd never heard this word. "That's really a thing?"

"Yeah. Some places are using it for everyone now. To be inclusive."

"Okay, let me talk to Dad about changing the plans." It was a shift, but it could work. The caterer and DJ could come to the backyard, so she'd only lose the deposit on the venue. Jess stood up. "Ready to go see Grandpa?"

They started back down the trail. Jess gave herself a mental pat on the back. She'd let go of her own expectations and listened to her child. Maybe she'd inherited that from her mother. Rhonda Schorr had always made time to sit and listen. A pang of grief shot through Jess. She couldn't believe her mother was really gone, that she wouldn't be there for Vox's big day. Jess wasn't sure her father would be there either. She'd see how he was doing today and decide.

As Vox walked along the trail, their steps seemed lighter. Clearly the pressure of the B-mitzvah had been weighing on them.

"Mom, look!" Vox pointed up the hill. Near the top, there was a large dark form, partially obscured by bushes. Vox took out their phone, zooming in to get a clear shot. Jess recognized the creature immediately. It was the bear who had been haunting her dreams. He ambled uphill, growing smaller and smaller until he reached the summit and disappeared over the ridge.

"I got it." Vox said. "I'm going to put this on TikTok."

As they made their way back to the car, Jess couldn't stop thinking about the new plan. It made so much sense. In the comfort of their home, Vox would be able to celebrate the milestone their way, free of pressure to conform to others' expectations.

Now she would need to get Drew on board. He liked to stick with traditions. When Maddie was up on the bimah, Drew had been overcome with emotion. Jess would have to convince him a ceremony in their backyard would be just as special, a unique experience for their second snowflake.

○   ○   ○

"Happy birthday, Dad." Jess placed the vase of flowers on the window ledge. Her father had never been big on celebrating birthdays, but Jess couldn't allow the day to pass unacknowledged.

"Birthday?" Her father gave her a blank stare from the bed. Even if he knew today's date, it wouldn't ring any bells. Since Jess had visited last month, he was even thinner, his eyes more sunken.

She took a seat in the chair next to the bed. "It's yours, Dad. November 13th."

Vox leaned over the side of the bed to give her grandfather a hug.

"Oh, how nice." His inflection made it clear he had no clue what was going on.

"I'm going to the art room," Vox said.

When Jess first moved her father here right after her mom died, she'd insisted her children visit him once a week. It didn't take long for Vox to start finding reasons to escape the room, and Maddie soon refused to come altogether. Watching the grandfather they knew disappear before their eyes was too painful, and Jess gave them a pass. It was no picnic for her either, but she felt a sense of obligation. As his daughter, she had to make sure he was well cared for, that he was fed and properly washed.

Jess watched her father pick at his eyebrows. The stone weighed heavily in her stomach again. She felt she needed to tell him about the lawsuit. Though he wouldn't understand—he barely understood anything these days—she needed to get it off her chest. And maybe his confusion would be better than the unrealistic expectations he'd strapped her with for all those years. The ones she didn't think she would ever live up to.

"I'm sorry I haven't been to visit as often, Dad. I've had a lot going on at work."

"Oh, yeah? What kind of work?"

"I'm a doctor, remember? I deliver babies."

"To a mailbox?"

Jess stifled a laugh. "No, not that kind of delivery. I help women through childbirth, make sure babies come into the world safely."

"Wowee. That's looney tunes."

"I couldn't agree more. I still love the patient care, but the academic part is a real drag. I'm not sure I can do it much longer."

"Do what?" His eyes went blank, the brief window of lucidity gone.

Even if he couldn't comprehend, Jess needed to tell her father what was going through her head.

"The academic life," she said. "It's not what I want anymore. I dread the papers and the publishing."

"I'm not sure—"

"One of my patients is suing me. I think she's going to win. This whole thing has made me take a closer look at my job. I need to make a change." This was the first time Jess had said this out loud. The lawsuit had forced her to hold a magnifying glass up to her career and figure out what was truly important. To her surprise, the admission didn't feel scary. Instead, it felt like a relief, as if she'd been carrying water on her back for a ten-mile hike and had finally stopped to take a rest. "I need to get off the treadmill. This path isn't for me anymore."

"Well, sweetheart, life's too short." He looked straight at her, fully present. The father she'd known would have been mortified to hear of her tarnished reputation. He would have pushed her to aim higher and go for the brass ring, to not be satisfied until she made full professor. So much of her father's personality had morphed with the dementia. "You do what feels right for you, not what other people expect."

"You really think so?" Jess felt tears collecting in her eyes. She hadn't known she wanted her father's blessing, but it felt like a precious gift. What next? Leaving her profession outright wasn't a possibility—someone had to pay the mortgage and college tuitions—but there were other options. Valley Health wasn't the only place to work. There were plenty of jobs that put the focus on people rather than status, that didn't require churning out journal articles and striving for titles she cared nothing about. Could she take the leap? How would it feel to step away from the career she'd worked so hard to build? She wasn't in a rush, but Jess would keep her eyes open for opportunities.

"I know so." Her father took her hand in his and rubbed his thumb over her palm. She couldn't remember him ever taking her hand before the dementia. The warmth from his touch travelled up her arm and for a moment she felt as if it might melt away the heaviness in her stomach.

Jess wiped her eyes with a tissue. "I brought you something." She reached into the paper bag at her feet and presented her father with a clear plastic container wrapped in a red bow.

"For me?" His eyes widened. It was a generous slice of cheesecake, the graham cracker crust layered with a dense layer of cheese filling and cherry topping. She helped him open the container and handed him a plastic fork.

He took a bite and slowly chewed, a dreamy smile on his face. "Good?" Jess asked.

He kept eating, creamy cheese smeared at the corner of his mouth.

"So, what are you going to do with the rest of your special day? Will they have a party for you?"

He scraped graham cracker crumbs from the bottom of the container. "Rhonda's coming. She likes to give me a birthday kiss."

"Oh, yeah?" Jess would never forget the day her mother died, the same day Hope Carlson was born. She could tell immediately from the gentle tone of the ER doctor's voice that her mother was gone. He went into an explanation about a heart attack and cardiac enzymes and too much muscle damage to recover from, but her mind went into overdrive. Still reeling from the tragedy of the Carlson delivery, she then had to arrange airline tickets, plan a funeral, and figure out how to care for her father. It was all too much. Her father recalled nothing of that day. Maybe it was better that way. The memories only prolonged the pain. A photo of her mom on the nightstand caught Jess's eye. She swallowed hard to clear the lump in her throat.

"Rhonda and I are going to the circus," he said. "She loves the flying trapeze. She holds her breath until they catch each other."

At the beginning, Jess used to correct him when he spouted nonsense, but no longer. His fantasy world seemed more satisfying than his real life.

"Sounds wonderful."

"Popcorn and candy apples."

"Delectable," Jess said.

Her father's eyes drifted closed.

Jess tossed the cheesecake container in the garbage.

"Will you give her a kiss for me?"

"Absolutely. I sure will."

In the car on the way home, Vox looked out the window, unusually quiet.

258

"You okay?" Jess asked.

"Yeah, I guess. It's hard to come here."

Jess couldn't agree more. Her father had always been so strong, so in control of everything, and now he was disappearing a little more every day. "You know he still loves you, right? Even if he's not able to say it."

"I know."

"I'm not sure he'll be able to come to your B-mitzvah. He won't know what's going on."

"I kind of figured that."

"I thought of an idea," Jess said. "I have the prayer shawl from his own bar mitzvah in the extra closet. If you want, you can wear his tallis for the service."

Vox looked over, their eyes glistening. "He can be with me in spirit. I'd like that a lot."

Chapter Forty

ABE

The social hall looked festive for the Hanukkah party, all decked out with blue and white streamers, the tables covered with blue tablecloths strewn with shiny silver gelt. Kids crowded around the platters of jelly donuts, and adults mingled in groups, holding glasses of wine, chatting and laughing. The aroma of deep-fried potatoes filled the air. Abe had always enjoyed this party, as had his children. When Ross and Eliza were young, they ate piles of latkes with applesauce until they were full to bursting. As they got older, going to synagogue on a Saturday evening hadn't been an easy sell, but this party was the one holdout.

Abe looked around for Ross and Gavin. He hadn't seen Gavin for a while. So busy with the Carlson case, it had been hard to fit in much else. He'd managed to meet Ross at the dog park a couple of times, but he was looking forward to catching up with his son-in-law. Abe spotted them and walked over.

"Hey, Dad. It's good to see you." Ross stepped forward for a genuine hug. Abe couldn't remember the last time Ross had embraced him this way. Being this close to his son felt nice.

"Happy Hanukkah," Gavin said, a broad smile covering his face.

Abe clapped Gavin on the back. "Thanks. You two are in high spirits tonight."

"We sure are," Ross said. "We have major cause for celebration. Why don't you share, Gav? It's your news."

"I got a phone call from my attorney earlier today. I've been dropped from the lawsuit."

Abe felt immediately lighter. After he'd declined to get involved, Abe had avoided asking questions about the case. "You must be so relieved."

Ross pulled Gavin in for a kiss. "Just in time for Hanukkah."

An upbeat song played through the wall speakers, the lyrics about believing in miracles and coming out of the darkness into the light. Ross shimmied, bumping his hip playfully into his husband's. Clearly, Gavin's lawsuit had been casting a shadow over their lives.

"Let's get some food," Gavin said. "I haven't eaten well in months."

Abe got in line at the buffet, motioning for Ross and Gavin to go in front of him. "Go easy on the latkes. It might be a shock to the system." Abe helped himself to several potato pancakes, a large spoonful of applesauce, and a few donut holes.

Fran Gans stood across from him, fixing herself a plate. "Fancy meeting you here."

"A can't-miss event. So much fried food in one place." Abe wasn't sure what to do. Ross and Gavin had settled down at a table. If he asked Fran to join them, Ross might jump to conclusions.

"Where are you sitting?" she asked.

Abe pointed to the table. He'd have to let this one sort itself out.

Fran set her plate down and introduced herself. Her dangly blue earrings were shaped like miniature menorahs.

"Nice to meet you," Ross said in a monotone.

Gavin shot Ross a pointed look. "Yes, welcome."

"I don't want to intrude," Fran said. "Naomi Margolis has a seat over there."

"Don't be silly." Abe felt himself blushing. "This is my son Ross and his husband Gavin. Fran's in my Torah study class."

Ross took a bite of a jelly donut and examined the internal contents. "Remember when Eliza used to suck the jelly out of the middle and leave the donut?"

"Of course." Abe relaxed a little as Gavin and Fran chuckled over Eliza's childhood silliness. He picked up his water glass but found it empty.

"So Fran, are you new in town?" Gavin asked.

"She's a recent transplant from the Midwest. Right, Fran?" Abe said.

"Yes, from Illinois. I'm enjoying the year-round sunshine."

"Quite a change," Gavin said. "Do you have connections out here?"

"My daughter and her family. It made sense to take the plunge."

"On your own?"

"Yes, but this congregation has helped me meet people. I've joined every club and even volunteer for the caring committee. I delivered a gift basket to your dad, in honor of your mom's Yahrzeit."

Ross took a gulp of white wine. "We were sorry to miss that."

"So thoughtful," Abe said. He knew this must be odd for Ross to see his father with a woman, even if she was just a friend.

"So, what do you do when you're not at Congregation Shalom?" Gavin asked.

"When it's not too hot, I take walks outside, and otherwise I watch a lot of Netflix."

"Any particular show?"

"Recently, I binged *Shtisel.*"

Ross put down his wine glass, his eyes sparkling. "I *love* that show."

"It's so good, right? I watched the whole thing in two days."

"Shulem is one of the most complex characters ever written for television. Such a fascinating mixture of good and bad."

"Ruchami had me captivated. Her story nearly broke my heart."

"Believe it or not, I wanted a more tragic ending for her. A more fitting way to tie up the story."

While the two of them continued trading thoughts, Abe got up to refill his water glass, Gavin following behind.

"Not a fan of Israeli television?" Abe asked.

"Not so much. After staring at a screen all day, the last thing I want to do is read subtitles. Requires way too much concentration."

"I hear you. I'm not a fan either, but I'm glad they found something to talk about."

"She's nice," Gavin said. "Level with me. Is something going on?"

"No, not at all." Abe brushed away the question.

Gavin raised a hand in the air. "Apologies. I didn't mean to overstep."

Abe filled his water glass from the pitcher and then topped off Gavin's. "Not yet anyway." The words were out before Abe could think. Gavin stared at him, then burst out laughing. Abe gulped down his water, trying not to choke.

Chapter Forty-One

JESS

"Thanks for coming in today." Angela folded her hands together on the pristine desk. Her office was neat and organized, just like the attorney herself. "We have a lot to discuss."

"Of course," Jess said.

"Listen, I'm not going to beat around the bush here. I've gone over your case ad nauseam. No matter which way I look at it, I come up with the same conclusion."

Jess felt a flutter in her chest. She had a sense of what Angela was about to say, but she still didn't feel prepared. "Okay, and what is that?"

"I strongly advise settlement," Angela said. "For many reasons, but most importantly, the jury won't look favorably on dishonesty. You can't talk your way out of that."

"I don't think I—"

"Let me finish first. Also, the jury would find the gifts confusing. Quite frankly, I'm not sure what to make of them either."

"I'm still not sure how Kendall Carlson knew they were from me."

"That's irrelevant at this point. They *were* from you, and that doesn't look good. In light of these factors, taking your chance in court would be a mistake. At this point, we can push for a settlement under your malpractice limits. With a jury, all bets would be off."

"Can I have a few days to think it over?"

"Yes. As soon as I hear from you, I'll contact the plaintiff attorney and start hashing things out. Any other questions for me?"

So many questions flashed through Jess's mind, but she couldn't form a coherent thought. She thanked Angela and somehow managed to drive home.

In her bedroom, Jess put on her favorite pajamas, the ultra-soft ones with the holes in the underarms. It wasn't even dinner-time yet, but all she wanted to do was crawl into bed. Maybe if she closed her eyes, she could block out the world. How had her well-ordered life become such a mess? She'd had it all, and now everything was at stake. Sometimes it didn't seem real. If she shut her eyes tight, maybe she could pretend it had all been a bad dream. As Jess climbed into bed, the rumbling sound of the garage door jangled her nerves. Drew was home early. Jess wasn't ready to face him yet. Angela's words pounded aggressively in Jess's temples. *SET-TLE, SET-TLE, SE-TLE.* Pressing her fingers against her head, she tried to make the pain go away. What would settling mean for her future at the hospital? Would her colleagues lose respect for her, stop asking for her opinion on cases? And what about her patients? Jess imagined women cancelling their appointments in droves, her schedule glaringly empty all of a sudden.

Jess burrowed under the covers, breathing in the warm darkness. Even that simple task proved challenging. The more she focused on breathing, the harder it became. The air got caught in her throat before it reached her lungs. She was standing in front of a firing squad and there was nowhere to hide. Her only choice was to throw her arms out and let them take aim.

Had Jess been dishonest? She didn't think so. Maybe writing the addendum in Kendall's chart hadn't been the smartest choice, but she'd done what she thought was right. For the sake of her career and her family. And the presents had nothing to do with honesty. The presents were for Hope, to help her blossom into the bright little girl she was meant to be. How to put her compulsion into words? Jess wasn't sure. All she knew was that when she came across a toy for Hope, she was helpless to pass it up. Her intentions were honorable, but maybe Angela was right. A jury wouldn't understand.

Jess squeezed her eyes shut, trying to push away Angela's words. With her mind revving at warp speed, sleep wasn't going to happen. She grabbed her phone and opened her email. There was one from her chairman, something about adding another weekly teaching conference for rotating med students and changing the manufacturer for portable Doppler units, surely to save money. It was a recurring theme: do more with less. The next email caught her eye, a job alert from the American College of Gynecology and Obstetrics.

Obstetrician/Gynecologist
Garfield Free Clinic, Phoenix, Arizona

Seeking board-certified OB/GYN to staff nonprofit clinic for pregnant teens. Generous state funding and federal grants assure the best possible care for our patients. Full-time clinical position. No research requirements.

As Jess finished reading the details about hours, salary, and benefits, her heart lifted. Maybe this was a sign, just the kick in the pants Jess needed. No. She tamped down her excitement. It was too good to be true. And anyway, Jess couldn't leave Valley Health now, not with rewrites of the article due, dozens of pregnant patients scheduled to deliver with her, and the OR scheduled out for months. Plus, if the case did settle, it would be smarter to stay put. She couldn't imagine another facility would be excited to take on a doctor who'd just settled a big suit. Dropping her phone back on the nightstand, she pulled the covers back over her head.

The door clicked open, the scent of Drew's cologne filling the room. "Jess? You in here?"

Maybe if she stayed still, Drew wouldn't notice the lump under the covers.

"Jess?"

She held her breath.

Drew lifted the comforter from over her head, the cool air assaulting her skin.

"What are you doing? The kids are asking what's for dinner, and I didn't know what to say. I thought you were making chili."

The thought of cumin and beans made Jess's stomach turn. "I didn't get around to it."

Drew sat down on the side of the bed. "What's going on? You don't seem yourself."

Jess sat up and rested her back against the headboard. "It's not good, Drew. I don't know how to say it."

He brushed sweaty strands of hair from Jess's forehead. "Tell me a story."

She closed her eyes and tried to breathe. Maybe she'd feel better if she said her piece, got everything out in the open. "I met with Angela today, and she came down pretty hard. She wants to make a settlement offer. She doesn't think going forward is an option."

"It's your right to go to trial if you want."

"I know, but—"

"She can't tell you what to do. If you want to fight this battle, it's yours to fight."

Jess put her hand on his arm to stop his rant. "I know I can, but I'm not sure I should."

"What do you mean?"

Now was the time to come clean. Though Jess would never feel ready, she had to tell Drew everything she'd been hiding from him. The way things had played out on the day of the Carlson delivery, the addendum in Kendall's chart, reading Hope's medical chart, and the presents. So many presents. Drew knew nothing about the many gorgeously wrapped gifts Jess had delivered to the Carlsons' doorstep over the past two years, but it was time he found out. Otherwise, he would never understand why settling was the only choice that made any sense. Jess took a step off the cliff and went into free fall, explaining everything to Drew as clearly as possible. Once she got started, the words tumbled out like water at the Blue Wash trailhead, flowing freely downhill with gravity.

Jess let out a long sigh. "Now you know."

Drew sat with his hands folded in his lap. "That's a lot to digest," he said after a long pause.

"I know. I thought I could handle it on my own, that everything would be okay, but you need to know. You should have known all along."

"You've been carrying around a lot."

"I feel so guilty," Jess said. "I can't stop second-guessing every decision I made that day and whether it would have changed anything. What if I hadn't taken Opal to the vet? What if I hadn't answered my mom's call and the car accident never happened? Or what if I told Eve about the accident earlier? Maybe she could have found another doctor."

"It's so much to think about," he said. "And you care so much about your patients. It must be hard to push down the guilt, to keep on going as if everything's fine."

"It's been so hard," Jess said. "Every time I deliver a baby, I think about the time things went terribly wrong. It plays over and over in my mind."

Drew leaned in and gave Jess a soft kiss. "That means you're a good person. One of the many reasons I love you."

"Sometimes I'm not so sure."

"So, that gift on the floor of your closet, all Christmas paper and tinsel? That's for the baby?"

"Oh, I thought I'd hidden it."

"The red and green caught my eye."

"I can't give it to her. Not anymore. But wrapping them makes me feel better."

"I thought the store had run out of Hanukkah paper or something. That it was for Maddie or Vox."

"Oh no." Jess opened the calendar app on her phone. Exactly as she'd feared. "Hanukkah starts tonight."

"And we have nothing?" Drew asked.

"Unless you've been doing some stealth shopping, which I doubt. How did I let this get away from me?"

"Is that a rhetorical question? You've had a lot on your plate."

"I'm going to call Angela and tell her to make an offer. I can't live in limbo anymore."

"You sure that's what you want? Admitting you did something wrong?"

"I did," Jess said. "Maybe not on purpose, but I did. It's time to own up to it. Not just for the Carlsons, but for us as well. I am so sorry for everything, and they need to know that. It won't change what happened, but at least it's a small step to make things right."

"Are you sure?"

"Yes, we need to put this thing behind us."

Drew enveloped her in his arms. Jess took a moment to breathe in his cologne. She still had Drew and the kids. Together, they would find a way to heal.

"After I make the call, we need to put our heads together. Come up with a last-minute plan to save Hanukkah."

Chapter Forty-Two

KENDALL

Holding the handle of the tricycle, Kendall pushed Hope down the sidewalk for a post-dinner walk, the sun low in the sky. As she walked, Kendall took stock of the neighborhood. The house on the corner boasted a new terra cotta roof, the one across from the community pool had a new manicured rock garden, and the Herreras had just planted a towering saguaro next to the family room window.

"Ba-ba, ba-ba," Hope babbled. Ba-ba was her newly discovered sound. These days, when she discovered a new one, she practiced it non-stop.

Kendall adjusted the padded Bottega Veneta hanging from the back of the trike. Ever since she had let her daughter play with it last week, Hope had insisted it go with them everywhere. The yellow fabric was scuffed with dirt and ripped at the corner, but Kendall didn't care. Only a bag, it was bringing Hope joy, and that was what was important.

At the end of the walk, Kendall stopped to assess her own house. Paint flaked off the adobe, weeds crowded the garden beds, and one of the gutters was hanging off the roof. Everyone was having a glow-up, except the Carlsons. Kendall sighed. With the sorry state of their finances, a makeover wasn't in their future.

A beat-up Toyota pulled into her driveway. Had Troy invited one of his coworkers over for an after-dinner drink? She hadn't straightened up for company. To her surprise, Attorney Silverberg got out of the car.

"Good evening, Mrs. Carlson," The attorney held his briefcase in one hand and a cellophane-wrapped flower bouquet in the other. "I tried calling, but I couldn't get you."

Kendall patted her back pocket. She must have left her phone on the counter.

"Is Mr. Carlson home? It won't take long."

"Yes, of course. Come on in." Kendall pushed the tricycle to the front door and began the tedious process of unbuckling the restraints. When she'd freed Hope, Kendall opened the front door and led the attorney inside.

"These are for you," he said. "Your house is lovely." He gestured to the living room, a Christmas tree in the front window, and red stockings hanging from the mantle. "Did you do the decorating?"

"Oh, thank you. Always, yes." Kendall wouldn't admit it was a fake tree. In the desert, real ones cost as much as a designer purse.

Troy came in from the garage, his workout clothes stained with sweat. He removed his earbuds and wiped his forehead with the sleeve of his shirt. "What's going on? Do you have an update?"

"I do indeed. May I have a seat?"

They gathered around the kitchen table. The attorney took an accordion folder from his briefcase and removed a packet of papers. Troy leaned forward and rested his forearms on the table. Wrapping herself around Hope, Kendall closed her eyes for just a moment.

Abe thumbed through the papers. "I come bearing good news. The defense has made a settlement offer. I think you'll be pleased."

"How much?" Troy asked.

When the attorney shared the number, Kendall couldn't believe her ears.

"Is that enough?" Troy asked. "I don't have a context for what's typical."

Kendall's mouth dropped open. It was plenty of money. Why was Troy trying to drag this out? In some ways, Kendall felt like she didn't deserve any compensation. If she'd allowed cervical checks, maybe Dr. Schorr would have recognized the prolapse earlier and taken her for surgery sooner.

"I'd say it's more than fair," Abe said. "But it's your prerogative to say no. I have to warn you, though, with delays at the courthouse, a trial wouldn't be scheduled for at least a year. And you'd have to bring Hope to the courtroom every day."

Kendall had no desire to use Hope as a prop. The pity party would be too much to bear. Maybe they could get more money from a jury, but at what cost? This was more than enough.

"We can't leave anything on the table," Troy said. "Hope is—"

"Hope is worth everything," Kendall interrupted. "She's the reason I get up in the morning and the reason I keep pushing forward when I don't think I can take another step. She makes me laugh and cry every day, sometimes both in the same minute. She's my reason for…well, everything. Troy, please. For Hope and for me, this has to end now."

Troy started to say something, then stopped. He met her eyes with a nod.

"Tell them we'll take it," Kendall said, drawing Troy into a hug, Hope sandwiched between them.

"Ba-ba," Hope said. "Ba-ba-ba."

Kendall's eyes brimmed with tears. "I can't believe it."

"Nothing makes me happier than winning a case that deserves to be won," the attorney said.

Kendall blew her nose into a paper napkin. "We can't thank you enough. This changes everything."

"It was truly my pleasure. Consider it my holiday gift to you."

Chapter Forty-Three

JESS

The line at the party store spilled out the door. Jess took her place at the end, tapping her foot with impatience. She didn't have time for this today. With Vox's B-mitzvah two weeks away, she had a bunch of errands to take care of—pick up her father's tallis from the dry cleaner, finalize the catering menu, and call the photographer to confirm the timing.

Jess looked over at a display of Happy New Year paraphernalia on sale after the fact, paper banners, headbands, and light-up glasses all going begging. The guy at the front of the line argued with the clerk, yelling some nonsense about a soccer team banquet. The clerk looked like he wanted to hide behind the counter. The woman in front of Jess smoothed her blond hair with manicured nails and adjusted a designer purse on her shoulder. She was vaguely familiar, maybe from the organic aisle at the grocery store or the nail salon a few doors down. Hopefully, she wouldn't pick a fight with the clerk as well.

Pulling out her phone, Jess opened Instagram. One of her med school classmates stood with her wife in front of the Taj Mahal, a clerk from labor and delivery beamed at the finish line of a race, a silver medal around her neck, and Drew's boss held a glass of scotch up to the camera. The line crept forward, now four people ahead of Jess. *Come on already.* Looking back at her phone, Jess noticed a graphic from The American College of Gynecology and Obstetrics. It was an ad for the same job Jess had gotten an email about a few weeks ago, the position at the nonprofit clinic for pregnant teens in downtown Phoenix. This job kept finding her. Maybe she'd give them a call later. It couldn't hurt to get more information.

Finally, the woman in front of Jess stepped up to the counter. "I placed an order for KC Events," she said.

Did she say KC Events? As the clerk went to retrieve the order, the woman turned to the window. Jess dropped her phone to the floor. Holy crap. It was Kendall Carlson. KC was Kendall Carlson? Her breath caught in her throat. Was this why the party planner had ditched her? But why did she take the job to begin with?

The woman bent down and picked up the phone. "Are you okay?"

Jess took it, looking at Kendall in shock. Her makeup was flawless and her hair blown to a sleek shine, but there was something darker hidden underneath. This woman shellacked her outer veneer so no one would see her buried pain.

"Oh, it's you," Kendall said. "This is weird. Are you stalking me?"

"What? No, I didn't know you ran KC Events. I never would have called you if I had any idea. You have to believe me. I—"

"I know that now."

"What?"

"When I first figured it out, I thought it was a trick. Like you were spying on me."

Jess felt dizzy. She gasped, trying to get more air.

"I saw you. When you delivered the trike."

Jess thought back to that day. She'd parked in front of Kendall's house. Jess remembered resting the phone down as she finagled the box out of the trunk, the chatty neighbor asking annoying questions. Of course. KC had been on speaker.

"You were just trying to plan a party," Kendall said. "Nothing more than that."

"I was. It's in two weeks."

"Congratulations, I guess."

The clerk returned, trailing a large cluster of green and yellow balloons. Kendall handed him her credit card, then stepped aside with her order.

"Next in line," he said.

Jess managed to spit out her name. When the clerk disappeared into the back room, she watched Kendall maneuver the gaggle of balloons out the door. No. Jess couldn't leave it here. She had more to say.

Jess ran out to the sidewalk. "Wait!"

"Haven't you done enough?"

"I could go into a long story about what happened that day. Why I was late. Everything that prevented me from getting to you. I tried. I really did—"

"But you failed."

"I know. I think about Hope all the time."

Kendall looked out to the parking lot.

"What I want to say is this." Jess steeled herself. "I regret the part I played in your life and the struggles you're going through because of me. I should have apologized to you a long time ago, on the day Hope was born even, but I didn't. Well, today is that day. I am truly, deeply sorry. You deserve to hear this."

For a moment, Kendall allowed her eyes to meet Jess's. In that instant, Jess felt something—not forgiveness *per se*, but a split second of understanding between two mothers, a tenuous common bond—and then just as quickly, it was gone. Kendall turned and walked away, the balloons bobbing along behind her.

Chapter Forty-Four
ABE

Abe sorted through his closet, trying to find a shirt that sent the right message. Casual, but not too casual. He held a blue Brooks Brothers shirt up to his chest and checked his reflection. No, that wouldn't work. It was meant to be paired with a tie, and that would read too stiff. He didn't want to seem like he was trying too hard. When Fran had called last week with New Year's wishes, the conversation had flowed naturally. They'd chatted for a good half hour. When they were about to hang up, Fran had thrown him a curveball and asked him out for dinner.

Back in Abe's dating days, men had always done the asking, but that was ages ago. Not only had Fran made the overture, she had also booked the reservation, and even offered to drive. Abe suggested they meet at the restaurant instead. He wasn't prepared for this whole new world. Should he open the door for her? What about the bill? He wanted to pay, but he also didn't want to offend her.

Abe settled on a casual golf shirt, a pair of navy-blue slacks, and a braided belt Risa had picked out a few years back. Wearing something connected to Risa seemed appropriate—a reminder he would always love her, even if he was taking a step forward. Risa would want him to be happy, but Abe felt pulled in two directions. He wanted to heal from his grief without forsaking the memory of his beloved wife. Abe turned on the local news to distract himself. He tucked in his shirt and fastened his belt.

"And now, breaking news," said the newscaster. "Everyone in Maricopa County has been following Bear 311. He's popped up on cul-de-sacs, in front of Trader Joe's, and has even been known to take a dip in a few neighborhood swimming pools."

A film loop showed footage of the bear's travels. In the last shot, he climbed into a dumpster outside Bashas' grocery store while several employees in red polos took videos on their phones.

"Earlier today," she continued, "the months-long saga came to a fitting conclusion. This afternoon, the Maricopa County Animal Control team sedated the bear and transported him to Prescott National Forest. This adventurous bear will surely be safer there than in our backyards. A new year brings a new home for Bear 311. Safe travels!"

On the screen, a team of animal control officers maneuvered a tranquilized bear onto a stretcher and into a van.

"Safe travels," Abe repeated out loud, turning the TV off.

In the living room, Bea was splayed out on the couch, a mopey look on her face. She knew whatever was happening didn't include her. Such a smart girl. He gave her a kiss on the snout. "It's okay, Bea. You'll always be my number one."

She emitted a high-pitched bark.

Abe wouldn't pick up the rope. She'd be fine alone for a few hours, and by the time he got home, she'd be fast asleep. He grabbed a peanut butter-filled toy from the freezer.

"Come on. Into the crate you go."

Grabbing a light jacket from the hall closet, Abe headed to his car. When he pulled into the entrance of The Four Seasons, Abe wished he'd opted for the shirt and tie. The grand driveway was lined by palm trees, and the valets wore crisp black uniforms and matching hats. He stopped under the porte cochère, handing his keys to a valet.

"Here for dinner, sir?"

"Yes, at Talavera."

"Wonderful choice. Go straight through the lobby, and you'll find it on the other side of the courtyard. You're in for a treat."

"Thank you." Abe's stomach gurgled, his mind spinning with second thoughts. He didn't know if he'd be able to eat anything.

He walked into the lobby and found the men's room. Standing in front of the mirror, he looked himself in the eyes. What had made him think he was ready? Had this whole thing been a mistake? Maybe he needed more time to mourn Risa before trying his hand with someone new, but there was no turning back now. Say what you will about him, but Abe was a man of his word. He'd promised Fran he would be there, and so he would. He smoothed his goatee and pushed open the door.

The lobby was decorated in Southwestern style with weathered wood floors and rustic chandeliers. Exiting through doors at the back of the lobby, he shivered in the cool air. He rubbed his upper arms and breathed hot air into his palms.

"Good evening," the hostess said. "Do you have a reservation with us?"

"Silver—" he started. "I mean Gans. I believe it's under Gans?" After over forty years of marriage, it felt odd to have a reservation under another name. So much of this evening felt foreign, and it had barely even begun.

"Yes, the other member of your party has already been seated."

Abe followed the hostess through the restaurant, his mind again spinning with doubts. How should he greet Fran? Should he shake her hand? A hug would be too intimate. What would they talk about? Awkward lulls in conversation drove Abe crazy. He walked by diners, their table covered with glasses of wine and plates of beet salad and grilled shrimp. Their talk and laughter echoed in his ears, and the aroma of garlic made him queasy.

The hostess stopped at a table outside by the railing. The light was gorgeous, the setting sun casting a golden hue over the landscape. Fran stood up. Lovely as ever, she wore a blue sundress and a jean jacket, her graying hair in a loose bun. As soon as Abe saw the warm smile on her face, his worries melted away. The hug she offered felt completely natural. They took their seats and arranged their napkins on their laps.

Abe looked over the railing at the unobstructed view of Pinnacle Peak, the natural landscape dotted with saguaros. A bottle of red wine stood on the table, both of their glasses full. Fran must have taken the liberty.

"This place is a little off the beaten track," Abe said. "You found it okay?"

"Easy peasy. I plugged the address into my trusty GPS and off I went." Fran's mother-of-pearl butterfly earrings swayed as she talked.

"Very impressive," Abe said. Fran had moved clear across the country, yet she seemed so at ease. Abe could barely figure out how to start the dishwasher. "Were you always so independent?"

"In the end, you're all you've got. Sounds corny, but I take that old saying to heart."

"You sure do." Abe opened his menu. "So many choices. It all looks wonderful."

"My daughter said it's one of the best restaurants in town for a date."

Abe's face paled at her mention of the word. He'd known what Fran had in mind, but hearing it made him squirm in his chair.

"Is everything all right?" Fran asked.

Abe's stomach churned with unease. "I think so. Maybe I'm just hungry."

"We could order appetizers. The tuna ceviche and blue cheese salad are supposed to be divine."

Raw fish and moldy cheese sounded far from divine. Abe wasn't sure what was going on with him. One minute, he was having a lovely time and the next, his stomach was threatening to revolt. Abe tasted bile in his throat.

"I think I need to make something clear," he said, his voice quivering. "I don't want to mislead you in any way."

"Mislead me?"

"I'm not sure I'm ready to date. Between losing Risa and learning to run my firm, I'm dealing with a lot. I'm still figuring out how to go it alone." His stomach quieted a bit. He hoped Fran wouldn't take it personally.

"Feeling like you need to be on your own for a bit before hitching up your wagon? I completely understand."

"I'd like to start as friends, if that's okay with you."

Fran lifted her glass. "To new friends."

"And to standing on our own two feet, no matter how difficult."

They clinked glasses, taking in the view of the sun dipping behind the mountains.

O O O

Stripping off his shirt, Abe spread it out on the washer and grabbed the Spray 'n Wash. It was just like him to dribble wine on his best golf shirt. At least Fran had been a good sport, laughing it off as no big deal. She was a good woman. Maybe one day he'd take her out on a real date. He spritzed the red splotches liberally, then threw the shirt in the basin. He couldn't run a load with just one shirt. Abe didn't believe in signs, but maybe this was one, of sorts. In his bedroom, he pushed open Risa's closet, steeling his nerves. As he bent to lift the hamper of dirty clothes, his knees made a clicking noise. Once he'd emptied the contents of the hamper into the washer along with a capful of detergent, Abe set the dials and pressed start. No time for second thoughts. With the sound of running water, Abe beamed with pride. He'd done it, gotten over his mental block about Risa's closet and successfully started the washing machine. He was no master of household tasks, but he was building momentum. One of these days, he might even resurrect the vacuum cleaner from the hall closet.

When Abe opened Bea's crate, the dog burst forth and joined him on the couch, covering his face with wet kisses. Abe pulled her onto his lap and scratched behind her ears, exhaling with a sigh. It was time.

Abe stood up and unfolded the wheelchair. He posed it in the center of the room under the overhead lights and snapped a photo. Grabbing his laptop from the other room, he settled back on the couch next to Bea. He pulled up Craigslist and typed *Phoenix* into the search bar. A gallery of miscellaneous items filled the screen—boats and air fryers and used shoes. Was there a market for all of these things? He clicked on *for sale* and selected the health and beauty category. Abe recalled how happy Risa had been the day he'd first brought the wheelchair home. Her face had lit up, and she'd wrapped her arms around him, her embrace noticeably weaker than a few weeks prior. Using a wheelchair meant she could still get out into the world, take in fresh air, and socialize with neighbors.

Picking up his cell phone, Abe dialed Norah. He wanted to bounce this decision off someone.

"It's the weekend," she said. "Everything all right?"

"Yes, can you spare a minute?"

"For you? Always."

"I owe you an update," he said. "With the Carlson case put to bed and last year in the books, the firm is doing better than expected."

"That's nice to hear."

"I wanted to thank you for everything you do, for the firm and for me. Tomorrow, I'll have a bonus check for you."

"That's amazing. Thank you."

"You're welcome. You deserve every penny," he said. "And Norah, can I ask your opinion on something? Not exactly firm-related."

"Of course."

"I might be ready to sell Risa's wheelchair. Do you think that's okay?"

"More than okay," Norah said. "Grieving is about you. If you feel ready, that's all that matters."

Abe thanked her and ended the call. That's exactly what he had needed to hear. On the screen, he typed in his information and the details about the make and model of the wheelchair. When it came to setting the price, he had no idea what would be fair. He'd paid a fortune, but he couldn't ask for anything close to that. There must be someone out there who desperately needed this item and couldn't afford to pay, an opportunity for tzedakah. He set the price to free and hovered the arrow over the finish button. Once he posted the ad, the wheelchair could be gone in a flash. Was he ready for this? Abe couldn't help feeling conflicted, as if he were betraying Risa. Enough with the mishegas. Risa wouldn't want the wheelchair collecting dust in the corner when it could be put to good use.

"Should we do this, Bea? Bark once for yes and twice for no."

The dog turned her face up to him, her earnest brown eyes filled with love.

"You don't want to weigh in?"

Bea leapt up and gave him a generous slurp on the lips.

"I'll take that as a yes." He clicked finish and watched his ad fill the screen. With any luck, someone in need would see the ad and give him a call. Abe would be honored to pay it forward.

Before he went to bed, Abe had one more call to make. He selected Marty's number and waited for him to answer.

"Howdy, partner, "Marty said. "It's late. Everything okay?"

Abe wouldn't usually call after ten, but this couldn't wait any longer. If he was going to successfully stand on his own, he had to dissolve the partnership once and for all. He'd been kicking the can down the road for much too long.

"All good," Abe said.

"Listen, I owe you a dinner invite. Gladys keeps reminding me."

"We have to talk," Abe said.

"This sounds serious."

"Until today, I've been timid, but we need to make a change. It's time for you to step away from the partnership."

"Is that what has you all hot and bothered? Don't be so hasty. I give you advice, so it could be good for you to keep me on the ledger. I don't want you to do something you might regret."

"I'm doing the work, Marty. Not you. It makes sense to make a clean break."

"It's going to be complicated. There's a lot to unravel."

"Regardless, it has to happen."

"All right already. Whatever you need," Marty said. "Friend-ship trumps business every day of the week."

"I'll have Norah call you in the morning. Get a meeting on the books."

"I look forward to hearing her pretty voice."

"I bet you do." After Abe hung up the phone, he bent his neck from one side to the other, feeling a release with each crack.

Chapter Forty-Five

KENDALL

"What does a lion say?" The librarian turned the book around to show the illustrations to the children.

"Roarie, roar, roar!" a little boy yelled, a hearing aid tucked behind each ear.

"Liam, we're at the library. Inside voices," his mom said. "Sometimes he doesn't know how loud he is."

Hope seemed quite content in Kendall's lap. After saying no to Dr. Hill so many times, Kendall had finally decided to give the playgroup for children with special needs a try. There was nothing to lose. Looking around, Kendall wasn't so sure about her decision. Yes, it felt good to know there were other kids in the community who were struggling, but it also made Kendall sad. Did she need a weekly reminder of how many ways a child could be disabled, how many unfortunate challenges innocent children could be forced to face?

A girl on the other side of the room had a disproportionately large head, there was a baby to her left with Down syndrome, and a little boy behind her had a cleft palate. Seeing all these kids in one place made Kendall want to sob about the hills they took much longer to climb, the milestones they may never reach. On the other hand, it was inspiring to see these kids getting out into the world, making silly faces and animal noises, dancing, and having fun.

"How old is Liam?" Kendall asked.

"Two and a half. I'm Molly, by the way," she said. "Welcome to the three-ring circus."

"Thank you," Kendall said.

"At first, I wasn't sure about this group either."

"Was it that obvious?"

"I saw the look on your face. It's overwhelming, but it's good to have people to lean on. Keeps me sane amidst the craziness."

The librarian pointed to a drawing of a silver hippopotamus. "Okay, folks, this is a tough one. What sound does a hippo make?"

A boy on the other side of the room banged his head against the wall.

"That's his thing," Molly said. "How he gets his energy out."

"Anyone?" the librarian said. "What does a hippo say?"

"Is this a trick question?" Molly whispered.

"That would be cruel and unusual."

Molly covered her mouth to hide her laughter.

The boy behind Kendall made a snorting sound. It sounded more like a pig, but Kendall was certainly no expert.

"Someone's been studying up." The librarian turned the page. "Excellent job, Alex."

Alex grinned with pride.

"How old is your little cutie?" Molly asked.

This mundane question triggered Kendall. In the old playgroup, she was constantly fielding questions about Hope's progress, but this group was different, she reminded herself. The parents here didn't see Hope as an anomaly, but as a child like any other.

Kendall cleared her throat. "She just turned two."

"Get ready for the terrible twos."

"I can't wait," Kendall said. Temper tantrums sounded delightful. She would welcome each and every one. Her phone lit up with a text from Jeanine.

"Still on for lunch tomorrow?"

Kendall replied with a thumbs-up emoji. She looked forward to connecting with Jeanine, away from the pretense and judgment of the old playgroup.

The librarian showed the children an illustration of a butterfly, the wings a mix of watercolor shades, two black antennae protruding from the top. "Does this creature make a noise? Anyone have ideas?"

The boy across the room stopped his head banging, coming in for closer inspection of the illustration.

"Noooooooooo," a little girl said.

Hope sat up in Kendall's lap, her eyes fixed on the book. "Buffly… buffly."

At first, Kendall wasn't sure what was happening. She held her breath, waiting for more.

"Buffly, Mama."

Kendall hadn't been imagining it. It was really happening. She gathered Hope and squeezed her tight, raining kisses on her cheeks and surrendering herself to the joy of the moment. "Yes, my love. Yes."

"Great job, Hope. This is a butterfly," the librarian said. "The noise comes from the fierce beating of her wings."

Kendall squeezed Hope tight. "You keep beating those wings, my little monarch. No matter what people say."

Chapter Forty-Six
JESS

"Baruch atah, Adonai, notein haTorah," Jess sang the end of the familiar Hebrew blessing, Drew and Maddie's voices joining with hers. As they finished the last line, Jess stepped back to watch Vox complete the final section of their Torah portion. Here in their backyard, the focus of the B-mitzvah was on the rite of passage, not on keeping up with the Cohens. No expensive open bar, personalized sweatshirts, or larger-than-life video displays.

Paring down the invites from nearly two hundred to less than thirty had been much easier than Jess had expected. When she scanned the list, she immediately knew who must be included. Drew's parents, his sister and her family, who'd flown in from Maine last night, Eve and Mai, a few of Drew's friends, and a handful of Vox's classmates looked on from two rows of chairs. Just the people most dear to Vox in the comfort of their own home. To Jess's surprise, Drew had gone along with the change right away. They'd both known it was the right choice for Vox.

Vox held a pointer against the scroll, Cantor Hirsch guiding their hand along. They looked sharp in a navy-blue suit and tie, hair parted to the side and slicked down with gel, their grandfather's blue and white tallis over their shoulders. Vox's voice sounded strong, the nervous tremble from a few minutes ago a thing of the past. Rabbi Glasser's chin bobbed in rhythm with the chanting. Though Jess didn't understand the meaning of the words, the tropes were ingrained in her, a part of her DNA. She closed her eyes, allowing the familiar melodies to wash over her. On the last note, Vox's voice rang out across the yard, a broad smile covering their face.

"Yasher Koach," the rabbi said. "You should be supreme-ly proud of yourself. And I can tell by your parents' faces that they're bursting at the seams. Hugs all around."

Jess took a tissue from the pocket of her dress and wiped happy tears from her face. She joined Drew and Maddie sur-rounding Vox in a circle of love, covering them with kisses.

"You never cease to amaze us," Jess said. "We couldn't be any prouder."

Maddie gave Vox a fist bump. "That was fire."

"Is that a good thing?" the rabbi asked.

Vox laughed, adjusting their grandfather's tallis around their neck.

Cantor Hirsch pulled her guitar strap over her head. "We'll conclude this service with my favorite part. It's time to pass the Torah." She invited Drew's parents to stand and join them in a line. A hole opened in the center of Jess's chest. Her parents should be here today, standing next to Drew's and passing the Torah down into her open arms. The generations felt incomplete. As the cantor strummed the first few notes, Jess felt her eyes fill up again. This song got her every time.

The cantor sang the first line, her right hand strumming the chords. "L'dor vador nagid godlecha."

The rabbi dressed the Torah in royal blue velvet and two silver crown toppers, lifted it from the table, and settled it in Drew's father's arms. Her father-in-law swayed to the music with his eyes closed, and then passed it on to his wife. When Jess accepted the Torah from Drew, she wrapped her arms around its girth, com-forted by the weight against her chest.

The cantor sang the English line about being carriers of wisdom. Sometimes Jess didn't feel so wise. How had she spent so long in a job that wasn't right for her? So many years subscrib-ing to the publish or perish mentality, sitting in a room by her-self writing articles instead of seeing patients. Maybe the lawsuit hadn't been all bad. It had forced her to open her eyes, to shine a spotlight on what was truly important.

Tears dampened the collar of her dress. She passed the Torah into Vox's arms. While the cantor strummed the final chords, the rabbi retrieved the Torah and rested it back down on the table. "I've done countless mitzvahs. Today ranks up there with the best of them. A special day for all."

The servers began milling about, offering mini potato pancakes topped with gravlax, tuna tartare on rice crackers, and at Vox's insistence, pigs in a blanket galore. The baking-themed centerpieces of mylar balloons in the shape of donuts, cupcakes, and chocolate chip cookies brought Jess back to the run-in with Kendall at the party store. The apology hadn't gone well, but what had Jess expected? That Kendall would accept her apology with a generous smile? No. Jess didn't deserve to be let off the hook so easily.

"Let's take some photos." The photographer's voice snapped Jess back to the moment.

Jess gathered her family by the fence, the natural beauty of the McDowell sanctuary serving as the backdrop. The photographer stepped in to start arranging the shots.

"Wait a second," Vox said, disappearing into the house. Where were they going? The photographer was ready to begin. Vox returned cradling Opal in her arms. If it were anyone else, the cat would have squirmed away, but she'd always allowed Vox to baby her. "Opal has to be in the pictures."

Jess hadn't thought to include the cat, but it made perfect sense. Opal had been Vox's support animal, their source of unconditional love, for nearly ten years. Jess had a flickering memory of her nightmare about Opal and the bear, the cat narrowly escaping his gnashing jaws, but she brushed the thought away. With Opal safe in Vox's arms, Jess felt secure for the first time in a while.

Vox took their place by the fence, Maddie at their side, and their paternal grandparents on either end.

Eve came up and put an arm around Jess, planting a kiss on her cheek. "Mazel Tov. You're raising a truly incredible child."

"Thank you." Sending Eve an invitation had been a no-brainer. Despite the lawsuit, Eve would always be her friend, one who was more like family. Sometimes you didn't like them, but you always loved them.

"You should be so proud of Vox, and of yourself as well," Eve said.

"What do you mean?"

"For making it through the last few months. It's been beyond stressful, and I didn't help the situation."

"You doubled down, but you told the truth. How could I fault you for that?"

"Thank you for inviting me. I was shocked I made the cut."

"You're on my A list, forever and always," Jess said.

Mai joined them, holding a plate of hors d'oeuvres. "Am I on your list too?"

"Only if you quit hocking me about stepping off the academic treadmill."

Mai took a bite of a goat cheese crostini. "Touché."

"I'll still read all the articles you write, no matter how horribly dull."

Mai reached out her hand. "You strike a hard bargain, Dr. Schorr, but you've got yourself a deal."

Jess clasped Mai's hand with a smile.

"When do you start the new job?" Eve asked.

"In a month. It's nice to have a little break."

"We're going to miss you at Valley Health," Eve said.

"I'll miss it too, but it's time for something new." The pay cut would take some getting used to—fewer restaurant meals, less frequent vacations, and maybe Drew would take over the gardening and pool maintenance—but they'd make it work. Filling out the claims history form for the new job hadn't been comfortable, but Jess wasn't the only doctor who'd ever been sued. It happened all the time. Hopefully, the fresh start would reinvigorate her and help her see things from a fresh perspective.

"Look at Vox," Eve said. "They're radiant."

"Now everyone say *LATKES!*" the photographer said.

"LATKES!" Vox yelled, their face lit up with joy. Though Jess had taught her children many things, they both had taught her so much more in return. Vox was a shining example of being true to yourself, of living your life authentically rather than following the well-trodden path. If Jess could embody this lesson even half as well as her younger child, she'd consider herself a success.

Jess walked to the fence and pulled Vox into a hug. "I want you to promise me one thing," she said in Vox's ear.

"What?"

"Never stop being who you are." Jess brushed a lock of hair out of Vox's eyes. "You're spectacular."

"Mom, you're so extra."

"Extra what?"

"It's a saying," Vox said. "It means you go above and beyond."

"Who, me? It was nothing." Of course, that was far from the truth, but now wasn't the time to go on about how much she'd sacrificed for her family, about the peaks and valleys of the past few years, and the toll it had taken on her. On Vox's special day, Jess would immerse herself in the moment and enjoy the celebration.

The End

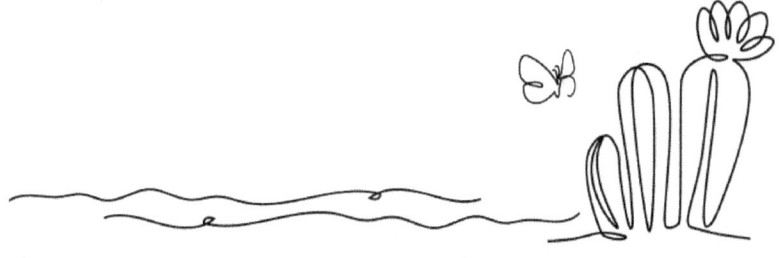

Acknowledgments

I had hoped writing a novel would get easier every time, but I've learned that is not the case. Like children, each novel is delivered into the world in a unique and unexpected way. This time around, personal challenges made it difficult to find the time and mental fortitude to sit down and write. It may have taken a little longer, but I finally got it done.

Michael T. Braun and the staff of Ten16 Press, I am so glad you fell in love with and decided to champion this story. I am thrilled with our new partnership. Dana Breunig, your gorgeous cover design and creative layout fit the story perfectly. Julie Ceresnie, your expertise in PR and enviable tenacity helped lift this book to new heights.

I couldn't have written this story without the incredibly supportive community at the Westport Writers' Workshop. Julie Sarkissian, I am thankful for our connection and always take your insightful feedback to heart. Chris Belden, you never fail to ask the right questions to elevate my writing to the next level, and Sally Allen, you encouraged me to step out of my comfort zone and begin my first novel over ten years ago.

Getting the story onto the page is hard, but revising can be even more difficult. Thank you to Michele Montgomery and the Women's Fiction Writers Association (WFWA) members at the daily write-ins who kept my tush in the chair and to my WFWA critique partners for their honest and clarifying feedback. To the brave obstetricians from Physicians Mom Group Book Club who spoke with me about their experiences with medical malpractice, you helped deepen and authenticate this story. Allison Dickens and Kathleen Barber, editors extraordinaire, you both pushed me to improve this novel in different and important ways.

One of the most incredible things about becoming an author is the friendships I've cultivated with other authors far and wide. I couldn't possibly list all the authors who have guided me, taught me, and lent a helping hand when I needed it most. For this book, special thanks goes out to Galia Gichon, Emily Liebert, Sarahlyn Bruck, Jackie Friedland, Laurie Frankel, Rea Frey, Kim Hooper, Dara Levan, Hadley Leggett, Samantha Greene Woodruff, and Lisa Montanaro. There are so many others, more than I could possibly name, who have offered words of advice and encouragement and for that I am truly grateful.

Book influencers, booksellers, and librarians are a special brand of people. The support you give to authors is truly priceless. Suzy Leopold, the best part of publishing a new book is knowing my book baby will embark on a curated Suzy Approved tour once again.

To my friends and family who don't completely understand this writing thing but know it's important to me: Joan, Marvin, Corey, Justin, Lev, Stephanie, Alli, Marisa, Michele, Margie, Deborah, thank you for listening and cheering me on. To the greatest boss, Ari Jonisch, and my colleagues at Main Street Radiology, you've had my back as I juggle two demanding careers, and to Stacy, for doing all the errands I have no time to do.

Finally, the Frimmer clan deserves a standing ovation. Benjamin, Shea, and Ari, you let me talk through plot points, listen to me complain, and respect my writing time at all costs, maybe even taking the dog for a walk on occasion. You three are the loves of my life.

Discussion Questions

1. *Always Hope* is told from the alternating perspectives of Jess, Kendall, and Abe. Did you identify or empathize with one character more than another? Was there one character you had a harder time connecting with? Why?

2. Do you think Jess is responsible for Hope's disability? If so, why? Does anyone else deserve part of the blame as well? Kendall, Troy, Eve? Anyone else? Did your feelings about this change as the story unfolded?

3. What is your opinion of doctors? Do your feelings lean positive or negative? Do you think of doctors as fallible human beings? Did this story make you reassess your feelings on this topic?

4. Did Vox's coming out take you by surprise, or were there clues along the way? What are your thoughts on Jess's reaction? Drew's? What was your response to the change in pronouns for the rest of the novel?

5. Kendall has a hard time accepting Hope as she is. Did you see her views change over the course of the story? What do you think is next for Hope and Kendall?

6. Abe is having a hard time dealing with the loss of his wife and the retirement of his business partner in the same year. How does the trial affect his grief experience? What was your response to Abe's burgeoning relationship with Fran and his decision during their dinner date?

7. Each of the main characters is literally keeping a secret in the closet. Jess hides her gift-wrapping supplies, Kendall hides her designer purse collection, and Abe hides his deceased wife's dirty laundry. Why do you think each character is keeping things hidden? How do each of the secrets come to light?

8. What role do the minor characters play in the novel? How do each of these characters deepen or expand the story—Drew, Troy, Vox, Eve, Fran, Ross, Marty?

9. What did you learn while reading? Did you learn anything new about obstetrics, cerebral palsy, or medical malpractice law? Were you inspired to read further about any of these topics?

10. Did you pick up on any symbolism in the book? How do butterflies lend significance to the story? What about the Arizona setting and desert landscape? The bear? Did you notice any recurring themes?

11. In many ways, this is a story about Hope. Not only Hope, the two-year-old girl, but also hope for her future, hope for the continuity of Jess's career, hope for healing, growth, and fulfillment. How do you think hope plays into each character's journey?

12. The novel concludes at Vox's B-mitzvah celebration. How do you feel about this conclusion for Jess's story? What about the endings for Kendall and Abe? Were you happy with the case settlement or were you hoping the case would go to trial? What do you imagine happens next for each of the main characters?

13. If this novel were adapted for film or TV, who do you picture as Jess, Kendall, and Abe?

14. What message do you think the author wanted you to take away from this novel?

15. Did *Always Hope* remind you of other books you've read? Which ones and in what way?

www.ingramcontent.com/pod-product-compliance
Lightning Source LLC
Chambersburg PA
CBHW070849260626
47170CB00007B/2550